WORLD'S END

Gordon Anthony

First published in paperback in Great Britain by
Pen Press an imprint of
Indepenpress Publishing Ltd., 2012
ISBN 978-1-78003-368-6

Cover design by Philip Anthony
Cover image courtesy of Shutterstock.com

For my mother, Moira,
who has waited a long time to see Calgacus in print.

Britain
circa 50 A.D.

Note on Place Names

With one or two exceptions, the concept of living in towns and cities was one that arrived in Britain with the Romans. Prior to the invasion of 43 A.D., the Britons tended to live in small, rural communities or, for the more powerful leaders, in hill forts which were protected by banks and ditches. Very few Iron Age towns, as we would recognise them, have been discovered. While archaeology continues to reveal traces of Iron Age settlements, very few are documented in ancient writing, although this may be because the Romans wished to portray the Britons as uncivilised savages.

The following brief descriptions provides some background on the places mentioned in this story, some of which are marked on the accompanying map.

Caer Caradoc

This battle site is not marked on the map as the precise location has never been positively identified, even though a description was recorded by the Roman writer, Tacitus. The battle is believed to have been fought somewhere on the upper reaches of the River Severn, although Tacitus merely says there was "a river", so even this "fact" is not certain. There is a hill named Caer Caradoc in Shropshire but it is almost certainly not the site of the battle. "Caradoc" is the Welsh form of "Caratacus" so anywhere that Caratacus built (or briefly occupied) any sort of fortification could easily attract the name Caer Caradoc.

Caer Gobannus

A fictional settlement loosely based on the site of a fort known as Hirllwyn, just north of the Brecon Beacons National Park in South Wales. The actual remains at Hirllwyn are possibly medieval rather than Iron Age, but this region is dotted with the remains of many Iron Age settlements, so there may have been some sort of fortified village here in the First Century. There is a stone circle nearby.

Camulodunon / Camulodunum
The Celtic / Roman forms respectively of a settlement which occupied the site of modern Colchester. The name means, "the fort of Camulos". Camulos was the war god of the Catuvellauni. The original, Iron Age settlement was reputedly founded by King Cunobelinos (Shakespeare's "Cymbeline") when he conquered, subdued or assimilated the neighbouring tribe of the Trinovantes. The Romans regarded it as the "capital" of the Catuvellauni and established their own colony there soon after the invasion.

Deva
The River Dee in north Wales and Cheshire.

Gaul
A province within the Roman Empire roughly equivalent to modern France.

Glevum
A Roman military fort established on the site of modern Gloucester.

Hafren
The Celtic name for the River Severn.

Isuria
The Romans established a town they called "Isurium Brigantum" which was built on the site of the modern village of Aldborough in North Yorkshire. The settlement of Isuria in this story is a fictional Iron Age town set in roughly the same location.

Lindum
A Roman fort built on the site of modern Lincoln.

Londinium
A Roman port and trading settlement built on the site of modern London.

Medu
The River Medway.

Mona
The Roman name for the island of Anglesey.

Sabrina
The Roman name for the River Severn.

Tamesas / Tamesis
The Celtic / Roman names for the River Thames.

Ynis Mon
The Celtic name for the island of Anglesey, once the spiritual home of the druids.

Prologue

Extract from a letter dated 21ˢᵗ September, in the Year 43 AD. From the Roman Imperial Archives.

To His Imperial Majesty, Tiberius Claudius Caesar Augustus Germanicus,

From Aulus Plautius, General commanding Your Imperial Majesty's forces in the island of Britannia.

Written on the tenth day before the Kalends of October, in the Seven Hundred and Ninety Sixth Year since the founding of the city of Rome, Claudius Caesar and Lucius Quinctilius Crispus being consuls.

"Aulus Plautius sends greeting to Claudius Caesar and has the honour to provide the following report on military operations in Britannia.

"On our arrival in Britannia, King Verica of the Atrebates fulfilled his promise and raised his people to join us. In addition, King Cogidubnus of the Regni swore allegiance to Caesar and provided troops to assist us. Many other barbarian tribes submitted without offering any resistance.

"As Caesar had anticipated, we were opposed by the tribes of the Catuvellauni and the Trinovantes who were led by King Togodumnus and his brother, Caratacus. They gathered their forces on the banks of a river named Medu, where they opposed our crossing. By sending a detachment of Batavian troops upriver, our forces were able to outflank the enemy. The barbarians fought most vigorously but were ultimately routed thanks to the bravery of our soldiers. The enemy were scattered with great loss of life.

"King Togodumnus fled north to the river named Tamesis but our allies, Verica of the Atrebates and Cogidubnus of the Regni, trapped him there and slew him.

"Your army now stands a short distance from the enemy's capital of Camulodunum. In accordance with your instructions, Caesar, we have not yet attacked this stronghold but await Your Imperial Majesty's arrival to accept the surrender of the various kings of Britannia.

"Now that the Catuvellauni and Trinovantes have been crushed, the majority of the other tribes have agreed to swear allegiance to you, Caesar. Only Caratacus has refused. Together with his younger brothers and a handful of followers, he has fled to the far west, vowing not to surrender. However, his army has been destroyed and I do not expect that he will prove to be anything more than a minor nuisance.

"Caesar, may I be the first to congratulate you on adding Britannia as the newest province of Your Imperial Majesty's mighty empire."

Extract from a letter dated 2ⁿᵈ June, in the Year 51 AD. From the Roman Imperial Archives.

To His Imperial Majesty, Tiberius Claudius Caesar Augustus Germanicus Britannicus,

From Publius Ostorius Scapula, Governor of the Imperial Province of Britannia

Written on the fourth day before the Nones of Junius, in the Eight Hundred and Fourth Year since the founding of the city of Rome, Claudius Caesar and Cornelius Sulla Faustus being consuls.

"Caesar, You wished to be kept informed of my progress in hunting down the rebel, Caratacus, who has continued to defy us and has waged war against us for the past eight years. As my previous letters have indicated, this Caratacus has proved most elusive, launching small attacks, then vanishing into mountainous terrain. However, my spies inform me that he has now called together a number of tribes with the intention of launching a major assault on our province.

"Having subdued the Cornovii and the Dobunni, I am now leading elements of the Fourteenth and Twentieth Legions into the territory of the Ordovices with the intention of bringing Caratacus to battle and ending his rebellion. I am informed that the enemy numbers in excess of forty thousand troops but our own soldiers are eager to close with Caratacus' army. I anticipate locating the enemy's forces within the next few days and will write again to confirm once we have gained victory over the barbarians."

3

Chapter I

Calgacus closed his eyes, allowing his other senses to soak in the pulsating atmosphere that surrounded him.

He could smell the grass, still damp from the overnight rain, now being crushed and trampled beneath the feet of thousands of men. He could smell those men, their rank body odour, the leather of their jerkins, shoes and shields, the damp wool of their cloaks.

The faint tang of lime reached his nostrils, telling him that some of the men had spiked their hair into white manes to make themselves look taller and more ferocious.

He could smell the freshness of the broad river that flowed only a few paces from where he stood. If he concentrated, he could almost feel the soft, comforting reassurance of the water as it cooled the air, creating a gentle breeze that caressed his face like a lover's kiss.

He could smell and he could feel but, above all, he could hear.

The tumult that surrounded him was almost deafening, seeming loud enough to shake the ground that he stood on.

The warriors were chanting their war songs, thumping their spears against their shields, stamping their feet. Drums pounded a frantic rhythm like a constant roll of thunder, while druids screeched curses or shouted magic spells to drive away the enemy.

Louder than all of these was the cry of the war horns. Carnyx players blasted raucous, ululating calls across the hillside, blaring their defiance. Calgacus could visualise the tall, winding carnyxes, rising like serpents above the heads of the trumpeters, each great horn culminating in the image of an animal's head. There were bears' heads with snarling jaws, boars with carved tusks and glinting, jewelled eyes, wolves' gaping maws. Each carved mouth had small, moveable parts which the carnyx players manipulated to create the horns' eerie, unearthly wails. Now they were competing to see who could produce the most terrifying call, the most ferocious blast of hate.

It was, Calgacus thought, magnificent. If he kept his eyes

closed, if he only felt, smelled and heard the war host, he could almost believe that they would win.

At last, he opened his sapphire blue eyes. He turned to look back, up the steep slope behind him to where the women and children had gathered to watch the battle that would determine the fates of every free man, woman and child among all the tribes of the Pritani.

Still detached from his surroundings, he kept his gaze moving, looking skywards. Overhead, a blanket of grey clouds hung low over the hilltop, forming a ceiling that seemed to amplify the sounds of the drums, horns and war chants. The clouds hemmed in the land below, making the hills appear more starkly majestic, more grim and threatening than usual. They also promised further rain to add to the overnight downpour that had left the grass slick and wet but, for the moment, they did no more than threaten.

Taking his time, Calgacus looked to either side, to the vast throng of warriors who had thrown off their traditional rivalries to unite against the common enemy. Lining the river bank were men of the Ordovices, of the Silures, the Deceangli and the Demetae. There were refugees from the Dobunni and the Cornovii. There were even a few hundred survivors from the Catuvellauni and Trinovantes who had fled to the west with the Great King, Caratacus.

Calgacus was counted as one of the Catuvellauni. He wore a long, drooping moustache as a sign of his heritage, although on this momentous morning he had chosen to stand in the midst of his adopted tribe, the Silures.

Calgacus was twenty-one years old. He had been a warrior since the age of thirteen, had killed his first Roman when he was fifteen, and had led his first raiding party at eighteen. He was experienced in war but he had never seen anything like this huge war host. It was the greatest gathering of tribes since the Romans had first crossed the sea from Gaul eight years earlier.

He continued to study his surroundings, casting a critical eye over the wall in front of him. The tribesmen had laboured for days to pile rocks and boulders along the bank of the river. Now the wall was as tall as a man's chest and thick enough that it would need a long stride to walk across it. The men had grumbled because a true warrior should not hide behind a wall but Caratacus, the Great King, the War Leader, had told them it would help keep

5

the Romans at bay. Calgacus' fingers were still raw from heaving and piling stones to create the barricade that the Great King had demanded.

The druids said that the wall was not necessary because their ghost fence would prevent the Romans crossing the river. They had set stakes into the ground at intervals of twenty paces, stretching along the river bank in the thin strip of grass between the wall and the water. Atop each stake was a human skull, its eyeless gaze turned towards the enemy, daring them to come and join it in death.

Finally, almost unwillingly, Calgacus looked across the river. The smells, the sounds and the sights of the mighty war host should have filled him with confidence but when he looked over to the far bank of the broad, fast-flowing Hafren, he saw the Romans mustering, forming up into their organised ranks, and his doubts returned.

"What's bothering you?" Runt asked him.

Calgacus shook his head, frowning. "We are doing this all wrong," he said, bending to shout into Runt's ear so that his friend could hear him over the bedlam that surrounded them. "This is what we did at the Medu."

Rhydderch, standing on Calgacus' right, heard him. The veteran warrior, whose wrinkled face was daubed with blue war paint, said, "I thought you lads were too young to have been at the Medu."

"We were," Calgacus replied. "But I have heard all about it from my brothers."

"So have I," Rhydderch said. "But this time it is different. The Romans cannot get round our flanks because of the other hills and woods. They must come straight across the river."

"That is what they are good at," Calgacus said.

"But we have a wall and a ghost fence," Rhydderch pointed out.

"The ghost fence won't stop them," Calgacus said scornfully.

"You'd better not let Cethinos hear you say that," advised Runt. "He hates you enough as it is."

Calgacus shrugged. Whatever the old druid, Cethinos, might say, Calgacus had witnessed too many sacrifices that had failed to halt the Roman advance to have any confidence that the ghost fence would be an effective barrier.

"Have you told Caratacus what you think?" Runt asked.

"Of course I have. But he said we must fight. He said that the druids have worked for years to build this alliance, so if he doesn't give the tribes a chance for glory and plunder, they won't stay."

"He's right there," Rhydderch growled. "That's why we came. The lads are looking forward to taking some Roman heads as trophies. Although I must admit that I don't much like standing alongside the Ordovices. I'm more used to fighting the bastards." He spat, showing his opinion of the tribesmen who held the right of the line. "They'll probably run as soon as the Romans come at them," he added sourly.

Runt nudged Calgacus' arm, jerking his head towards the slope behind them.

"Here he comes," the little man said.

The warriors turned to watch a small group of men traversing the slope behind them. Slowly, the songs subsided, the horns and drums faded. Then the men's chants turned to cheers at the sight of their chieftains.

Watching the small group on the hillside, Calgacus saw the tall figure of his brother, Talacarnos. He recognised Cadwallon, king of the Ordovices, short-legged and pudgy, wearing an ostentatious torc of gold around his throat. He saw Vosegus, king of the Deceangli and the hulking Emont, king of the Demetae. Behind the chieftains, he saw the gaunt, angular figure of old Cethinos. The grey-bearded druid's face was marred by its permanent scowl of disapproval, his dark eyes and hatchet nose prominent even at this distance. Cethinos scanned the war host, his brooding gaze seeming to fix on Calgacus.

Calgacus looked away, ignoring the druid. Like all the warriors, there was only one man in that group of chieftains whom he wanted to see.

The tall, long-haired, moustachioed Caratacus raised an arm, calling for silence.

The Great King had given this speech once already when he had addressed the Ordovices. Now he repeated it for the men who stood at the centre of his war line.

"Are the Silures ready to win?" he called.

A roar of agreement greeted the question. Spears and swords were raised high.

Caratacus said, "My friends, we have been waiting for this day

7

for eight years. Today, here on the hill of Caer Caradoc, we will decide the fate of the free tribes of the Pritani. Today we will smash the Romans and drive them back, all the way to the sea and beyond!"

He paused as another reverberating roar of approval echoed across the hillside.

"The Gods are with us!" Caratacus shouted when the cheers had died away. "Sacrifices have been made to Nodens and to the spirit of Hafren, whose river guards us. With their aid and with your bravery, we will destroy the invaders." He pumped a fist into the air. "Victory!"

"Victory!" the warriors bellowed.

The Great King treated them to a relaxed, confident smile. Pointing at Calgacus, he said, "I see you have my little brother among you. I want you to take care of him because, as you know, he is a delicate soul."

The Silures hooted with laughter at this joke. Most of them were relatively short, stocky men, with swarthy skin and dark hair. Calgacus also had dark hair, as black as a raven's wing, but in size he towered over the warriors around him. He was broad-shouldered and massively muscled, bigger even than his famous brother, the Great King, Caratacus. The Silures laughed at Caratacus calling him delicate because he had fought alongside them for several years and they knew how fearsome he was in battle.

Calgacus joined in the laughter. Caratacus met his gaze, exchanging a brief moment of companionship in a look that told Calgacus all he needed to know. The Great King, his brother, had complete faith in him.

When the laughter had died down, Caratacus thrust his fist skywards again. "Victory!" he repeated.

"Victory!" the men of the Silures echoed.

Then Caratacus moved on to repeat his speech to the men who held the left of his defensive position.

Watching his brother walk casually along the slope as if he were merely going for a stroll, Calgacus felt his doubts fade away, dissipated by Caratacus' confidence and enthusiasm. He trusted his older brother implicitly, trusted his skill, his experience and his ferocity in battle. He knew now that he should not have doubted Caratacus' plan. The Great King would not have fought if he did

8

not think he would win.

They had created an almost impregnable position on the slopes of Caer Caradoc. If the Romans attacked, they would lose; blocked by the river and the wall. If they retreated, they would be harried and pursued all the way to the distant sea. Most of the warriors thought the legions would not dare to attack because they were outnumbered more than two to one by the great war host that had assembled to face them. The Romans had trekked through the hills for weeks in an attempt to find Caratacus, the man who had defied them for eight years. Now they had found him and he had prepared a trap for them. Here, at Caer Caradoc, the invaders would meet their match at last.

It was almost time. The chieftains were splitting up, hurrying to join their tribesmen. The war horns blared again, the drums boomed their defiant beat, the men chanted their songs.

Rhydderch scowled when he saw the pudgy Cadwallon trot along the hillside behind them. "Bloody Ordovices," he growled. "The man's no fighter."

"All the more glory for us then," said Calgacus.

Rhydderch's muttered reply was lost in the cacophony of sound.

Runt pointed across the broad river. He said, "I think they are getting ready."

Calgacus held out his left arm to take his shield from his friend. This was a large rectangle of densely woven wicker, covered by a thick cowhide and with a small, domed, iron boss in the centre. He slipped his arm through the first strap that was fastened to the inside of the shield, wrapped his fist around the second, then drew his longsword from his back.

"Let them come," he said. "We are ready."

But the Romans did not come. Instead, their artillery began to fire, sending great stones arcing across the river to crash down on the wall and its defenders. Men were crushed or had limbs smashed by the great rocks of heavy limestone. Other missiles struck the wall, shattering into thousands of sharp fragments which caused dreadful cuts and lacerations when they sprayed into the densely packed mass of warriors.

Calgacus ducked when a stone flew just beyond him. As he did so, he felt a whirr of air as something else flew over his head like a giant insect. He heard a scream and turned to see the man behind

9

him falling backwards with a long, iron-tipped wooden bolt buried in his belly.

Another bolt slammed into the wall, flashing high into the air as it ricocheted from the stones. Then a third whizzed past his shoulder, slamming into the leg of another man, breaking bones and spraying blood.

Runt shouted, "They are aiming for you! They can see your breastplate!"

Calgacus glanced down at the bronze breastplate he wore. It had been a gift from Caratacus, a reward for a successful raid on a Roman supply column the previous year. It was functional, plain and undecorated but it shone with a dull gleam.

"Get down!" Rhydderch snarled as another bolt thudded into the wall, quivering as it wedged between two stones.

Calgacus ducked behind the wall, raising his shield over his head.

"Come and fight like real men!" he shouted at the distant Romans.

Still the Romans did not come. Their artillerymen continued to wind the massive horsehair ropes, dragging back the heavy throwing arms of their catapult using huge ratchets. Then another massive limestone ball would be placed in the leather cradle at the end of the wooden arm, the restraining lever would be knocked clear of the ratchet and the arm would leap forwards as the tension in the ropes was released, hurling the boulder across the river. As soon as it had been thrown, the catapult crew would begin the process all over again.

While the catapults bombarded the defences, other soldiers shot the iron-tipped bolts from huge crossbows that were mounted on wooden stands, aiming and firing with astonishing accuracy. Bolt after bolt flashed across the river, driven with such force that some were capable of passing completely through a man's body.

For the tribesmen, there was nothing to be done except endure the bombardment and pray that the Gods would keep them safe.

The barrage seemed to last forever but it eventually stopped because the Roman foot soldiers were advancing at last.

They came in three massive columns, each one eight men abreast, plunging into the dark waters of the Hafren, raising their shields high as the water reached their waists. It did not stop them. Slowly, inexorably, they advanced towards the tribesmen. Their

10

standards bobbed above their heads, small flags on cross-poles of wood. Far back in one column, Calgacus saw a silver eagle perched on a pole that was decked with bright ribbons. It seemed to drive the legionaries on, urging them to ignore the cold, swirling water.

Freed from sheltering from the artillery, Runt drew his sword. In his left hand he held a long hunting knife. With the skill of a master juggler, he idly tossed the two weapons from one hand to the other, swapping them over, then throwing them back again, catching them with nonchalant ease.

"Stop showing off, Liscus," Calgacus said to him.

Runt grinned. "I'm just trying to decide the best way to kill them," he replied cheerfully.

Calgacus returned his friend's smile. He knew that Runt was not boasting. As his nickname suggested, Liscus was a small, slightly-built man, shorter than most of the Silures. The top of his head barely reached the middle of Calgacus' chest but he was a fearsome fighter, incredibly fast and equally skilled with either hand.

It was almost time for him to show that skill. When Calgacus peered over the wall, he saw that the nearest Romans were barely twenty paces away. He could make out their faces beneath the iron helmets, could see the red and yellow patterns of their massive shields. He also saw what the leading men were about to throw.

"'Ware javelins!" he yelled.

The Romans threw their dreaded pila, long hafts of wood topped by an iron spike that formed almost a third of the javelin's length. When a pilum struck, the wooden peg that secured the iron spike to the haft of the javelin would snap, causing the soft metal of the pointed shaft to bend where it joined the haft. Nobody could throw a pilum back at the Romans. But this time the weapons did little damage. Waist deep in swirling water, the legionaries could get no purchase to power their throws.

Then Caratacus gave the signal the tribesmen had been waiting for. Carnyx horns blasted the command across the hillside, unleashing a torrent of missiles. Javelins, darts and rocks were hurled at the men in the water, the sound of them striking shields and metal armour creating a furious, rattling thunderclap.

Calgacus shouted with delight while Runt yelled insults in Latin at the men in the water and the warriors hurled more and

11

more missiles.

A few soldiers went down, claimed by the river, victims for the goddess Hafren who ruled these waters, but most of the Romans simply lifted their shields to form a protective roof and ploughed on.

They reached the river bank, hauling themselves out of the water. The posts of the ghost fence were cast down, toppling the skulls into the river. The druids screamed in outrage and disbelief as the ghost fence was overwhelmed, but the Romans quickly moved on, launching themselves at the wall.

Now the warriors learned why Caratacus had insisted on building the barricade. The short swords of the Romans could not reach across the wall but the long, ash spears of the Pritani could. They stabbed and thrust, driving legionaries back.

The centre column had reached the wall just to Calgacus' left. He could not reach the soldiers but he saw that they were spreading out, grabbing at the wall, trying to dismantle the barrier one rock at a time. They died as they ripped at the loose-fitting stones but more and more Romans were forcing their way across the Hafren and the wall was crumbling as they tore at it with their bare hands.

Then a Roman soldier jumped into a space where his comrades had made a low gap in the wall. He died as two spears thrust up beneath his shield but another legionary sprang up, and another. They leaped across the wall, shoving Silures aside, stabbing with their short swords, using their enormous shields to create space for themselves. Now, at close quarters, they could kill the unarmoured tribesmen while their own armour protected them from the spears. More Romans clambered over the wall to join them.

Calgacus ran at them, shouting at warriors to get out of his way. Charging at full speed, he smashed his shield into a Roman, knocking the man over, then swung his huge sword at another, catching the man's leg, bringing him down. A third soldier faced him but Calgacus bludgeoned the man down, smashing his sword onto the Roman's iron helmet. The Silures ran in behind him, finishing off the fallen men.

Calgacus screamed his war cry, invoking the war god of the Catuvellauni.

"Camulos!"

He leaped onto the wall, hurling back another soldier who was

12

trying to cross from the other side, then he jumped down to face the column. His sword swung left and right, his shield parried and barged. Another legionary went down with blood streaming from his face, then another with his right arm half severed by the massive blade. A third was barged back into the river, vanishing from sight as his armour pulled him beneath the water.

Runt arrived, his sword and knife darting like quicksilver, sending down another Roman. Then more warriors surged across the wall, throwing themselves at the Romans, forcing them back into the water that was now running red with blood.

"We're beating them!"

It was Rhydderch, wild-eyed and grinning like a maniac, his blue-painted face now smeared with dark splashes of blood from the men he had killed.

Calgacus paused to catch his breath. It was true, the Romans were falling back.

A huge cheer billowed downriver. Calgacus looked to his left to see his brothers, Caratacus and Talacarnos, leading a ferocious charge to rival the one he had made himself. The northernmost column of Romans was hurled back from the wall, its head crumpling and disintegrating under the ferocity of Caratacus' attack.

Then Calgacus heard another loud cheer from his right. This time, the sound came from the collective voices of the Romans.

Rhydderch swore, his voice full of dismay. "Bloody Ordovices! I knew they'd run!"

To the south, the Romans had breached the wall. Legionaries were flooding across and the men of the Ordovices, led by their king, Cadwallon, were fleeing up the hill.

"What do we do?" Rhydderch yelled. Around him, the Silures were suddenly anxious. They had been on the verge of winning a victory that was now in danger of turning into a defeat.

"Give me half the men," Calgacus said instantly. "You hold here and I'll try to stop that lot."

"Good luck to you, lad," Rhydderch said. He waved his arms frantically, signalling to the warriors.

Calgacus and Runt re-crossed the wall, jumping down to join the Silures who had not been able to reach the central Roman column. The warriors were nervous now, looking to Calgacus for reassurance.

13

"Don't worry," he called out. "We have thrown them back once. We can do it again."

The Romans who had broken the Ordovices were forming up behind the shattered, crumbling wall. They were making no effort to pursue the fleeing tribesmen. Instead, they intended to force their way along the river bank to attack the remaining Pritani from the flank and rear.

Calgacus knew there was only one way to stop them.

"Charge!"

His cry was taken up by several hundred men of the Silures as they raced to meet the challenge. Calgacus threw himself at the wall of shields that faced him. He had broken a Roman formation only a few moments earlier but this time the men were in ranks, were braced and ready, standing on relatively level ground. He heaved with his shield and he slashed with his sword but he could not break through.

Three times his shield and breastplate saved his life. A fourth time it was Runt who knocked aside a thrusting Roman sword. The warriors hacked and cut but for every Roman that went down, another took his place and at least two of the unarmoured Silures were cut down by the savage, thrusting short swords of the legionaries.

Needing room to swing his sword, Calgacus found himself facing two legionaries at a time. They pushed forwards, working together, stabbing with their short blades, forcing him back.

Back, back. Step by blood-soaked step, the warriors were driven back.

From far behind him, the carnyx blared a signal. Calgacus knew instantly what it meant.

"Run!" he yelled. "Up the hill! Form at the top!"

The tribesmen needed no encouragement. They turned and ran.

It was a painful, awful climb. The hill was so steep that Calgacus was often on all fours, hauling himself up, hampered by his sword and shield. Runt was beside him, gasping for breath as they scrambled frantically up the hill, away from the Romans.

Half way up the long slope, Calgacus risked a brief look back. The Romans were not chasing them, so he stopped to catch his breath, trying to see what had happened elsewhere. For those awful, blood-filled moments, his world had been limited to the space immediately around him, to the men beside him and the

14

enemy in front of him. He had not known anything except the desperate fight he was involved in.

What he saw when he looked around dismayed him. The dead were piled in heaps around the wall. Most of them were Pritani warriors. All three Roman columns were across the river and the hill was dark with desperately fleeing tribesmen.

He saw Vosegus, king of the Deceangli, his face pale, hand clasped to his side, vainly trying to staunch the blood that was pouring from him. Two of his men were dragging him up the hill.

As he staggered past, Vosegus gasped, "They attacked again. We could not hold them." He looked distraught as he added, "Emont of the Demetae is dead. We have lost."

"No. We will stand at the summit," Calgacus told him. He could not countenance defeat. "But you should get away. Find a druid to help with that wound."

As Vosegus' men hauled him away, Runt said, "They won't stand now."

"We must," Calgacus insisted.

It was a vain hope. Rhydderch had disappeared, Emont of the Demetae was dead, Vosegus was badly wounded and Cadwallon had fled. Without their chieftains, the warriors would not stand. Once panic set in, there was no stopping a rout. Calgacus felt tears of frustration sting his eyes as he resumed the long climb.

Caratacus was at the summit, vainly trying to restore order. The Great King's armour was scratched and dented, his face streaked with blood, but his eyes were blazing. He, at least, had not lost heart.

"What happened?" he demanded when he saw Calgacus.

"Cadwallon ran."

"Bastard! We nearly had them beaten." He gazed at Calgacus, frowning when he saw the blood that spattered his clothes and breastplate. "Are you hurt?" he asked.

"Just winded." Calgacus was bent over, hands on his knees, his breath rasping in his throat.

"Good. We stand here."

The summit was broad and flat, the approach steep and difficult. Caratacus sent Talacarnos, accompanied by a hundred warriors, hurrying across to the women and children, telling them to get away to safety. Already, some Roman troops, not legionaries

15

but lighter armed men, were climbing the hill towards the families in an attempt to cut them off from the warriors. Further down the slope, the main Roman force was formed again and slowly climbing to where Caratacus was trying to force the warriors into a battle line.

The Great King bellowed his orders in vain. The Ordovices were already gone; the Silures, feeling betrayed by their traditional rivals, did not wait to be cut down by the advancing Romans. They ran.

Calgacus saw Rhydderch, blood streaming from a cut on his arm, staggering away. Other chieftains, wounded or not, fled, taking their warriors with them.

The Deceangli, without Vosegus to lead them, also lost heart and the men of the Demetae ran with them. Mixed among them were druids, their faces stricken by terror as they fled the hill.

Caratacus yelled and screamed at the men to stand, but they ignored him as they ran across the broad summit, rushing down the shallow slope of the far side, heading for the safety of the forests beyond. Weapons were discarded so that the men could run faster.

Caratacus swore, kicking at a stone in frustration as his army disintegrated around him.

Abellio, his shield-bearer, approached the Great King, his grey moustache stained dark with sweat and the blood of the men he had slain, his eyes filled with tears of sadness and despair.

"You must flee, Lord," Abellio said to Caratacus. "We will hold them to allow you to escape."

Caratacus looked around. The Roman auxiliary troops were now between the warriors and their families, threatening to circle round behind the few men who still held the summit, while the legionaries were climbing ever closer. In a few moments the remnants of Caratacus' army would be trapped.

"We should all run," the Great King said, reluctantly conceding that the battle was lost.

Abellio gave him a sad smile. "I am too old to run," he said. "We are tired of running. Go. Now." He looked at Calgacus. "Make him go."

"You are the best of men, Abellio," Caratacus said as he clasped the old warrior's hand.

"Go!" Abellio urged them.

Calgacus wanted to stay, wanted to fight rather than flee, but

Caratacus was their only hope and must not be taken by the enemy. Calgacus could not abandon his brother. He grabbed Caratacus' arm and they ran, with Runt following close behind, his short legs pounding the turf as he struggled to keep up.

Glancing left, Calgacus saw his other brother, Talacarnos, waving frantically, urging them to escape. Then the Roman troops closed in and Talacarnos vanished from his sight.

Caratacus shouted in anguish when he saw his daughter, Rufinna, being seized. He stopped, staring helplessly back towards her but Calgacus grabbed his arm again.

"Come on!" he shouted. "We cannot help them now."

Swearing, Caratacus allowed himself to be dragged away.

Cethinos appeared from a fold in the ground to their right. The old druid beckoned them, desperately waving his arm. "Over here!" he shouted. "There are horses."

They ran. In a small hollow they found Cethinos waiting anxiously with six men of the King's personal guard. They held a score of horses.

"Hurry!" Cethinos shouted as a warrior helped him mount one of the sturdy ponies.

Runt, lithe and agile as ever, ran to a free horse and vaulted up into the saddle with one bound. Calgacus boosted his brother onto another horse then grabbed for the nearest free pony. He had no mounting step but the horse was one of the small, shaggy-coated breed that he was used to. He was tall enough to mount without a step if necessary.

It was necessary now. Sheathing his sword, he grabbed for two of the pommels and leaped upwards, swinging his right leg high. The horse skittered and danced when he landed heavily on the saddle but he quickly brought it under control. His long legs dangled loosely on either side of the beast but he was held securely by the tall saddle which had four rounded pommels, one at each corner, and a high front and back to hold him in place. He grabbed the reins, raised his heels and jabbed his mount into motion.

Cethinos was already galloping away. The others followed, the warriors huddling protectively around Caratacus. From the top of the hill, the sounds of fighting reached their ears, taunting them as they galloped away from Caer Caradoc.

Calgacus felt sick. His worst fears had come true. Once again, victory had turned to bitter defeat.

17

Chapter II

Publius Ostorius Scapula, Governor of the province of Britannia, sat in his campaign tent, leaning over the small table that served as his desk, scratching at the writing tablet with his iron-tipped stylus. He had secretaries who could have written the despatch but there were some messages that were so important, he felt it necessary to write them himself.

The Emperor Claudius had been waiting for a long time to hear that Britannia was finally subdued. Of course, the Emperor had celebrated the conquest of the island years before, marching through the streets of Rome in triumphal procession after the majority of the island's tribes had submitted to him. But there had never truly been peace. The rebel, Caratacus, had waged a guerrilla campaign for years, hiding in the hills and forests of the west, constantly stirring up trouble.

Scapula considered the Empire's newest province to be nothing but trouble. He had been appointed Governor a little over three years previously. He recalled with a sense of annoyance that it had been the Emperor's freedman, Narcissus, who had actually given him his briefing before he had left Rome. That still rankled with Scapula. A former consul of Rome should at least receive the courtesy of being briefed by the Emperor personally. But Claudius, Scapula knew, was a witless old fool, dominated by his slaves, his freedmen and his wife. Galling as it had been to be given instructions by a mere freedman, Scapula conceded that he had probably got more sense out of Narcissus than he would ever have got out of the bumbling Claudius.

And so here he was, at the end of the world. His predecessor, Aulus Plautius, had conquered the main part of the island, subdued the tribes who had opposed the invasion, and cowed those who had thought better of fighting. Plautius had done a competent enough job, Scapula conceded, but he had never been able to deal with Caratacus. When Plautius' term of office had expired, it was Scapula who had been sent to complete the task. Now, at last, he

18

had succeeded.

He scraped a few more carefully chosen words. This victory, he hoped, might persuade the Emperor to recall him to Rome, to award him triumphal regalia for finally crushing the rebels. Then Scapula could enjoy the fruits of his success far away from this pestilential island with its barbarian inhabitants and its almost total lack of civilised amenities.

He detested Britannia. Other ex-consuls were sent to the east, to the wealthy provinces of Asia or to Greece, which at least had some culture that a civilised man could enjoy. Africa would not have been so bad either. Scapula would even have been moderately happy in Gaul, which was largely civilised now. But here he was in Britannia, a land of rain, wind and fog, of summers that promised warmth but then delivered days of endless rain, and of winters that promised cold and brought it in abundance. The damned place did not even have decent snow, he thought miserably. In Germania he had seen deep drifts of snow, covering the land in a thick, white blanket. It made life difficult but at least you knew what you were getting with German snow. In Britannia, snow was inevitably mixed with rain. It lay wet and slippery on the ground, quickly degenerating into slush and puddles of cold, muddy ice. Scapula hated the cold.

In his darker moods, the Governor often wondered whether he had upset the Emperor in some way, or perhaps, more to the point, had annoyed Claudius' wife, Agrippina. He could not recall doing or saying anything untoward, but it was hard to tell what offence the imperial family might take at even an innocent remark. He supposed there was probably nothing sinister in his appointment. If he had offended Agrippina, she would have had him executed rather than sent to Britannia. The Emperor's wife was not a woman who took half measures.

So here he was, Governor of the Empire's most unruly province. Narcissus had explained that the Emperor wanted a man of action in charge of Britannia, a man who would complete the conquest of the whole island. Perhaps that really had been the reason for sending Scapula to this distant, otherworldly province. But during his first three years as Governor, Scapula, the man of action, the bold and decisive general, had barely managed to advance Rome's dominion at all. Such a lack of success, he knew, looked bad on his record.

19

But things would change now. Caratacus had been defeated at last, the tribes of the west routed. Britannia would be at peace. It was important that the Emperor knew who was responsible for this great achievement, so Scapula wrote his own despatch, choosing his words with infinite care, not wishing to appear boastful while still ensuring that there could be no doubt where the credit lay.

The flap of the tent's door opened, admitting Scapula's aide, Lucius Anderius Facilis. The Tribune gave a smart salute, then removed his plumed helmet which he tucked under his arm.

Scapula looked up. "Do we have him?" he demanded impatiently.

Facilis maintained an impassive expression as he admitted, "No, sir. He seems to have escaped."

Scapula slammed the stylus down on the table. "Escaped?" he barked. "How in Jupiter's name can he have escaped?"

Facilis was used to his commander's temper. He replied calmly, "The terrain was unsuitable for our cavalry, sir. By the time they got across the river and over the hill, most of the rebels had got away into the trees."

Scapula held up the writing tablet. "Do you know what this is, Facilis?" he snapped. Before Facilis could answer, he went on, "This is a letter to the Emperor, telling him that we have finally crushed the rebels. This would have allowed me to return to Rome. Now you are telling me that Caratacus, the man who has single-handedly defied us for eight years, has escaped?" The final word rose to a high-pitched shriek of rage as he slammed the tablet down on the table in frustration.

Facilis knew better than to offer platitudes. Telling the Governor that he was sure they would soon capture the rebel leader was pointless. Such an unfounded claim would only rouse more invective about his naivety. But Facilis had come prepared.

"There is some good news, sir," he said stoically.

"Really?" Scapula asked, his voice heavy with sarcasm.

"Yes, sir. We have captured Caratacus' wife, his daughter and his brother. All alive and unharmed. We are also certain that Caratacus himself has no more than a dozen men with him. The rest of his army has scattered. The alliance of tribes has been smashed. I am sure the Emperor will be delighted to hear that."

"Don't presume to tell me what the Emperor will be delighted to hear," Scapula said. His tone was harsh but Facilis could see that the Governor's temper had been mollified by the news of their prisoners.

"His wife, daughter and brother, you say?" Scapula asked.

"Yes, sir."

"Which brother? He has two."

"The older one, sir. His name is Talacarnos."

"What about the other one? What is his name again? The young one who keeps ambushing our supply wagons."

"That would be Calgacus, sir," Facilis replied. "There is no sign of him. He may be dead, or he may be among the men who escaped with Caratacus."

"Well, at least we have the rest of the family," Scapula said grudgingly. "That is better than nothing."

"Yes, sir. What would you like done with them?"

"We will send them back to Rome, of course," Scapula said. "As proof of his utter defeat. Make sure they are well guarded. I want no harm to come to them." He gave Facilis a sharp look. "The girl hasn't been raped, has she?"

"No, sir."

"Good. Make sure she stays that way. Keep them all under a close watch."

"Of course, sir. And the other prisoners?"

"If they can walk and are not badly maimed, we'll sell them into slavery as usual. Kill any who are badly wounded or disfigured."

"Do you want them crucified, sir?"

"No, just use the sword. Get it over with quickly. I don't want to stay here any longer than we have to."

"Very good, sir. Speaking of which, the Legates are wondering what your intentions are now. Do we press on in pursuit of the rebels?"

Scapula picked up his stylus, tapping the end against his teeth. He had brought the Fourteenth and the Twentieth legions with him, along with elements of the Second and a score of auxiliary units. With an army that size, he could defeat any force the barbarians might muster. Somewhere beyond the rugged hills and steep-sided valleys was the island of Mona, the home of the druids. That was a tempting target, a prize that would ensure his reputation for all time if he could seize it.

Scapula knew he was often accused by his rivals of being a

21

hothead, a man who rashly charged into any situation. He acknowledged that the accusation was partly true but three years in Britannia had helped to temper his boldness.

After some consideration, he said, "No. We will withdraw. We are a long way from our supply bases. I have no wish to go blundering around in the hills for weeks on end while Caratacus dances round us. Besides, you know this damned island as well as anyone, Facilis. If we stay here, trouble will flare up somewhere else."

"Yes, sir. I shall inform the Legates."

"We'll build a chain of forts to keep the western tribes under observation," Scapula decided. "I'll put the Fourteenth Legion near the northern end and the Second near the south. The Twentieth we will hold in reserve. They are under strength anyway and need time to recruit and train more men."

"Yes, sir. I will have the orders drafted for your approval. Do you have any orders for the Ninth Legion?"

"No. They should remain at Lindum for the time being. I need them to watch the northern frontier." He rubbed his chin pensively. "By Jupiter, we are stretched thin. It's just as well we have disarmed the tribes in the south and east."

"Yes, sir," Facilis replied flatly, managing to conceal his private thoughts. He recalled with chilling clarity that one of the Governor's first decisions when he had arrived in Britannia was to order the conquered tribes to hand over their weapons. It had almost led to a full-scale rebellion. The Iceni, in particular, had been incensed. Their king had declared that he was an ally of Rome, not a subject. When Scapula had stubbornly insisted that every tribe should be prohibited from bearing arms, the Iceni had renounced their allegiance. Only a brutally swift and bloody campaign had suppressed them. Their king had had his head removed and a new, more amenable, ruler had been installed in his place.

Governor Scapula had regarded the revolt as little more than an inconvenience but Facilis was not so sure. It was true that the new Iceni ruler, Prasutagus, was very pro-Roman, or at least too afraid to be anti-Roman, but many in his tribe remained angry. Facilis could still vividly recall the fiery gaze of Prasutagus' wife, the tall, red-haired woman named Bonduca. She had said very little when her husband had been elevated to the kingship, but when he had seen the spark of defiance in her eyes, Facilis had been thankful that it was her husband and not she who had been chosen by the Governor as the new ruler. Like many of the other conquered tribes, the Iceni were a simmering pot, ready to boil over at the slightest provocation.

Facilis sighed inwardly. Like so many Romans, Ostorius Scapula neither knew nor cared what the local inhabitants wanted. Their choice was simple. As far as the Governor was concerned, they would become civilised or they would be killed. Rome brought many benefits but she did not tolerate dissent. Facilis knew this, which was why he could already guess the Governor's response to the next problem. He braced himself for another outburst of temper.

"We have received a letter from the Procurator, sir," Facilis said. "He sent it from the new colony at Camulodunum."

Scapula frowned. Facilis could tell that the Governor wanted to concentrate on his despatch to the Emperor. Reluctantly, Scapula asked, "What does he say?"

"It's the new temple, sir. The one you persuaded the local chieftains to build in honour of the Emperor."

"I know which temple you are referring to, Facilis," Scapula said testily. "What about it?"

Facilis cleared his throat. "According to the Procurator, the barbarians are complaining about the taxes being raised to pay for the construction."

"It is the Procurator's job to collect the taxes," the Governor replied. "I have other things to worry about. He knows the barbarians must pay, so tell him to collect what is due. It was the locals who wanted to worship the Emperor in the first place. If they are going to do that, they will do it properly, in a proper temple, not in some muddy forest clearing or a ragged circle of stones. They should stop grumbling and pay up."

"Quite right, sir," Facilis said smoothly. "But the Procurator and the Town Council have already pointed that out to them without much success. It seems there has been some violent resistance to the tax collectors. Nothing too serious. A few broken bones and a little blood spilled, but the Procurator is not pleased. He has asked that you send some soldiers to restore order and ensure the taxes are collected."

Scapula sat back on his chair, shaking his head wearily. "What

23

did I tell you, Facilis? Turn your back on these Britons for a moment and they cause trouble."

"Yes, sir, What would you like me to tell the Procurator?"

Scapula gave his aide a cold, hard stare. "Tell him I shall send an auxiliary cohort. But I don't want the taxes collected."

Facilis blinked in surprise. "You don't?"

"No, Facilis. I want the trouble-makers put in chains. If they won't pay their taxes like free men, they can build the temple themselves as slaves." He gave a humourless smile. "Tell the Procurator to seize their properties as well. That should help defray the costs and will encourage other people to pay their taxes promptly."

"Yes, sir."

"Is there anything else?"

"No, sir."

"Good. I need to finish this despatch. I don't want to be disturbed unless you can bring me news of Caratacus' capture."

Facilis placed his helmet on his head, thumped a fist to his chest in salute and left as quickly as he could. All things considered, he felt that he had escaped quite lightly.

Outside, a few spots of light rain moistened his cheeks as he looked across the river to the scene of the morning's fighting. Soldiers were gathering weapons and plundering the bodies of the fallen. Prisoners were being herded into the camp and wood was being gathered for funeral pyres. Not that the barbarians would be cremated, of course; they would be left to rot. Only the Roman dead would be burned.

Facilis watched a cavalry patrol splash across the river, heading up the steep slope on their way to search for the rebel leader, Caratacus. He knew they were unlikely to find him. The man had a talent for vanishing into the wilderness, and one thing Britannia had plenty of was wilderness. The island was crammed with hills, forests and swamps that could conceal an army, let alone one man.

It was disappointing that the rebel leader had escaped but Facilis was not overly concerned. Caratacus had evaded them for years but now that his army had been destroyed, the myth of his invincibility had been shattered. He could hide from them, but he could no longer trouble them. The simple truth was that Caratacus had nowhere left to go.

Chapter III

Calgacus was dreaming of defeat.

It was not the humiliating flight from Caer Caradoc that troubled his sleep but an earlier battle, one that had been fought when he had been a boy of thirteen, not yet old enough to be declared a man despite the fact that he was bigger and stronger than many who were older than he was. It was frustrating. While boys he had known for years had already been acknowledged as men, Calgacus was still regarded as a child.

The dream had not troubled him for several years. In the early days after Caratacus had taken him away to the far west, it had often visited him, disturbing his sleep, but as time had passed it had gradually ceased to torment him. Now, triggered by his feelings of loss and failure, it had returned and the memories were as vivid as ever.

He had wanted to go to war but he had been left behind in Camulodunon when Togodumnus and Caratacus had led the war host to fight the newly arrived Romans at the Medu. Runt, who claimed that he was already fourteen, had been given a spear by Togodumnus. Calgacus had accused his friend of lying about his age but Runt had insisted that he was old enough to be counted as a man. Because he was an orphan, and had not been with the tribe very long, nobody could argue with him, so he had proudly carried around a heavy spear that was almost twice as tall as he was, while Calgacus was not permitted to carry a man's weapon.

With the war host gone, taking many of the families with them, the two boys had waited for news, trying to avoid the chores that Verran, Togodumnus' wife, had given them.

"If you want fresh bread baked," she had said, "You will need to grind the flour. It won't do itself."

Calgacus hated the daily grind. He thought it was women's work but Verran often made him turn the heavy quern stones because, even at thirteen, he was stronger than most of the women.

Little Beatha had been sitting at Verran's knee, holding a small spindle as she tried to copy Verran's deft movements, spinning wool that would be woven into clothes and blankets.

All golden hair and blue eyes, eight-year-old Beatha had asked, "Where is your spear, Calgacus? Liscus has got one."

Calgacus had scowled at her but Verran had hushed Beatha into silence. Beatha stuck her tongue out at Calgacus, grinning because she knew he could not get his own back while Verran was around.

Cethinos looked up from his iron divining rods and collection of carved knuckle bones to say, "The boy does not need a spear. He is to be trained as a druid. His father agreed to it on the day he was born."

"I don't want to be a druid!" Calgacus had protested. "I want to be a warrior like my brothers."

"Your half-brothers," Cethinos corrected automatically before adding. "You cannot escape your destiny, boy."

Verran, acting peace-maker as she so often did, had changed the subject by asking Cethinos, "What about Togodumnus? Is there any news?"

The druid, sitting cross-legged outside the roundhouse, had been casting his arcane divining rods and knuckle bones all morning, examining the way they landed in an attempt to read the future in their patterns. Prompted by Verran's question, he tugged thoughtfully at his long, grey beard while he studied them again.

"Great things are happening," he replied after a long pause. "But the will of the Gods is unclear."

"That means he doesn't know," Calgacus whispered to Runt.

Cethinos looked up sharply, his dark, brooding eyes narrowing as he stared at Calgacus. The druid may have been more than fifty years old but there was nothing wrong with his hearing.

"Do not try my patience, boy," he hissed. "If you had paid any attention to the lessons I have been trying to beat into you for the past few years, you would know that it is not an easy matter to interpret the will of the Gods."

"I am sure Calgacus meant no disrespect," Verran said, trying to soothe the old man's habitual bad temper. "We just wanted to know whether the Romans had been beaten yet."

"There is one way to discover the truth," Cethinos said, giving Calgacus a malevolent stare. "I could open the boy's fat belly and read the future in his entrails."

26

"Cethinos!" Verran said abruptly.

Calgacus swallowed nervously, but he was more annoyed at being called a boy than at the threat of being sacrificed. Cethinos would offer a human sacrifice whenever possible but he would not dare touch a son of the great Cunobelinos.

Runt gave a sudden shout of excitement as he pointed towards the west. "Look!"

"They are back!" Calgacus said. "The Romans have been beaten already." He shot Cethinos a triumphant look but decided it would be sensible not to ask the druid why his divining rods had failed to reveal the imminent return of the war host.

Everyone rose to their feet as a line of chariots appeared at the far edge of the wide settlement.

Verran was wringing her hands nervously, her wool discarded on the ground, her expression a mixture of apprehension and expectation. Little Beatha hovered near her, seeking some protection behind Verran.

Calgacus waited, unable to still his racing heart as he saw the chariots hurrying through the wide spaces of Camulodunon, curving between the roundhouses, avoiding plots of sown earth, scattering geese, sheep, goats and pigs as they approached the king's home.

"The ponies look exhausted," Calgacus observed.

"The drivers and warriors, too," agreed Runt. "Where is Togodumnus?"

"It's Caratacus!" Calgacus said. "He's hurried back to tell us of the victory."

"Hush, Cal," Verran whispered.

He glanced up at her, saw the fear in her face. Instinctively, he reached out to hold her hand. Verran had been like a mother to him, as she had been to Runt and Beatha.

"Togodumnus will come soon," he assured her.

The leading chariots wheeled to a halt ten paces from the door of the house. When Caratacus stepped down, the haunted look on his face was enough to drop Verran to her knees with a wail of anguish.

"Where is Togodumnus?" Calgacus called.

Caratacus walked slowly towards them, his expression bleak. His coat of chainmail was battered and dusty with travel, spattered with mud and dark stains of dried blood. His huge longsword hung

27

on his back, the hilt half-hidden by the tangled, matted masses of his untamed hair. His long moustache could not conceal the pain of his distress.

Talacarnos dismounted from the second chariot. He, too, seemed unwilling or unable to answer the question. He held back, standing beside the chariot with his head bowed while Caratacus approached Verran.

"Where is Togodumnus?" Calgacus repeated, his voice catching in his throat. He already knew the answer; he could see it in the men's faces.

"I am sorry, Little Brother," Caratacus said, his own voice thick with emotion. "He is dead."

"No!" Calgacus' cry was drowned by another heart-rending wail from Verran.

"He almost beat them," Caratacus said, addressing Verran even though she was oblivious to his words. It was as if he needed to tell the story, to share the burden of his grief.

"He led a charge into the midst of their army. They should have broken and run. Any normal men would have fled but these Romans—" He broke off, shaking his head at the memory.

"The war host?" Cethinos asked, his own voice not immune to emotion, although it was horrified disbelief rather than grief that afflicted him.

"Destroyed," Caratacus said grimly. "We were betrayed. After they threw us back from the Medu, we broke off to re-group. Togodumnus was still alive. We fell back to the Tamesas, hoping to stop them there. He sent me into the marshes, to ambush the Roman advance while he went upriver, to guard the ford. We ambushed them well enough, killed a good few, but then we heard the news."

Calgacus felt as if his heart was about to burst with agony. Togodumnus could not be dead. Must not be dead.

Caratacus went on, "Three traitors joined the enemy. They were waiting at the ford. Togodumnus never had a chance. His force was outnumbered five to one. Only a handful escaped."

"Who?" Cethinos demanded. "Who betrayed us?"

"Our own brother, Adminius, came across the sea with the Romans," Caratacus spat. "As did Verica of the Atrebates. As soon as they arrived, Cogidubnus of the Regni joined them."

"The Gods will punish them for their treachery," Cethinos said darkly.

"I will punish them," Caratacus vowed. Then he stiffened as his eyes settled on Beatha who had placed an arm around Verran's shoulders, trying to comfort the distraught woman.

When she saw Caratacus glare at her, the blonde-haired girl put a hand to her mouth, her eyes opening wide with terror.

Verran shrieked, "No!"

Caratacus stepped forwards, one hand reaching back over his shoulder to draw his famous longsword.

"Move aside, Verran," he ordered harshly. "She was given as a hostage for her brother's loyalty."

Verran was still on her knees, scrabbling through tear-stained eyes to ward Caratacus away while Beatha stepped back, edging towards the door of the roundhouse.

Calgacus jumped in front of his brother. "Do not do this!" he shouted.

"Out of my way, Little Brother," said Caratacus. "Cogidubnus betrayed us after pledging loyalty. What is the good of taking his sister hostage if we do not kill her when he breaks faith?"

"It is not her fault," Calgacus said desperately. "She is our friend. It was her brother who betrayed us, not her."

"Her brother killed Togodumnus!" Caratacus shouted.

"I know. But killing her won't bring him back," Calgacus replied defiantly.

Like all the sons of Cunobelinos, Caratacus was a tall man, a trained warrior. He could easily have knocked Calgacus aside but he said, "I must do this, Little Brother. Stand aside."

"No." Calgacus stood his ground. "You are our king now. If you cannot spare her, then who can?"

Caratacus paused. He was plainly tired, almost exhausted, his brain dulled by shock, grief and lack of sleep. He looked down at Calgacus.

"If I am the king," he said, "you must do as I say."

"Beatha has done nothing wrong!" Calgacus insisted. "Togodumnus would not kill an innocent girl. Can you not show mercy?"

"Mercy?" Cethinos snorted. "Kill the girl and be done with it! Her death will appease the Gods."

The druid's words only strengthened Calgacus' resolve. "A druid will always call for death," he said to Caratacus. "A king should know when to show mercy." He looked up at his older brother, held his blue eyes, pleading with him. "You never know when you might need someone to show you some mercy. How can you expect it to be granted to you if you do not give it yourself when you are able? Please, Brother. Togodumnus treated Beatha like his own daughter. Do not betray his trust."

The massive blade in Caratacus' hand dropped. He closed his eyes for a moment, sighing deeply.

"A fine start to my kingship," he said softly, "My army destroyed and my family defying me." Wearily, he sheathed his sword. "Very well, for the sake of my brother, I will spare her life. But she cannot come with us. She must stay here and face whatever Rome brings."

Cethinos muttered in disgust but Calgacus breathed a sigh of relief. He wanted to turn to Beatha, to make sure that she was safe but Caratacus' words were too important.

"Go?" he asked. "Where are we going?"

"I don't know," Caratacus admitted. "But we cannot stay here. Camulodunon cannot be defended by the few men we have left. The Romans could be here in a matter of days. We must leave."

"We should go to the Iceni," Calgacus told him. "Bonduca is there."

"The Iceni refused to join us when we called for their aid," Caratacus said, his mouth twisting in anger at the memory. "They have already taken Roman gold as the price of peace. They would not welcome us, even if our sister is married to one of their king's cousins. We cannot go there."

"Then where?" Calgacus wanted to know.

"We should go west," Cethinos said. "The druids of Ynis Mon will ensure the western tribes resist the invaders. There are hills and valleys where the Romans will not dare venture."

Caratacus made up his mind quickly. "Since there is nowhere else, that is what we will do. We will raise another army."

He went to his chariot, picking up a long spear, a smooth piece of ash that was tipped by a wickedly sharp, leaf-shaped blade. He tossed it to Calgacus who caught it deftly.

"For me?" Calgacus asked, scarcely believing that he was holding such a potent weapon.

"I think what you just did proves you are a man," Caratacus said. "Now gather up your things and let us be off. We must get away from here."

Calgacus turned to grin at Cethinos. He held the spear up, showing it to the druid who spluttered, "He is to be sent to Ynis Mon on his fourteenth birthday! Your father promised he would be trained as a druid."

Caratacus shook his head. "Our father is long dead, Cethinos. I am king now and I need every warrior I can get. Besides, you are always complaining that Calgacus cannot remember your lessons. Now hurry, or we'll leave you behind as well. You know what the Romans do to druids."

The threat was enough to silence Cethinos' arguments. Without another word, he rushed off to his small roundhouse to gather his belongings.

They were ready in only a few moments because almost everything was to be abandoned. They piled chariots and ponies with food and weapons, spare cloaks and some iron tools but there was no time to take much else.

Caratacus did not order everyone to leave. There were many who wished to stay, to risk surrendering to Rome. Verran was among them. She refused to leave the home she had shared with Togodumnus, refused to abandon Beatha. Caratacus did not argue with her. He embraced her, kissed her forehead and climbed aboard his chariot, stepping up beside Calgacus.

The driver flicked the reins, urging the tired ponies into motion. Calgacus looked over to Runt who shared a chariot with Talacarnos. Both boys proudly held their spears, ready to defend themselves should the Romans attack.

As the chariots rolled towards the gates of Camulodunon, Calgacus turned to look back. Verran stood with one arm around Beatha's shoulders. He had saved the young girl's life but he knew what the Romans did to women and children when they stormed a town. Everybody knew. Beatha's life, like Verran's would not be a long one.

Calgacus had a spear and was counted as a man. He had avoided the fate that Cethinos had decreed for him. It should have been the greatest day of his young life but it was not. All he felt was the crushing weight of loss and the certainty that the world he had grown up in had ended.

Calgacus jerked awake when someone kicked him.

"What is it?" he asked groggily.

He sat up, blinking in the darkness, not quite sure where he was. His nerves were still tingling with the sense of dread that his dream had inspired and it took a few moments for his mind to disentangle the present from the vivid memories of the past. Part of him hoped that the awful defeat at Caer Caradoc had been part of his dream, but one look at the haggard faces of the men around him told him that it had been all too real. Eight years had passed since Togodumnus had died and little Beatha had been abandoned to her fate, but the crushing sense of failure and defeat was the same now as it had been on that awful day.

"Is something wrong?" he asked as he came fully awake.

"You were having a bad dream," Caratacus said.

Calgacus pulled himself up, awkwardly adjusting the folds of his cloak.

"I'm sorry," he apologised as he moved to sit beside his brother.

"Don't be. My own dreams were too bad to give me much sleep." Caratacus was sitting with his back against the trunk of a large oak tree, his hands clasped around his upraised knees. The Great King's eyes held a haunted look.

Other men were stirring as the gloom of the forest they had hidden in was lifted by the first glimmerings of a dull, grey dawn. The warriors had lit a small fire and were boiling some water to make a herbal tisane but there was nothing to eat. They had spent hungry nights in the forests before, but the previous night had been infinitely worse because they were weighed down by the oppressive burden of their defeat. That burden showed no signs of lifting with the sunrise.

"What do we do now?" Calgacus asked.

Caratacus did not appear to have heard the question. He stared at a distant nothing, lost in a dream as if his eyes could no longer bear to look upon the real world.

Cethinos left the fire and stalked over to them, planting his long staff on the soft grass in front of him as he stood over the two brothers. The dark eyes above his hatchet nose glared down at them.

"We should go to Ynis Mon," he told them. "The Druid Council must be informed of what has happened."

When Caratacus did not reply, Calgacus said, "They will hear of it soon enough. Other druids survived. They were running faster than anybody."

Cethinos' scowl deepened. "Nevertheless, we should go there," he insisted, letting the jibe pass for once. "We can seek guidance from the Gods."

Anger, frustration and the acrid taste of defeat made Calgacus' temper flare. "The Gods did not help us yesterday," he snapped. "What makes you think they will help us now?"

"Insolent whelp!" Cethinos snapped. He jerked his staff towards Calgacus, as if to strike him but Calgacus knocked it aside with his forearm. He pushed himself upwards, intending to surge to his feet but Caratacus thrust out an arm to restrain him.

"Sit down, Little Brother!" the Great King commanded. Glaring up at the druid, he said, "Leave us for a while. I must think."

Cethinos glowered at Calgacus, his nostrils flaring. "You should learn some respect, boy," he hissed. "It is because of you and others like you that the Gods abandon us. Why should they help us when you mock them with your insolence?"

Caratacus said, "Please, Cethinos. Let me speak to my brother. He meant no disrespect. He spoke harshly because he is young and hurting."

"We are all hurting," Cethinos replied scathingly. He stood there for a long moment but eventually realised that Caratacus was not going to speak until he had left. After giving Calgacus another frosty stare, he turned away, returning to sit by the fire.

"I don't need you to speak for me, Brother," Calgacus said softly when the druid was out of earshot.

"Yes, you do," Caratacus told him. "You should know better than to antagonise Cethinos. He has ambitions to become a member of the Druid Council."

"Then we would be rid of him," Calgacus retorted.

"No. Then he would be even more influential than he is now. It is not wise to make an enemy of such a man. Especially now, when we need all the help we can get."

Calgacus felt chastened by his brother's gentle reprimand. "All right," he said, "I will try to curb my tongue. But I don't think we should go to Ynis Mon. The druids have failed in everything they have promised us. Their ghost fence did nothing to stop the Romans."

"Something you had best not mention when Cethinos can hear you," Caratacus warned. "Especially because you are right."

Calgacus gave a bitter laugh. "Being right does not help when you are dealing with Cethinos. I learned that a long time ago."

"You were right about the battle, too," Caratacus said softly. "We should not have fought them that way. They are too strong. Flesh and blood cannot win against metal armour in a head-on fight."

"What else could we have done? You said it yourself. The tribes wanted a battle."

"There were lots of things we could have done," Caratacus said ruefully. "We could have lured them deeper into the hills. We could have ambushed them on the march, attacked their camps, harried their supply trains." He shook his head sadly. "Anything except what we did. I should have listened to you, Little Brother. I forgot the lesson I learned when we faced them on the banks of the Medu eight years ago. That battle cost us our brother, Togodumnus. This one has cost me almost everything else."

Calgacus did not know what to say. Apart from Calgacus, Caratacus had lost his entire family to the Romans. There were no words that could hope to be adequate to console him. Yet Calgacus knew his brother. Caratacus did not require consolation. He required vengeance.

"So what do we do now?" Calgacus asked again, knowing he would receive an answer this time.

"We must find somewhere we can raise another army."

"Where? Back to the Silures?"

"No. The tribes of the west will not rise again. Not yet, anyway."

"Then where?"

"We must go north," Caratacus stated firmly.

Calgacus could not hide his astonishment. "North? To the Brigantes? They are savages."

"We thought that about the Silures when we first joined them," Caratacus said with a wry smile. "But the civilised tribes of the south, including our own, fell to the Romans in only a few months, while the Silures have resisted for years. Perhaps we need to recruit some more savages."

Runt raised another objection when he heard what Caratacus

34

proposed.

"The Brigantes were one of the first tribes to make peace with Rome," he pointed out.

"That was when the Romans were a long way from them," Caratacus said. "Now, the Empire has pushed north, to the very fringes of their territory. The Cornovii and the Coritani have already been conquered. The Brigantes will be next to fall, you can be sure of that."

Cethinos was not convinced. "We should go to Ynis Mon," he said again. "The Brigantes are friends of Rome. I have heard that all druids have been banished from their territory."

"A political decision," Caratacus insisted. "You know how the Romans feel about druids. They would not allow any tribe to harbour a druid. But the people will not have given up their beliefs."

"Unlike some," Cethinos muttered darkly, giving Calgacus a sidelong look.

"Perhaps you could go to Ynis Mon while we ride to Brigantia," Calgacus suggested hopefully.

They all knew that Caratacus had made up his mind. There was no question of any of the warriors disputing his decision. Only Cethinos would need persuading.

The druid snorted in disgust when he heard Calgacus' suggestion. "Whatever you may think, you will need the support of the druids if you are to continue to fight." He turned to Caratacus. "I served your father, the great Cunobelinos. I will not abandon you now. I will accompany you to the north if that is where you wish to go."

Calgacus exchanged a resigned look with Runt. He had hoped the druid would refuse to come with them but it seemed they were doomed to be dogged by his stark disapproval. Runt gave a slight shake of his head, warning Calgacus to say nothing.

Caratacus appeared pleased by Cethinos' decision. "Good," he said. "If you can help bring the Brigantes into the war, the Druid Council will be impressed."

"I do not act for my own selfish ends," Cethinos said frostily. "I do what I do for the good of the free tribes of the Pritani."

"Then we are agreed," Caratacus said smoothly. "We will go to the Brigantes. What can you tell us about that tribe? It is years since I met old Volisios, their king."

"Volisios is dead," Cethinos replied. "I heard the news only a few moons ago."

"So who rules the tribe now?"

Cethinos shrugged. "That is uncertain. You know that the Brigantes inhabit a very large territory, almost all the northern part of what we regard as the civilised part of the island. Beyond them live the wild tribes of the far north, the Caledones and other Picts."

"Maybe we should ask them to join us, too," ventured Calgacus.

"The Caledones have no interest in anything but their own affairs," Cethinos said. "To an extent, the same is true of the Brigantes. They are more a loose confederation of related people than a unified tribe. They are often at war among themselves."

"That doesn't sound encouraging," Runt said, earning himself an angry look from the druid.

Cethinos continued, "Sometimes they do come together under one chieftain whom they acknowledge as their king. If one of their leaders is strong enough, he can persuade the others to obey him. Volisios, who governed them for the past twenty years, was such a man."

"But now there is no single ruler?" Caratacus guessed.

"There may be. If I recall what I heard correctly, Volisios had a daughter. Her name is Cartimandua. I believe she has proclaimed herself Queen of the Brigantes."

A slight frown crossed Caratacus' brow. "That could either help or hinder us," he said pensively. "If she is able to hold the tribe together, we might be able to influence her more easily than we could an older, more experienced ruler. But a young, inexperienced woman is unlikely to inspire the tribe's loyalty. If she shows any weakness, the other chieftains will be like a pack of wolves around a dying stag."

"From what little I have heard," Cethinos said, "she is far from weak. She had an older brother who would have been king, but he died unexpectedly a year or so ago. There are rumours that it was not accidental."

"She killed her own brother?" Calgacus asked, appalled at the thought.

Cethinos shrugged. "Who can say? There was another sibling as well, a sister, I think. But she has . . . disappeared."

"So there are no rivals to dispute Cartimandua's inheritance?"

36

Caratacus asked. "That is very convenient for her."

"I did not say there are no rivals," the druid replied. "I simply have no knowledge of who might dispute her rule. But I believe we can be confident that she is strong-willed enough to rule the Brigantes on her own."

Caratacus took a deep breath. "It is not as if we have much choice," he said. "We will go to Brigantia and meet this new, young queen." He slapped Calgacus on the shoulder. "Maybe you could marry her, Little Brother. That would bring her onto our side."

"What if she is ugly?" Calgacus asked.

"Even more reason for you to marry her," Caratacus laughed. "She will be desperate for a husband."

Everyone joined in the laughter except Calgacus and Cethinos. It was the first time Calgacus could remember ever agreeing with the old druid.

Chapter IV

The journey north was a slow and dangerous one because much of the territory they needed to cross was under Roman control, dotted with small forts and guarded by cavalry patrols. But Caratacus and his companions were used to travelling unseen. They rode on the higher ground, slipping from forest to forest, avoiding villages and keeping well clear of any Roman forts. Caratacus was impatient at their slow progress but stealth was more important than speed.

Food was their greatest problem. Water was plentiful, for the streams and rivers were in full flood, fed by snow-melt and the recent heavy rains. The ponies could crop the long grass whenever they halted for the night but the men went hungry unless they could catch some small fish or unless Runt, who was a skilled marksman with his sling, could bring down a plump bird.

They raided birds' nests for eggs or young chicks, picked early berries when they could, and visited isolated farmsteads where Caratacus traded small ringlets of iron or bronze, the universal currency, for what food the farmers could spare.

Cethinos remained out of sight on such visits, for none of them wanted news of a druid to be passed on to the Romans.

Calgacus and Runt rode at the rear of the group, maintaining as much distance as possible from Cethinos, who rode beside Caratacus, deep in conversation.

Eight days into their journey, as they were ambling along a low ridge, Runt gave his friend an inquisitive look.

"What is bothering you now?" he asked.

"Nothing," Calgacus replied.

"Don't give me that, Cal. I've known you too long. You don't think this is a good idea, do you?"

"I trust Caratacus," Calgacus said defensively.

"But you don't agree with him," Runt accused.

"I'm not sure."

"What are you not sure about?"

Calgacus sighed. "I just think we would be better off with the

Silures. We know them and we know the land."

Runt shook his head. "The Silures are beaten, remember?"

"For the moment. But they would join us again. A lot of them got away."

"Cethinos says the Brigantes can summon an army of fifty thousand," Runt pointed out. "He also says that the land to the north is rugged, with lots of hills and valleys. It sounds ideal for us."

"Cethinos says a lot of things," Calgacus grumbled. "How does he know? He's never been here before."

"He's a druid," said Runt. "Druids know things."

"All Cethinos knows is how to slit the throat of a captive or how to read the Gods' will in the entrails of a dead prisoner."

Runt laughed. "You can't disagree with something just because it is Cethinos who says it. Anyway, this was Caratacus' idea. Cethinos wanted to go to Ynis Mon. Would you rather go there?"

"You know I wouldn't."

"Then we don't have much choice. We either go to Brigantia or we surrender to the Romans and I'm never going to do that." The little man spat for luck. "I've been a Roman slave once before. I'm never going back to that. I'll kill myself first."

Calgacus was not surprised by the vehemence in his friend's voice. Runt had been born a slave and had spent the first years of his life being whipped and abused by his master, a travelling merchant. When the trader had crossed the sea from Gaul in an attempt to make his fortune among the Pritani, Runt had run away. With Calgacus' help, he had been welcomed by the Catuvellauni but he had never forgotten his brutal upbringing which had left him with an abiding hatred of all things Roman.

Sympathetic to his friend's mood, Calgacus tried to make light of the subject. "The way things are going," he observed, "the Romans will probably kill us all anyway."

Runt gave a short, mocking laugh. "By Toutatis, Cal. I'm glad you are thinking positively. I'd hate it if you were feeling depressed."

Calgacus did not answer. His eyes were fixed on the other riders who had come to a stop on the top of a low rise up ahead. He urged his pony into a trot, bending his knees to lift his feet from the long grass. With a resigned shake of his head, Runt followed.

Caratacus was pointing at something when they arrived, leaning to one side to speak to Cethinos in low tones. Calgacus reined in beside him, looking out across a wide, lush, heavily wooded plain. Cethinos had said that Brigantia was a land of steep hills and deep valleys, of moorlands, rocks, caves, rivers, swamps and forests, but the vista that lay before them was as far from that description as anything Calgacus had ever seen.

Ploughed fields and grassy pastures covered the broad flatland, interspersed with clumps of woodland. Oak, elm, ash, rowan, larch and a dozen other species competed for space among the fields. Scattered roundhouses marked the homes of the farmers, some of them tall, two-storey buildings where the families would sleep on an upper level above their livestock. On this bright afternoon, Calgacus could see that the fields were home to cattle and sheep, goats, pigs and small herds of ponies.

He took all this in with a single glance but what drew his attention, what Caratacus was pointing at, was a vast area surrounded by a fence of tall, wooden stakes set on an earth embankment. A wide entranceway with an open set of tall, double gates led into the massive enclosure.

Off to the left, a tree-lined river ran eastwards, then curved to the south, disappearing beyond the man-made ramparts, its path marked by the distant tops of the tall trees that grew along its banks. The line of the river revealed just how large an area the earthworks and fence enclosed.

Calgacus shaded his eyes to peer through the open gates. What he saw almost took his breath away. Beyond the gateway were dozens, perhaps scores or even hundreds of roundhouses. It was the largest village he had seen since he had left Camulodunon eight years previously. No, he corrected himself, it was much more than a village, it was a town.

He could see that the houses were smaller than the farm buildings that lay outside the ramparts. Inside the protective perimeter, the buildings were huddled together with little space separating one from the next. A faint haze of blue-grey smoke shimmered in the air above the town, the escaping fumes from the hearth fires that had seeped through the thick, straw thatch of the pointed rooftops.

People were coming and going in and out of the town. On the river, a small coracle bobbed lazily. It was as peaceful and idyllic a scene as Calgacus could recall.

Caratacus turned in his saddle. "Well, Little Brother, we are here." He pointed to the distant settlement. "That is Isuria, home of the rulers of Brigantia. Let's go and stir them up, shall we?"

They attracted many fearful looks as they rode towards Isuria. Women called to their children, ushering them inside the spurious protection of their homes while farmers fetched axes and stood watching warily until the riders had passed.

They approached the town from the west, passing a line of ancient monoliths, massively tall stones that must have stood for countless generations as a meeting place, a sanctuary, a place of open-air worship. Cethinos nodded approvingly at this sign that, whatever the Romans might have decreed, the people still clung to their old beliefs.

Calgacus was more interested in the town's defences. As he drew closer, he could tell that the ditch, rampart and fence, although impressive, were not as formidable as they first appeared. The ditch was not deep, the embankment less than the height of a man, the fence only slightly taller. The defences seemed designed more to mark the perimeter of the settlement than to protect it. Calgacus wondered whether this was because the Brigantes were confident that nobody would dare to attack Isuria, but as they rode closer, they encountered a series of wide ditches, ploughed land, irrigation channels and low hummocks that barred their way, forcing them towards the massive gates.

"Chariot traps," Caratacus observed as they passed another narrow, steep-sided ditch.

When he heard this, Calgacus took a closer look at the apparently random ditches and patches of soft earth. He realised that Isuria's defences were predicated on the assumption that any attacking force would be mounted on chariots which would be unable to cross the obstacles. Blocked by these irregular lumps and dips, they would be forced to head for the gaps where the warriors would leap down, swords in hand, to challenge the defenders to open combat.

Calgacus almost burst out laughing. He had not seen a chariot used in warfare since he had been a boy. Caratacus had done away with his chariots years before because the small, two-wheeled vehicles were expensive to maintain and required a great deal of practice to use properly. Worse, they were useless in the rough terrain that Caratacus had used to fight the Romans during the long years of his resistance. The Great King had favoured ambush from woodlands and mountains where a chariot could not be used effectively.

Even on open ground, chariots were obsolete now. Roman cavalry were faster and Roman infantry stronger. A chariot could carry a driver and one or, at most, two warriors. But the men could not fight from the platform of a moving chariot, except to hurl javelins. The chariots main purpose was to deliver the warriors to the battlefield where they would dismount to fight on foot. It was a tactic that had worked well enough in the days when the wealthy warriors of rival tribes also employed chariots but the Romans had changed the rules of warfare.

A Roman infantry cohort could throw a hail of their own javelins at a passing chariot, overwhelming the charioteers. If the warriors dismounted, the odds against them were even greater. To match the five hundred legionaries of a cohort would require at least two hundred and fifty chariots to deliver the same number of fighting men. At the height of his power, Caratacus could have afforded such a luxury but he had quickly learned that warfare based on prestige and display was no match for the way the Romans fought. The Romans would not be intimidated by two well-groomed ponies pulling a polished chariot bedecked with bells and ribbons; they would not be frightened by a big warrior shaking a spear at them as he rode majestically up and down in front of them. When the Romans fought, they simply put as many heavily armed men in the field as possible and slaughtered whoever dared stand against them. Chariots, Calgacus knew, were little more than a relic of a world that had changed.

Caratacus was obviously thinking along the same lines. As they drew near to the gates, the Great King said, "It is just as well the Brigantes are at peace with Rome. If the legions ever come here, they will take the place without breaking sweat."

There were guards at the gates, four big men who carried heavy, wooden cudgels. Calgacus saw no sign of any blades except the small knives that everyone carried at their waist. There were no spears, no swords in evidence.

The men stared at them uncertainly, their eyes nervously taking in the war gear, the swords, the dusty, travel-stained clothes.

42

Their expressions turned to outright alarm when they saw Cethinos, who sat sternly beside Caratacus. The druid seemed to frighten them more than the sight of nine armed warriors on horseback.

One burly guard stepped forwards, holding his massive club across his chest in both hands.

"Who are you?" he demanded gruffly. "And what do you want?"

The man's accent was so atrocious that Calgacus thought he was speaking a different language. It took a moment for the mangled vowels to transform into Brythonic.

Caratacus seemed to have no such trouble. Still sitting on his high-pommelled saddle, he leaned forwards to say, "My name is Caratacus, son of Cunobelinos, King of the two tribes of the Catuvellauni and the Trinovantes, War Leader of the free tribes. I have come here with my brother, Calgacus, and with Cethinos, a druid, to speak to Queen Cartimandua."

The sentry stared at them blankly for a moment while he tried to assimilate this information. Behind him, the other guards shifted restlessly. A small crowd was gathering just inside the open gateway, peering nervously out at the strange visitors with their long moustaches and their unfamiliar, southern accents.

After thinking for what seemed an age, the guard said, "Wait here. I will send word."

Caratacus nodded his thanks, settling back to wait while the guard sent one of his companions running into the town. The watching crowd grew larger as word of the visitors spread. Murmurs of astonishment and curiosity reached Calgacus' ears as more men, women and children thronged to the gates, pointing and whispering.

Caratacus turned to the half dozen warriors who sat patiently on their ponies.

"Remember we are here to find friends and allies," he warned them. "I want no trouble. Is that understood?"

The warriors nodded their assent.

Cethinos turned to Calgacus. "That applies to you as well, boy," he hissed. "Keep your mouth shut and leave the talking to your elders."

Calgacus bristled angrily. It applies to you, too, he thought to himself as he stared back at the druid. He knew that Cethinos'

43

brusque manner was capable of antagonising anyone. It was already evident from the expressions on the faces of the guards and the assembled townsfolk that the old man was creating a stir simply by being there. The druid, though, paid no attention to the stares and whispers, simply sitting, stiff-backed, on his pony, looking around as if he found Isuria a rather disappointing place.

The ponies grew unsettled and restless, stamping their hooves and shaking their heads. Calgacus could sympathise. It was unnerving to sit inactive under the eyes of more than a hundred people. Fortunately, they did not have long to wait before the messenger returned, bringing another man with him.

The newcomer was stocky, broad-shouldered and walked with the confident, light-footed gait of a warrior. His long, brown hair was combed back from a broad, honest, clean-shaven face. He wore a finely-made tunic and trousers, with a broad, leather belt that was fastened by a silver buckle. He had no cloak but a shining, silver brooch was pinned to his tunic.

The man stopped a few paces in front of Caratacus, showing no fear at being faced by so many armed men when he carried nothing more than a small dagger at his waist.

"I am Garathus," he announced, inclining his head in welcome. "I am shield-bearer to Cartimandua, Queen of the Brigantes. Welcome to Isuria."

Caratacus patiently introduced himself and his companions again. "I must speak with Cartimandua," he told the shield-bearer.

Garathus gestured vaguely towards them. "You must surrender your weapons first. That is the law."

"A strange law," Caratacus observed.

"It is Roman law," Garathus explained without any hint of embarrassment. "No man is permitted to carry arms."

Calgacus thought that his brother was going to argue but Caratacus swiftly looped his sword belt over his head and held out his sword to Garathus.

Calgacus was astonished. Caratacus' sword was a marvel of the smith's art. Its gleaming, golden scabbard caught the sunlight, highlighting the thin, silver strip that ran down its entire length. The scabbard alone was a thing of beauty, although Calgacus knew that the metals were actually bronze and tin rather than gold and silver. Still, the effect was dazzling, telling the world that the man who carried this weapon was more than a simple warrior.

44

But it was the sword itself that was precious. Iron tools were hard and strong, capable of retaining a sharp edge for a long time, but blades could be brittle and could break or bend out of shape. Calgacus' own sword was already dented and slightly twisted following the fight at Caer Caradoc. He had no qualms about handing it over because he needed a new one anyway, but Caratacus' sword was different.

Every so often, perhaps once in every ten thousand attempts, a smith would produce a sword of such quality that the blade would not bend or buckle under constant use. It would remain strong yet flexible, able to retain its shape. Such swords were prized more than gold. Caratacus' sword was one of those marvels, yet he surrendered it without question. Following his example, the rest of his party did the same.

Garathus signalled to the guards to take the weapons away. "They will be returned to you when you leave," he said. "Leave your horses. There is a paddock nearby where they will be cared for."

Caratacus dismounted, signalling to his companions to do likewise. "What now?" he asked the stocky shield-bearer.

"A house has been set aside for you. I will have someone lead your men there. You and your immediate companions should come with me. I will take you to Queen Cartimandua."

Caratacus handed his shield to one of his warriors, a scar-faced man named Pencoch.

"Remember," the Great King said. "No trouble. See that the horses are cared for, then go to the house that has been offered and wait for me."

Pencoch nodded. "As you command," he said, accepting the shield with pride.

Caratacus turned to Garathus. "Lead on," he said.

Garathus led the way through the gates. Caratacus and Cethinos followed, with Calgacus a step behind. Runt, uninvited, came with him.

Calgacus was amazed by Isuria. Beyond the gateway, a wide path took them into the town, curving and twisting between the closely packed houses. Every so often, other pathways branched off, leading deeper into the town, busy highways that had no pattern but wound their way among the roundhouses like rivers seeking the easiest path through stony ground.

Between the homes were narrow, shadow-filled alleyways from which drifted a concoction of smells and noises.

Every home had a doorway facing east to greet the morning sun. Some had a second, west-facing door to catch the afternoon light. On this fine day, all of the wooden doors were open, the people sitting outside, taking advantage of the warm, summer sun.

Many of the townsfolk lined the path to watch their visitors pass. The voices were strange, the accents harsh to Calgacus' ear, giving the town a foreign, unfamiliar feel. Yet the people were much like any others he had met. Most of them wore their hair long and had clothes that were brightly-coloured in shades of red, blue and green as well as the more drab browns and greys of homespun wool and linen.

There were women spinning wool, grinding barley or oats, or weaving wicker baskets. A smith was hammering iron on a huge anvil, tanners were treating leather and hides, potters were shaping clay pots and bowls to bake in their ovens, carpenters were sawing and shaping wood.

The smell of baking bread mingled with the sharp tang of tannin, competed with the odour of fresh fish, the stink of the cesspits and the pungent smell of herbs.

Small dogs roamed the narrow alleyways while cats, essential for keeping rodents under control, lay languidly in the sun or stalked the sloping, smoke-hazed rooftops, gazing imperiously down on the throng of humans below.

The people chattered noisily to one another, pointing at their strange-looking visitors. Men stopped working to watch the small procession pass, while others muttered to one another in their coarse dialect, laughing as they ran fingers down the sides of their mouths in a gesture that mocked the long moustaches of the Catuvellauni warriors.

Children stared in excitement at the presence of a druid while the women noted the armour that Caratacus and Calgacus wore and turned knowing, anxious glances to each other.

One young woman was holding a basket of freshly-cut herbs and flowers. She blushed and turned away when Runt blew her a kiss.

"We are not to cause trouble," Calgacus reminded his friend.

"I have no intentions of causing trouble," Runt replied with a broad smile. "I was just being friendly."

"Yes, and knowing you, you'd like to get more friendly with her. But she's at least seventeen years old, so she'll have a husband who probably won't be so friendly if you try anything."

"He wouldn't need to know," Runt said blithely.

"If you must go chasing women, look for an ugly, unmarried one," Calgacus advised.

"Where is the fun in that? Anyway, I don't go chasing women; they usually come chasing me."

"Then send them away. You heard what Caratacus said. No trouble."

"You're just jealous," Runt teased.

Calgacus could not help smiling. Despite the strangeness of their surroundings, Isuria felt somehow reassuring. There were so many people there, so many craftsmen and artisans, women and children that it was difficult for him not to smile as he passed through the town. He had thought the Brigantes were savages but, apart from their unfamiliar accents, they seemed entirely normal and not unfriendly.

They reached another junction where Garathus turned to the right. Glancing left, Calgacus saw a wide space among the roundhouses where farmers were selling produce from the backs of wagons or small carts. The sight brought an unexpected feeling of nostalgia, although he did not know why.

Caratacus turned to look back over his shoulder. "Togodumnus would have loved this place," he said. "It is everything he wanted Camulodunon to be."

Calgacus could only nod his head in agreement. The nostalgia, he recognised, was not for something he had known, but for something he had never known except through the words and dreams of his brother, Togodumnus. Camulodunon, which Calgacus remembered only with the memories of a boy, had been a large settlement, but it was the home of a king and his warriors. The houses had been far apart, each one with its own plot of land for growing vegetables and barley. The iron-working, the pottery kilns, all the trades, had been spread outside the royal stronghold. Here in Isuria, the Brigantes had brought everything together. Caratacus was right. Togodumnus would have loved this place.

"It looks like we are there," Runt said, disturbing Calgacus' reminiscence.

Calgacus looked up to see that there was another open space

on the southern edge of the town. Beyond, instead of the smooth-sided slopes of a man-made defensive embankment, was a natural hill, steep-sided and covered by thick woodland. Facing them, on the lower fringes of the slope, built on a levelled shelf that was slightly higher than the rest of the town, was a massive, wooden-walled hall.

Cethinos stiffened as Garathus led them towards it. The hall was huge, towering above the rest of the town, but its most striking feature was its rectangular shape. The old druid muttered softly under his breath when he saw it. Among all the tribes of the Pritani, from the civilised south to the wild north, everyone knew that buildings should be circular. Circles were important; in art, in life, in all things. All life was a circle and tradition demanded that the people acknowledge that essential fact when they built their homes. Only the Romans thought in straight lines, with their straight roads and their square or rectangular, straight-edged buildings. The hall facing them was, to a druid, a betrayal of the Pritani way of life.

Calgacus could see that the very sight of the hall offended Cethinos. For that reason, he studied it more closely, determined to like it despite its foreign appearance.

The walls were straight and tall, unadorned but with small, square windows near the top, just below the overhang of the thatched roof. The roof itself was impressive, sloping up on both sides to meet in a high ridge that ran the entire length of the building. The hall was magnificent in its scale, dwarfing any building Calgacus had ever seen.

Two more heavy-set guards stood at the doors, each of them holding a long staff and doing his best to appear unimpressed by the visitors. Calgacus paid little notice to them because the massive, double doors of dark oak demanded his attention.

They were enormous, so tall that he would not need to duck as he went through them. More than their mere size, though, the elaborate carvings that covered them from top to bottom caught his eye. There were images of hunting scenes, of warriors, of chariots, of great bulls and bears, of eagles and horses; symbols of power that were intermingled with more arcane, abstract designs of swirling circles and jagged lines. The carvings were so detailed, so numerous and so vibrant that Calgacus knew the doors must have taken longer to create than the hall itself.

48

Garathus paused, allowing the four visitors to see the magnificence of the doors at close quarters.

"They are wonderful," Calgacus breathed.

"They are merely symbols," Cethinos scoffed. "Their purpose is to daunt any who come here. Ignore them."

Garathus frowned slightly at the druid's dismissal, but he made no comment. He gestured to the guards, who pushed the heavy doors open.

"Follow me," he told the four Catuvellauni.

The interior was a bewildering mix of gloom and light. The first thing Calgacus saw was a great fire burning in a rectangular, iron-ringed fire pit. The firelight and smoke obscured what lay beyond. To either side, he saw a row of thick, polished, wooden columns that vanished upwards into the fog of firesmoke to support the massive rafters of the roof. Shafts of sunlight shone through the high windows, dappling the interior of the hall in alternating patches of light and dark that baffled his eyes. Under his feet, the floor was a vast expanse of expensive wooden boards that were strewn with rushes and sweet-smelling plants which muffled his footsteps and masked the scent of the people who were gathered at the far end.

Following Garathus as they skirted the blazing hearth, Calgacus was able to make out shadowy figures which slowly transformed into a small crowd of living, breathing men and women. They were at either side of the hall, near the far end. Some were sitting on long, wooden benches, others standing behind those who were seated. All were looking at Caratacus and Cethinos as they walked the length of the long hall. Seeing their tense, disapproving expressions, Calgacus sensed that their welcome would be more hostile than that of the people in the town. He instinctively reached up as if to grip the hilt of his sword but lowered his arm when he remembered that he had no sword.

He cursed silently, knowing that they were helpless in here. Ahead of him he was dimly aware of a figure, dressed in white, seated at the end of the hall but he was more concerned with the men and women at either side. These would be the elite among the Brigantes, the warriors and their womenfolk. For all the apparent normality of the town, the Brigantes were alleged to be fearsome warriors, quick to take insult and even quicker to demand retribution. Walking into this great, cavernous hall was like going, unarmed, into a bear's den.

His eyes darted from side to side, trying to gauge whether there was any danger. He noticed some men standing in the shadows by the walls, big men who held long, wooden staffs. He counted at least six of them, three on either side. He tensed, feeling the sense of menace grow with every step he took.

Garathus stopped in front of a low dais that ran across the end of the hall. Stepping to one side, he announced, "My Queen, here is Caratacus, son of Cunobelinos. He has with him his brother, Calgacus, and Cethinos, a druid."

Calgacus cast a quick glance at Runt who had been excluded from the introduction but the small man did not appear to be concerned about being overlooked. He was staring straight ahead, his eyes bright with fascination and desire.

For the first time, Calgacus turned his full attention to the figure on the raised dais. When he saw her, his heart skipped a beat. There, sitting on a high-backed wooden chair was the most beautiful woman he had ever seen.

Cartimandua, Queen of the Brigantes, was young, perhaps only nineteen years of age, although her regal bearing gave the impression that she was several years older. She was of medium height, with a slim waist and full figure. Her skin was so pale she must have spent a lifetime avoiding the sun. Her long hair, as dark as Calgacus' own, fell down her back almost to her waist. She wore a dress of white linen that left her slender arms bare, revealing thin bands of gold encircling her upper arms and wrists. Around her waist she wore a wide belt of dark leather that served to accentuate her hips and bust. Nestling round her delicate throat was a torc, the symbol of her power and authority. It was made of many long, thin strips of gold twisted together like the braided strands of a rope, the two ends culminating in small globes of solid gold. It was a thing of beauty, yet it looked dull and ordinary compared to its wearer.

Calgacus was mesmerised. Cartimandua's face was as finely carved as one of the images on the doors of her hall, her cheekbones high but not overly prominent, her lips full and sensuous. The eyes with which she regarded her famous visitors were blue and piercing, radiating strength and intelligence. She was, Calgacus thought, perfection in human form.

50

When she spoke, Calgacus barely noticed the words. Her voice was as smooth and rich as honey, as inviting as a summer morning, yet with an unmistakeable hint of iron.

"Welcome, Cousin," she said, addressing Caratacus by the honorific title used among ruling families. "I confess that I did not expect to see you here. May I ask why you have come to me?"

Caratacus stood tall and proud. If he was offended by the fact that she remained seated in his presence, he did not show it. Speaking loudly, so that everyone in the hall could hear, he announced, "I have come to both seek and to offer aid."

Cartimandua's delicate eyebrows rose as if in surprise.

"I hardly think you are able to offer aid, Cousin," she said. "Word of your defeat has preceded you."

Caratacus hesitated for a moment, caught off balance by her words. He rallied quickly, saying, "Then you must know that the Romans have conquered almost all of the free tribes. They will turn their eyes to Brigantia next."

"I do not think so," she replied calmly. "We are friends of Rome."

Cethinos was unable to restrain himself. He barked, "No tribe among the Pritani should befriend the Romans. They seek to destroy our religion, to tear apart our ancient heritage, to rule everything. It is your duty to resist them, to follow the instructions of the Druid Council and to fight our common enemy."

Calgacus had seen Cethinos bring strong warriors to the point of abject terror but Cartimandua merely turned a frosty stare on the old man.

"Be silent, Druid," she said coldly. "My duty is to my people. Your presence here endangers all of us. I will not hear you."

"Do you dare to insult me?" Cethinos breathed furiously. "Have a care, girl. The Gods—"

"—Are honoured here," Cartimandua interrupted. "But it is plain for even a blind man to see that the Roman Gods hold sway now. I say again, your very presence is a danger to me and my people. You may not speak to me. Be silent or I will have you thrown out."

Caratacus placed a warning hand on Cethinos' arm. The druid, unused to being touched, visibly flinched, but the Great King's gesture distracted Cethinos from arguing long enough for Caratacus to say, "We must speak, Cousin. In private. What

51

Cethinos says is true. The Romans are a threat to us all. Rome has no friends, only subjects. Soon, they will turn their attention to you and you will be crushed. I can help you defeat them."

From any other man, that statement would have been judged as nothing more than an empty boast but from Caratacus, it was a simple statement of fact. His reputation was such that nobody uttered so much as a whisper of scorn or disbelief.

Cartimandua's blue eyes studied him for a long moment. Then she shifted her gaze over Cethinos, quickly passing on to Runt before settling on Calgacus. He shuffled his feet, looking defiantly back at her. Their eyes locked for a moment, as if testing each other's will, then he saw the tip of her tongue gently moisten her lips as her eyes roamed from his head to his feet. He felt that she was studying him the way he and Runt would stare at young women, admiring them, imagining what they would look like without their clothes. Under Cartimandua's predatory gaze, it was Calgacus who felt suddenly naked.

"What do you say, warrior?" she asked him.

Calgacus felt the eyes of the hall turn on him. Cethinos turned his angular face towards him, eyes blazing with anger and indignation, as if the old druid was trying to will him to silence.

Cethinos' anger gave Calgacus confidence. He had never seen anyone treat the old man the way the Queen of Brigantia had done. She was strong-willed, confident and unattainable, yet he found that he wanted her approval. More than that, he wanted her.

But he reminded himself that he owed his brother everything. Trying to ignore the way she was watching him, he said, "I follow my brother in all things. I cannot add to what he has told you."

"How unimaginative," Cartimandua said, bringing a ripple of mocking laughter from the audience. "I had hoped you might be more than a mere follower. Do you have no thoughts of your own?"

Calgacus felt his cheeks flushing. He thought he detected a hint of amusement behind her impassive mask. She was, he decided, playing a game with him, testing him. It was the sort of game he had encountered before. Cartimandua may have been a queen, but she was a young woman and he was sure that she was using a ploy that other women tried when they wanted to show their power over a man.

Holding her gaze, Calgacus replied "I have plenty of thoughts.

But I do not think you want to hear them. Not here, with all these people listening."

That brought some stifled gasps and muted, uncertain laughter. Cartimandua regarded him appraisingly, then seemed to dismiss him, as if his taunt had not affected her.

She turned back to Caratacus. "You have placed me in a difficult position by coming here, Cousin," she told him. "I must think about what I am going to do. In the meantime, the rules of hospitality mean that you are under my protection. I will have food and drink sent to the house I have set aside for you. You are free to go anywhere within Isuria but I must ask you not to pass beyond the gates."

"Are we your prisoners, then?" Caratacus demanded.

"You are my guests," Cartimandua replied smoothly.

"I must speak to you privately," Caratacus insisted.

"Perhaps later," she said. Then she signalled to her shield-bearer, Garathus. "Show them to their lodgings," she commanded.

Garathus inclined his head in a bow, then turned towards Caratacus. He spread one arm, inviting the Great King to leave. As he did so, half a dozen of the queen's guards emerged from the shadows of the pillared hall, their thick staffs held ready.

Caratacus turned a questioning eye on Cartimandua. "Is this how you treat guests?" he asked.

"It is how I treat problems," she told him.

"We are not your enemies," Caratacus told her.

Cartimandua looked at him, unsmiling. "If you were my enemies," she said, "you would be dead by now."

She waved an arm, dismissing them.

Caratacus spun on his heel, marching away, anger radiating from every pore. Cethinos, after giving the queen a look of barely-concealed menace, followed him.

Calgacus stood for a moment until Cartimandua looked at him quizzically. Slowly, deliberately, he moistened his lips with his tongue. Then he gave her a defiant bow before turning to follow his brother out of the hall.

53

Chapter V

"Insufferable wench!" Cethinos declared when they reached the roundhouse where their warriors were waiting. "She is testing us. Did you notice the way she looked at us?" He frowned, his bushy eyebrows meeting at the bridge of his nose. His left hand tugged at his long beard in a gesture that signalled he was trying to resolve some problem. "She was testing us," he repeated.

"What do you mean?" Calgacus asked. He was surprised at the old man's reaction. He had expected Cethinos to be full of outrage, ranting at the disrespect he had been shown. Instead, the druid's anger was chillingly cold and brooding.

Cethinos treated him to the look of scornful disapproval he seemed to reserve for Calgacus.

"I would not expect you to notice," he said darkly. "Standing there with your tongue hanging out like a dog after a bitch in heat."

Caratacus said, "She is a clever one. But I think Calgacus dealt with her better than either of us did."

Cethinos snorted. He sat down on a small stool beside the newly-lit hearth fire. He stroked his beard again.

"Aye, she is a clever one. She understands the power of symbols. The question is, how much of what she said was for show and how much did she really mean?"

"We will learn that when I speak to her," Caratacus said. "At least she meant it when she said she would have food brought to us."

The food had been delivered by a group of servants. It was plain but plentiful. There was fish, roasted meat, some bread, cheese and honey and some ground oats for making gruel. The warriors were already heating a pot of water over the slate-lined fire pit of the hearth. Barta, the youngest of the warriors, had been elected to cook.

The others sat on small stools or squatted on the earth floor. Above their heads, tendrils of smoke from the fire were already gathering in the rafters. Before long, the roof would be hidden by a

54

dense cloud of smoke that would help to keep the house warm as well as keeping the thatch free of vermin. Hearth fires were usually kept burning even through the warm days of summer but Calgacus was already feeling the heat. With Runt's help, he unbuckled his heavy breastplate and laid it on the ground beside one of the bracken-filled mattresses that Cartimandua's servants had brought for them to sleep on.

Pencoch, who now viewed himself as Caratacus' new shield-bearer, said, "There are men watching the house. I tried going out earlier on. They didn't stop me, but a couple of them followed me."

Caratacus nodded. "Cartimandua says that we are guests, not prisoners. I expect we will be watched closely, though."

"What is she like, then?" Pencoch asked. "Is she pretty?"

"You had better ask Calgacus," Caratacus said with a grin.

Calgacus gave a weak smile. "I didn't really notice," he said.

Runt laughed. "Not much," he chuckled. He opened his mouth, letting his tongue loll out. Pencoch and the others joined in the laughter.

Caratacus said, "It may work to our advantage, Little Brother. I think she likes you. You should try to get close to her. It might help persuade her to join our cause."

Calgacus looked uncertain. "If that is what you want," he said.

"I don't think it would be a hardship," Caratacus told him. "A woman her age should have married years ago. She must be looking for a husband. Why not you?"

Calgacus grinned self-consciously but his mind wandered to thoughts of what it would be like to hold Cartimandua in his arms. No, he decided, it would not be a hardship at all.

Garathus arrived while they were hungrily devouring their meal. The queen's shield-bearer enquired as to whether they required anything else.

"Some fresh clothes would be welcome," Caratacus said.

"I shall see to it," Garathus replied. "The Queen has instructed me to invite you to a private dinner this evening. Just you and your brother."

Caratacus nodded in satisfaction. "Tell her we are grateful for the invitation," he said.

Once they had satisfied their hunger, they stripped off their old, tattered clothes, washing in water heated on the fire, using small lumps of soap made from tallow and ashes to clean away the accumulated grime of several days' travel. Then they shaved, using iron razors plundered from Roman soldiers they had killed. Romans never wore beards and most soldiers had a razor in their pack that was far superior to the old-fashioned bronze shavers the tribesmen had once used. Calgacus sharpened a new edge on his razor using a small whet-stone, then sat patiently while Runt scraped the blade across his cheeks and neck. It felt good to be clean again.

An assortment of fresh clothes arrived; cloaks, tunics, linen shirts and undertrousers, leather jerkins, woollen trousers, and some leather shoes. To Calgacus' surprise, he was able to assemble an outfit that was large enough to fit him.

"You're lucky," Runt said as he flapped the sleeve of a shirt that was much too large for him.

Fed, washed, shaved and dressed, Calgacus felt refreshed. He rummaged through the shoes that the cobblers of Isuria had made but decided to keep his old, comfortable boots. He sat in the doorway, scraping and wiping the leather clean before tugging them on to his feet. He stood, looking down uncertainly at his new clothes. The shirt was plain but well-made. The short-sleeved, leather jerkin warm and supple, the trousers patterned with blue and green squares.

Runt looked him up and down. "If she doesn't fall for you now, she never will," he said.

Calgacus said nothing. Remembering the hungry looks Cartimandua had given him, he felt like a victim being prepared for sacrifice.

"Let's go, Little Brother," Caratacus said. "The rest of you stay here until we get back."

As soon as the two brothers ducked out of the low door, two of Cartimandua's warriors appeared. They silently led the way back to the hall. Calgacus was aware of many more stares from the townsfolk as they made their way along the winding pathway. Most people were preparing or eating their evening meal, sitting cross-legged on the ground outside their homes to take advantage of the fine summer evening. One or two young children raced along beside the brothers, calling questions or shouting cheeky insults. The two Catuvellauni ignored them.

The hall was almost empty this time. The high windows had been shuttered, leaving most of the great space in shadow. The gloom was lit only by the central fire and by candles which were set on niches cut into the tall columns that lined the hall.

A table had been set up in front of the low dais, with six wooden chairs arranged beside it. Cartimandua was there, with Garathus standing a few paces behind her. Two other men waited beside the table, their expressions hard and unfriendly.

Calgacus wondered who these surly men were and why they were waiting with the Queen, but his attention was diverted when Cartimandua greeted him and Caratacus with a smile.

"Welcome, Cousins. I offer you the hospitality of my house."

"Thank you, Cousin," Caratacus replied formally. "We are honoured."

Cartimandua gestured towards the two strangers who were waiting near the table. "This is Venutius," she said, introducing the first. "And his shield-bearer, Vellocatus."

The man named Venutius nodded a curt, grudging welcome. He was about Calgacus' age, little more than twenty years old, of medium height and build, with the typical long hair and clean-shaven face of the Brigantes. His hazel eyes stared out from beneath a sullen brow, every glance displaying his hostility. He wore finely made clothes and a great deal of ostentatious jewellery, including finger and arm rings of gold. A pendant of dark jet hung from a gold chain around his neck. The dagger at his belt had a sparkling, jewelled hilt.

Vellocatus, the young nobleman's shield-bearer, was a tall, handsome man a few years older than his master. He, too, was finely dressed although he lacked the display of gold trinkets that Venutius wore. His greeting was no warmer than that of his chieftain.

Cartimandua affected not to notice the boorish welcome. She gestured for them to sit, then clapped her hands, summoning servants who brought plates piled with a variety of foods.

There was a long, awkward silence while the servants placed the platters on the table. Calgacus again felt the strangeness of the surroundings. He was used to carving his meat from a communal plate, fresh from the fire, or scooping broth or gruel from a cooking pot. Here, the food had been prepared elsewhere, brought into the hall and laid on the table as if on display. He noticed that the serving girls were entering through a door that was concealed by a wooden screen. They hurried to and fro, delivering more and more food, far more than six people could possibly eat.

Calgacus studied the growing collection of dishes. There were traditional roasted meats, succulent lamb and beef, along with goose and swan, all of them garnished with mint, sage or onion. There were platters of fish, chicken, wildfowl and eggs, plates of dark bread and goats' cheese, piles of honey-flavoured bannocks. Bowls of mushrooms, kail and beans were brought. Then, when Calgacus thought there must be an end, plates of other, unfamiliar food arrived. Olives and figs, sheep's brains garnished with dill and rosemary, chaffinches stuffed with melted cheese, and a bowl of a hot, pungent fish sauce which Cartimandua poured liberally over her food.

"I thought we would give you the opportunity to sample some Roman food," she said with an innocent smile. "There is wine as well." She signalled to a girl to pour wine into tall, silver goblets.

"Unless you would rather drink heather ale or beer," Venutius said sarcastically.

The girl pouring the wine hesitated but Caratacus signalled to her to continue.

"We do not mind Roman food and drink," he said brusquely. "We traded with them for years before they decided to steal our homes from us. Since then, we have simply taken what we wanted from the bodies of the Romans we have killed."

He did not give Venutius an opportunity to respond but raised the goblet, pouring a small libation onto the floor.

"To Camulos," he said.

"To Camulos," Calgacus repeated.

After a short pause, Cartimandua echoed the toast, then poured a libation of her own.

"To Brigantia," she declared.

All of the guests dutifully repeated the invocation. Seeing Calgacus' puzzled expression, the Queen explained, "Brigantia is the spirit of our land and people. She watches over us." She gave a faint smile. "I have heard that some of the poorer folk believe I am the incarnation of Brigantia."

Calgacus, remembering his brother's earlier instructions, said, "I am sure you are more beautiful than any spirit could ever be."

Cartimandua smiled again. "Such pretty words from a man of

war," she said. "Perhaps you do have thoughts of your own, after all."

"Thoughts he should keep to himself," rasped Venutius. The look in his eyes suggested that he would have liked nothing more than for Calgacus to choke on his food.

"You should be more civil to our guests, Venutius," Cartimandua chided gently. She treated Caratacus to another radiant smile. "Venutius' family have long been the most important in the north of Brigantia," she explained.

"The North?" Calgacus queried. "That would explain his lack of manners then. I have heard that the northern tribes are barely civilised."

Venutius stiffened at the insult but Cartimandua raised a hand, signalling for calm. "We are not here to insult one another," she said firmly. "We are here to show my Cousin, Caratacus, that he should consider renouncing his hostility to Rome."

"Why should I do that?" Caratacus wanted to know. "If a thief comes to my home and steals my horse, I do not go after him and invite him to keep it, nor to offer him my cattle and gold as well."

"You cannot defeat the Romans," Venutius muttered darkly.

"I can try," Caratacus rejoindered. "Better that than crawling to them on my belly."

Again Cartimandua soothed the tension. "My father went to Rome when he was a young man," she said. "He told me all about it. He was very impressed, bewitched almost. He told me there are many buildings of marble and stone, great temples and palaces." She gestured around the shadow-dark room. "That is why he built this hall in the style of a Roman hall, with outbuildings for the cooks and servants."

"Why did he not build it of stone if he wanted to be a Roman?" Calgacus challenged.

"Do you know anyone among the Pritani who has the skill to build in stone?" she countered. "I have heard that the Romans have had to bring masons from Gaul to help construct their new towns in the south."

"Towns they build over our old homes," Caratacus said. He finished chewing, took a sip of wine, then placed his goblet firmly on the table. "Soon, the conquered tribes will be calling themselves Britons instead of Pritani."

"A name is just a name," Venutius argued. "Why worry about

things like that?"

Caratacus ignored the young Brigante. He turned his attention to Cartimandua. "Let me speak plainly, Cousin," he said. "I will not surrender to the Romans. Instead, I would urge you not to be blinded by the material wealth they offer. They are trying to buy your allegiance. This is their way, to divide the tribes, to prevent us uniting so that we cannot oppose them effectively."

"The tribes have always been divided," Cartimandua said. "You yourself defeated the Atrebates and the Regni, did you not? You forced Verica to flee and you cowed Cogidubnus into submission. In what way was that different to what the Romans have done?"

Caratacus pursed his lips. Calgacus could see that his brother, nearly fifteen years Cartimandua's senior, had not expected such perceptive argument from her. The Great King could not deny her accusation. He said, "That was different. We fought to defend ourselves. Verica seized land and enslaved people who were under our protection."

"Yet you did far more than simply reclaim your land," Cartimandua countered. "You turned the Atrebates and Regni into subject tribes."

Caratacus face was flushed with rising anger. He said, "That is all in the past. When times change, we should change with them. The Romans are a threat to us all. They have already shown their hunger for conquest. They will not leave you in peace."

Seemingly unaffected by the Great King's anger, Cartimandua said, "But, as Venutius has already pointed out, they cannot be defeated in war. Surely it is better to surrender some liberties and remain on friendly terms?"

"They can be beaten," Caratacus said.

"Apparently not by you, though," Venutius mocked.

Caratacus kept his temper in check. He stared at the young Brigante chieftain.

"Perhaps you are right," he said softly. "But Calgacus knows how to beat them. If he had commanded at Caer Caradoc, we would have won."

Calgacus lowered his eyes, embarrassed by his brother's unexpected praise. It was the way of many warriors to boast of their prowess but Calgacus had learned from his brother that it was better to accomplish deeds than to boast about them. He wondered whether Caratacus' claim was part of a ploy to spark Cartimandua's interest. If so, it seemed to work.

Clearly intrigued, she said, "Is that so? There must be more to you than meets the eye, Calgacus."

Caratacus said, "My brother is the finest warrior I have ever seen. He has a talent for war that I think is greater than even he suspects."

"I learned from the best," Calgacus said modestly.

Cartimandua turned to Venutius. "Perhaps you should be careful what you say," she warned him. "I suspect Calgacus is not a man you should upset."

"Neither am I," Venutius replied with a scowl.

Calgacus did not bother looking at him. He turned away, catching a glimpse of Garathus' face. Cartimandua's shield-bearer, normally stolid and impassive, seemed to be enjoying Venutius' discomfiture. Calgacus guessed there was no love lost between the two men.

"All that aside," Caratacus said, "it seems we disagree on what should be done, which does not help any of us."

"No, but there may be a solution," Cartimandua said. She paused, making sure she had their full attention before continuing. "My father pledged peace to the Emperor," she said. "I intend to maintain that position. Perhaps I could use my influence to broker a peace arrangement between you and the Romans."

The suggestion hung in the air for a long, drawn-out moment before Caratacus asked, "Why should I agree to that? What would I gain from such an arrangement?"

"Your life," Cartimandua replied. "Your family. Who knows what Rome might offer? They may restore some of your lands."

"Or they may take me to Rome to be ritually strangled," Caratacus said grimly. "I know what the Romans do to their enemies."

"We will not know until I ask the Governor," Cartimandua said. "One thing is certain, you cannot remain here for long."

"Oh? Why is that?"

"I have offered you my hospitality," she said. "That means you are under my protection. But the Romans have a fortress not far from here. A Roman army could march to Isuria in less than a sennight, as they surely will when they learn that you are here. When they come, I will not be able to protect you."

61

Calgacus felt a cold shiver run down his spine. He had known the Romans had pushed the boundaries of their province close to Brigantia but if men could march to Isuria in less than seven days, horsemen could arrive much sooner. Refusing to look at Venutius, he asked, "How would they learn we are here?"

The look that Cartimandua gave him was one of disappointment. "Really, Calgacus, I thought you were supposed to be clever. How do you think I heard of your defeat? I have spies in Lindum who tell me everything that is happening in the Roman fortress. It would be naive to think that the Romans do not have their own informants here."

Calgacus felt his cheeks flushing at her reproachful comment. Once again she had made him look and feel foolish.

Caratacus rescued him by saying, "Then we will not remain here for more than a few days. Whatever we decide to do."

"So you will think about my proposal?" she asked.

"I will think about it."

It was dark by the time they left the hall, the moon and stars hidden by a mass of clouds that had rolled in from the west, threatening rain. Venutius and Vellocatus stalked off into the night without a word, Vellocatus holding a burning torch to light their way.

Garathus followed Caratacus and Calgacus to the doors of the hall. He instructed one of the guards to lead Caratacus back to the roundhouse but said to Calgacus, "The Queen asks that you speak to her privately."

"Me?"

Garathus nodded, his face betraying no emotion.

Caratacus laughed softly. "I will see you later, Little Brother," he said as he walked away into the night with his escort. "Enjoy yourself."

"This way," Garathus said to Calgacus, leading him round the side of the hall, towards the tree-covered hill that lay behind the building.

Moving beyond the hall they entered a small, open space nestled in the shelter of a cove in the hillside. Here, Calgacus saw the dark outline of a small roundhouse.

"The Queen's private dwelling," Garathus informed him.

There were two more guards standing a discreet distance from the doorway of the house. They made no comment as Garathus and

Calgacus passed them.

Garathus knocked once on the wooden door, pushed it open, then stepped aside, gesturing for Calgacus to step inside. The shield-bearer's face remained an impassive mask, giving no indication of what Calgacus could expect when he went through the low entrance.

Half suspecting a trap, half hoping for something much more, Calgacus ducked through the arched doorway, hearing Garathus close the door as soon as he was inside.

He paused to take in his surroundings. A few candles stood on carved ledges on the main wall timbers, their light reflecting from a silver pitcher and goblets that stood on a table at one side of the house. A hearth fire crackled in a pit at the centre of the house, the smoke forming a warm and cosy blanket above his head.

The floor was made of large flagstones that were another display of Cartimandua's wealth and status, for stone was difficult to work and awkward to lay properly. Most roundhouses had floors of hard-packed earth, sometimes covered by a layer of daub, a concoction of mud, straw, lime and dung that was mixed with animal blood so that it would set into a hard, smooth surface that was durable and easy to sweep clean. Some wealthy people would have wooden floorboards but few would go to the trouble and expense of having a stone floor laid. Cartimandua, it seemed, wanted only the best. Instead of rushes or sweet-smelling flowers, her floor was carpeted by scattered furs, thick sheepskins and richly-decorated rugs.

Two large chairs stood near the fire. Beyond them was a great pile of furs, blankets and pillows spread over a thick mattress. In front of the bed stood Cartimandua.

"Don't look so perplexed," she said. "There is more than one way out of my hall."

Calgacus' tongue felt too large for his mouth, preventing him from speaking. He stared at her, all too aware of her beauty.

She moved to the side, towards the table. Lifting the pitcher, she poured wine into the goblets. Taking one for herself, she passed the other one to Calgacus.

He took it, sipping thirstily, even though he had emptied several goblets during the meal.

"Sit down," she said, gesturing towards the chairs.

When he was seated, she stood in front of him, holding her

goblet in her right hand, her left arm across her body, just beneath her breasts, the hand supporting the elbow of her right arm. The sight of her sent his pulse racing. Why was he here? He hoped it was for the reason he wanted.

She sipped at her wine then fixed him with a hard stare. "Will Caratacus agree to my proposal?" she asked.

The question caught him off guard. He had been thinking of more earthy matters than their earlier discussion. He had to force his attention away from the swell of her breasts, the inviting curves of her hips.

"I doubt it," he replied eventually.

She nodded. "I thought as much." Another penetrating look, then she fired another unexpected statement. "You don't like Venutius."

"There is not much to like."

Her mouth twisted in a faint smile. "He is a very powerful young man. A chieftain who commands thousands of warriors."

"That does not make him a man to admire."

"No, but perhaps you should respect him."

Calgacus laughed scornfully. "Respect should be earned," he said. "It is not a right."

Cartimandua's blue eyes shone as if the answer pleased her. Then she asked, "Do you know why he is here?"

Calgacus shook his head. "No."

"He wants to marry me."

The statement surprised him. She seemed to be able to constantly surprise him. To give himself time to gather his wits, he took another sip of wine, receiving another surprise when he found that the goblet was almost empty.

He looked up at her, knowing what she had said had aroused his jealousy. Venutius wanted to marry her?

"You could do much better than him," he told her.

"That depends," she said. She waved her arm, her hand moving from her forehead down to her legs, indicating her body. "Most men want only this," she said frankly. "But Venutius wants Brigantia. If I marry him it will unite all the people of our tribe. It is the simplest way to remove him as a threat to my rule."

"There is another way to remove him," Calgacus suggested meaningfully.

"Oh, I know that," she replied. "But it would alienate half of

64

my tribe. I would rather have him near me, where I can control him." She gave a conspiratorial grin. "My father taught me that I should keep my friends close, but keep my enemies closer."

"I would rather keep my enemies far away," Calgacus said.

She laughed, the first time he had heard her utter a sound of genuine amusement. "I like you, Calgacus. You are an uncomplicated man in a complicated world, yet you have something about you, just like your famous brother." Another pause, another shift of mood and another question came at him. "Are you really as talented in war as Caratacus says?"

Calgacus decided it was time for him to do some boasting, time to impress her.

"Yes," he told her.

"It is a pity your are not of the Brigantes," she mused. "Then I would be able to marry you."

He could not tell whether she was joking, testing him again. The wine made him abandon caution.

"You could marry me anyway," he said.

She laughed again, crushing him. "That is not a good idea, Calgacus," she said. "I think I like you and I would hate to spoil that." Another laugh. "Oh, don't look so petulant. I am not a nice person, you know. I cannot afford to be. You would hate being married to me."

He suspected she was right but desire drove him on. He had spoken of marriage because Caratacus had suggested it but all he really wanted was her body.

He said, "You are very beautiful. Who could hate being married to you?"

She moved to the table, setting down her goblet. Then she turned back to him, an unreadable expression on her exquisite face.

"You are only seeing the outside," she said softly. Tapping a finger to her temple, she added, "The real Cartimandua is in here and she is not a nice person at all. She will do whatever is necessary to keep her people safe. Could you do whatever is necessary, Calgacus?"

"Yes."

"Really? I don't think you could. I am good at reading people. I think you are too honest, too honourable, to be ruthless."

Before he could protest, she came towards him, dropping to her knees in front of his chair. He swallowed, his nerves tingling

65

with anticipation as she reached out her right hand. To his surprise, she gripped his knife, drawing it from its sheath at his belt. She held the blade in front of her face.

Firelight flickered from the sharp metal and from her blue eyes. She looked at him, still holding the dagger upright between them. He watched, entranced, as her left hand moved to her shoulder, pushing down the white material of her dress. Switching the knife to her left hand, she pushed down the other shoulder, letting the dress slip down her body, leaving her naked from the waist up.

He stared as she took his hand in hers, placing the handle of his dagger in his grip, then guiding the point until it rested between her perfect breasts.

"What are you doing?" he managed to ask. He could not move. He could feel the stirring in his loins at the sight of her but the dagger was touching her flesh, threatening her life.

She looked him in the eyes. "If I told you that all you needed to do to defeat the Romans was to kill me, would you do it? Could you do it? If my death would guarantee that the Brigantes would join you, guarantee that all the tribes would unite and drive the Romans out, would you kill me?"

He wanted to pull the knife away but she had both of her hands around his, gripping him tightly. If he moved, the blade might pierce her flawless skin.

He said, "This is a foolish game. Your death cannot guarantee anything."

"No? If I die, there will be civil war among the Brigantes. Some here oppose Rome. Others will appeal to the Emperor for help. If you kill me, you will get your war." She stared into his eyes. "All you need to do is kill me now. Can you do that, Calgacus?"

"Killing women is druids' work," he said after a long pause. "I am a warrior."

Her grip loosened, releasing his hand. She stood up. He expected to see scorn on her face, derision for his weakness, but she gave him only a sad smile.

"As I thought, you are not ruthless enough," she told him. "If things were the other way around, if I could guarantee the safety of my people by killing you, or killing anyone, I would do it in a moment, without even thinking about it."

Slowly, he pushed his knife back into its sheath. He believed her. The knowledge of how far she would go to protect her tribe appalled him. Yet still he could not take his eyes from her body.

"Now you see why marrying me would not be a good idea," she told him.

He asked, "If marrying me would guarantee the safety of your people, would you do it?"

She laughed again. "Oh, Calgacus, you are cleverer than you look. But that is a game we cannot play. We both know that it would never work. I need to unite the Brigantes, not divide them."

"Then perhaps I should leave," he said, although he made no effort to rise from the chair.

"Not yet," she said softly.

With both hands, she pushed her dress down over her hips, allowing it to slide to the floor. She stepped out of it, entirely naked, moving towards him.

"I am sorry, Calgacus," she said. "I did not mean to argue with you. I invited you here for another reason all together." She smiled invitingly as she added, "I think you have had enough of Cartimandua the Queen. Now you can know Cartimandua the woman."

Chapter VI

Calgacus returned to the roundhouse as the sun was beginning to edge over the horizon. He was greeted by some ribald cheers and coarse laughter.

"Did you sleep well?" Runt asked with a grin.

"Hardly at all," Calgacus replied, unable to keep a smile from his face.

Caratacus, wiping sleep from troubled eyes, asked grimly, "Never mind that, Little Brother. Do you think you will be able to convince her to join us?"

Calgacus knew the answer but something prevented him from telling the truth. "I'm not sure," he replied cautiously. "We didn't do a lot of talking."

Cethinos grunted in disapproval. "Even you should be able to persuade her," he said. "It is well known that a young girl will fall in love with the first man who takes her, as your diminutive friend has demonstrated many times."

Runt responded with a salacious grin. "I can't help it if women fall in love with me," he said.

Calgacus shook his head. "Cartimandua is very strong-minded. I don't think it will be easy to persuade her."

"Keep trying," Caratacus said. He looked weary, almost lost. Calgacus had never seen his brother so low in spirits. He guessed that the suggestion Cartimandua had made, that they surrender themselves to Rome, was weighing heavily on Caratacus' mind. He also guessed that his brother had not mentioned the proposal to anyone else, certainly not to Cethinos, for whom the idea of submission was unthinkable.

Cethinos said, "Of course, perhaps you are not the first man she has taken to her bed. That might make things more difficult."

Calgacus felt the irrational tug of jealousy again. He suspected that Cethinos might be right but the impersonal way the druid spoke annoyed him. The old greybeard's words suggested that Cartimandua was not a real person. And yet Calgacus knew that she, too, was capable of manipulating people. In her own way, Cartimandua was just like Cethinos, prepared to do anything to achieve her ends.

With a rueful sigh, Calgacus recognised that he was trapped between the two of them. Both the druid and the queen would lay claim to his allegiance, would use him for their own purposes; purposes that would inevitably conflict. Yet all he could think of was the warmth and softness of Cartimandua's body and the passion of her lovemaking. He did not want to think about where that passion might lead him, nor about how many other men had shared her favours, had caressed her flawless skin and kissed her perfect lips.

Caratacus had other priorities. He said, "We have no alternative. We must convince her to renounce her allegiance to Rome."

"She says that she is thinking of marrying Venutius," Calgacus told him, hating himself for admitting it.

Caratacus regarded him bleakly. The Great King turned to Cethinos. "Can you cast any spells on her?" he asked.

"Such things are not easy," the druid replied. "In times past, a ruler would heed the advice of a druid but things have changed. If I offer sacrifices to the Gods, they may influence her, but the spirit of Brigantia is strong in her."

"You must try," Caratacus urged.

"I will visit the stones," Cethinos said, referring to the ancient monoliths that stood to the west of the town. "Perhaps I will receive some guidance."

The four massive stones stood in a long, widely-spaced line, running from the north-west to the south-east. They were imposingly enormous, the largest more than three times the height of a tall man. Irregularly shaped and exposed to the elements, these huge menhirs exuded a sense of permanence, as if they had always stood there. In a way, Cethinos knew, that was true. The stones may have been placed quite deliberately but they had stood there for millennia, set up so long ago that nobody could remember when or why they had first been erected. What mattered was that they marked a place of importance in the landscape, a place where people would come to speak to their ancestors or to offer sacrifice to the Gods.

The ancient menhirs lay close to the town but the wide field was deserted when Cethinos stepped between the two central stones. A heavy, constant drizzle fell from a grey, overcast sky, serving to keep people away. Even the Brigante guard who had followed him from the town had stayed well back, unwilling to intrude on a druid's business, especially in such a sacred place.

Cethinos was thankful that he was alone. He needed solitude.

He stood with his long staff clutched in his left hand, his right arm extended to the side and his head tilted to the heavens, blinking drops of rain away from his eyes. He had a great deal to think about. Here, in solitude and silence, he hoped that the Gods would give him a sign.

Letting his mind drift, he found himself wondering how things had gone so badly wrong. For years he had served the Great King, Cunobelinos, when the Catuvellauni had expanded their influence, subduing their traditional foes, the Trinovantes. Those had been great days. With Cethinos at his side, Cunobelinos had united the two tribes under one rule. Following Cethinos' advice, the Great King had taken a Trinovante princess as his bride. That had been a master-stroke, Cethinos recalled. Instead of warring, the two tribes had lived peacefully side by side.

Cunobelinos had even built himself a new home at Camulodunon, in the heart of Trinovante territory. When his wife had produced four sons, his dynasty had seemed secure. Even when his wife died, he had taken another Trinovante bride, siring two more children in his old age.

Cethinos frowned when he considered Cunobelinos' later offspring. The girl, Bonduca, had been married to a prince of the Iceni. That had secured peace with the Catuvellauni's northern neighbours but despite the marriage alliance, the Iceni had remained aloof when the Romans invaded, choosing to make peace. The girl, Cethinos thought, had been a disappointment.

As for Calgacus, the youngest of Cunobelinos' sons, he had always been a trouble-maker, intransigent and argumentative, always questioning the old ways, always challenging.

Cethinos felt annoyance stir within him when he thought of Calgacus. The boy should have been sent to Ynis Mon to train as a druid. If he had failed the stringent tests, which seemed more than likely in spite of the propitious time of his birth, he would have been sacrificed and that would have been an end of him. Instead, he had forsaken his destiny and become a warrior, a dull-witted fool whose only real talents were wielding a sword, getting drunk and bedding young women.

Cethinos pushed his irritation aside, letting the fine rain wash his face, allowing it to cool his thoughts. Calgacus apart, Cunobelinos had produced fine sons. When the old king had died, Togodumnus and Caratacus had carried on his work. They had continued to expand their influence, bringing other tribes under their control. And Cethinos had been there with them, advising, directing.

Those had been good years but the memories caused more pain than pleasure, taunting him with visions of what might have been. He should have been a member of the Druid Council long before now; would have been if the Romans had not come. Now, the Catuvellauni were crushed, the other tribes falling one by one to the invaders. The druids were slowly being strangled, their power and authority waning as their sacrifices failed to halt the Roman advance.

As for the sons of Cunobelinos, Adminius had joined the Romans, Togodumnus was long dead, Talacarnos a prisoner of Rome, and Caratacus was a beaten man, a failed War Leader. Everything had gone wrong; all the power of the Catuvellauni swept away as if it had never existed.

Cethinos allowed his thoughts to wander, seeking solutions instead of going over the problems. He had come to the stones in search of an answer. When it came, it was simple, yet also difficult to accomplish. He clung to it, nurtured it, thinking it through. The more he considered it, the more sense it made.

He understood where the fundamental problem lay. He, and every druid he knew, had offered sacrifice after sacrifice to the Gods, yet the Romans had not been stopped. The Gods had not heeded the offerings. For Cethinos, that could only mean that the sacrifices had been deemed unworthy. The Gods demanded more.

Cethinos had always believed that Caratacus was the hope of the Pritani, that there was no other man who could lead the tribes to victory. After the disaster at Caer Caradoc, that belief had been shattered. Now, for the first time in his long life, Cethinos knew doubt. The uncertainty appalled him. He had followed Caratacus to Brigantia because he had hoped that the Great King might be correct, that the Brigantes could be roused out of their submission

71

to Rome. That hope, too, was fading. Caratacus had been unable to sway the upstart Queen and Cethinos doubted whether she could be persuaded. He placed no confidence in Calgacus. The boy was obviously smitten by Cartimandua, bewitched by her physical charms, blinded to anything else. No, he thought, Caratacus had failed again.

Cethinos pondered the solution that had come to him. It was drastic, a bold, desperate step, but there was no other option. Great disasters required great sacrifices. In times of danger, the most precious things should be offered to the Gods. The most precious things or the most precious people. Only then would the Gods grant their aid to the warriors.

He lowered his arm, knowing what he must do. Caratacus must be taken to Ynis Mon. There, Cethinos would persuade the Druid Council to shed the Great King's life. Offering their most famous War Leader, the people would display their devotion to the Gods.

Calgacus would also be sacrificed, Cethinos decided. He would only cause trouble if his older brother was sent to the Gods. The young man, though troublesome, was still of royal blood. He would make a good sacrifice and his death would rid Cethinos of an irritation that had plagued him for years. The boy had turned his back on the ancient lore. Let him see that it was not wise to cross a druid.

Cethinos lowered his head, tugging his cloak around his shoulders. The Gods had answered him. He knew what he must do. It would take time and persuasion but he could be patient when required. Satisfied that he knew how to save the free tribes of the Pritani, he left the stones, tramping back across the sodden meadow towards Isuria.

Calgacus and Runt stood under the shelter of the trees that lined the river bank, looking at the wide ford that lay to the east of Isuria. Rain pattered on the leaves above their heads, rippled the water that flowed past them, and kept most people under cover.

"Why are we here?" Runt asked plaintively. He pulled the hood of his cloak tighter.

"Because I don't want to be in the same house as Cethinos any longer than I have to. Did you see the way he looked at me earlier?"

"He always looks at you like that," Runt said morosely.

"I suppose. But I'm fed up listening to him harping on about going to Ynis Mon. That's the last place we should go. We should return to the Silures."

"We should go back to the house," Runt said. "It is cold and wet out here. I hope you don't intend to stay here all day."

Calgacus shrugged.

"So will Caratacus go along with Cartimandua's idea?" Runt asked.

"I don't think so. But he is worried about his family. The thought of seeing them again must be tempting him. I've never seen him so worried."

"Me neither." Runt sighed, looking pensive. He looked along the wet, deserted riverbank then nudged his friend's arm. "Watch out. Here comes trouble."

Calgacus turned to see Venutius and Vellocatus trudging along the grass at the side of the river, skirting a bed of reeds, their shoulders hunched against the rain as they tried to stay beneath the overhanging shelter of the trees. They stopped when they came to within a few paces of the two Catuvellauni warriors.

"What do you want?" Calgacus demanded.

"To give you a piece of advice," Venutius replied, his voice hard and unfriendly.

"What advice would that be?"

"Stay away from Cartimandua," Venutius said menacingly. "She will marry a man of the Brigantes, not a renegade outcast like you."

"I think she will marry whoever she pleases," Calgacus said sharply. "Although I doubt it will be you. She told me she prefers real men."

Venutius ignored the taunt. "You have been warned, Renegade. I will not warn you again."

Runt stepped forwards belligerently. "Do you want me to kill him, Cal?" he asked.

Venutius' lip curled in a sneer. "Who are you, little man?" he asked.

"My name is Liscus. My friends call me Runt. You can call me Liscus."

Calgacus gently placed a restraining hand on Runt's shoulder. "Leave him. He is not worth it."

Venutius glared at him for a moment then, without another

word, he turned and walked away. Vellocatus treated Calgacus to a sly smirk before following his master back to the town.

"What in Andraste's name was all that about?" Runt asked.

"He has a serious problem," Calgacus said.

"So are you going to stay away from her?"

"What do you think?"

Calgacus walked to the Queen's private roundhouse at nightfall. He had not received an invitation but he needed to get away from Cethinos. The old druid was still arguing that they should return to Ynis Mon, dismissing Calgacus' suggestion that they should return to the land of the Silures. Caratacus had listened to both arguments but would not be swayed by either of them.

"We will wait a few more days," the Great King said eventually. "Perhaps Calgacus will be able to persuade Cartimandua to change her mind."

Cethinos had turned away in disgust but Calgacus had been delighted. "I will do my best," he promised his brother.

The two warriors who guarded the approach to the Queen's private dwelling stood aside wordlessly, allowing him to pass. He supposed that meant he was expected. Knocking on the door, he pushed his way inside.

"Hello, Calgacus." She was already under the covers of her bed, one bare arm stretched languidly out towards him. "I have been waiting for you."

He needed no second invitation. In moments, he had stripped off his clothing and joined her.

"I missed you today," he told her between kisses.

"I was busy. It is not easy, governing a tribe like the Brigantes. But never mind that. I am all yours now."

And she was. They spent the night entwined together, revelling in the feel and closeness of their bodies. The fire had died low by the time they lay back, exhausted and spent.

After a while, Cartimandua slipped out from the covers to place some more wood on the fire. Then she went to the table to pour herself some wine.

Calgacus, drowsy after their lovemaking, watched her, enjoying the sight of her naked body. She made no effort to conceal herself from his gaze. When she had drained the goblet, she walked seductively back towards him.

74

He pushed the heavy blankets aside to welcome her but she stopped when she reached the pile of discarded clothing he had left on the floor. She bent down, picking up a shining coin.

"What is this?" she asked, holding it up to the faint firelight.

The coin was gold, with a leather thong passing through a small hole that had been drilled through it, slightly off-centre.

"You had it around your neck," she said.

"It is a coin of my father's," he told her. "All of my brothers were given one. It reminds us of who we are."

Intrigued, Cartimandua studied the coin more closely.

"A horse on this side," she said, "and a wheatsheaf on the other. Symbols of power and fertility. And this writing . . . Cunobelinos."

"You can read?" he asked, astonished.

"Of course. Can't you?"

"No. What use is reading?"

"What use is thinking?" she shot back. She moved to the bed, looping the coin over his head so that it lay on his chest. Then she knelt over him, straddling him.

"So who are you?" she asked, jabbing a teasing finger at the gold coin.

"I am Calgacus. A warrior. A man who loves you."

She frowned. "Do not speak of love, Calgacus. I told you yesterday, that can never be."

"So why am I here?" he asked, annoyed at her dismissal of his declaration.

"Because you are big and strong and a good lover," she told him. "A very good lover. But no more than that, so do not get ideas that we can share anything more than bed sport."

Calgacus sought a way to fight back. "Venutius threatened me today," he told her. "I think he is jealous."

She shrugged. "He does not need to be."

"You think not? He knows about us. Any man would be jealous of another who has shared your bed."

"That is because men's brains stop working when they see a pretty face."

"You should be careful of him. He is not to be trusted."

"You have only known him for two days," she said.

"That is long enough to know he is a snake."

"I think he is more like a fox," Cartimandua said.

75

"What? Smelly?"

"No," she giggled. "He is crafty. But forget him. We still have plenty of time before dawn. If you are ready for more." She looked down, then frowned, tapping a delicate finger against a small blemish on his thigh.

"What is this mark?" she asked. "I never noticed it before."

He could not remain angry with her. "I have always had it," he explained. "People told me that when I was born, Cethinos saw it and announced it was a star. I was born at midwinter and he was still covered in blood after making the sacrifice when he burst into my mother's house, demanding to see me. It was that mark which convinced him I should be a druid."

"Clearly he was wrong," she said as she gently traced the pink mark with her finger. "I don't think it is a star," she said thoughtfully. "I think it is a sword."

Calgacus pushed himself up on his elbows to look down at the birthmark. "You are right," he agreed. "It is a sword."

She giggled, leaning forwards to kiss his lips. Laughing, he grabbed her around the waist, pulling her towards him, his mouth searching for her breasts. She arched her back, reaching out to seize his head, holding him close, encouraging him.

"I love you," he mumbled as his lips and tongue caressed her.

"Yes!" she gasped.

As they made love, he told her again and again that he loved her, taking her "Yes!" as his answer. When they at last fell asleep, with her head on his shoulder and one of her long legs draped across him, he was convinced he had won her over.

He woke before dawn, disturbed by Cartimandua who had slipped from the bed and hurriedly washed. She was pulling her long, white dress over her head when he wiped the sleep from his eyes.

"I have a lot to do today," she said, her tone matter-of-fact. Picking up an antler comb and a mirror of polished bronze, she began to comb her long, dark hair.

"You should talk to Caratacus again," he told her.

She did not look at him but kept her eyes on the image in her mirror.

"Why?" she asked absently. "To hear the same arguments again?"

"If need be. You are a Brigante, one of the Pritani. How can

76

you turn your back on your people?"

"The Catuvellauni are not my people," she replied, her tone sharper now. "I owe nothing to anyone except the Brigantes. The Pritani you speak of have never been united. It is nothing more than a name."

"What about the druids? Your people must still follow them."

Cartimandua tugged furiously at her hair. "There have been no druids in Brigantia for several years. The people survive without them." She turned her head to face him. "And you have defied them. You became a warrior against the wishes of your own druid. What gives you the right to demand that I obey the greybeards?"

Calgacus had no answer to that but he could not give up.

"You must help us," he said urgently, almost pleading.

Cartimandua's own temper was rising. "What would you have me do, Calgacus?"

"Marry me,." he said. The words were out before he could stop them.

"No," she said flatly. "I cannot."

He sat up on the bed, leaning towards her. "You don't need to love me," he said. "You do not love Venutius, yet you say you will wed him. Why not marry me? Together, with Caratacus to lead your war host, we can defeat the Romans. I know how to do it."

Cartimandua turned away, resuming her efforts to comb her hair.

"You are not of the Brigantes," she said, her voice hard as iron. "If I marry you, Venutius would raise a rebellion against me. So do not mention marriage again. It is not possible."

"You are a queen. Anything is possible for you. As for Venutius, I will kill him for you."

Tugging angrily at her hair, she snapped, "If you believe that will solve things, you are more foolish than I thought."

"You don't love him."

"No. But I need him. I need the allegiance of the northern chieftains." She turned her blue eyes on him. They glinted like ice. "I do not need you," she told him.

"But last night—" he protested. "Does that mean nothing to you?"

He could see that she was angry now. She laid down the comb and mirror, turning towards him again.

"Last night was fun, Calgacus, nothing more."

"So what happens now?" he demanded angrily. "Do I spend my nights here until you grow tired of me? Do I stand aside while you wed Venutius? Or do you really want me to hand myself over to the Romans?"

"I think you should leave now," she said, her cheeks flushing slightly. "And do not come back here. Tell your brother he must decide today whether he wishes me to speak to the Governor. If he does not, you should all go."

"Go where?" he snapped.

"Anywhere! I don't care! You should never have come here in the first place. Now get out!"

She bent down, scooped up his clothes and threw them at him. He caught them awkwardly. Her furious stance left him in no doubt that there was nothing to be gained by exchanging more angry words. Pushing himself out of the bed, he dressed hurriedly, his mind racing, his temper driving a thumping pulse in his temple. She watched him silently, her eyes like seething sparks of fire.

Pulling on his boots, he strode for the door.

"I think you are right," he growled as he passed her. "Cartimandua the Queen is not someone I could ever love."

"Just go!" she retorted, waving her arm towards the door.

He had hoped to see tears in her eyes but there was no sign of them, just blazing anger. If she had cried, he would have gone back to her, would have put his arms around her and held her close but she was Cartimandua, the ruthless queen, and she had discarded him. He yanked the door open, stepped outside and slammed it shut behind him.

He paused, taking a deep breath, waiting in case he heard the sound of crying from behind the door, but the house was silent. Muttering dark curses, he stalked away, ignoring the curious glances of the two sentries.

The sky was just beginning to lighten in the east, the blue-black of night turning to grey, the stars slowly fading. A cock crowed somewhere in the distance, greeting the dawn. Calgacus did not care. He marched round the corner of the great hall, oblivious to everything except hurt and anger.

The world exploded as something hit him on the back of the head. He staggered, his eyes dazzled by lights of pain and shock that danced like stars, blinding him. A foot lashed out, tripping him. Hands pushed at him, then blows began to rain on his back and head. He tried to push himself up, to slide away but there were too many assailants. He was surrounded and the blows would not stop.

From somewhere far away, just as he began to lose consciousness, he heard a voice laughing.

"I warned you, Renegade. You should have stayed away from her."

Chapter VII

Aemilia was bored. She had spent most of the day in the stifling confines of the carriage, then been forced to sit listening to her mother talk for hours to a woman Aemilia did not know, the wife of one of the centurions whose soldiers manned a small fort out in the middle of nowhere. There had been warm milk to drink, and watered wine, and some freshly baked bread and biscuits. That had been nice, but she had been utterly, utterly bored. Now, half way back to the legionary fort, the wagon had lost a wheel. That meant they would be forced to wait while the soldiers tried to repair it. It would mean another few hours of boredom.

Already the sun was starting its slow descent towards the horizon and Aemilia knew it would be dark by the time they got home. She decided she must get away from her mother for a while.

"Mama?"

"What is it, dear?"

"I need to answer a call of nature."

Her mother frowned. She looked around, then pointed to some tangled bushes that covered the long, empty slope to the south.

"Go over there," she said. "But don't be long. Come back as quickly as you can."

"I will," Aemilia promised.

"Carilla will go with you."

"Mama!"

"No arguments, Aemilia."

Her mother signalled to the young optio who commanded the soldiers. "Send two of your men to watch over my daughter. Discreetly. They must maintain a respectful distance."

"Yes, ma'am," the optio replied. He signalled to two soldiers who resignedly lifted up their large shields and javelins.

Aemilia hurried off, not waiting for the soldiers or for Carilla. The fat, elderly slave woman was supposed to look after the young girl, but as far as Aemilia was concerned, all Carilla ever did was scold her. Laughing happily, Aemilia skipped away from the trackway, heading towards the forest of scrub while Carilla huffed behind her.

The two soldiers followed at a sedate pace, chatting to each other while they walked, scarcely paying attention to the girl. They were just glad to avoid the heavy work of lifting the wagon while the repaired wheel was fitted.

Aemilia danced her way among the gorse and brambles, pleased to get away, even if it was for only a few moments. Ever since her father had brought the family to Britannia, it had felt like a prison. She hated this wild, barbarian country.

When she had first heard that her father was being sent to command a legion, *Legio IX Hispana*, she had been pleased. Hispania was a warm province, almost as civilised as Italy. Then she had learned that, despite its name, the legion was based in Britannia, an island at the end of the world, shrouded in perpetual mist and rain, and inhabited by barbarians and monsters.

Her friend, Servilia, had assured her that Britannia was home to all sorts of flesh-eating creatures who stalked the wild forests in search of human prey. Her stories had frightened Aemilia, although she would never have admitted it, especially not to Servilia.

Naturally, Carilla had scolded her when she had ventured to ask about the one-eyed giants and the men who could transform themselves into bears or wolves. Carilla's clinching argument was that, at ten years old and never having travelled further than Ravenna, Servilia could hardly be regarded as an expert on Britannia.

"But there are monsters," Aemilia had protested. "Papa says he saw a bear in the amphitheatre. It was from Britannia. He said it was the largest bear he had ever seen."

"Bears are dangerous beasts, right enough," Carilla had said. "But they are not monsters. Besides, there will be plenty of soldiers to protect us."

Aemilia's mother had been more worried about the barbarians than the alleged monsters. "The Britons are said to be most savage people," she had confided to one of her friends when she thought Aemilia could not hear her. "But I suppose that is why we are going there; to teach them how to be civilised. Still, it will be hard being away from Rome."

Her friend had offered sympathy and both women had talked

about duty and the need for self-sacrifice. To Aemilia, Britannia sounded a dreadful place. It had no temples, no libraries, no shops, and no theatres. Apparently it did not even have any proper towns worthy of the name. She had wondered whether Servilia might have been right after all.

It was true that Aemilia had not actually seen any monsters since she had arrived on the island. In fact, she had not even seen a bear or a wolf, but there were certainly lots of barbarians. They lived in horrible, circular houses built of mud and sticks, with thatched roofs that sloped low to the ground and rose to a point at the top in a most un-Roman way.

They also spoke a disgusting, barbarous language which Aemilia could not understand at all. And they smelled. They had no bath houses and never seemed to wash. She hated them.

She hated the damp, cold weather which seemed to last for most of the year, and she hated that there were few roads. Whenever her mother took her anywhere, which was not often because there were few places to visit, they sat in their carriage being shaken and jostled on simple, rutted trackways.

Today had been no different. Aemilia was glad that the wheel had broken. At least it stopped the uncomfortable bumping for a while.

As she darted between the bushes, trying to evade Carilla, she thought about the other things that she hated. Living in an army fortress was one of them. There were very few other children because only the centurions were allowed to marry and bring their families. In Lindum, there were no other girls of Aemilia's age. She was never allowed to leave the fort to play, not unless Carilla and some soldiers went with her, which spoiled the fun anyway.

She found that she even disliked the soldiers. She had thought they would be mostly Spaniards, because that was what the legion's name meant, but she had discovered that more than half of them were from Gaul. They were all Roman citizens, of course, but most of them had never seen Rome and, in Aemilia's young eyes, they were little better than the barbarians. They were rough, coarse men who enjoyed fighting and drinking and playing at dice. Sometimes, they did all three at the same time. She knew they would never harm her, because she was the Legate's daughter, but she did her best to avoid speaking to any of them if at all possible.

"Aemilia! Where are you?"

That was Carilla, annoyed and hectoring as always.

"I'm over here!" Aemilia called back. She immediately darted away, ducking low to dodge among the bushes while Carilla blundered through the tangle after her.

Aemilia covered her mouth with one hand, stifling her laughter. It was nice to have some fun, especially at Carilla's expense. She was glad she had made the excuse about needing to relieve herself. That had been a lie, but one her mother could hardly argue with. Still, now that she was here, she decided she might as well take advantage of the screen of bushes. It would be several hours until they reached home.

Seeking some privacy, she wound her way towards a stand of trees. She could hear Carilla calling her but the slave woman was well out of sight now. Finding a secluded spot, with tall bushes all around her and the trees only a few paces away, Aemilia squatted down. She looked around, surveying her surroundings, checking that it was safe to pull down her undergarments without fear of being interrupted.

Her heart lurched when she saw eyes staring back at her from behind the thick undergrowth in the woodland.

She froze, her mouth and eyes opening wide. Before she could scream, there was a guttural shout from someone hiding in the trees, then the bushes were shoved aside as men exploded out into the fading daylight.

They were long-haired, half-naked men, wearing long trousers and dark cloaks, with blue paint all over their faces, their arms and their bare chests. Before Aemilia could move, one of them grabbed her, flinging an arm around her waist, sweeping her up. She screamed as he carried her off, charging back the way she had come, towards the trackway.

She was aware of other men running alongside, cloaks flapping wildly as they charged through the scrub, yelling fierce war cries. They all carried long spears.

Jostled in the man's arms, tears of fright filling her eyes, Aemilia's world was restricted to brief images of what was happening around her. As if in a dream or a nightmare, she saw one of the wild men stab Carilla in the belly, throwing the old woman to the ground. Carilla screamed as she fell, and Aemilia, terrified, screamed as well, calling Carilla's name while frantically trying to wriggle out of the barbarian's powerful grip. He hit her across the cheeks, barking at her, but she could not understand the harsh words.

The two soldiers who had followed her, caught unawares by the unexpected attack, threw their javelins then hastily drew their swords. The barbarians easily dodged the hurriedly thrown javelins and swiftly surrounded the two legionaries. Spears flashed in the slanting rays of the setting sun, came back up, red and bloody. Aemilia saw the legionaries crumple to the ground.

The barbarians ran, crossing the trackway in a wild rush of triumphant screams and ferocious yells. The man holding Aemilia was shouting orders, waving his free arm. He had seen the other soldiers who were escorting the carriage, seen them grabbing shields, forming up. He obviously decided not to stay to fight, so the barbarians ran, heading north, charging towards the trees on the other side of the track.

"Mama!" Aemilia screamed.

The man slapped at her again, warning her to silence.

The barbarians charged across the tussocky grass. Bouncing on her captor's shoulder, Aemilia managed to see that some of the men were weighed down by plunder. She saw one struggling under the weight of a sheep's carcass that was slung across his shoulders. Another had several dead chickens strung on a long line while yet another was dragging a young woman behind him. All were running as fast as they could.

Despite the threats and the slaps, Aemilia shouted, calling for help, screaming for the soldiers to rescue her. They threw some javelins, but the barbarians were too far away, moving too quickly in the fading light. The man carrying Aemilia hit her again, then awkwardly clamped his free hand over her mouth to stifle her cries. She tried to kick him but he was too strong. Then she tried to bite his fingers. He responded by punching the side of her head and shouting at her.

Dazed, Aemilia could no longer struggle. Tears flooded her eyes. Blinking through them, she looked back towards the trackway. She caught a glimpse of her mother, standing beside the carriage, frantically waving her arms, calling her name. Then the trees obscured her view and she knew there was no chance of being rescued.

Laughing and calling to one another, the barbarians ran on, ever deeper into the forest.

Chapter VIII

Calgacus woke to a world of pain. His head ached, his back throbbed and his sides pulsated with dull agonies. The fingers of his left hand screamed in nauseating protest and his jaw felt swollen and raw.

"Calgacus?"

The voice came from far away. He knew he must be dreaming, for it sounded like Cartimandua. He blinked, turned his head, wincing as he did so.

"How are you feeling?" she asked.

He looked around, trying to understand where he was. Cartimandua was sitting beside his low bed, with Garathus, her shield-bearer, standing protectively at her shoulder. Beyond Garathus, he saw Runt and Caratacus, both of them looking at him with anxiety etched on their faces. Cethinos was also there, stern and disapproving as ever. There were other people too. Pencoch, Barta and the other warriors, all of them angry and concerned.

"What happened?" he asked, the words muffled by his tender jaw and bruised lips.

Cartimandua said, "It was Venutius. He and some of his men attacked you."

"You were lucky," Runt told him. "If the Queen had not stopped them, they would have killed you."

Calgacus peered at Cartimandua. "You stopped them?"

She nodded. "Yes. My guards heard them and came to fetch me."

He lay back, half closing his eyes. "Why didn't you let them kill me?"

Her voice took on a hard edge as she said, "You are my guest. I offered you my protection."

He was too tired, too sore to argue. He wanted to ask her whether there might have been another reason she had stopped the beating, but he could not face another confrontation. It was enough that she was here.

Cethinos said, "There is no serious damage done. You have a remarkably thick skull, as I have often observed. There are no broken bones, simply bruising. You are fit and strong. If the Gods will it, you should heal in a few days."

"He may have concussion," Caratacus said. "Or he may be bleeding inside."

Cethinos gave an uncaring shrug. "Then the Gods will decide his fate," he said.

Cartimandua stood up. "I am sorry this happened," she said. "I did not know Venutius intended you harm."

"I did," Runt muttered darkly. He asked Calgacus, "Do you want me to kill him now?"

"I'll do that myself when I've recovered," Calgacus said wearily.

"There will be no killing," Cartimandua stated firmly. She turned to face Caratacus. "I think it is time you left, Cousin. As soon as Calgacus is able to ride, you must leave Brigantia. Unless you wish me to approach the Governor on your behalf?"

Cethinos' ears immediately pricked up. "What is this?" he demanded.

"Nothing," Caratacus said quickly. "The Queen suggested that we should surrender to Rome, but I have no intention of doing that. We will leave when Calgacus is able to travel."

Cethinos' eyes narrowed but he nodded. "Good. We will go to Ynis Mon. I shall speak to the Druid Council and we will decide what must be done."

"Then I will leave you," Cartimandua said. "I suggest you all remain in this house until you are ready to leave. It will be safer for everyone." She turned to look down at Calgacus. "I am truly sorry about your injuries, Calgacus, but perhaps this is for the best. It could never have worked between us."

She turned, nodding a curt farewell to Caratacus, then walking serenely to the doorway with Garathus a step behind.

Calgacus looked up at his brother. He thought Caratacus looked ten years older than he had before they had come to Isuria.

"I am sorry, Brother," Calgacus said.

Caratacus shrugged. "I am sorry too, Little Brother. I did not think Venutius would dare such a thing."

"It does not matter. What do we do now? Where will we go?"

Caratacus gave a smile that was replete with exhaustion. "We will go to Ynis Mon. Cethinos is right. We need the support of the Druid Council if we are to raise another army from the western tribes. That is all we can do."

Calgacus saw Cethinos nodding in approval.

The druid said, "That is good. When we get there, you will see the true power of the Servants of the Gods."

Wearily, Calgacus lay back, closing his eyes. He was tired and sore, a headache rampaging through his battered skull. Perhaps that was why Cethinos' words sounded like a prophecy of doom.

For two days, Cethinos grudgingly mixed herbal drinks for Calgacus and applied soothing poultices to his bruised body. By the third day, much of the swelling on his face had reduced and he was able to eat something more substantial than gruel or broth.

"I'm well enough to ride," he declared.

"Are you sure?" Caratacus asked.

"I'll be fine," Calgacus assured him.

"Then I suppose we should go and say goodbye to our hostess," Caratacus said with little enthusiasm.

"Not before time," grumbled Cethinos. The druid had fretted and fussed for the past two days, anxious to set off for the sacred island of Ynis Mon.

"Do you want to come to the hall?" Caratacus asked him.

The druid shook his head. "I have nothing to say to that woman," he growled.

Leaving the others to pack their few belongings, Calgacus accompanied his brother to the Queen's hall. Two of Cartimandua's guards fell into step behind them as soon as they left the roundhouse.

The sky was clear and blue, only a few cumulus clouds drifting lazily across the heavens. The summer sun was warm and bright but the fine weather did not match the Great King's mood.

"I made a mistake coming here," Caratacus admitted as they made their way along the winding path that led through the roundhouses.

"We had to try," Calgacus replied.

"But now we have run out of options," Caratacus said gloomily.

"We are not beaten yet."

Caratacus gave a forced smile. "No, Little Brother, we are not.

But I confess that it is difficult to see how we can win now."

"Do you want to surrender?" Calgacus asked, dismayed at his older brother's grim mood.

"No. Not until there is no other choice."

"Good. Then let's get this over with and get away from here. The sooner we are among friends, the better."

They emerged from the gaggle of roundhouses into the open space in front of the hall. As they approached the doors they met Garathus who was walking briskly out of the hall, his broad face creased in an uncharacteristic frown. He stopped abruptly when he saw them, the frown giving way to a look of concern.

"Get inside!" he said urgently. "The Romans are here."

Calgacus whirled, looking around for the enemy, but Garathus grabbed at his arm, tugging him towards the doors.

"Be quick. You must hide," the shield-bearer said as he ushered them towards the doors.

"Where are they?" Caratacus demanded.

"On their way. Get inside and stay in the shadows. Try to keep out of sight."

The shield-bearer bundled them through the doors, pointing them towards the side of the great hall.

Calgacus asked, "Are they here for us?"

"I don't know," Garathus said. He pushed them to the side, beyond the row of tall pillars. Other men were already there, the big warriors who acted as the Queen's guards. Garathus shoved the two brothers to the back, then hurried away to the door.

The hall was crowded, the far end crammed with men and women who clustered round the Queen's dais. The air of anxious tension was palpable.

Cartimandua sat on her tall chair, a ghostly figure in white among the shadows. She was too far away and too shrouded in gloom for Calgacus to make out her face but she sat stiffly, unmoving. Calgacus knew that she could not have failed to see Garathus bringing him and Caratacus into the hall although she gave no indication that she had noticed anything untoward. Everyone else, though, was regarding the two Catuvellauni with expressions that ranged from curiosity to outright fear. Around Calgacus, the guards shifted uncomfortably, giving the two brothers nervous looks, as if they were unsure whether they were supposed to be hiding them or taking them captive.

"What do we do?" Calgacus whispered to his brother.

"We wait."

A clatter of hooves sounded from beyond the open doors. From the sound, Calgacus guessed that at least a dozen horses had arrived. A short while later, Garathus reappeared, striding into the hall, his expression as stoic and impassive as ever. Behind him came a Roman officer, complete with breastplate, a skirt of metal-studded leather strips, a red cloak flowing behind him and a helmet with a red-dyed horsehair plume. At his left hip was a short, Roman sword. He had removed his helmet, holding it in the crook of his left arm, revealing a young, intelligent face topped by brown hair that was cut short in the Roman fashion. He followed the shield-bearer, looking neither to left nor right as he walked the length of the hall, moving from light to shade as he passed through the patches of bright sunlight formed by the high windows.

A third man, short and dark-haired, wearing British-style tunic, trousers and hooded cloak, trailed nervously behind the Roman.

Calgacus ducked his head, knowing that his long, dark moustache marked him out as a foreigner among the Brigantes but the Roman officer did not glance in his direction and the small Pritani who followed him seemed too anxious to take any notice of his surroundings. Following Garathus, the two men passed on to the far end of the hall where they halted in front of the dais.

Garathus announced, "My Queen, this is Anderius Facilis, a Tribune of Rome. He has been sent by the Governor, Ostorius Scapula."

The hall was virtually silent, only the soft crackle and hiss of the hearth fire audible. It was as if the assembled nobles and warriors of Brigantia had held their collective breath while they watched and waited to hear what the Tribune had to say.

Cartimandua remained calm. "Welcome Anderius Facilis," she said, her voice echoing through the silent hall.

The little, dark-haired man translated the Queen's greeting into Latin. Facilis inclined his head in a cursory bow.

Although Calgacus could only see the back of the man's head, he gained the impression that the Tribune was quite unafraid. All around were Brigante warriors, yet Facilis paid no attention to them. Calgacus could sense that the Brigantes were more nervous than the solitary Roman. He understood their fear. If they were found sheltering enemies of Rome, there would, as Cartimandua had predicted when they had first walked into her hall, be trouble. It was evident that the Brigantes were afraid of Facilis, not for his own sake but because of what he represented. He was only one man, but he had the unimaginable power of the Empire behind him.

Apart from the Tribune, Cartimandua was the calmest person in the hall. She ordered a drink brought for her guest, although she made a point of making him stand while she remained seated on her raised chair. If Facilis objected to this obvious statement that she was in charge, he did not show it. He may have been standing before her like a petitioner, but he treated her with the same haughty, disdainful attitude that all Romans reserved for foreigners.

Cartimandua, well capable of playing the Roman game, affected not to notice his contempt for his surroundings.

"To what do we owe this unexpected visit?" she asked sweetly.

Calgacus could feel sweat on his palms and a dryness in his throat. But at least everyone was now watching Facilis, not looking at him and Caratacus. He wondered whether they should try to slip out of the door, but the faint sound of horses outside told him that there were more Romans beyond the doors. He waited.

Facilis' voice was stern. He spoke in clipped Latin which the interpreter translated. "Do you not know?" he asked.

"How should I know?" Cartimandua responded innocently.

Facilis rattled out a string of Latin, pausing every so often to allow the interpreter to relay his words in Brythonic. The little man said, "Four days ago, some tribesmen raided into the province of Britannia. They attacked a small party of Roman nobles and killed three people; two soldiers and a slave woman. They also kidnapped a young girl."

The silence in the hall seemed to intensify as Facilis spoke again. "The girl is the daughter of the Legate of the Ninth Legion."

Relief washed over Calgacus. He almost laughed aloud. The Romans had not come for the Catuvellauni after all. Caratacus gripped his arm, squeezing it in silent celebration.

In contrast to Calgacus' joy, Cartimandua was plainly worried by the news.

"This was not done with my knowledge or consent," she said. "I will have men search for her. The culprits will be punished and the girl will be returned."

Facilis listened while the interpreter translated. He gave a slight nod of his head, then he made his fateful reply. "Governor Ostorius Scapula is in Lindum. He has ordered me to tell you that the girl must be returned, alive, unharmed and well, within twenty days. If she is not, Rome will view this as an act of war. Is that clear? In twenty days she must be at the legionary fort at Lindum or Rome will destroy the kingdom of the Brigantes."

Nobody spoke. Cartimandua stared fixedly at the Roman emissary, a distant look in her eyes. The interpreter had to ask her twice if she had understood.

"Yes, I understand," she replied at last, her tone flat.

"I should warn you that the Governor is not a patient man," Facilis said. "I would advise you to return the girl as quickly as possible."

"I do not know where she is," Cartimandua said, trying to keep her voice firm.

"Then find her," was the Tribune's reply. "You have twenty days."

Cartimandua could only nod her head in acknowledgement. Satisfied, Facilis gave the slightest of bows, spun on his heels and marched out, his companion scurrying after him. Calgacus saw a look that might have been relief on the Roman officer's face as he passed. He realised that, despite his outward confidence, the man must have been worried about venturing into Cartimandua's hall. Glad to have delivered his message and got away, Facilis swept past, clearly in a hurry to depart. In his wake, he left a stunned chamber.

Caratacus whispered, "Say what you like about the Romans, that took some balls. Coming in here alone to make a demand like that."

"He's probably too stupid to understand the danger," Calgacus replied, relieved that the Romans apparently had no idea that they were there. Privately, though, he agreed with his brother's assessment. The Tribune had displayed a great deal of courage and boldness.

The large doors closed behind Facilis, bringing an immediate uproar as everyone tried to speak at once. Some men shook their fists, clearly ready for a fight. Others looked scared, their faces pale. The women, too, were alarmed and vociferous, some for war,

91

some against. Calgacus noticed Venutius among the crowd, his hazel eyes wary, one hand rubbing thoughtfully at his cheeks.

Cartimandua stood up, clapping her hands to demand their attention. The room fell silent.

It was Cartimandua the Queen who addressed them. Her stance revealed her outrage as she spoke in a voice that was hard and utterly determined. "You have all heard this ultimatum," she announced. "I want every man who has a horse to ride out and search for news of this girl. I want the brigands who carried out the raid to be found and brought to me. I do not care whether they are dead or alive. Above all, I want the Roman girl returned here to me. My father worked hard to maintain peace with Rome and I intend to do the same. I will not have that peace threatened. The girl must be found. Go now and prepare. I want everyone riding out before noon. Visit every farm and village. Search every house if you have to. Find her!"

She pointed a commanding finger to the door. Instantly, men began to head outside in response to her orders. There were no arguments, no questions. It was a monumental task they faced, for the kingdom of Brigantia was vast and the girl could be anywhere. But the Queen had spoken and her subjects, understanding the consequences of failure, hurried to obey.

Caratacus maintained his grip on Calgacus' arm, holding him still while the Brigantes pushed their way to the doors. When the Great King spoke, there was new fire in his voice.

"This is our chance, Little Brother. The Gods are smiling on us at last. Come, we must speak to Cethinos."

"Wait," Calgacus said. He nodded to two men who were walking past them. Venutius and Vellocatus paused when they reached the two brothers.

"Are you still here, Renegade?" Venutius asked, a cruel smile on his lips.

"I am not easy to kill," Calgacus replied.

"Well, perhaps next time Cartimandua won't be around to save your filthy southern skin," Venutius rasped.

"Next time I will be ready for you," Calgacus promised.

"There will be no next time," Caratacus said firmly. "It looks as if the Romans have decided to bring war to the Brigantes, just as I predicted. We are on the same side now."

Venutius treated the two brothers to a look of contempt. "I

doubt that we will ever be on the same side," he said scornfully. "If it comes to war, the Brigantes are capable of fighting without help from a handful of exiled brigands who have already been defeated."

Caratacus' rejoinder was silenced when Cartimandua arrived.

"What is going on here?" she demanded. Her face was still flushed with anger.

Caratacus said, "Greetings, Cousin. I had come to tell you that we were leaving but I think now that we will stay a while longer. If you do not find this Roman girl, you will need our help."

"We will find her," Cartimandua replied. "Venutius was just leaving to help in the search. Is that not so?"

Venutius exhaled a short breath of resigned irritation. "I shall leave immediately," he said brusquely. With a mocking wave of his arm, he turned, leading the tall figure of Vellocatus outside.

Caratacus turned to Cartimandua. "You should prepare for war, Cousin," he told her.

"Perhaps."

Calgacus cut in, saying, "There is no perhaps. Rome intends war. The girl probably does not even exist. This is just a ploy. The Governor wants to destroy the Brigantes while the western tribes are unable to trouble him. He has invented this excuse."

"What do you mean?" Cartimandua asked.

"I mean that this emissary did not say where the girl was kidnapped. How old is she? What is her name? He did not say. How do they know it was Brigante tribesmen who took her? He did not say."

"Roman girls are not very common around here," Cartimandua replied. "There will only be one. She will not be that difficult to find."

Caratacus said, "Nevertheless, we need to talk. It is foolish to rely on only one strategy. Search for this girl if you must, but you should also prepare for war so that you are ready if it comes."

Cartimandua studied the two brothers thoughtfully. Seeing her now, Calgacus was aware of just how young she was for such responsibility. She concealed her inexperience behind a mask of self-assurance but he had come to know her intimately, and he recognised that she was, for the first time since he had met her, unsure of what to do.

"I must oversee the arrangements for the search," she said after a while. "Come to my house this afternoon. Both of you. And bring your druid."

Cethinos was surprisingly unexcited about the news but Caratacus, who had flung off the depression that had gripped him over the previous days, was bursting with enthusiastic energy.

"She has no choice now," he told them. "The Romans do not make idle threats. In twenty days, they will attack." He slammed a fist into the flat of his other hand. "Then the whole tribe will rise up."

"What if the Brigantes find this Roman girl?" Runt asked. "They might be able to do that. If she exists, it won't be easy for anyone to keep her hidden. Word will get around."

"Not that quickly," Caratacus said. "But you are right, we should take a hand in the search. If we find her first, we can ensure the Romans declare war."

Calgacus gave his brother a look of concern. "What do you mean?"

Cethinos muttered, "It is simple enough, boy. Find the girl and kill her."

"No," Calgacus said. "I will not kill a child."

Cethinos rolled his eyes in exasperation but Caratacus waved a conciliatory hand. "Don't worry, Little Brother. You won't need to kill her. Just find her, then find somewhere to hide. Keep her until the Romans attack. After that, we can take her close to a Roman camp. Runt speaks Latin, so he'll be able to get her close enough to return her safely. By that time, it won't change things."

Cethinos said, "That is not necessary. If we find her, we should offer her to the Gods."

"You would like that, wouldn't you?" Calgacus asked sharply. "Slitting the throat of another innocent."

"The Gods demand sacrifice!" Cethinos barked, rounding on him. He jabbed a long, bony finger at Calgacus chest, his voice rising to a querulous shout. "You should remember that. The Gods will have vengeance on those who show disrespect."

"Enough!" Caratacus demanded. "The girl will not be harmed. If we find her."

"Has defeat turned you soft?" Cethinos hissed at the Great King. "Sacrificing a Roman child will please the Gods."

Caratacus' eyes blazed. He held the druid's gaze as he replied in a low, hoarse whisper, "I am not growing soft, Cethinos. But my own wife and daughter are prisoners of the Romans." He glanced at Calgacus as he went on, "I learned some years ago that I cannot expect mercy if I do not show it. For the sake of my family, I will not harm a Roman child."

"Your wife and daughter are Roman slaves by now," Cethinos muttered angrily. "The legionaries will have used them for their pleasure, then put them in chains. If we find this Roman girl, you should avenge their fate."

"I am a father," Caratacus replied. "I will not harm another man's daughter. I will pray that the Gods will see this and will protect my own child. Rufinna is precious to me."

Calgacus wanted to hug his brother for defying the old druid. Rufinna, the Great King's young daughter, had been a favourite of all the warriors. The thought of her being raped by Roman soldiers was one that none of them had voiced. If preserving the Roman girl could help Rufinna, none of the warriors would harm her.

Calgacus wanted to say all this but there was something more important that needed to be said.

"There is a problem," he told them.

"What is that?" Caratacus asked.

"Cartimandua is no fool. She will never permit us to leave to search for this girl. She knows we would never hand her over to prevent the war."

Caratacus smiled. "Don't worry about that, Little Brother. I have an idea that will allow you to leave Isuria unhindered."

They watched the searchers depart. Horsemen galloped out of the town, heading in all directions. Chariots were harnessed and some men went out on foot to visit the nearer villages, farms and hamlets. Cartimandua stood by the eastern gates, watching them go, calling encouragement. When the last man had ridden out, she nodded to the Catuvellauni delegation and led them back to her private dwelling.

Inside, the roundhouse was just as Calgacus remembered it. He glanced at the bed, then looked away hurriedly, trying to force down the memories. Then he looked at Cartimandua, her hair slightly ruffled by the wind, her cheeks still tinged with anger. Her soft, white dress clung to her as she moved, exciting more memories. She had spurned him but he still wanted her. She,

95

however, looked at him as if he were a stranger. Perhaps that was just as well, he thought. Her indifference towards him would turn to hatred if she ever learned how they were about to betray her.

"Well, Cousin?" she asked Caratacus.

The two rulers sat on the tall chairs beside the hearth. Garathus stood behind the Queen, his arms folded across his burly chest, while Calgacus and Cethinos took up positions behind the Great King.

Caratacus said, "Perhaps you will find this girl and perhaps not. If you do, then I will depart. If you do not, then I will remain here. I offer my services as War Leader."

Cartimandua nodded. Her face was calm now, her eyes watchful and pensive. "Thank you, Cousin," she said.

"In the meantime, you should begin preparations for war. Isuria cannot be defended against Rome. The land around here is too flat, too open. It is the type of terrain the Romans love. You must abandon this place and take to the hills."

Calgacus had expected her to protest but she simply nodded her understanding. "Go on," she said.

"I can advise you on how and where to fight but it would help if I knew the land better. I know that hills and valleys lie to the north and there are high moorlands to the east, but I need a pair of eyes to locate the best hiding places, the best spots to trap a Roman army."

"I cannot permit you to leave Isuria just now," Cartimandua said, her tone light and reasonable. "You must know that."

"Of course. I will remain here. I can advise you on what supplies and equipment should be readied, on how to move your people quickly to places of safety. Cethinos will also stay here. But I told you once before that Calgacus has a talent for these things. I would like you to allow him to ride north, to seek out a place where we can defeat the Romans."

Cartimandua's eyes turned on Calgacus. She said, "If I were a suspicious person, I would suppose that you intended to look for this missing Roman girl. If she dies, the war you crave is certain."

Calgacus had to force indignation to his face to cover his fear that she had seen through Caratacus' plan. But his brother had foreseen this and they had discussed how he could best respond without lying.

Speaking proudly, he said, "For one thing, I do not believe this

Roman girl exists. For another, I have told you that I do not make war on women and children. If I happen to come across this Roman child, which I doubt, I swear on my father's coin that I will return her unharmed." He tugged the coin from under his shirt, holding it up for her to see. "By this token, I give my oath," he added decisively.

She regarded him thoughtfully for a long time before returning her attention to Caratacus. "Very well, Cousin," she said. "I trust Calgacus' word. I also agree that it would be wise to plan for all eventualities. It shall be as you suggest."

Chapter IX

"I can't believe she went for it," Runt said as they rode out of Isuria only a short while later.

"I think she wants rid of me," Calgacus replied. "Or maybe she wants to believe me. I didn't actually lie to her. I just didn't say when I would bring the girl back."

"Do you think that will make any difference if she finds out?" Runt asked. "If you think she was angry before, it will be nothing to what she does if she learns you found the girl and hid her. She won't forgive that, Cal. Believe me, women don't ever forget things like that."

"She hates me anyway," Calgacus said. "Besides, we have to find the girl before we start worrying about how Cartimandua might react."

Runt gave a soft laugh. "I don't think she hates you," he said. "You should have seen her face when she thought you had been killed by Venutius."

"Forget her," Calgacus snapped. "We have a job to do."

He tried to push thoughts of Cartimandua to the back of his mind. She was beautiful and intoxicating but she was too driven, too intent on being a ruler. He could have loved Cartimandua the woman, but he knew that Cartimandua the queen would always remain beyond him. Now he was attempting to betray her, using her inexperience in war and her fear of losing her high status to trick her into allowing him to roam her land. He knew that, if their positions had been reversed, Cartimandua would have done the same to him without hesitation, but the thought of going behind the back of someone he could have loved left a bitter taste on his tongue.

"Let's get moving," he said, urging his pony into a canter. He winced as the movement of the horse jarred his bruises but it felt good to be on horseback, to have his sword on his back again. He was glad to escape the stifling confinements of Isuria, where he had felt trapped by the need to please such charismatic characters as Caratacus and Cartimandua, not to mention old Cethinos. Now, at last, he would be able to do what he did best; lead a war band into hostile territory.

Twisting round in the saddle, he checked that the six warriors were following close behind, then waved a hand to Caratacus who was standing by the western gate, watching them go.

The Great King's parting words had been, "It is all up to you now, Little Brother. May the Gods favour you."

Calgacus understood the responsibility he had been given but he accepted the challenge. The fate of the free tribes depended on him accomplishing a seemingly impossible task and somehow preventing Cartimandua from discovering his betrayal. It was a last, desperate gamble but, as Caratacus had told him, they had no choice but to risk everything. They could not afford to think about the consequences of failure, so Calgacus concentrated only on how to achieve the impossible.

He raised a hand in farewell to his brother. He hated leaving Caratacus behind but he knew there was no other choice. The Great King stood tall and proud, unbending despite the fact that he was effectively being held as a hostage. He trusted Calgacus to do whatever was humanly possible but Calgacus knew that his brother would never blame him should he fail. That was not the Great King's way. Caratacus was a great man, a noble man. Calgacus wanted nothing more than to emulate him, to be worthy of his praise and trust.

Pencoch had wanted to stay with the Great King but Caratacus had insisted he would be safe enough and that the veteran warrior would be of more use with Calgacus, so eight of them now rode out of Isuria, turning north-west, angling away from the river towards the distant hills of Brigantia.

"So where do we begin looking?" Runt asked as they rode at a steady canter.

"We go north first, until we are away from Isuria and any of the other search parties, then we go east."

"Why east?"

"Because most of the Roman province lies to the south and east of here. The girl is supposed to be the daughter of the Legate, so it is likely that she was taken somewhere south-east of Isuria."

"You're guessing," Runt observed. "She might have been in the west."

99

"I doubt it. The Cornovii were conquered fairly recently. The Coritani to the east submitted to Rome some time ago. She's more likely to have been in the peaceful part of the Province."

"I suppose so," Runt said with a considerable lack of conviction.

"So, if the raiders were to the south-east, they are hardly likely to have come towards Isuria, not with a Roman prisoner when they know Cartimandua wants to be a friend of Rome."

"Unless they are very stupid. You shouldn't overestimate their intelligence."

"Don't complicate things," Calgacus said. "If they are that stupid, one of Cartimandua's other search parties will soon track them down. We must assume they would avoid coming near Isuria."

"So they would go straight north or north-east," Runt said.

"That's my guess."

"It will still be like looking for a four-leafed clover in a bed of nettles," Runt said.

"Then let's hope the Brigantes have the same problem. As long as she is not found, the war will begin."

They saw several of Cartimandua's search parties. The Brigante warriors were spreading out from Isuria, heading in all directions, like ripples in a pond. On foot, on horseback and on chariots, they scoured the land for signs of the kidnapped girl.

Calgacus ignored them. If the girl was found nearby, there was nothing he could do about it.

The eight Catuvellauni rode all day, climbing into steep-sided hills and winding river valleys. Once he was reasonably sure that they had out-distanced the other search parties, Calgacus turned towards the east.

Now the search began. They stopped at every farm, every village, to ask whether anyone knew of a Roman girl who had been taken prisoner. Their long moustaches and southern accents brought them some suspicious looks although there was no outright hostility. But everywhere they asked, the answer was the same; nobody knew anything. In some places, they discovered that Cartimandua's men had already passed that way, asking the same question.

A second day passed, then a third, and Calgacus became all

too aware of the enormity of the task facing them. There was so much land to cover, so many places to visit. As far as possible, he had tried to search methodically, riding north, then east, then south before heading east again to repeat the pattern. It was slow, painstaking work and it proved to be utterly fruitless. Gripped by a growing sense of frustration, he decided to concentrate his efforts on searching the higher ground, hoping that anyone who had taken a Roman girl captive would want to remain hidden and would stay somewhere remote. It was, he knew, a plan born of desperation.

It brought no success.

On the evening of the fourth day, they were riding along a high ridge, moving slowly as the horses carefully picked their way along the uneven ground. Everyone was tired and frustrated. They had climbed so many hills, plunged down into so many dales, only to have to climb the far side again. Now they had reached a wide expanse of rugged and windswept upland moors, great swathes of land covered by long grass or by endless vistas of bracken and heather. Low hills bounded the horizon in every direction, their slopes dotted by small caves or jumbled piles of rocks. They passed dense clumps of woodland, splashed through small streams and clambered their way across sudden dips in the ground.

"You could hide an army up here," Runt said.

"We may have to," Calgacus replied.

Runt said, "I think we should find somewhere to camp. The sky's getting dark behind us."

Calgacus turned to look over his shoulder. One glance at the sky told him that his friend was right. Away to the west was a mass of towering, dark, menacing clouds. There was a storm coming their way. He looked around, seeking shelter. They were high on a wide, undulating ridge. To their left, the land fell, then rose again into a stretch of upland moor, devoid of shelter for as far as he could see. To their right, the hillside dropped away steeply, into a narrow valley. At the foot of the high slope, hundreds of feet below them, was a small river, twisting its way out of a thick patch of trees. Ahead of them, the ridge turned sharply to the right, the slope becoming even steeper where it did so. The high hills on the other side of the narrow valley also twisted, creating a dogleg in the valley. Even from this height, he could not see what lay beyond the woodland that crowded round the stream far below.

He glanced back at the western sky, pulling his horse to a stop.

Pointing down to his right, he said, "We'd better go down there."

Runt eyed the descent dubiously. "That's pretty steep," he said.

"It's either that or stay up here and let the storm hit us."

Runt nodded. "Down it is, then."

The slope was so precipitous that they were forced to dismount, leading the horses slowly, picking their way cautiously down the rock-strewn hillside. It was slow, difficult work and more than once men lost their footing, sliding down the hill for a way before they could regain their feet. Their ponies were more sure-footed but moved extremely carefully.

Somehow, after what seemed an eternity, they all made it to the foot of the slope without serious mishap, but the sky overhead was dark as the storm, pushed by gusting westerly winds, overtook them. They could see the gloom of the rain coming towards them, could hear the distant rumble of thunder. Calgacus led them into the trees just as the first heavy raindrops splattered onto the ground.

In single file, they pushed into the thick woodland. There were no paths that Calgacus could see. The undergrowth was thick, snagging at his arms, legs and ankles as he forced his way through the woodland. Low branches obscured his view ahead, forcing him to duck as he shoved his way between the trees. The rain was now drumming on the leafy canopy over their heads. They were protected from the worst of the rain, but large drips fell heavily through the trees so they drew their cloaks tightly around themselves in an effort to stay dry.

The sky was dark now, turning the evening to premature night, then a flash of lightning briefly illuminated the trees, followed after a few heartbeats by the reverberating crack and rumble of thunder.

Calgacus pushed doggedly on. They may have been sheltered from the worst of the rain, but there was nowhere to stop. The trees offered no open spaces. This was ancient woodland, overgrown and almost impenetrable. He suspected they might well be the first people who had ever come this way.

The hill to his left became a cliff, turning sharply, forcing them to the right, into the dogleg he had seen from the ridge. He trudged onward, wet now as the rain drove down heavily, breaching the thick woodland canopy above their heads. Another bright flash seared the sky, another deep rumble of thunder vibrated all around them, making the ground at their feet tremble.

The horses whinnied in terror, tugging at the reins, forcing the men to calm the beasts before they could coax them onwards. Yet the men were near panic themselves. To be caught outdoors during a thunderstorm was one of their greatest fears, for they had been taught from childhood that there was a risk of the sky falling on their heads. Calgacus knew that was a folk tale to frighten children but knowing did not prevent his own fear. Yet he also knew that if he showed that fear, his men would truly panic, so he shouted at them to remain calm, to steady the horses and to follow him. Step after weary step, he forged on through the dense woods.

Abruptly, the trees came to an end. In the dim light, Calgacus could see a wide, grassy meadow, bisected by the narrow river. To his right, on the far side of the stream, were steep hills. Ahead were more trees, another thick patch of ancient woodland. On his left was an almost vertical rock cliff with a wide overhang jutting out to create a shelter. It was less than a cave, but it was the best cover they were likely to find. He called for his men to follow as he pushed his way out of the trees, through the drenching downpour, and then into shelter under the massive ledge of rock.

He shook himself dry. There was easily enough room to stand upright and just enough space for the eight of them and their horses to stay out of the rain. The shelter was completely open on two sides, and only partly protected by the woodland on the third side, but it was as welcome as any roundhouse.

The storm was upon them now. The rain hammered down in torrential sheets, churning the surface of the small river, soaking the ground, drumming loudly as it struck the earth, while the wind blew the trees wildly and drove the rain on ever harder. Lightning flashed again. This time the thunder was directly overhead, echoing around the small bowl of the valley, ferocious enough for the men to feel the shock of it in their bones. They struggled to calm the terrified horses who reared, their eyes rolling in panic. The noise of the rain, the wind and the thunder was so loud that they needed to shout to one another to make themselves heard.

Calgacus knew they had a miserable night ahead of them. The only good thing was that the storm was moving on quickly. Taranis, god of thunder, liked to spread his terror as far and wide as he could, so he rarely lingered in one place for long. The darkness of the storm gradually faded, to be replaced by the darkness of night. The wind still blew but the rain eased, then eventually turned to little more than a light drizzle as the booms of thunder faded into the distance.

Every one of the men breathed a sigh of relief, grateful that the storm had passed. In its wake, the air felt fresh and clear, cleansed by the thunder. Calgacus sent some men into the wood to try to find some sticks that were dry enough to start a fire. They returned with armfuls of damp wood which eventually produced a smoky, feeble flame.

"Just like home," Calgacus told them. "What more could we want?"

Then his blood ran cold when he heard the deathly sound of the Underworld.

Everyone froze. It was a low, ghostly moan, an ululating groan that spoke of anguish, pain and terror, chilling them to the bone with its awful sound. Calgacus leaped upright, his hand reaching for the hilt of his sword. He peered into the darkness. The wail was coming from the far end of the valley, beyond the second woodland. Primeval fear gripped him, making his legs shake, silencing his voice.

"It's Dis!" groaned Pencoch.

Calgacus swallowed hard. If it was the Lord of the Underworld come to claim them, there would be no escape for them. No man could fight a god, especially not Father Dis. He stood, facing the sound, dreading what might materialise out of the trees. From behind, he heard men offering up hurried, whispered prayers. Once again, they fought to control the terrified horses. He turned to see some men preparing to lead the animals away.

"Stand!" he shouted. "Whatever it is, we'll face it together. If it is Dis, running won't help. We won't get far through that forest."

The men stopped, their faces ashen, their eyes wide with fear. Calgacus shared that fear, but he would prefer to face whatever it was where he could see it, not try to run through that thick forest where he could see nothing.

Runt edged his way to stand beside Calgacus. He had his sword held ready. "Whatever it is, it's not getting any closer," he said, almost managing to hide the tremor in his voice.

"Are you sure?"

104

Runt did not answer, but as time passed and the mournful wail continued, Calgacus began to think that his friend was right. The sound echoed through the trees, swirled along the valley, but though it sometimes faded and sometimes grew louder, it was always distant.

The moon rose, occasionally shining through gaps in the heavy clouds that were whipped raggedly across the sky by the wind. Still the doleful sound went on, but nothing more happened. Eventually, the effort of standing, straining to see and hear, began to tell.

"We should rest," Calgacus said. "Whatever it is, it's not coming this way. Two men on watch. We'll leave at first light."

He lay down, trying to set an example to the men, trying to show them that he was not afraid. He wrapped his damp cloak around himself, rested his head on his arm and closed his eyes.

The sound of the Underworld moaned all around him. He tried to dismiss it from his mind, forced himself to think of something else, something more pleasant. He thought of Cartimandua.

The eerie sound faded away at some point during the night. The new day dawned fresh and clear, the air clean after the thunderstorm. The wind had died away to a mere light breeze. Birds chirped noisily in the trees and the men, rousing themselves after a miserable night, felt their spirits rise.

The fire was still burning, so, although the damp wood produced more smoke than heat, Calgacus decided they should eat some warm food before leaving. They boiled some water to make a thin oatmeal gruel. It was bland, lumpy and unappetising but it was hot and they felt better for it.

Once they had eaten, they led the horses to the river to drink, allowing them to crop the lush grass of the meadow while the men extinguished the fire and packed up their things.

"Which way do we go out?" Runt asked. "That's a steep slope to climb up again."

Calgacus nodded. "We'd best go through the valley, I suppose." He nodded towards the trees at the far end.

"That's where that sound came from," Runt pointed out, clearly not keen on going in that direction.

"Whatever it was, it has gone now." Calgacus looked eastwards, towards the far woods. Then he looked again. A movement from the trees caught his attention. To his surprise, a man walked out of the woods, following the course of the river, walking on the far side of it from where they stood watering their horses.

The man stopped, obviously surprised to see them. He wore an old tunic of plain linen, which fell to his knees, tied at the waist with a simple cord. His shoes were of worn, faded leather, bound with thin cords. His windswept hair and long beard were grey, almost pure white. In one hand he held a wicker basket.

Calgacus' warriors edged away. He heard someone whisper, "It's Dis!"

"Quiet!" Calgacus snapped. "Gather the horses. Wait here." Moving slowly, he walked along the river bank, heading towards the old man who was watching him warily from the far bank.

Runt, ignoring the command to stay behind, followed Calgacus. "Be careful," he whispered. "What if it is Dis?"

"I think a god would come armed with something a bit more dangerous than a basket," Calgacus replied.

The man waved a hand in a cautiously friendly welcome. "Good morning. How did you get here?"

Calgacus stopped opposite him, only the river separating them, a distance of no more than ten paces.

"We came in that way," he said, pointing towards the western end of the tiny valley.

The man's bushy eyebrows waggled. "Really? That's a difficult way to get in."

"We were trying to find shelter from the storm," Calgacus told him.

"Yes, of course. Well, welcome to my home. My name is Myrddin." If he was afraid of eight armed men appearing in his valley, he did not show it.

"I am Calgacus, son of Cunobelinos. You live here?"

Myrddin nodded. "Just me. Some people call me Myrddin the Hermit."

Calgacus gave a small laugh. "Some of my men thought you were Dis. We heard a strange noise last night."

Myrddin shook his head, his expression serious. "I am just a man. But you were partly right. There is an entrance to the Underworld near hear. The God permits me to live nearby. You get used to the noise after a while." He gave Calgacus a meaningful look. "I should warn you that he does not like strangers wandering through his valley, especially men who threaten violence."

"We are no threat to you," Calgacus said.

"Then you should be safe enough," Myrddin replied. "But keep your swords in their scabbards."

Calgacus was intrigued by the old man. "Why would a hermit live near an entrance to the Underworld?" he asked.

"I didn't say I was a hermit," Myrddin responded. "I said some people call me a hermit."

Calgacus had heard this sort of thing before. "Are you a druid?" he asked suspiciously.

"Me? No. I'm not a druid. Come, let me check my nets, then we will go back to my home. We can exchange news and then I will show you an easier way out."

He walked along the river to where a small, curved inlet in the bank formed a deeper pool. Here he knelt, tugging up some ropes to reveal a small net of willow strands. Working quickly, he flipped two tiny fish into his basket. While they flopped noisily, he replaced the nets. He looked over to Calgacus. "Breakfast!" he said, pleased with himself. "Come on, you'll need to cross the stream. Follow me."

Runt and Calgacus exchanged glances. Calgacus shrugged, fetched his horse and splashed across the river. His men, still nervous, followed his lead.

Myrddin led them along a narrow path through the thick woods. The place was alive with wildlife. A squirrel shot up a tree trunk beside the path, birds chattered noisily in the branches. Underfoot, Calgacus saw the prints of roe deer, badgers and foxes on the muddy path. The woodland was thick, the bushes of the undergrowth dense and heavy with leaves. The path seemed to go on for a long way, twisting and turning through the trees, but at last the woodland came to an end, suddenly giving way to a rocky gravel underfoot. Here, the valley split in two, one narrow path curving left, another, wider defile leading right.

Myrddin stopped and pointed down this valley. "There's Dis's realm," he said in a harsh whisper.

Calgacus looked across a barren, stony pass, strewn with shale, boulders and gravel. At the far end, some hundred paces distant, was a low, steep hill with a dark cavern lurking at its foot. The entrance was black, impenetrable, staring back at him ominously.

107

A chill ran through his bones.

Myrddin nudged his arm. "You see that rock about half way there?" He pointed to a tall, upright rock standing in majestic isolation in the middle of the pass. It was about the height of a man and had a disconcertingly human shape.

"That's the last person who tried to go in," Myrddin warned. "Whatever he saw, it turned him to stone. We are safe enough in daylight here, but go no closer."

"Can we move on?" Calgacus asked anxiously. The dismal entrance to Dis's realm filled him with dread.

Myrddin nodded. "Come on, then." He led them left, following the curve of the valley which soon widened out into another grassy meadow, bordered by trees and overlooked by high hills. To the right of the meadow was a rocky shelf in front of the steep hillside, and here Myrddin lived in another cave.

Picketing their horses near the river, they joined the old man on the wide, flat surface of the ledge where he had a fire set in the centre of a ring of large rocks that served as seats. The cave behind him was snug, filled with furs and an assortment of tools and utensils. A wooden frame had been set at the entrance, weighted leather curtains hanging from it to allow Myrddin to close off the cave.

"You have lived here a long time?" Calgacus asked.

"More than thirty years," Myrddin replied as he gutted the fish with a small knife before tossing them into a small pot on his fire. He sprinkled some herbs into the pot, stirring the contents with a long twig.

"Why?"

"I like it here," Myrddin said with a grin.

"Don't you get lonely?"

Myrddin laughed at that. "I've never been a great one for mixing with other people which is just as well, seeing as the God discourages visitors. There is a village a little way down the hill, out to the east. I go there every so often for supplies. But I can get by on what the valley provides. Let's see what I can find for you to eat."

"Thank you, but we've eaten. Save your supplies for yourself."

Myrddin nodded his thanks. He stirred the pot as he gave Calgacus an appraising look. "So you are Calgacus. The brother of Caratacus?"

"You are well informed for a hermit," Calgacus said.

"I told you, I am not a hermit. So why are you here, I wonder?" He held up a hand. "No, don't tell me. Either you are fleeing from the Romans or you are here seeking help from the Brigantes, trying to raise an army for your brother. Am I right?"

Calgacus could not help smiling. "Perhaps a little of both."

"The last I heard, you were living down among the Silures," Myrddin said. His eyes narrowed as he studied Calgacus. "Has there been a battle?"

Calgacus nodded.

"I see from your expression that the Romans won again," Myrddin said softly. "That explains why you have come north. What about your brother? Is he dead?"

"No, he is still alive. We went to see Cartimandua."

"Ah, her. She's the new queen, isn't she?"

"That's her."

"I see. So you asked her for help. But she refused you?"

Calgacus was perturbed at the old man's uncanny ability to tell what had happened. "What makes you think that?" he asked.

"Because if she had agreed to help you, you wouldn't be out here in the middle of nowhere," Myrddin explained. "I suppose you are on your way to see the Parisi next?"

"No," said Calgacus, relieved that the silver-haired old man was not infallible. He had been starting to suspect that Myrddin was a sorcerer of some sort. "We are looking for someone."

"There's nobody here except me," Myrddin said happily, scooping a mouthful of his fish soup up in a wooden spoon and tasting it. He smacked his lips. "And I don't have anything worth stealing," he added carefully.

"We are not thieves, we are warriors."

Myrddin nodded, his eyes looking sad. "Yes, I can see that."

"You disapprove of warriors?"

Myrddin gave a weary shrug. "My approval makes no difference. But, in my experience, warriors are among the least useful members of any society."

"Warriors are the elite," Calgacus replied indignantly. "We protect the people from our enemies."

"But can you make anything?" Myrddin asked. "Do you have the skill to forge one of those swords you carry with such pride? Can you make a pot from a lump of clay? Or make a brooch from

109

bronze or silver?" He shook his head, adding, "No. Warriors know only how to destroy. Why should a man who fights be valued more highly than a man who grows the crops that feed an entire village?"

"Because there would be no village without someone to protect it," Calgacus said.

"There would be no village without someone to feed it," Myrddin countered.

Calgacus threw up his hands. "I have no time to argue over such things," he said.

Myrddin gave him a faint smile. "I am sorry. I don't get guests very often. I apologise for any insult. So tell me, who are you looking for?"

Calgacus took a deep breath, calming himself. The old man's arguments had been irritatingly thought-provoking. He had never heard anyone question such things before and he found it unsettling. But perhaps the strange old character could help.

"We are looking for a Roman girl," he said. He outlined the story, telling the old not-a-hermit of the ultimatum the Romans had delivered to Cartimandua. Myrddin listened intently.

When he was done, Calgacus asked, "I don't suppose you have heard anything of a Roman girl being taken captive?"

Myrddin shook his head. "No."

"Then we had best be on our way. We do not have much time to find her."

"Wait!" Myrddin held up a hand. "What will you do if you find this girl?" He stared at Calgacus, his eyes searching the tall warrior's face.

Calgacus thought for a moment. Something in Myrddin's manner demanded a truthful response and suggested that he would instantly detect a lie. Calgacus decided that there was no harm in telling the truth because there was nobody the old man could inform.

"We will keep her hidden until the war starts," he answered. "After that, we will let her go."

"It would be better to kill her, would it not?" Myrddin asked in a quiet voice.

Runt sniffed loudly, signifying his agreement with the sentiment, but Calgacus replied, "I do not make war on children."

Myrddin gazed at him for a long moment. Slowly, the old man

110

nodded. "You are an unusual man, Calgacus, son of Cunobelinos. Tell me, what will happen if the war starts? Lots of people, including children, will die. You and I may be among the dead."

Calgacus did not know why he felt compelled to justify himself to the old man, but he said, "If the Brigantes fight, Caratacus will be able to defeat the Romans. With my help, he will drive them back across the sea. Then everyone will be free."

"Everyone?"

"Of course."

"Well, that is a noble aim, to be sure. Is that why you fight? To be free?"

"Of course it is. The Romans want to enslave us all."

"So even the slaves will be free?"

"What?" Calgacus was puzzled by the question.

"Have you ever been a slave?" Myrddin asked him.

"I have," said Runt with feeling. "I will not be one again. That is why I fight."

Myrddin looked at the two of them. "The Catuvellauni had slaves, did they not? Your father and brothers conquered other tribes, seized their land and cattle, took slaves."

"You know they did," Calgacus said, growing angry. Myrddin's accusation was the same argument that Cartimandua had used against Caratacus. He added, "Every tribe takes slaves."

Myrddin smiled as if he had just realised something. "Ah! I see. So it is not slavery that you object to. It is your own slavery that you fight to avoid."

"I have no time for this!" Calgacus snapped. "Slavery is the way of the world. Do not mock me because I seek to stay free. The Romans are the enemies of all the people of this island, and I will fight them for as long as it takes to drive them out."

Myrddin waved a hand, calming him. "Sit down, young man. You are quite correct. Slavery is the way of the world. It does not make it right, though, does it? You would not like to be a slave, so what makes you think anyone else does?"

"You want me to change the world?" Calgacus asked scornfully.

"Why not? You have changed my world already, just by being here. A man like you can do many things, I am sure. Everyone changes the world of the people around them. Some men, like your brother, like you, can cause great changes."

111

"You are a druid," Calgacus accused, narrowing his eyes.

"No, I am not," Myrddin said emphatically. "I am merely trying to show you that if you succeed in starting a war, you will change the lives of many people. Many of them for the worse, I dare say. You might not make war on children, but children will suffer and children will die because of what you intend to do."

"Then that is how it will have to be," Calgacus growled. "I will not bend my knee to Rome. Now, we have wasted enough time. We will be on our way."

"In a moment!" Myrddin said sharply. His voice was so full of command that, despite himself, Calgacus remained where he was. The old man said, "I have seen what Rome does. They are a warlike people, the Romans, always afraid of anyone different, always desperate to take over so that they can make everyone like themselves." He stared into the fire. "They make war on everyone, regardless of age. I am not a warlike man, but I know that there are times when war is necessary." He looked up at Calgacus with sad eyes. "I think you are an honourable man, Calgacus, son of Cunobelinos. You have not touched your nose once while we have been speaking."

Calgacus blinked. "What?" He reached up, gingerly touching his nose then looking at his fingers in puzzlement.

Myrddin gave him a sad smile. "When people lie, they have a habit of touching their nose, or sometimes their ears. A druid told me that once. It is one of their tricks, you know, to watch how people use their hands, how they stand. They call it magic, but it is not; it is just a way of reading people. You did not touch your nose once, so I know you have been telling me the truth. The truth as you see it, anyway."

"Is there a point to this?" Calgacus asked, anxious now to be on his way.

Myrddin sighed. "I know nothing of a Roman girl being taken. But I have heard that Riccinatos, a young chieftain of the Parisi, has been carrying out small raids into the Roman province. He is a young, boastful man. Very foolish too, in my opinion, for knowledge of his actions is becoming commonplace. If I have heard of it, the Romans will surely learn of it before long."

"The Parisi you say?" Runt asked, his voice betraying considerable interest.

"Yes. They are subject to Rome, of course, but Riccinatos does

112

not like being subject to anyone. You could do worse than go and see him. At the very least, he may send men to join your brother's army when the war begins."

Calgacus nodded his thanks. "So where do we find this Riccinatos?"

Myrddin waved a hand eastwards. "Go out the valley and down the hill. You'll see the village I mentioned. You have to pass it. There's an old drove road at the foot of the hill. Go east. On horseback, it should not take you more than a day to reach the land of the Parisi. Riccinatos lives somewhere near the borders of their land. I am sure you will find someone who knows where his village is."

"Thank you, Myrddin," Calgacus said with a respectful nod of his head.

"Don't thank me. I am just an old, foolish man who wants nothing more than to be left alone. You are young, and strong, and full of ideals. Off you go and change the world."

Chapter X

Riccinatos was worried. He had washed the blue paint from his body as best he could, but the tell-tale stain was still there on his skin. His warriors bore the same marks and the messenger from Mardix, king of the Parisi, had been suspicious. Riccinatos had claimed that he and his men had been out chasing bandits who had raided their flocks. He was not sure whether he had convinced the man. Mardix was like an old woman, terrified of the Romans, and Riccinatos would not normally have cared what the old fool thought. But the news the king's messenger had brought was serious. The girl he had snatched was the daughter of somebody important; so important that the Romans wanted her back. They had threatened war if she was not returned.

The Parisi were a small tribe, living in widely scattered villages. If the Romans turned on them, Riccinatos knew that there would only be one outcome. His people were descended from a tribe who had once lived in Gaul. Generations ago, they had fought against the first Caesar, the one the Romans called Julius and who was now worshipped by them as a god. In his days as a mortal, Julius Caesar had utterly defeated the Parisi. Most of the tribe had been killed or enslaved. Only a few thousand had escaped, crossing the sea to the rain-shrouded land of the Pritani. There, they had wandered until they had found a place to live in the cold north, between the moors and the sea, where they had settled. Here, they had thought, they would be safe from Rome. That safety had lasted barely four generations.

Riccinatos wandered to the small pen where he had chained the girl. He lifted off the wooden boards that concealed the tiny cage. Looking inside, he saw her sitting, her arms clasped round her raised knees, her face pressed down against them.

"What am I going to do with you?" he asked aloud.

She glanced up, her eyes sullen and red-rimmed. She could not understand him, he knew. He wished he had never taken her. It had been an impulsive act, one he regretted now. She was too young to

114

take to his bed, too wilful and haughty to be a decent slave. And with the news he had now heard, he knew that he could not keep her here. He suspected the messenger might return, with some of Mardix's warriors, demanding to search the village.

Riccinatos rubbed his chin thoughtfully. If he killed her, the Romans would destroy his people. If he kept her, the same would happen, or Mardix would find her and would have Riccinatos killed. Or perhaps the old king would hand him over to the Romans to be crucified. None of those options appealed to Riccinatos. But if he simply let her go, she would never find her way back home on her own.

He decided that all he could do was take her to Mardix and claim that he had found her being held captive by some bandits. Mardix might believe that, he supposed. The old king was certainly stupid enough to believe it. It would help, of course, if Riccinatos could take some heads with him, proof that he had killed her captors. The girl would not be able to betray him, he felt sure; she had no idea where his village was, and she could not understand what he was saying. He thought it might still be best if he laid low for a while afterwards, though. Perhaps he would go further north, to visit one of his cousins.

He tossed the various thoughts around in his mind, still unsure of what to do, but knowing he must do something. He was still no nearer a decision when one of his warriors ran to find him.

"We have guests!" the man gasped.

"Who? Romans?" Riccinatos felt a pang of fear shoot through him.

"No. Strangers. Eight men on horseback. They are Pritani, but they all have moustaches and they speak with a strange accent."

Riccinatos gestured towards the girl. "Cover the pen," he told the man. Then he went to see who these strange visitors might be.

Calgacus, Runt and their six warriors sat amongst Riccinatos' men, all of them in a circle around the hearth fire. Riccinatos entertained them royally, supplying copious amounts of ale.

Calgacus, wanting to stay alert, drank sparingly. He instinctively liked the young Parisi chieftain. Riccinatos was friendly, and made it plain that he had no love for Rome. Calgacus noticed the faded blue tint to his skin where the swirling designs of war paint had not yet washed out. Several other men had the same bluish hue to their skin.

Riccinatos was immensely proud that Calgacus had visited him. To have the brother of the famous Caratacus as his guest was a great honour.

"How can I serve you?" he asked.

"My brother is trying to raise a new army. He has heard that Rome threatens war against the northern tribes."

"I have heard that, too," Riccinatos said. There were nods and mutters of agreement from the other men around the fire.

Calgacus asked, "If the Romans attack, would you be willing to join us?"

Riccinatos, his tongue loosened by the ale, said, "I would be glad to join you. How many men does your brother need for this army he is trying to raise?"

"Fifty thousand," Calgacus said. "More if we can find them."

Riccinatos spluttered into his ale. With a laugh he wiped the spilled liquid from his trousers. "I can bring twelve," he said with a smile.

"Twelve thousand is a good number," Calgacus nodded soberly.

Riccinatos shook his head. "No. Twelve. Twelve men. But all have their own spears, even though the Romans say that we are not supposed to carry weapons any more."

Calgacus could not help smiling. "Well, twelve men would be welcome, so thank you. What about other villages? Could you get more men from there?"

"Perhaps," Riccinatos said thoughtfully. "Maybe a few hundred."

"That would be good. When the war begins, bring as many men as you can to Isuria. If you join the Brigantes, we will be able to defeat the Romans."

"How?" Riccinatos asked. "Nobody has been able to beat them yet."

"By fighting them our way, not theirs," Calgacus told him. "There is no point in facing them in open battle but we can beat them if we lure them into the high country, if we trap them where they cannot manoeuvre. By attacking their supply columns and wearing them down."

Riccinatos nodded his head sagely. "I suppose that might be possible," he conceded. "You seem certain that there will be war."

116

"I am sure of it," Calgacus told him. "When it comes, you must join us."

"That may not be easy," Riccinatos said thoughtfully. "The Romans will be quick to attack us."

"They will not be quick enough," Calgacus assured him. "Someone like you will be able to avoid them easily enough. I am sure you are used to crossing hostile territory unseen to raid your enemies."

Riccinatos gave a conspiratorial wink. "Yes, we've been known to do that sometimes," he admitted, bringing a knowing laugh from his warriors.

"Have you done it recently?" Calgacus asked him, watching carefully.

"Recently? No." Riccinatos brushed the fingers of his left hand against the tip of his nose.

Calgacus glanced at Runt, who gave an imperceptible nod. He had seen it too. Calgacus wondered whether old Myrddin had been right about that. Before he could ask any more questions to test the theory, Riccinatos hurriedly changed the subject. He jabbed a finger at Runt.

"So what is your story, my little friend? You say you are of the Parisi? How did you come to be with this giant here?" he asked, waving his mug in Calgacus' direction.

"It's a long story," said Runt.

Riccinatos replied, "What are the evenings for if not good food, good company and good stories?"

Calgacus had been eleven years old when the Roman trader had arrived at Camulodunon. The merchant had sailed across the sea, up the rivers, then had his slaves carry his goods to the king's home. Togodumnus, always keen to trade, had welcomed him cordially.

Calgacus sat in the crowded roundhouse for a while, listening to the news. He always enjoyed hearing stories from far away places, even if he had only the vaguest idea of where those places were.

The trader said his name was Rubius. He spoke their language because he was from Gaul, even though he claimed to be a Roman.

He told them that Gaius Caesar was dead, assassinated, along with most of his family. The Emperor who had once threatened to cross the sea to invade the lands of the Pritani, had fallen victim to the endless intrigues of Rome. His uncle, who had more names than was good for any man but who was usually referred to as Claudius, was now Emperor of Rome. Rubius let slip that the new Emperor was a cripple and partially deaf, a man more accustomed to books and learning than to warfare. Togodumnus had been pleased at that news; a deaf cripple was hardly likely to cause trouble for the Pritani.

Rubius had no more news, so Calgacus wandered outside. He had no interest in the bartering which he knew would go on for a long time. He strolled idly down the line of Rubius' slaves, noticing the guards who watched over them; big, tough men who carried swords, clubs and whips. The guards watched him in turn, as he made his way down the long line. He stopped to admire Rubius' horse, a big beast, much larger than the small horses the Catuvellauni were used to. The horse snorted at him, making him jump quickly away in case it kicked him.

He was near the end of the row of slaves when he saw a boy dart across the path in front of him, ducking behind a roundhouse. The nearest guard was watching Calgacus, facing away from the boy who had been wearing a Roman tunic and sandals. Intrigued, Calgacus quickly turned and walked round the other side of the roundhouse, hoping to intercept the boy. They collided as the runaway hurtled round the curved wall, running straight into him. The boy struggled to get away but Calgacus grabbed him. Calgacus was bigger and stronger, able to hold him easily.

"What are you doing?" he asked in a harsh whisper.

The boy gave him a withering look. "What do you think I'm doing? I'm running away. Can you hide me?"

Calgacus thought for only an instant. "Follow me!"

Careful to take a route that kept buildings between them and the Roman guards, he took the boy some way across the town to the pig sty. "You can hide in there," he said.

The boy looked at the filthy mud. "Are you serious?"

"They'll never look in there for you," Calgacus assured him. "Or you can always go back."

The boy thought about that. "Never!" He opened the rickety gate, stepping into the churned mud with a squelch. He ploughed his way across to the tiny wooden sty. The pigs grunted noisily, moving reluctantly out of his way. At the small doorway, he turned, looking back to ask, "What is your name?"

"Calgacus."

"I am Liscus. Thank you, Calgacus." He crawled into the darkness of the sty.

Feeling immensely pleased with himself, Calgacus walked back to Togodumnus' roundhouse. It took an age for Rubius to conclude his dealings with the king, but at last the Roman prepared to leave. He inspected his stock, counted his slaves, frowned, counted them a second time, then shouted, "Where is he? Where is the boy?"

Togodumnus looked perplexed. "What boy?"

"My slave! He has gone. You must search for him."

Togodumnus gave the trader a stern look. "It is not my fault that you cannot look after your slaves."

"You must find him. I insist!"

Togodumnus was a patient man, not easily roused to anger, but he was a king and this guest was only a merchant. "I will not have my people's houses searched for a runaway," he said.

"But he is my property!" Rubius wailed.

Togodumnus turned to Cethinos. "Can you find this runaway with your magic?" he asked the druid.

Cethinos shook his head. "Not unless I have some item of his clothing."

"He is a slave," Rubius said bitterly. "He has only what he wears."

Cethinos shrugged, indicating that there was nothing he could do. Calgacus was pleased about that. He suspected that all Cethinos would have done was to fetch some of Togodumnus' hunting dogs and let them sniff out Liscus, then claim that he had found the boy by magic.

Togodumnus looked around thoughtfully. A small crowd had gathered, wondering what had caused the commotion. Togodumnus' gaze fell on his youngest brother's face and Calgacus saw the king's face twitch slightly. His heart sank. He knew that expression well. It was almost impossible to hide something from Togodumnus.

The King looked away, turning to address the small band of onlookers. Raising his voice, he said, "If any man knows where this runaway slave is, let him speak now. Any man who knows where the boy is and does not reveal it, will be sentenced to slavery himself. I am Togodumnus! I have spoken!"

He waited. Nobody spoke. Rubius looked around frantically. "Somebody must know where he is!"

Togodumnus said firmly, "I suggest you leave before you lose any more slaves."

Reluctantly, cursing his luck, Rubius had mounted his big horse and ridden off, his slaves and guards trudging after him. When he was safely out of sight and the crowd had begun to disperse, Togodumnus walked over to Calgacus.

"Where is he, Little Brother?"

"In the pig sty."

Cethinos' face darkened. "You dared to defy your king?" he asked. "On pain of enslavement?"

Togodumnus waved a hand, dismissing the druid's protest. "Calm down, Cethinos. I said that any man had to tell me. Calgacus is only eleven. He is not yet a man, as you are so fond of telling me yourself."

"You play games with words," Cethinos said, his dark eyes regarding Calgacus with their usual expression of annoyance.

"Yes. It is a trick I learned from you," Togodumnus replied.

Cethinos inclined his head, as if acknowledging a compliment, while Calgacus gave him a triumphant grin.

"Come then, Little Brother," Togodumnus said. "Take me to him."

Calgacus led him to the sty, where he called Liscus' name. The small boy crawled out, covered in filth and mud. He slowly crossed the quagmire to stand before the king.

"Well, well," said Togodumnus with a broad smile. "It looks like our litter has a new runt."

Riccinatos laughed. "That is a good story, my friend. My cousin, I should say. You really are of the Parisi?"

"From four generations of slaves," Runt said. "But my mother taught me our language and told me of our history."

"And now you are free. Tell me, cousin, what is the best thing about being free rather than a slave of Rome?"

"Wearing trousers instead of a tunic," Runt replied without hesitation. That brought another round of drunken laughter.

"Well, I am glad you are here," Riccinatos told him. "I must find a suitable gift to honour you. And you, too, my giant friend," he said to Calgacus.

"There is only one thing we would like," Calgacus said instantly.

"What is that?"

"We are looking for a Roman girl. She was taken by some tribesmen several days ago. The Romans want her back."

Riccinatos hesitated. Frowning, he looked into his mug as if seeking inspiration. His left hand tugged nervously at the lobe of his ear.

"So why do you want her?" he asked eventually.

Calgacus gave the young chieftain a serious look. "To stop anyone else from handing her back. To bring the Brigantes into the war."

Riccinatos rubbed his nose. "If the Romans wage war, our people will suffer."

"Rome will attack you sooner or later anyway," Calgacus said earnestly. "Why not let it be sooner? Half their army is still in the west."

Riccinatos nodded, his expression sombre. "You would keep the girl hidden?"

Calgacus nodded. "And I would tell no-one where I found her."

Riccinatos inhaled deeply, then released a long, slow breath. He saw his warriors watching him, waiting for his decision. He turned to Calgacus. "Come with me."

Chapter XI

Aemilia was asleep when the boards were hauled away from her tiny pen. She woke up in a fright, her eyes dazzled by the light of flaming torches being held above the small cage. The door was opened and rough hands fumbled for the lock on her leg irons. She almost cried at the relief as she felt the manacles fall away. Someone pulled her out, lifting her to her feet. Bewildered and frightened, she staggered, almost falling.

There were men's voices all around her, harsh, incomprehensible. She knew they were talking about her, but the words were just barbarian nonsense, like the bleating of sheep. Then there was a face in front of her as one man squatted down to peer into her eyes.

"Hello," he said. "What is your name?"

Aemilia blinked in astonishment. This man was dressed like the others but he spoke Latin. His accent was rather coarse, not educated at all. In fact, she thought, he sounded like some of her slaves. But he had spoken to her in Latin and it was the first thing she had understood for more days and nights than she could remember.

"Aemilia," she said.

"Hello, Aemilia. My name is Liscus. We are going to take you away from here."

"Are you taking me home?" she asked, hope rising within her at last.

"Soon. You will have to stay with us for a while, then we will take you home."

"If you don't take me home, my father will come and kill you all," she told him earnestly, hoping that the threat would be enough to make him take her back to her mother and father immediately.

He laughed at that, which puzzled her. She had never seen anyone laugh when threatened with the might of Rome.

"He will have to find us first," Liscus said. "But don't worry, I will take care of you for a few days and then we will take you

122

home."

"Are you going to kill these men who captured me?" she wanted to know.

"No."

"Why not?"

"They are not my enemies. I only kill Romans."

She was frightened then. The way he said it, she knew it was not bravado. He really meant it. He touched her face gently, pushing back a strand of her hair which had fallen down. "But I don't kill little girls," he told her.

Giving her a reassuring smile, he led her away. She was still afraid but she stayed close to him because he spoke her language. He was a strange man, she thought, part Roman, part barbarian. But he gave her some food and some warm milk to drink, then he spoke to another man, a huge giant with black hair, a dark moustache and sparkling, blue eyes, who told some of the women to give her a bath and to treat the sores on her ankles where the manacles had cut her skin.

She was frightened when the women took her away but she allowed them to help her wash, and sat bravely while they dabbed at her raw skin with foul-smelling salves. After she had been fed and bathed, the women took her back to Liscus and the dark-haired giant. Liscus sat beside her until she fell asleep.

In the morning, he took her to his horse, lifting her so that she sat in front of him. There were eight men on horses, she saw. The leader was the dark-haired giant. Now that she could see him in the daylight, he seemed very fierce, especially now that she could see the massive sword he carried. Aemilia looked away because he frightened her.

The horsemen waved farewell to the villagers then they rode westwards, setting a fast pace, taking her away from her captors. She did not know where they were going, but she was glad to be out of that horrible cage. Liscus put his arms around her, telling her to hold on tightly.

"We have a long way to go," he told her.

Calgacus pushed the horses as hard as he dared. One of the few things he recalled from the lessons Cethinos had tried to beat into him when he was young was that horses had the largest hearts of any animal in proportion to the size of their bodies. It was this

123

which gave the beasts their remarkable stamina, but it also meant that, if pushed too hard, a horse was more likely to suffer heart failure than any other animal. The trick to travelling a long distance quickly was to find the balance between keeping the horses alive and pushing them as hard as he could.

He felt a thrill of satisfaction that they had found the girl, but he knew that they could not afford to be seen with her, so they avoided using the old drove road, travelling instead across the open countryside, circling wide of any farms or villages.

He had decided to head back to Myrddin's valley. When they had left, Calgacus had seen how the entrance, even the one Myrddin claimed was the easy way in, was so well concealed by the shape of the hills and jumbles of massive rocks that it was virtually invisible from all directions. It was, he had decided, the ideal place to hide. But for his plan to succeed, they needed to get there quickly, to avoid detection by Cartimandua's roving bands of searching warriors.

Several hours of hard riding across moors and through dark woods left the men as tired as the horses by the time they saw the tiny village that sat at the foot of the hill. Calgacus looked to the sky, judging the hour by the position of the sun. Runt, still holding the girl, Aemilia, urged his horse alongside.

"There's still a lot of daylight left," the little warrior said.

"I know."

They had debated whether to pass the village in darkness but had decided that it would be too difficult to find the entrance to the hidden valley without light. Calgacus had wanted to get there late in the evening but he had misjudged their speed. Now, their choice was to head up to the valley in broad daylight, or find somewhere to hide for several hours. Calgacus did not like either alternative.

He waved his arm, pointing towards the hills. "Let's climb the hills here, away from the village. We can approach the valley from the high ground."

"The villagers will probably still see us," Runt pointed out.

"Yes, but from a distance. They won't know who we are, and they won't see her," replied Calgacus, waving a hand in Aemilia's direction. Tugging his mount's reins, he led them up the slope.

Once they reached the high ground they slowed, taking care that the horses did not stumble on the uneven terrain. There were so many rocks and boulders, some the height of two men that they were soon forced to dismount and lead their horses along the treacherous slope. As they picked their way along the hillside, Calgacus heard Aemilia complaining loudly about something. He looked back, snapping at Runt to keep her quiet. The girl hid from him, ducking behind Runt's legs.

"You've scared her," Runt chided.

"Just as long as she stays quiet, I don't care."

A sudden noise of movement made Calgacus jump nervously. He cursed when he saw that they had merely startled a few sheep that had been grazing on the sparse heather, sending the animals into a headlong rush down the hill. Shaking his head, he pressed on.

Soon, he saw a combination of boulders, a piled, irregular shape that he recognised. Pushing his way past them, he found the narrow trail that led down into Myrddin's valley. He heaved a sigh of relief. They had done it.

The old man was nowhere to be seen as they approached his cave. His fire still burned on the rock shelf, but his cave was deserted. Then Calgacus heard a call from the opposite side of the stream where he saw Myrddin creeping out from the bushes, a sheepish expression on his face. The old man crossed the water using some stepping stones and walked over to them.

"I wasn't sure who was coming," he explained. "You can't be too careful." Then he saw Aemilia standing beside Runt. "By Esus! You found her."

"You were right. Riccinatos had her."

Myrddin's expression grew sad. "And now you will start your war, I suppose."

"We need somewhere to stay," Calgacus told him. "If we can remain hidden for another eight days or so, the Brigantes will be committed."

Myrddin nodded. "Then you'd best go back to the place I first found you. There's more room there for you and your horses." He did not seem pleased at the prospect of them staying.

Calgacus led his men on, scrambling along the narrow path, hurriedly passing the barren devastation that stretched out from Dis's cave, then along the winding path through the woods, eventually coming out into the meadow. They selected a site opposite the overhanging shelter they had cowered under on their first night, making camp on the southern side of the tiny, narrow

125

valley, in a hollow of the steep hillside. It was a good spot, sheltered on three sides and with plenty of room.

The men quickly got to work. The horses were tethered near the trees at the western end of the valley. Two men were sent to rub them down and see that they were fed and watered. Others hacked wood from the trees and set about building small shelters of intertwined branches. Stones were gathered to create small hearths where fires could be lit, and their dwindling supplies of food were stacked inside the shelters.

Runt unravelled long cords of leather he had stashed in his pouch. It was his sling, a weapon he was uncannily accurate with. He whirled it experimentally in his hand then stooped to gather up small stones.

"I'll see if I can get something extra to eat," he said.

Calgacus looked at Aemilia. "What about her?"

"I've explained that there is nowhere for her to go. But if you sit at the fire, she won't move. She's scared of you."

Calgacus glanced over to Aemilia. The young girl immediately dropped her gaze.

"Don't be long," he told Runt.

By the time night fell, they had settled in. Runt had downed a wood pigeon and two crows, so they had a little fresh meat. Calgacus had also raided Myrddin's nets where he had found three small fish. He felt a pang of conscience at taking them, but they were all hungry and they had a long time to wait in the valley.

He was sure that nobody could find them here, but he insisted that one man stay on watch at the eastern woods that led to Myrddin's cave. That was the way anyone would approach. If anyone did brave the steep descent down to the western woods, the route they had used on the night of the storm, the horses would give warning. He could not think of anything else they had to do except wait.

The low moan of Dis's cave began at some point during the night. Aemilia began crying, cuddling into Runt. The others were unable to sleep, huddling near the fires for warmth and comfort. Pencoch, who had been taking his turn on watch among the trees at the end of the narrow path, came hurrying back to the camp.

"I'm not staying out there on my own," he said. "It's dangerous enough being alone at night but this place is the worst I've ever been in."

126

Calgacus wanted to offer to stand watch among the trees but the tormented moans of the Underworld chilled him to the core of his being. Pencoch was right. Night was when evil spirits prowled the land in search of victims. Everyone knew stories of people who had ventured out alone at night and never returned. Sometimes a body would be found, sometimes the person would vanish without trace. With Dis's cave so near, only being close to a fire would keep a man safe in this remote place.

"All right," he told Pencoch. "Keep watch from here. Nobody will come this way at night anyway."

None of them slept much that night. The wail persisted during the morning, then died away around mid-day. It returned intermittently throughout the afternoon before fading away completely as evening drew on.

"Maybe we should find somewhere else to hide," Runt suggested.

"We are safer here than anywhere," Calgacus said. "Myrddin said nobody ever comes here."

"Nobody would be that daft," Runt said.

"But he's been here for years."

"He's a crazy old man. How do you know he's not lining us up as sacrifices to Dis?"

Calgacus shrugged. "I trust him."

"You hardly know him," Runt challenged. "He could be planning anything."

"I'll go and talk to him," Calgacus said, pushing himself to his feet. "You stay here."

"Don't worry, I'm not moving from this spot."

Calgacus picked his way through the woods, past the defile that led to Dis's realm and on to Myrddin's cave. There was no sign of life. The old man's fire had gone out. Calgacus knelt, touching his fingers to the ashes. They were cold.

Rubbing the ashes from his hands, he stood up. He looked all around but there was no clue as to where Myrddin might have gone. Calgacus felt a tingle of fear. If Runt was right, if he had mis-judged the old man, they could all be in danger. Calgacus would face a legion of Roman soldiers without fear but the threat of dark magic and evil spirits was enough to bring a cold sweat to his palms and set the hairs on the back of his neck tingling.

He glanced upwards, checking the sky. It was too late to try to find another camp now, and a bank of grey rainclouds was edging in from the east. Offering up a silent prayer to Matrona, the mother goddess, to protect them, he made his way back to the camp.

"What did he say?" Runt asked when he reached the shelters.

"He's gone. His fire is cold."

Runt swore softly. The other warriors exchanged anxious glances.

Pencoch asked, "What do we do now?"

"We stick to the plan," Calgacus replied with as much confidence as he could muster. "We wait."

Chapter XII

Venutius was angry and growing ever more exasperated. For twelve days he had led his men on a fruitless search for the missing Roman girl, criss-crossing the country, stopping at every house; asking, searching. There was no sign of the girl. There was always the possibility that some other party had found her, of course, but he did not dare rely on that hope. He had to keep searching. Not only to keep the Romans from attacking, but because he wanted to be the one who took the girl back to Cartimandua. With a prize like that, he could demand the right to marry the queen.

He knew Cartimandua was wilful, but if he found the missing girl, the Queen would not be able to refuse him. All the chieftains would support him. He would be the man who had saved them from destruction.

Venutius had no love for the Romans, but he was a pragmatic man. He had a long term strategy and the first step was to become king of the Brigantes. A war with Rome would ruin everything, so it was essential to find the girl.

But he could not find her anywhere.

Time was running out. He and his men were circling back towards Isuria now, tired and sore from the constant searching. He waited while his men went into the little, nameless village which sat huddled at the foot of high, rocky hills. He glanced up, watching the gathering rainclouds. Perhaps he should stay here for the night, he thought. He could throw some of the peasants out of one of the houses. That would allow him to stay dry, at least.

"Lord!" It was Vellocatus, striding towards him, his hand gripping the collar of a boy, half dragging the lad to where Venutius waited. "This wretch says he saw some men."

Venutius looked at the boy. He was probably around eleven years old. His hair was filthy and matted, his clothes ragged and dirty.

"So?" Venutius asked.

"He was on the hills, looking for some sheep that had strayed.

He says he saw some men. There was a girl with them. A girl who spoke a foreign language." Vellocatus looked meaningfully at his master. "I thought maybe it was Latin the boy heard."

Venutius looked down at the boy. "Where did you see them?"

"Up there, Lord." The boy pointed to the hills to the north. "They went into the hermit's valley."

"When was this?"

The boy said, "Yesterday afternoon."

Venutius frowned. "They'll be long gone by now, but maybe we can pick up their trail."

The boy shook his head. "No, Lord. There is only one way in to the hermit's valley and they have not come out."

"Are you sure?"

"Fairly sure, Lord. I would have seen them, I think."

"You said they had a girl with them. Are you certain of that?"

"I saw her, plain as day," the boy nodded, anxious to please. "They did not see me because I hid among the rocks until they had passed."

"And she spoke Latin?"

"It was not our language she spoke," the boy answered with a slight shrug.

"What were the men like? How many of them were there?"

"They had swords. And they wore long moustaches on their faces." He held up his hands, counting on his fingers, holding up eight for Venutius to see.

"Calgacus!" breathed Venutius exultantly. "He's found the girl and he's hiding her. The treacherous bastard."

"We have only twelve men," Vellocatus pointed out. "It will not be easy to take her from them."

"Round up some men from the village," Venutius ordered. "Offer them some copper coins. If they can carry an axe or a scythe, that will do." He looked up at the hills, smiling for the first time in many days.

"I'm coming for you, Renegade," he whispered softly.

It was raining heavily by the time a group of eleven village men led Venutius and his warriors up the difficult climb to where they said there was a narrow entrance into a small valley. They told him that an old hermit had lived in that secluded place for many years, but that few of them ever went into the valley because of the ghosts that stalked the place. Venutius' men were alarmed at that, but he snarled at them and at the reluctant villagers, telling them that if Calgacus could go in, so could they.

"It will soon be dark, Lord," Vellocatus pointed out.

"Then they won't see us coming," Venutius snapped. He could see the glints of fear in the men's eyes but finding the girl was too important to be delayed. The Gods were being kind to him. If he acted quickly, he could find the girl, kill Calgacus and marry Cartimandua.

Most of the villagers were armed with spears. Venutius was not surprised that they had found weapons. The Romans had ordered the tribes to surrender their arms and forbidden them from carrying weapons, but most men had something hidden away in case of need. They would be useful now. The villagers would have little chance if they faced Calgacus and his trained warriors in battle, but with their numbers and the element of surprise, he was confident they would be able to overwhelm the renegade prince.

They scrambled over the slick, wet stones that concealed the narrow defile leading down into the valley. Venutius sent two men ahead while he and the others waited in the pouring rain, pulling their cloaks tightly around them in a vain attempt to stay dry.

The scouts soon returned. One of them told him, "There is a cave. It looks as though somebody lives there, but it is empty."

Venutius nodded. "Let's go."

The path was narrow, barely wide enough for two men to walk side by side. It twisted its way down between steep hills, beneath the overhanging boughs of tall trees, and then to an open glade where a stream trickled past a rocky ledge that lay in front of a large cave with a wood-framed entrance. As the men had said, the cave was deserted.

"Keep going," ordered Venutius. "They must be here somewhere."

Wet and cold, and with night drawing ever closer, they followed the twisting combe until they found a split in the way. Branching off to their left was a defile that was nothing but a rocky wasteland with, at the far end, a dark cave mouth. The villagers muttered anxiously when they saw it, making protective signs to ward off evil spirits. They pointed to the figure of a man they said had been turned to stone when he went too close to the place.

"It is Dis's realm!" one of them whispered fearfully. "We

cannot go that way."

Venutius did not like the look of the dark cave. The villagers' fear was genuine and when he looked at the dismal cavern, he could understand why. He hesitated, wondering whether Calgacus might have dared to go that way. He glanced right, towards a thick woodland that barred the way west.

"Check over there," he told his scouts.

In only a few moments they were back. "There are footprints. And a path."

Venutius grinned triumphantly. He sent the scouts to follow the path. The rest of the men crowded into the trees, seeking some shelter from the steady downpour and, just as importantly, to get away from the sight of the dark cavern that dominated the rocky pass.

By the time the scouts returned, twilight was turning to full darkness.

"We saw the light of some camp fires beyond the trees," they reported.

Venutius turned to his shield-bearer, the tall warrior Vellocatus. "What do you think? They will have at least one man on watch."

"Wait until most of them are asleep," Vellocatus suggested. "Attack under cover of darkness."

Venutius nodded thoughtfully. Nobody liked fighting at night. The dark was dangerous enough, with wild animals and ghosts wandering the earth, but the prize for success was immeasurable.

"We'll do that," he decided.

It would be a cold, wet, miserable wait. But he knew where the girl was now. He could put up with a few hours of discomfort if it meant getting hold of her. Killing Calgacus would be a pleasant bonus.

The rain was relentless. The clouds formed a blanket across the night sky, obscuring the moon and the stars, plunging the small bowl of the valley into utter darkness. There was no wind to blow the clouds away, so the rain went on and on, soaking everything.

Calgacus took his turn on sentry duty, huddled by the one fire that was sheltered enough to remain alight. He knew that he did not have to stand watch, but the men appreciated that he took his share of the duties, especially on a miserable night like this. He stood under the twined branches of the shelter, staring out into the darkness.

He shivered. There was nothing to see except rain and impenetrable night. The only light came from the spluttering fire beside him. There was nothing to hear except the constant pounding of the rain drumming on the branches above his head and hissing as it struck the water of the stream.

As he stood there, he realised that he had created a problem for himself. If he remained hidden, holding the Roman girl captive until the war started, Cartimandua would know that something was wrong, that he had betrayed her. He was supposed to be searching for a place to fight the Romans. She would expect him to return before the Governor's deadline passed. But he could not go back, not now that he had found the girl.

He wrestled with the problem. Perhaps he should send some of his men back with a message while he and Runt remained here. He soon shook his head, dismissing that idea. The warriors would not be able to keep the secret. Their grins and laughter would betray them. No, he decided, he and Runt would need to go back in person. They would circle north, scout out some likely spots for ambushing the Romans, then return to Isuria. He would leave Pencoch and three others here to watch the girl. Later, once the war had begun, he would return and they would take her home. Cartimandua would never know what he had done.

He hoped his plan would work. There was a slim chance that the Romans might call off their attack once the girl was returned, but he doubted that. Once the Romans began a war, they usually saw it through.

There were, though, other unpredictable factors, not least of which was Venutius. If the war began and Calgacus remained among the Brigantes, could he bear to watch Cartimandua go through the hand-fasting ceremony with the Brigante chieftain? Then he worried that the Brigantes might not agree to fight under Caratacus. Venutius might insist on leading the war host. If he did, he would probably try to fight Rome the old-fashioned way, with his warriors driving their chariots and standing in the open, daring the Romans to attack them. That, Calgacus knew, would be a disaster.

He offered up a silent prayer to Esus, god of the air, who could see everything. That was what Calgacus needed now; to see

133

everything. He was trying to second guess too many people. There was no profit in worrying about such things, he told himself. He could only face problems when they became real. He had made up his mind. In the morning, he would ride back to Isuria to complete the deception and bring about the war.

The rain sluiced down, the cold chilled him and the night passed slowly. By the time he roused one of the warriors, a man named Luscovius, to relieve him, Calgacus was still no nearer to resolving his worries.

"Is anything happening?" Luscovius asked uncertainly, peering into the darkness.

"Nothing," Calgacus replied.

Luscovius took his place beside the fire. "Miserable night," he said. "But I think it is clearing."

"Let's hope so," Calgacus replied. "Even the animals are staying under cover tonight."

He crept further into the shelter. Pencoch stirred and sat up sleepily.

"Something wrong?" he asked.

"No. Go back to sleep."

Calgacus stepped carefully towards a space on the ground, took off his wet cloak to shake the worst of the rain from it, unfastened his breastplate and sword, then lay down and tried to sleep.

He did not know how long he had slept but he was woken by the sound of a man screaming in pain. Calgacus was on his feet in an instant, grabbing for his sword in an automatic reaction. For a brief, horrible moment he did not know where he was, did not know who had screamed or why. Then dark shapes were running at him from the darkness beyond the fire. He saw a sword blade, reflecting dully in the orange firelight and saw another man rising from one of his sleeping warriors, a bloody dagger in his hand.

Calgacus came fully awake in an instant. His sword swung in a wide arc, knocking his assailant's blade aside. Calgacus yelled, trying to scare the man, then backhanded his blade, feeling it strike home. He twisted it free, jumped to the fire and hacked at another swordsman.

He had time to see Luscovius lying in a pool of blood beyond the fire, sightless eyes staring into the night sky. It had been his scream that had woken Calgacus. Had he not given that last, terrified death cry, they would all have died while they slept.

Now Pencoch was up, grappling furiously with a spearman. Another man, Barta, was there, wielding his sword to Calgacus' left, and Runt, thankfully, was on his right, his sword ready, his hunting knife reflecting dull orange in the flickering firelight. But the four of them faced five times their number.

The attackers came in a screaming, yelling rush, urged on by a vaguely familiar voice from the rain-lashed darkness. Calgacus slashed, parried, slashed again. Runt, more economical with his moves, swiped his blade across a man's belly. Barta head butted his opponent, then stabbed him as he fell. Calgacus' opponent reeled back, crying in pain as Calgacus' sword hacked three fingers from his right hand.

For one glorious moment he thought they would hold them. Then spears flew out of the darkness. Runt, reacting more quickly than Calgacus would have believed possible, threw up his left arm to knock away a spear that would have buried itself in Calgacus' belly. Barta was not so lucky. A spear thumped into his chest, sending him staggering back, falling to his knees. Then men with swords were charging into the gap where Barta had stood. Pencoch went down, screaming defiance as two men hacked at him.

Calgacus threw back a swordsman, then saw dark shapes running past him into the shelter.

They were after the girl!

He turned to chase them, heard the warning shout from Runt too late and staggered as a blow like the kick of a mule caught him in the back, just above his waist on his right side. He fell to the ground, unable to stand, trying to twist away from the pain, hearing himself scream as he went down. Pain like fire lanced through him. He was dimly aware that there were men around him. Desperately, he rolled, saw spears coming for him as he tried to twist away. The pain in his back was awful, threatening to consume him, but he had to avoid the men who were coming for him.

A spear plunged into his left shoulder, sending more shards of sharp pain stabbing through his body. The spear jabbed again, coming for his eyes. He flailed his sword, twisted away and the edge of the spearpoint gouged the side of his head instead of driving into his skull. The spear thumped into the earth beside his ear.

135

He could feel blood everywhere but another blade was threatening to impale his right thigh. He flung his arm at it, knocking the spear away with his sword. The spear vanished from his blurred vision. He knew its sharp tip had pierced his skin but it had not gone deep. The next blow, though, would certainly kill him.

He could hardly move. Dimly, he heard Aemilia screaming as she was carried past him, kicking her legs wildly. He could do nothing to stop the men from taking her. He looked up, saw the spears coming for him again and tried to yell at the men, to show them that he was not afraid to die. No sound came.

Then Runt was there. He had a gash on his forehead and blood was pouring down his face, but the wound did not slow him. His sword and knife flashed, the men fell back and Runt planted his legs on either side of Calgacus, standing over him. Another spear was thrown, but Runt batted it away with contemptuous ease. It clattered to the ground several paces away.

Then there was silence. A man groaned in pain somewhere outside the shelters but the fight was done.

Calgacus, struggling to stay conscious, lying in a spreading pool of his own blood, gasped to Runt, "The girl! Get the girl!"

Runt looked down. "She's gone, Cal." Then his face paled. "Oh, by Grannos! What have they done to you?"

Calgacus lost his grip on his sword as his fingers refused to obey him. He closed his eyes, only dimly aware of Runt's desperate calls to him, telling him to stay awake, not to die. He tried to obey but Runt's words slowly faded down a long, dark tunnel.

Chapter XIII

The atmosphere inside Cartimandua's great hall was thick with tension. The Queen of the Brigantes sat at a table that had been set up in front of the low dais but this time there was no meal for her guests. She sat with Garathus, Caratacus and Cethinos, discussing what had been done so far and making plans for what needed to be done next.

Several chieftains stood nearby, waiting to receive orders or to deliver reports. A handful of Cartimandua's guards lurked in the shadows while others manned the doors, ensuring that nobody was admitted without the Queen's permission.

Caratacus rubbed at his chin, his eyes pensive. "We have three priorities," he said. "Food, shelter and weapons. Shelter is the least of these. Temporary huts are easy enough to build and, from what you say, there are many caves we can use."

Garathus said, "There are also a lot of small dwellings in the hills. The people move up to the high ground in summer so that their cattle and sheep can use the high pastures."

"Good. Weapons stores are being prepared?"

"They are," Garathus confirmed.

"We could do with some places where new weapons can be forged. Places the Romans will not find easily."

"We can trade with the tribes to the north for weapons," Cartimandua suggested. "The Votadini and the Novantae are no great friends to us but they will provide weapons if we offer enough gold and silver. They also prize jet stones and, through Venutius, we control the only supply."

"That is a good idea. So, food, as always, is the main problem."

Cethinos interrupted, saying, "We must send word to Ynis Mon."

"Only when we know that we are committed to war," Cartimandua said. "There is still time for the Roman girl to be found." She gave Caratacus a stern look. "Do not think that

137

making these plans means that I am determined to fight the Romans. I still hope to avoid that."

"I understand," Caratacus said, though his eyes told a different story.

Cethinos said, "If war comes, sacrifices must be made."

Cartimandua inclined her head, acknowledging the druid's words. Privately, she still felt uncomfortable at having him here. Druids had not been seen in Brigantia since she was a girl, but she knew that his presence would encourage her people if war came. Allowing him to participate in their planning was a pragmatic solution although his contributions had, so far, been of little practical help.

"Do you have prisoners?" he demanded.

Cartimandua shook her head. "Brigands and cattle thieves are executed by those who catch them," she said.

"Then we must select some suitable people as soon as possible," Cethinos declared. "In the meantime, offerings can be cast into the rivers and marshes at sacred spots. Gifts of gold, silver and weapons will alert the Gods to our plight."

Cartimandua exchanged a quick look with Caratacus, trying to gauge his view, but the Great King betrayed nothing. She said, "We will need our gold and silver to trade for weapons."

"And we need our weapons for fighting," added Garathus.

Cethinos scowled at them. "You must honour the Gods before using valuables to meet earthly needs. You must—"

His words were cut off by a loud commotion at the great doors. They were flung open, admitting a glare of sunlight that silhouetted three figures.

"My Queen!" shouted Venutius. "I have the girl!"

A babble of excited voices greeted the young chieftain as he and Vellocatus strode confidently towards the table, leading a small girl between them. She wore a long, Roman-style dress that was dirty and torn, her long hair hung lankly around her tear-stained face and fear had rendered her legs barely able to support her. The two men, oblivious to her terror, dragged her through the hall towards the Queen.

Everyone stood. Cartimandua moved quickly round the table to meet Venutius.

"Is it truly her?"

"I am sure of it. She does not understand our language."

Cartimandua bent down to face the terrified girl. She could feel her heart thumping and her nerves tingling but she forced herself to remain calm. Searching her memory for the Latin that her father had insisted she learn, she asked the girl, "What is your name?"

The girl would not look at her but kept her head lowered. "Aemilia," she said in a barely audible whisper.

Cartimandua was not used to speaking to children. She sensed that she should try to comfort the girl but there was too much at stake to spend time soothing Aemilia's fears.

Cartimandua asked, "Who is your father?"

"Quintus Aemilius Pudens. He commands the Ninth Legion."

Cartimandua closed her eyes as relief flooded through her. She stood up, placing a hand gently on the girl's shoulder. "Then we will take you to him," she said.

Aemilia looked up at her then, as if she did not believe what she had heard. Cartimandua confirmed her statement with a nod that triggered a flood of tears from the young girl.

Cartimandua had no time to console the child. There were too many questions that demanded answers. She turned her attention to Venutius who was grinning fiercely, glowing with pride at what he had accomplished.

"It is her," Cartimandua confirmed. "Where was she?"

Venutius cast a sly look at Caratacus before replying. "She was a day's hard ride to the east," he announced. "Calgacus had her and was hiding her so that we could not return her."

Cartimandua stiffened. The watching chieftains gasped and muttered in angry surprise.

"Tell me what happened," Cartimandua said coldly.

Venutius could not prevent a smile spreading across his face as he recounted, "We heard news of her being taken to a remote valley. We found Calgacus and his war band there, hiding her. There was no doubt about his intentions. He was not bringing her here." He turned a triumphant grin on Caratacus. "We had to take her from him by force."

"Where is Calgacus?" Caratacus asked, his face turned grey by concern and the certain knowledge of defeat.

"He is dead," Venutius said with undisguised glee. "One of my men put a spear through his head."

With deliberate slowness, Cartimandua turned to face

Caratacus. Her expression was dark with rage.

"You knew about this," she said accusingly, her voice hard. "You planned this with him."

Caratacus stared back at her, saying nothing, his silence an admission of his complicity.

"You betrayed me," Cartimandua said, her voice rising angrily. "You lied to me!"

"Calgacus did not lie," Caratacus said with weary resignation. "He would have brought the girl back eventually."

"But too late to prevent the war?"

Caratacus nodded. "It was my idea," he admitted.

Cartimandua signalled to her guards. "Seize him!" she barked. "Put him in chains and guard him closely."

Caratacus made no attempt to resist as two big men loomed out of the shadows to grab his arms while a third searched his clothing. His dagger was taken from him, then manacles were brought. His wrists and ankles were quickly shackled.

"Check around his neck," Cartimandua ordered, her voice seething with icy fury and her blue eyes glinting dangerously. "There should be a gold coin."

"No!" Caratacus protested for the first time.

"Take it!" she snapped.

One of the guards tugged the coin loose. Holding it by the long cord of twisted leather, he handed it to the Queen.

She turned the coin over in her palm. "This reminds you of who you are," she said to Caratacus. "Now you are nobody."

"What will you do with him?" Venutius asked, his voice thick with gloating anticipation.

"We will take him to Lindum. When we return the girl, we will give the Governor an additional gift."

Cethinos, who had stood in impassive silence while Caratacus was accused and seized, took a step forwards. He did not look at the Great King but addressed Cartimandua.

"You must give him to me," he said. "I will take him to Ynis Mon. There, his life will be offered to the Gods."

Caratacus head jerked round. He gaped at the druid in disbelief.

Cartimandua shook her head. "You were party to this deception, Druid. He will be taken to Lindum and will help to save the Brigantes from destruction. As for you, I will not harm a druid

140

but you must leave here. I don't care where you go, but leave Brigantia. Do you hear me?"

Cethinos narrowed his eyes. "The Gods will punish you for this," he rasped.

With an effort of will, Cartimandua met the druid's malevolent gaze. She understood that his threat was a very real one but the Romans were a more immediate problem.

"I will make offerings of gold to the Gods," she said. "I will sacrifice cattle, goats and sheep. But Caratacus will be offered to the Romans."

Cethinos stared at her for a long time but he eventually realised that his disapproval would not break her resolve. He gave a curt nod. Without another word, he turned away, walking towards the doors. He did not give Caratacus a backward glance but stalked from the hall like a bird of ill omen.

Cartimandua felt her muscles relax when the druid had left. She turned to Caratacus. "Well, Cousin, I have saved you from that, at least," she said.

"You have only delayed my death," Caratacus replied, his voice flat and unemotional. "The Romans will not allow me to live. But at least I will be reunited with my family before I die. For that, I thank you." He cast a baleful look at Venutius. "Are you certain that Calgacus is dead?"

Venutius said, "Three spears took him. We were too busy rescuing the girl to wait around but Vellocatus saw him fall."

"No man could have survived those wounds," the tall shield-bearer confirmed.

Venutius said, "I only regret that it was a quick death, which is more than he deserved."

Despite herself, Cartimandua felt a sense of loss when she heard this. Rallying her composure, she said, "Then he is dead. Forget him. Now, we must leave for Lindum. Garathus, send a rider with a message to the Governor. Tell him we have found the girl and that we will bring another mighty gift for him. Do not mention Caratacus by name. We will keep that as a surprise."

Garathus nodded his understanding. "Yes, my Queen."

"And have my chariot prepared. We shall go to Lindum immediately."

"Yes, my Queen."

Venutius said, "There is one other matter we must discuss."

141

"What is that?" Cartimandua asked.

"Our hand-fasting ceremony. We should be married without delay."

Cartimandua hesitated. With so many witnesses, she could not snub him now. He had saved her. He had saved her people. She had always known she must marry him to secure the allegiance of the northern Brigantes. Now, she could not refuse him. And yet . . .

"As soon as we get back from Lindum," she promised.

If Venutius was disappointed by the delay, he hid it well. Smiling the smile of a man who had achieved all his aims, he said, "I shall look forward to it, my Queen."

Isuria was in uproar. People thronged towards the hall, wanting to see the Roman girl, wanting to see the Great King, Caratacus, in chains. The sudden change in fortunes was so bewildering that everyone wanted to learn the truth for themselves.

Those who had clamoured for war were stunned, those who had wanted peace were ecstatic. All of them hurried to witness the Queen taking the Roman girl and the famous Catuvellauni warlord to the Romans.

Ignored by the crowd, Cethinos retrieved his cloak from the now deserted roundhouse. Fastening it around his scrawny shoulders with his silver brooch, he took his staff and made his way through the town towards the gates where the horses were kept in a large paddock. Nobody tried to stop him. Those few who noticed him simply stepped out of his way, giving him a wide berth.

When he reached the paddock, Garathus was already there, issuing orders for horses to be harnessed to the Queen's chariot. He saw Cethinos approach and had a pony saddled for him. Cethinos nodded his thanks.

Garathus gave a polite bow, then left him, returning to the great hall.

While Cethinos was looking around for a mounting step, a voice called to him.

"Venerable One!"

He looked up to see Venutius hurrying towards him, with the tall figure of Vellocatus trailing him as usual. Venutius bowed his head respectfully as he reached the druid.

"What is it now?" Cethinos demanded harshly.

142

Venutius' tone was surprisingly humble as he said, "Venerable One, I wish only to assure you that there are still some among the Brigantes who honour and respect the old ways. Cartimandua has followed her father in suppressing all opposition but once I have married her, I will have much more influence." He gave the druid a conspiratorial look. "There are many who disagree with her attitude towards Rome."

"I thought you shared her beliefs?" Cethinos asked warily.

"Outwardly, I must," Venutius replied smoothly. "For the time being."

"So you will renounce the allegiance to Rome when you marry her?"

"It may take some time," Venutius said. "She remains the rightful queen. For the moment, I wish you to know that you still have friends among the Brigantes. Will you inform the Druid Council of this?"

"I will," Cethinos agreed.

"As for Caratacus, I agree with you. His life should have been offered to the Gods. But, as Cartimandua says, he is being sacrificed."

"Not in the correct way," Cethinos said stiffly. "And not for the right reasons."

"I understand, Venerable One. I am sorry I could not bring you Calgacus," Venutius said.

Cethinos snorted. "He is of no account. He has always been an insolent, disrespectful fool. He is no loss to anyone, least of all to me."

"But he would have made a valuable sacrificial victim. Cartimandua could not have objected if he were to be taken to Ynis Mon."

"That is true," Cethinos agreed. "But what is done, is done. Now, I must go. I have a long way to travel."

"I wish you well, Venerable One," Venutius said. He stooped, cupping his hands to help Cethinos heave his old bones into the saddle.

Once mounted, the druid steadied himself, nodded a farewell and jabbed his heels into the pony's flanks, setting it into a slow trot.

The two Brigantes stood by the open gates, watching him go.

"I do not understand, Lord," Vellocatus said. "What was the

point of all that?"

"It never hurts to have friends in both camps," Venutius said. "We cannot read the future, so knowing a druid may come in useful."

Vellocatus scratched his head, frowning. He often had trouble understanding his master's reasoning. "So what happens next?" he asked.

Venutius grinned happily. "That is simple. First, we go to Lindum to ensure that the girl is handed back, then I will marry Cartimandua. After a suitable time has elapsed, she will suffer an unfortunate accident, leaving me as the undisputed ruler of the Brigantes."

Vellocatus' smile matched that of his master. "How long will you wait?" he asked.

"That depends on how much I enjoy my nights with her. But I cannot act too soon. I need to gather as much support as I can. Perhaps next year."

"And then you will attack the Romans?"

Venutius sighed. "Of course not. Why would I do a foolish thing like that?"

Vellocatus' face fell. "But I thought you told the druid you were against Rome?"

"You should stick to doing what I tell you," Venutius told his shield-bearer. "Thinking too much will only give you a headache. I told the druid what he wanted to hear. It was a precaution. Nothing more."

"Against what?" Vellocatus asked.

"Against the unforeseen," Venutius answered. "The Romans are a mighty people but who knows what will happen. Their last Emperor was murdered. The same fate may lie in store for Claudius Caesar. If that happens, the legions may be recalled."

"That does not seem likely," Vellocatus ventured cautiously.

"It is extremely unlikely," Venutius agreed. "But the future is hidden behind a curtain. We can never tell what it will reveal. If the legions were to leave, the druids would seize power again. No doubt they would soon take their revenge on anyone who has opposed them. So, unlikely as this outcome seems, it is as well to have friends on Ynis Mon."

Vellocatus' handsome face brightened as understanding dawned. "What about Cartimandua?" he asked, "When the time

144

comes, how will you get rid of her?"

"I'm not sure. But it will be done while you and I are away somewhere, perhaps on a hunting trip."

"Then how—" Vellocatus paused, knowing he was likely to be mocked again.

Venutius laughed. "It is better that neither of us knows that. I will get Segomou to do it."

"Your cousin?"

"The very same. I will send for him once I have married the Queen. I expect he will insist on being showered with gold but it will be worth it. When the time is right, he will arrange Cartimandua's death. Segomou enjoys killing people and he is very good at it."

"You think of everything, Lord," said Vellocatus admiringly.

"I try. But we are getting ahead of ourselves. First, we must go to Lindum and make sure the Romans are appeased."

Chapter XIV

Two days before his deadline expired, Governor Ostorius Scapula sat on the open-air tribunal that had been set up in the parade ground at the centre of the legionary fort at Lindum. The tribunal was nothing more than a row of seats placed on a raised platform, with the legion's standards set up behind the chairs, but everyone knew that those who sat there were men who could dispense justice on behalf of the Emperor.

On the Governor's left sat Facilis and the Ninth Legion's Tribunes. On his right was Aemilius Pudens, the Legate, along with the Camp Prefect and the Aquilifer, the legion's standard-bearer. Stretching away from either side of the tribunal, forming the sides of a wide square, stood orderly ranks of legionaries in full armour.

"Will they be here soon?" the Legate, Pudens, asked for the hundredth time.

Scapula did not reply. He had already decided that Pudens should be removed from his position as commander of the Ninth Legion. Rome needed men of action in command of her armies, not mewling faint-hearts who fell apart at the loss of a child. As if that were not bad enough, Pudens' wife was among the fort's civilians who were clustered behind the tribunal, waiting for the British delegation to arrive. The woman was worse than her husband, constantly crying in a most un-Roman fashion which Scapula found both embarrassing and shameful. Roman matrons were supposed to be stoic and unflinching in the face of loss but Pudens' wife was behaving like some decadent Easterner with her wailing and sobbing.

Pudens leaned forwards to direct a question at Facilis. "What is she like, this Cartimandua?" he asked.

"She's late," Scapula said irritably, cutting off Facilis' reply.

"But can she be trusted?" Pudens insisted.

Facilis gave a slight shrug. "She is very young. I think she is afraid of us. That should make her trustworthy."

146

"They say she is very pretty," Pudens observed.

"Yes," Facilis agreed. "Very. But clever too, I think."

"A bad combination," the Governor observed. "Women should not rule. It only causes trouble. Mark my words, Facilis. This Cartimandua will cause us problems. Women rulers always do. Look at the trouble that she-devil Cleopatra caused."

"Yes, sir." Facilis knew it was best to agree with the Governor when he was in this sort of mood.

"She is late on purpose," Scapula grumbled. "Trying to prove a point."

"I don't mind, as long as she brings my daughter back," Pudens said.

A fanfare of trumpets sounded from the gates, spawning a buzz of excited conversation that swept the camp. In response, the centurions barked at the soldiers to be silent. The officer's wives and other civilians also obeyed the command.

They all looked down the length of the wide via principia, the main street that bisected the fort. When the massive gates opened, they saw half a dozen chariots slowly enter in single file.

Pulled by small ponies, the chariots were completely open at the front and rear, with semi-circular or rectangular wicker panels on either side of the main platform, offering the passengers something to hold on to. The panels were brightly decorated with coloured ribbons that fluttered as the chariots moved. The manes of the immaculately groomed ponies were also braided with red and yellow ribbons so that they resembled tightly corded ropes of alternating colours and their tails were neatly chopped short to prevent them flying in the faces of the chariot's passengers. Small bells on the ornate harnesses jangled as they trotted towards the parade ground.

Facilis studied the vehicles with interest. He had heard about British chariots but had never seen them. They made a spectacular sight yet, at the same time, they were barbaric and strange, nothing like the small, lightweight chariots used in the Roman races at the Circus. Yet he had heard that British chariots were surprisingly nimble, their drivers unusually skilled. Some of the veteran legionaries claimed that the British charioteers were so agile that they could leap off the platform and balance on the long pole that led between the ponies, even if the chariot was travelling at full speed. Facilis doubted whether the story was true but it was always

147

difficult to tell in Britannia. The strangest tales could sometimes turn out to be accurate.

There were no such displays of agility today. The chariots came on at a sedate pace, the ponies stepping high, the drivers keeping them under tight rein, the passengers standing tall, staring straight ahead as they passed between the long lines of tents and half-built barrack blocks which housed the Legion's soldiers.

The leading chariot had three occupants, a driver, a stocky, long-haired warrior whom Facilis recognised as the Queen's shield-bearer, and Cartimandua herself. She was dressed in white, with a cloak of blue and green patchwork round her shoulders. A golden torc glistened at her throat and her long, raven-dark hair was held back from her face by another thin band of gold.

The chariot stopped when it drew level with the end of the ranks of legionaries. Cartimandua dismounted gracefully, then walked slowly towards the tribunal. She came alone, walking barefoot like a supplicant, her head bowed. Under the eyes of three thousand men, she approached the Governor.

"By Jupiter, she's a rare beauty," one of the Tribunes said under his breath.

Cartimandua stopped in front of the tribunal, dropping to her knees. She looked up, her eyes fixed unerringly on the Governor. Speaking Latin in a clear voice, she said, "Lord, I come to affirm the agreement made by my father that the Brigantes will be friends of Rome. We will not bear arms, we have banished the druids. Tribute will continue to be paid. In exchange, we ask only for Rome's protection and goodwill."

Scapula cleared his throat. Trying not to be distracted by her stunning looks, he replied, "You heard my demands. Peace comes at a price. Where is the girl?"

Cartimandua rose to her feet. She waved a hand to the chariots before turning back to face the Governor.

"She is here. Unharmed. The men who took her are dead."

Her shield-bearer walked to the second chariot, then came forwards, leading a small girl.

"Aemilia!" Pudens gasped. He almost leaped to his feet but a sharp command from Scapula kept him in his chair. But from behind the tribunal his wife echoed his cry. The girl broke free and ran to her mother who hurried to meet her, dropping to her knees to fold her arms around her daughter. The watching legionaries gave a spontaneous cheer of approval.

Facilis sensed the Governor's irritation at the un-Roman display of emotion and at the soldiers' reaction to it. He wondered whether Scapula was considering breaking his word, whether he would decide to attack the Brigantes in spite of his demand being met. The Ninth Legion had taken no part in the recent campaign in the west and the men were always eager for conquest and plunder. Facilis knew his man and he could almost see the Governor's thoughts as Scapula weighed up how to react.

But Cartimandua had sent word that she had another gift. She waved her hand again. A man was dragged from the rear chariot, his wrists manacled in front of him, his ankles chained together. He hobbled along, half-dragged by two burly warriors.

"Who is that?" Scapula asked.

Cartimandua smiled. "This is my gift to you," she said. "I give you Caratacus, son of Cunobelinos, as a token of my good faith towards Claudius Caesar, Emperor of Rome."

A murmur of excitement raced round the crowd like wildfire as every Roman came alert. Pudens' daughter was almost forgotten because this was the man who had defied Rome for eight years, who had raided and killed, who had refused to surrender to them and, until now, had evaded every attempt to capture him.

The crowd behind the tribunal surged to the sides as people jostled and craned their necks to see the most famous adversary Rome had encountered since the Legions had landed in Britannia. Facilis felt a momentary unease as he wondered how the civilians would react next. Some of them, he knew, were Britons. In fact, some of the centurions' wives were Britons. What would they do at the sight of Caratacus in chains? Above the muted whispers of amazement, he heard one woman sob as the famous War Leader was led towards the tribunal.

Facilis tensed but there was no trouble. He realised that, Britons or not, most of the civilians probably belonged to different tribes and would owe no allegiance to a king of the Catuvellauni and Trinovantes. They were excited but it was curiosity that drove them to press forwards, not a desire to free the chained man.

As Caratacus drew nearer, Facilis studied him. The Briton was everything he had expected; tall, well-muscled, with long, unruly hair and a drooping moustache. He may have been shackled but he held his head high, no sign of fear or submission in his eyes. He

149

seemed resigned to his fate, yet his expression suggested that he regarded his captors with contempt. Walking onto the parade ground, with ranks of his enemies on either side, Caratacus paid no heed to his surroundings. His eyes were fixed on Cartimandua.

The Queen turned away from her prisoner. Addressing the Governor, she gestured with a flourish. "Caratacus is yours to do with as you please. I am assured that his brother, Calgacus, is dead. I trust that this gift will ensure many years of friendship between our peoples."

Facilis had to admire her. She was young but, as he had suspected, she was clever. By presenting Scapula with his greatest foe, she had ensured that the Governor could not go back on his word without showing himself to be untrustworthy, even if that word had only been given to barbarians.

Scapula signalled to a centurion. "Take him!" he ordered.

Facilis saw that the Governor had relaxed. He was actually smiling.

"On behalf of the Emperor, I thank you," Scapula said to Cartimandua. "I confirm that there will be peace between Rome and your people."

Cartimandua bowed her head while Caratacus was dragged away by half a dozen legionaries. Pudens rose, going down to meet his wife and his newly-returned daughter. The soldiers cheered again, acclaiming the Governor who stood to accept their applause. All tension evaporated, driven away by the handing over of Caratacus.

Facilis sat back in his chair, breathing a sigh of contentment. There would be no more fighting because Ostorius Scapula had effectively subdued all the tribes who lived in the southern half of Britannia. The Silures were defeated, the Ordovices routed. Cartimandua of the Brigantes had come to him in her bare feet, begging for clemency. Above all, Caratacus was a prisoner at last.

The Governor should be pleased, Facilis thought. Britannia had finally been conquered. There was nobody left to oppose them.

Chapter XV

Myrddin picked up a small, leather bag and slung it over his shoulder. Leaving his rocky home, he went down the trail, past the fork, ignoring the low moan from Dis's dark cavern, then plunged into the woods. When he reached a certain point he recognised from the notches he had carved long ago in the trunk of a gnarled old oak, he cut off the path, crouching low to follow a small animal trail until he came to the rock wall of the hillside.

He turned to his right, pushed through some thick bushes, skirted a patch of brambles and found the tiny cave in the rocky hillside to his left.

The whole valley was riddled with small caves, and Myrddin had long ago explored every one of them. Some were too small for a man to crawl inside, some were dangerously deep shafts, while others, like this one, were quite spacious. This particular cave was so well concealed that he had kept it as a hidden refuge in case of need. Years before, he had covered the entrance with a cow hide so that no animals or birds could get in. He had stored firewood, blankets and some utensils there and he occasionally used the cave when he wanted to be sure that nobody could find him. The wails and moans from Dis's cave were a good protection against unwanted visitors, but being invisible was even better.

He gave a low whistle as he approached the cave. The leather flap moved as a hand pulled it aside.

"It's only me," he called cheerfully.

Runt poked his head outside. The scar on his forehead was still red and ugly, but the wound was healing well.

"They have not come back?" he asked.

"No," Myrddin replied. "I expect they think you are dead."

"We would be if not for you," Runt said.

Myrddin turned to the figure lying on the floor of the cave, its bulk covered by a pile of furs and animal skins.

"How is he?"

"Getting stronger," Runt said. "Whatever you put in those

potions seems to be helping."

"Well, I had best check his wounds. We don't want them turning bad on us. If evil spirits get into them, they will become infected. Then he will die just the same."

He pulled back the covers and began gently unwrapping the strips of cloth he had used for bandages, humming to himself as he did so.

Calgacus wearily opened his eyes to peer up at the hermit. "Why are you doing this?" he asked in a faint whisper.

"Ah, you're awake. That's good. But I've brought some more medicine to put you back to sleep."

"I don't want to sleep. I need to get up," Calgacus croaked.

"You need sleep. You lost a great deal of blood," Myrddin told him, gently but firmly pushing his head back down. "You are lucky that I found you in time. Fortunately, your wounds, though serious, did not affect any vital organs, nor sever any major arteries. But they could still kill you unless you give them a little time to heal. So lie still and rest."

"The girl?"

Runt said, "She's long gone, Cal. There will be no war."

Calgacus slumped despondently. "Then you may as well let me die. I have failed."

Myrddin gave him a gentle slap on the cheek. "Don't be foolish! You should not say things like that. I will forgive you only because you are feeling unwell, but I don't want to hear it again. Understand?"

Calgacus blinked groggily, his eyes barely able to focus but he managed a slight nod.

Myrddin continued his lecture, saying, "You may have failed, young man, but you did what you thought was right and you did your best. What more can a man do? What makes you think life was meant to be easy? You claim to be a warrior, so you should fight this battle too, not give up like some craven coward."

Calgacus opened his eyes again. "Why are you helping me?" he asked drowsily.

"I'm a healer. It is what I do."

Calgacus tried to smile. "I thought for a moment there that it was because you liked me."

Myrddin grunted. "No, but I like your friend here and he asked me to save you. I suggest you be quiet and do as I say, or I might

152

change my mind."

Three days later, Calgacus felt strong enough to venture outside.
Supported by Runt, he clumped his way half a dozen paces to the
mouth of the cave, then cautiously stepped outside. Six more paces
took him to a tussock of grass where he sat down heavily,
breathing hard.

"It's good to see the sky again," he gasped.

"You'll be fine in a few more days," Myrddin said. "I will
need to cut out the stitches I put in your wounds but they seem to
be healing nicely. If you rest for the turning of a moon, you'll be
back to normal but the young are always impatient, so I expect you
will want to leave before then."

"As soon as I can ride," Calgacus confirmed.

"Humour an old man and wait a bit longer," said Myrddin.

"I'll see how I feel. Now, you two should tell me what has
been happening while I've been hibernating."

Runt's face grew serious. "It was Venutius. I recognised his
voice."

"They killed all the others?"

"Barta lasted a day," Runt said. "But it was a bad wound. He
had no chance. There were too many of them to bury, so we
burned all the bodies, including the ones who attacked us."

Myrddin said, "Three of the men you killed were from the
village. I went down there yesterday. It seems your friend Venutius
threatened them into helping him. I told them that Dis is displeased
with them and that they should stay away from my valley for a
while. I also said that you were all dead." He gave a sad smile.
"They are very afraid."

Runt said, "As things stand, we've got plenty of horses and
weapons but not much else. We had to burn your clothes. They
were drenched in blood. I got your old ones out of your pack."

Calgacus looked down. He had not noticed that he was dressed
in the old shirt, tunic and trousers he had worn at the battle of Caer
Caradoc. His hand reached inside the shirt, tugging out the gold
coin that still hung around his neck. Reassured, he pushed it out of
sight again.

He saw Runt give him a questioning look. "What are we going
to do, Cal?" the little man asked.

"I will give it a few days," Calgacus said. "Then we will return

153

to Isuria. I need to see Caratacus and I have a score to settle with Venutius. That is twice he has tried to kill me. I don't intend to let him try a third time."

Calgacus was never good at waiting patiently. Each day he pushed himself to do more and each day he felt stronger. His wounds were healing well although he knew he would be left with some large scars, especially on his lower back where the spear had gouged a deep gash. The skin there had been purple and tender but the bruise was already fading to blotchy yellow. His shoulder and thigh were less serious and his head wound, which would have killed him had the spear struck a finger's span to the left, barely troubled him. Myrddin had shaved away some hair to allow him to dress the cut but already it was growing back, concealing the jagged wound.

Physically, his wounds were healing but he was plagued by fears over what might have happened to Caratacus and remorse over his failure to keep the Roman girl hidden. But now that he had recovered from the worst of his injuries, these fears were outweighed by a burning desire for revenge against Venutius.

"I will take his treacherous head," he vowed.

After another few days, Myrddin suggested they move into his cavern. "It's bigger and more comfortable than this place," he explained. "And I don't think you need to hide here any longer."

Now that Calgacus was moving more freely, Myrddin told him he should exercise to build up his strength. The old man soon had him busy chopping enough firewood to last Myrddin through the winter. With Runt's help, Calgacus stacked the wood in a great pile by the rock ledge outside the old hermit's cave. The exercise left him feeling exhausted and sore although Myrddin seemed pleased with his progress.

In the evening, Myrddin made them help carve new utensils and make strings by twining strips of boiled willow bark which the old man then wove into new nets and traps he could use to catch fish in the stream.

"Doesn't it make you feel good to make things?" Myrddin asked.

Runt laughed but Calgacus merely scowled. "We should be making plans. I feel almost ready to leave."

"I will take your stitches out tomorrow," Myrddin told him. "If

154

your wounds are still fine, you can leave the following day. That is still much too soon but I expect you will ignore my advice. Still, until then, you can work. It will do you good. But don't do too much. You are young and fit but you will still be sore for a while."

The following day, Myrddin demonstrated how he supplemented his diet by showing them how he caught small birds. He began by handing Calgacus a few mistletoe berries.

"Chew these," he said.

Calgacus looked at the small, red berries sitting on the palm of his hand.

"They're poisonous," he said warily.

"I said chew them, not eat them. And try not to swallow the juice. A tiny bit will do nothing more than make you feel unwell. Too much and you'll be vomiting, or even unable to move. Just chew until you have a sticky mush, then spit it onto this plate." He handed over a small wooden platter, one of the new ones that Calgacus had helped him to make.

"Why don't you chew them?" Calgacus asked.

"Because you are here. I don't want to make myself ill, do I?" He grinned, waving a hand at Calgacus. "Go on. Chew."

Calgacus placed the berries in his mouth and chewed cautiously, more than a little apprehensive about the task. When he had turned the berries to mush, he spat them out.

"That's not nice," he said with disgust.

"Very useful plant, the mistletoe," Myrddin told him, ignoring his complaint. "Now, stretch it all out, like you are making a string. Roll it. That's right."

Calgacus did as Myrddin directed. As the mush dried, it grew sticky, clinging messily to his fingers.

Myrddin said, "That will do." He took the wooden plate then placed some bread crumbs alongside the paste. Ignoring Calgacus' curious gaze, he went outside. "Watch!" he said.

He crossed the stream, hopping to the far side on the large stepping stones to avoid getting his feet wet. Approaching the trees, he selected a low, thin branch that he could reach easily. Picking up the stringy paste of mistletoe berries, he worked it along the top of the branch. Once he had the long string in place, he carefully sprinkled the bread crumbs on top of the paste. Then he returned to the cave, giving Calgacus a broad wink.

"Now we wait," he announced.

After a while, the crumbs attracted small birds. Sparrows and finches flocked to this source of easy food. When they landed on the branch, they flapped their wings in panic as their tiny feet stuck in the paste. Myrddin gleefully ran from the cave, danced his way across the river and wrung their necks as quickly as he could. A few managed to escape, but he brought back three scrawny birds for the cooking pot.

"Useful stuff, mistletoe," he said happily as he set about cleaning the birds for the cooking pot. "The leaves have some healing properties, you know."

"It's a druids' plant," Calgacus said.

"It is merely a plant," Myrddin replied. "Part of nature. The druids just happen to know its secrets."

"So how do you know them?"

"I have had to learn a lot of things up here on my own," Myrddin replied enigmatically. "Now, strip off your shirt and let's get your stitches out while the birds are cooking."

Calgacus pulled his shirt over his head. Myrddin examined the wounds, clucking his tongue and pronouncing them healing very nicely. Using a small knife, he sliced the thin threads, tugging them free. Calgacus winced as the thread burned through the newly healed and still bruised flesh. The large gash on his back was particularly painful but once the stitches were out he felt much better, able to twist and turn, moving his arms more freely.

He turned to Myrddin. "Thank you," he said. "I owe you my life. I will not forget that. But I am not sure how I can ever repay you."

"Repay me by making the best use of your life that you can," the old man said.

"I will do my best." He paused, knowing that his thanks were inadequate for what Myrddin had done for him. "I suppose we should get ready to leave," he said.

"Give it another day," Myrddin said.

After breakfast the following morning, Calgacus put on his bronze breastplate. Runt helped him fasten the straps that held it in place. Then Calgacus looped his sword belt over his shoulders.

"That feels better," he said.

Myrddin said, "I suppose I will be wasting my breath if I tell you not to do too much for a few days."

156

"As soon as I've killed Venutius, I'll rest as much as I can," Calgacus promised.

"Fighting and killing," Myrddin mused sadly. "There is more to life than that."

"It is the only life I know," Calgacus told him.

Myrddin sat back, regarding him carefully. "Are you not afraid?" he asked. "It seems to me that you have many enemies. I would hate to think I have saved you only for you to be killed in another fight."

"Death is not to be feared," Calgacus said. "It is merely a gateway to the Underworld."

"So the druids teach us," Myrddin said. "And yet we all cling to life." He gave Calgacus an amused smile as he asked, "Did you ever know a druid to offer himself as a sacrifice? They are happy to send others to the Gods, yet they avoid that fate themselves, while telling us that there is nothing to fear in death."

Calgacus frowned. Myrddin always seemed capable of saying something that would confuse or challenge traditional beliefs.

"What are you trying to say?" he asked.

Myrddin chuckled. "I am trying to encourage you to see the world in a new light. Just because everyone says something is true, does not make it so. You are a resourceful man, Calgacus. I think you may be more capable than even you realise. But everyone has fears that need to be faced. I think you need to face one now."

"What do you mean?" Calgacus asked suspiciously. "I am not afraid of any man."

"I was not talking about a man," Myrddin said. He cocked his head to one side, holding a hand to his ear. "Can you hear the noise from Dis's cave?"

Calgacus listened. He had become so used to the sound over the past few days that he often ignored it, even when it was at its most mournful.

"Yes, I hear it."

"It is not too loud today," Myrddin said brightly. "I think you should go and see what causes it."

"Into the Underworld?" Calgacus asked.

"You just said there was nothing to fear in the Underworld," Myrddin pointed out with a wicked grin. "You don't have to go far. Just walk to the entrance and take a single step inside." His lined face turned blank, daring Calgacus to refuse him. "One step,

157

that's all. Or are you afraid of death after all?"

Calgacus' face grew stern. "I am not afraid."

"Then prove it." The old man stood up, inviting them to follow.

"All right." Taking a deep breath, Calgacus went to the rear of the cave to gather up his shield, then nodded that he was ready.

Myrddin led the way, Calgacus and Runt following close behind.

"What's this about?" Runt asked in a whisper.

"I have no idea," Calgacus confessed.

"Don't do it, Cal," Runt urged. "There may be nothing to fear in the Underworld, but once you go there, you can't come back."

"I don't think Myrddin would spend all that time saving my life just to see me dead," Calgacus replied.

"You don't know that. Maybe Dis wants a healthy sacrifice."

Calgacus had no answer to that. All too soon, they reached the fork in the way. Myrddin waved to the blank, barren defile that led to the cave. "There you are," he said.

The eldritch wail suddenly seemed louder and far more threatening. Calgacus looked at the old man's face, hoping for signs of a smile, an indication that this was a joke of some sort. Myrddin simply stared back impassively, waiting.

Gritting his teeth, Calgacus drew his sword with a flourish. Then he looped his shield over his left arm and started walking.

The rocks and gravel crunched under his feet as he picked his way over the uneven surface. Overhead a raven cried, its raucous croak echoing round the narrow pass. He heard footsteps behind him and knew that Runt was following. Up ahead, the dark maw of the cavern stared back at him, defying the bright sunlight with its impenetrable blackness. The familiar low moan of dead souls grew louder as every step took Calgacus closer.

He told himself it was just a cave. He had lived in a cave for the past twelve days. They had heard the sound so often that he had become used to it. Surely there was nothing to fear. But the inky blackness of the opening and the mournful sound that emanated from it, mocked him. He felt a shiver run down his spine.

His heart thumping in his chest, Calgacus reached the stone man, the last person who had come this far. He circled the pillar cautiously, half expecting the silent sentinel to spring to life and attack him. When nothing happened, he reached out, gently tapping his sword against the rock. There was no response except the sound of the iron blade rapping on stone.

Calgacus glanced at Runt who was watching nervously from a safe distance, his sword and long knife at the ready. Gesturing towards the stone man, Calgacus gave a bemused shrug.

He stepped closer. From the opposite side, it looked like just another block of stone. There was a vague outline that might have been a bulky head above broad, twisted shoulders, but there was no face, no arms. Whoever the man had been, he was nothing but stone now.

Drawing another deep breath, Calgacus moved on. Now he could see that there were two great boulders at the entrance to the cave, looking like nothing so much as the stumps of great fangs. He could see nothing but blackness beyond them.

He forced his legs to keep walking, taking care where he stepped on the jumbled stones beneath his feet. To his right, he saw that there was yet another part to the seemingly endless twists and turns of Myrddin's valley. Curving away out of sight was a narrow cleft, as if some giant or god had smashed down on the earth with a great axe to carve a cruel gash in the land. It was a ruined mess of boulders, as lifeless and barren as the place he now stood.

After only a few more steps, he was at the entrance to the cave. The noise of the ghostly wail was all around him now, the breath from the darkness blowing past him, ruffling his hair with its chill blast. Still there was no movement, nothing threatening him except the sound of tortured souls and the certain knowledge that to go any further would take him into the Underworld, from where there was no return.

He hesitated, gripped his sword tightly, then stepped between the two great stones that guarded the entrance.

Calgacus stood in the mouth of the cavern, waiting for some change, some sign that he had left the world of the living.

Nothing happened.

The moaning sound was loud, all around him, buffeting his ears. His hair and cloak moved in the wind that raced out of the cave, but there was nothing else. The floor of the cave was soft earth and gravel, the walls hard, uneven, ordinary sandstone.

He took another step, heading for the blackness in front of him. Still nothing happened. He took half a dozen steps, slowly, cautiously, holding his sword out ahead of him. The tip of the long blade scraped against the rear wall of the cave, a slab of dark rock rising sheer in front of him. The wind howled and moaned around him, coming down from above in an icy rush. He looked up, but saw nothing except darkness.

Puzzled, he turned. Runt was still standing outside, his expression radiating concern and fear, but Myrddin stepped inside the cave, smiling.

"The Cave of the Wind, I call it," the old man said with an expansive wave all around. His long hair and beard were fluttering around him.

"That's it? Just the wind?" Calgacus felt a mix of relief and foolishness.

Myrddin nodded. He pointed upwards to where the wind was whistling down at them, singing its dreadful song.

"There are tunnels up there. When the wind is blowing from the right direction, it comes through them. That's what makes the noise. It's a bit like a gigantic flute, or a horn." He grinned. "You could call it Dis's carnyx."

Calgacus lifted the tip of his sword to the old man. "You lied to us."

Myrddin laughed. "Come and sit over here." Moving back to the two great rocks that lay at the entrance, he sat down on one of them, gesturing to Calgacus to take the other.

"All I did was play on your fears," he said. "I simply told you what I wanted you to believe. Your minds did the rest, because you have grown up hearing tales of the Gods and the Underworld. Everyone knows that caves lead to the Underworld, and this one especially so, but as I told you, just because everyone says something, does not make it true."

"You lied to us!"

Myrddin shrugged. "Nobody tells the truth all the time. The trick to a good lie is to say it with conviction; convince yourself that it is close to the truth. It is a trick you will need to learn if you are going to fight the Romans. You must make your enemies see what you want them to see. Truth and honour will not win your war for you, I'm afraid. But I think you know that already."

"What is life without honour?" Calgacus asked.

"What is honour without life? But I am not saying you should live without honour. I am saying that you are young and you have a lot to learn. From what you have told me, it is plain that you have made a lot of enemies already, more than is good for you. If you want to defeat them, you need to use your head as well as your muscles. I am just trying to show you that what you think you see may not always be the truth."

He waved a hand at the stone man standing back down the pass. "That's just a rock," he said. "Nothing more, nothing less. It makes a good story, though, doesn't it?"

"You made fools of us," said Calgacus bitterly.

"You made fools of yourselves by believing what I said." Myrddin laughed. He slapped the rock he was sitting on and stamped his feet on the floor of the cave. "A man should always know what is around him, what is under his feet. This is just a cave."

Calgacus sheathed his sword and slung his shield over his back. "Well, I will not forget this lesson, old man."

"Shall I tell you a secret?" Myrddin asked unexpectedly.

"What secret?"

"The druids' secret."

Calgacus gazed into Myrddin's eyes. "I thought you said you weren't a druid."

"I'm not. But I was going to be. I started the training, but my teacher died when I was about your age, or perhaps a little older. He's buried under this rock I'm sitting on."

Calgacus stared at him in amazement. "You buried him here?"

"The grave won't be disturbed here," Myrddin said. "Nobody comes here. Even the animals don't like the noise of the wind. There's not a safer place I know of. He was an old man and, for some reason, quite worried that his bones might not be buried in a safe place. So I put him here. That was more than thirty years ago and I never got round to going anywhere else. I never completed my training. Everything else I know, I learned by myself."

"So what is the secret you learned?"

Myrddin sighed. "I suspect you know it already, although you may not have realised it. The druids control how the people speak to the Gods, yes?"

"Of course."

"So the druids have power, prestige and the right to command

161

even kings. Naturally, they want to keep these privileges."

Calgacus nodded. "I know all that."

"So what if I tell you that it makes no difference what sacrifices they offer? That the Gods do not listen to them any more than the wind does?"

Calgacus shifted nervously. Myrddin's words were uncomfortably close to his own, secret thoughts. "What are you saying?" he asked.

"I am saying that if, let's say, I wanted this noise to stop coming out of this cave, I could sacrifice a lamb, or a goat, or even you, and pray to Esus to make it stop. Such a sacrifice would be wasted, because the wind, while it might be Esus' breath, will still blow and the noise will still come. But if I climbed the hill above the cave and filled the holes that lead into the tunnels with earth and rocks, the noise would stop. If I was a druid, I would claim that Esus had come to me in a dream, showing me what to do. I would fill the holes, make a suitable sacrifice, and the noise would stop. That, of course, would justify the sacrifice."

He wagged a finger at Calgacus. "The druids need the people to believe that they can influence the Gods. It keeps them in power. If people stopped believing the druids make a difference, they would lose everything. But the druids, or some of them, know the great secret. They know that the Gods have little interest in the affairs of petty mortals. That is why anyone who challenges the druids, anyone who questions what they say, is a threat to them."

The two of them sat silently for a long moment, staring at each other. Eventually, Calgacus said softly, "That is heresy. It goes against everything we believe."

Myrddin shrugged. "Does it? It goes against everything you have been told, but I think you believe it already." He leaned forwards, fixing Calgacus with a steely gaze. "I want you to think about it. You are a good man and I know you are a brave one. But if we are to remain free from the Romans, we need men who can think for themselves, men who will not be fooled by believing everything they are told."

"You are saying I should not trust the druids?"

"Trust is a difficult thing to give," Myrddin said. "Trust must be earned. But if you wish to fight the Romans, you will need the druids' support. Whatever you may think of them, there is no avoiding that. What I am saying is that you should be aware of how they think and why they do the things they do. You will need their help but you should not be tricked into believing they can solve all your problems. You must think for yourself."

"I hear you," Calgacus said thoughtfully.

Myrddin stood up. "Now come, you should get ready to leave." He went back out into the sunlight. Turning, he said, "You know, not many men would have dared walk into this cave. I think you are learning already."

Calgacus sat thoughtfully for a moment before rising to his feet and leaving the cavern. "You teach a hard lesson, old man," he said. "But I will not forget it."

Myrddin turned to Runt. Laughing and pointing at Calgacus, he asked, "Did you see that? He went into the Underworld and came back out again. That is a sight you should remember."

Chapter XVI

Calgacus had a great deal to think about during the ride back to Isuria. Listening to Myrddin had sparked something inside him, awakened the questions he had asked himself for many years and had tried to ignore. He could not ignore them any longer.

As a boy, he had witnessed Cethinos sacrifice a war captive, a man of the Atrebates. It had been necessary, Cethinos had declared, because the Romans were said to be preparing an invasion force. Calgacus remembered how the naked prisoner, drugged and bound, had been tied to the sacred oak, how Cethinos had given him a message to take to the Gods and had then slit his throat with the ceremonial bronze dagger, sending a river of blood to drench the victim's bare chest.

The crowd who had assembled in the sacred grove had cheered but Calgacus, only ten years old, had been watching the prisoner's face and had seen the fear in his eyes.

"That is no way for a warrior to die," he had said to Bonduca, his older sister. "How could he take a message to the Gods when he was so frightened?"

"Do not say such things, Calgacus!" Bonduca had scolded. "Never say such things or Cethinos will accuse you of heresy. Then you would be next to be sacrificed."

Of course, she was correct and so, it turned out, was Cethinos. The sacrifice had worked. Camulos had terrified the Romans so much that they had not dared to board their ships. Their Emperor, the now-dead Gaius Caligula, infuriated at their cowardice, had ordered the soldiers to gather sea shells in their helmets, then had marched them back to Rome with this strange booty. Much as the young Calgacus had hated to admit it, Cethinos had saved the Pritani.

Faced with this evidence of the power of sacrifice, Calgacus had tried to forget the terror he had seen on the victim's face, had tried not to ask questions. He had never quite succeeded but had managed to keep most of his concerns and doubts to himself,

164

locking them away. When other sacrifices had failed, when druids' predictions were proved wrong, Calgacus had reminded himself of that powerful sacrifice that had scared away Caligula, and he had tried to bite his tongue. His doubts had persisted but he had told himself that was only because of his hatred for old Cethinos. Arguing with one ill-tempered druid was one thing. Questioning the people's whole way of life was quite another. Who was he, a young warrior, to challenge the beliefs of men and women who were older and wiser than he was?

But now Myrddin had opened the cage and let all his doubts free. The sensation was unsettling, yet liberating. For the first time in his life, Calgacus felt vindicated. Armed with his new freedom, he felt that he could achieve anything.

He had been a warrior, a leader of small war bands. He knew he had a talent for such things but he was honest enough to admit that he had treated it like a glorious game in which he had pitted his wits against the Romans. He had not concerned himself with strategy, had been content to leave grand plans to others while he had simply got on with the fighting.

Now he knew better. The past summer had shown him how much was at stake. The crushing defeat at Caer Caradoc had taught him a great deal, not least of which was that he should have stood up to Caratacus, should have defied the druids, and should have insisted that they fight differently. He had been right, but had allowed himself to be persuaded out of his convictions because of his love and respect for his older brother and because the druids had insisted that a battle must be fought. He vowed that he would not make that mistake again, not even if it meant arguing with the Great King and the Druid Council.

Caratacus had told him that he had been right about how to defeat the Romans; Myrddin had told him the druids' secret, confirming his own, private suspicions. But knowing these things was only a beginning. Myrddin had also told him not to waste his life. It was time he used the things he had learned.

"What are you thinking?" Runt asked as their ponies trotted across a wide expanse of tree-dotted plain. Behind them, they led a string of six more horses, each one laden with swords and shields, knives and spears, all wrapped in the cloaks of the men who had died in Myrddin's valley.

After a moment's thought, Calgacus said, "I'm thinking it is

165

time to take charge of our lives. It's time I started trusting my instincts instead of going along with what other people tell me to do."

Runt laughed. "You never listen to anyone, Cal. You never have."

"That's not true. I've always done what Caratacus told me."

"That's different," Runt said. "He's your older brother and your King. He's also a great War Leader."

"But he is not infallible. He has made mistakes. He admitted as much himself."

"Nobody is infallible, Cal. Not even you. That's why you need me to watch your back all the time."

"I know that. But now I am going to start doing things my way."

"So what's the plan?"

Calgacus frowned. "I'm not sure yet. It depends on what has happened at Isuria. Caratacus has probably left. He won't have stayed there once Venutius arrived with the girl."

"So we kill Venutius, then go after Caratacus?"

"Something like that."

"Oh, good. That sounds simple. All we need to do is march into Cartimandua's home, kill her most important and well-guarded chieftain and walk out without being stopped."

"That sounds good to me," Calgacus agreed. "Simple plans are always the best."

"It is certainly simple," Runt agreed. "It's also completely crazy, although I expect you know that."

"Just you watch my back and we'll be fine," Calgacus told him.

They rode slowly because Calgacus' wounds were still painful, his injured back chafed by the high back of the saddle, his wounded thigh aching as he used his legs to guide the horse. They stopped frequently to allow him to rest and to nibble on the meagre supplies Myrddin had given them for the journey. At night, they made camp at the fringes of a patch of woodland, far from any farms or villages.

The following afternoon, Calgacus decided they could not avoid people any longer. When he saw a small collection of roundhouses by the side of a small stream, he headed towards them.

166

"We'd better ask directions," he said. "I know we must be somewhere near Isuria but I'm not sure of the way."

The buildings turned out to be a farmstead, home to an extended family, but they quickly realised that there were few people there. Goats and sheep still grazed in the meadows, a donkey tied to a wooden post brayed when they passed but the only inhabitants were an old, half-blind man and two boys aged around eight or nine.

"Where is everyone?" Calgacus asked them.

The boys cowered behind the old man who peered at them through opaque, milky eyes. He said, "They have gone to Isuria. For the festival."

"Festival?"

The blind farmer frowned. "Lughnasa," he said. "Didn't you know that? The feast is tonight."

"We've been travelling," Calgacus explained. "We lost track of the days."

"You've been travelling a long way by the sound of your accent," the man observed.

"Yes. But we are headed for Isuria. The festival is tonight?"

"That's right. Most folk have gone there. Special occasion this year."

Calgacus felt a tightening of foreboding in his chest as he asked, "What occasion is that?"

"They say the Queen is marrying Venutius." The man spat on the ground. "Bad omens for a hand-fasting, though."

Calgacus frowned. "What omens, old man?"

"No rain today. If it rains on the feast day, it shows Lugh is pleased and will care for the crops, give us a good harvest and bring good luck. There's been no rain today, so things won't be so good this year. I reckon that will go for the marriage, too."

Calgacus nodded thoughtfully. Knowing the people involved, he suspected the blind man's prediction might well prove correct. Nevertheless, the news that Cartimandua was marrying Venutius, though not unexpected, left a bitter tang of disappointment in his mouth.

"Is there any other news from Isuria?" he asked. "We heard that a kinsman of ours was there."

"Another southerner?" the blind man asked. "The only one I heard about was that fellow Caratacus, the famous king. But he's gone now."

"I don't suppose you know where he went?"

The old man laughed. "I thought everyone had heard that by now," he said. "The Queen took him to the Romans, Handed him over in chains, she did."

Runt swore softly. Calgacus sat stock still in the saddle, unable to move, scarcely able to breathe as the enormity of the old man's news struck him.

The blind man said, "I can't see your face, youngster, but I can hear well enough. That wasn't what you wanted to hear, was it?" When Calgacus did not answer, the man went on, "Well, I have no great love for southerners but I've no love for the Romans either. I don't like what happened, but it happened, or so they say. If you take my advice, you'll stay well clear of Isuria. You'll find no friends there."

"I don't suppose we are going to listen to his advice?" Runt asked once they had obtained directions and set off again.

"No."

"I didn't think so."

It was dark by the time they came in sight of Isuria. Calgacus led them into a stand of trees on the eastern side of the river that bounded the north and east of the town. Tethering the horses, they crept towards the river.

"Is the plan still the same?" Runt asked as they squatted behind a stand of tall reeds.

"Yes. Except this time I might wring Cartimandua's neck as well."

Runt heard the savagery in his friend's voice. He said, "I thought you didn't make war on women?"

"I'm prepared to make an exception in her case. How could she do that?"

"She's trying to save her people from war, Calgacus," Runt said soothingly. "And we did try to fool her."

"But she's one of us! A Pritani." Even as he said it, Calgacus recognised the futility of his anger. Cartimandua had repeatedly told him that the Brigantes owed nothing to the Catuvellauni. It was the curse of the Pritani. The tribes stood apart, unable to put aside their differences, submitting or being conquered one by one.

"So what do we do?" Runt asked.

"We wait. Let them feast, let them get drunk. Then we will

168

sneak in. We'll climb the fence over there, well away from the gates. If there are any sober guards at the gateway, they won't see us."

"All right. But you can't kill Venutius tonight. Not on Lughnasa. Lugh will strike you down if you draw blood on his feast day."

"The day ends when the sun goes down," Calgacus replied grimly.

They returned to their horses, sitting down with their backs against the trunks of trees to wait. Borne on a mild, westerly breeze, the sounds of drums and horns drifted from the town. The orange glow of huge bonfires glimmered above the high earthworks. Within the bounds of Isuria there would be dancing and drinking, feasting and lovemaking. Outside, under the shelter of a copse, Calgacus and Runt drew out their whetstones and sharpened their swords.

Calgacus barely spoke. He was tired and sore, silently acknowledging that Myrddin had been correct; he had tried to do too much, too soon. Then he thought of Cartimandua, standing beside Venutius, their wrists being symbolically bound together in a hand-fasting ceremony. Anger gave him strength, banished his weariness.

They waited until they judged it was after midnight and the sounds of music had faded. Silently, they made their way to the river.

This was the most dangerous part of their approach because the town's gates overlooked the ford. Anyone on watch would have seen them as they crossed the river, but the gates were shut and there was no sign of a guard. They splashed through the knee-deep water, then cut to their right, away from the gates. Moving like shadows, they crept along the ditch until they had curved out of sight of the entrance.

They clawed their way up the embankment to the foot of the fence. Calgacus took off his cloak, folding it into a thick bundle. Then Runt made a stirrup with his hands, hoisting Calgacus up. He grabbed for the top of the stakes, pulling himself up. With Runt still struggling under his weight, Calgacus wedged his cloak over the sharp points of the wooden stakes, then heaved himself up to straddle the fence, where he sprawled on the padded cushion of his cloak. He leaned down, grabbing Runt's outstretched hand and helping him to clamber up the fence. Runt quickly wriggled past him, dropping lightly to the ground inside the fence. Wearily, Calgacus rolled off his precarious perch, pulling his cloak down with him. By the time he stood inside Isuria, he was panting heavily, sweat dripping from his forehead.

"Are you all right?" Runt asked in a low, concerned whisper. "You look dreadful."

"I'll manage. That's the hard bit over."

"This is a bad idea, Cal. You're very pale."

"I said I'll manage!" Calgacus snapped. "Just watch my back."

He took a series of deep breaths, then moved towards the shadowed gaps between the nearest roundhouses. Shaking his head, Runt followed.

There was no alarm. A dog barked somewhere off to their right, but they headed left, picking their way between the closely-packed roundhouses. Most of the homes were silent, the people sleeping off the effects of the plentiful food and drink. A baby cried as they passed one home but no voices called out to them, nobody challenged them. Navigating by feel and under the pale illumination of the moon and stars, they worked their way southwards, towards the great hall.

After what seemed an age, they crept round the circular wall of one house to see the open space and the hall beyond, its dark bulk just visible against the tree-studded hill behind it. The doors of the hall were open, firelight flickering within. They could hear the sounds of animated conversation and drunken laughter.

"She'll be in there," Calgacus said.

"She might be in her house," Runt replied. "With Venutius."

"Let's look inside the hall first."

"Andraste preserve us!" breathed Runt.

Calgacus strode out of the shadows, heading straight for the open doors. He had barely covered half the distance when a man staggered out of the hall, weaving drunkenly.

It was Vellocatus.

He stopped, his jaw dropping in bewilderment. His face went deathly pale when he saw the two figures approaching.

"You're dead!" he croaked, pointing one trembling finger at Calgacus.

"I was. I came back. For you and your master."

Vellocatus let out a wail of terror. He turned and bolted back inside the hall, shouting loudly that the spectre of Calgacus had come to Isuria.

"I suspect we've lost the element of surprise," Runt said bitterly.

"He seemed surprised enough."

"That's because you look like a ghost. Your face is paler than his."

Calgacus gave his friend a wicked smile. "Good. Let them see what we want them to see." Not waiting to hear any more protests, he walked towards the doors.

The laughter had stopped, replaced by an ominous silence. Calgacus could see the fire of the central hearth, could make out the shapes of long tables and the silhouettes of dozens of men and women who were sitting, staring at him in petrified terror. He clenched his teeth together and stepped to the threshold.

Garathus met him, holding a burning torch in his right hand. The shield-bearer's face was taut with suppressed fear but he held his ground, standing only a few paces in front of Calgacus.

"Halt, Shade!" Garathus shouted. "You have no business here."

Calgacus replied in a loud voice so that everyone could hear him. "I have business with Venutius, who killed me. And with Cartimandua, who betrayed my brother."

"This is the feast day of Lugh," Garathus persisted. "There is amnesty for all."

"It is night. The feast day is over," Calgacus countered. "Now stand aside so that I may find my enemies."

Still Garathus did not move. "You know I cannot let you pass," he said. "Whether you are mortal or spirit, I must oppose you. My duty is to protect my Queen."

Calgacus reached back over his shoulder. Weak as he was, he had enough strength to draw his sword. It rasped clear of the scabbard with a metallic ring. Women shrieked in alarm and he heard men whispering prayers to the Gods, asking for protection.

"I have no quarrel with you, Shield-bearer," he said to Garathus. "But if I must kill you to reach Venutius, I will."

"No!"

It was Cartimandua, dressed as usual in a long, white, sleeveless dress. She had a garland of flowers in her hair that seemed incongruous when matched against the look of grim

171

determination on her face. She walked slowly between the long tables until she stood shoulder to shoulder with Garathus. Calgacus could not help noticing the hint of fear in her eyes, nor the thin band of cloth around her wrist, the symbol that this was her wedding day. He turned a cold stare on her.

"You sold my brother to the Romans," he hissed.

"You tried to betray me," she countered. "You lied to me. Or your brother did on your behalf."

She took a step forwards, holding out an arm to signal Garathus to stay behind her. She peered at Calgacus' face.

"They told me you were dead," she said softly.

He continued to stare at her. The fear in her eyes was changing to uncertainty. He decided to stick to the ploy that had brought him this far.

"I was dead," he said. "I was released from the Underworld so that I could have my revenge."

"On me?" she asked.

He could not answer. Her blue eyes held his, challenging him. She raised both hands, tugging at the front of her dress, pulling the neck down to reveal the delicate shape of her neck and collarbone, exposing her throat to him.

"I gave you this opportunity once before," she whispered so that only he could hear. "I offer it to you again. Kill me if you really think it will solve all your problems."

She closed her eyes, waiting for him to strike. He stood there, the tip off his sword resting on the ground in front of him. He studied her face, the face he knew so well, looked at the rise and fall of her chest. When he had entered the hall he had wanted to lash out, to remove her head from her shoulders but, seeing her, he knew that he could not. No matter what she had done, he could not kill her in cold blood.

"It is Venutius I want," he told her.

She opened her eyes, lowering her hands to her sides. "You cannot have him," she replied. "I need him."

"I will not be denied!" he shouted.

Many in the watching crowd flinched at his outburst, but Cartimandua did not.

"You are sweating, Calgacus," she whispered. "I did not think that spirits had flesh to sweat."

"I must kill him," he breathed through gritted teeth.

172

"No," she said firmly.

He knew she had defeated him. He could have knocked her aside easily enough but he knew he would not do that. She had laid herself open to him and he had stayed his hand. He had lost his chance. Now she knew he was flesh and blood. He felt that blood pumping in his temple, throbbing as his resolve faded and the exertions of the night caught up with him.

"Venutius is a cowardly, treacherous dog," he told her. "You do not need him."

"Not the way you mean," she said. "But I still need him."

He felt his knees trembling, threatening to collapse beneath him. Steeling himself, he sought for arguments that would overcome her but he could think of nothing that would sway her.

"This is not over," he said weakly.

"Yes it is," she replied. "You cannot stay here. But I do not wish to see you killed. For the sake of what once passed between us, I would rather that you lived."

"Live where?" The words escaped his throat like a strangled sob.

"You should go back to the west, to where you can fight your pointless war."

He closed his eyes for a moment. When he opened them, he whispered, "Tell your worthless husband that I will kill him one day. That is a promise."

"But not today?" she asked.

"Not today."

She gave an almost imperceptible nod. Then she said, "In that case, there is one more thing I can do for you." She held out a hand to Garathus. Snapping her fingers. "Give me the coin," she ordered.

Garathus delved in his belt pouch, pulling out a gold coin on a thin cord which he placed in Cartimandua's hand.

Speaking in a loud voice, she said, "This is the feast of Lughnasa. No man may be killed during the feast. But I give you this as payment for what I did to your brother."

Calgacus stared at the gold coin that she pressed into his palm. It was the twin of the one he wore around his own neck. A thought came to him as he tucked it into his own pouch.

"Give me my brother's sword," he said under his breath.

"Do not be greedy, Calgacus," she replied softly. "Take the

173

coin and go, before Venutius recovers his wits and sends men after you."

He looked into her eyes and almost lost himself. "I wish . . ." Her lips twitched in a faint smile. "So do I. If things had been different, who knows?"

"I will not see you again," he said. "I will go back to join people who will fight the Romans, not surrender to them."

"That is probably for the best," she said. "Go now. But be warned; if you return to Brigantia, I will have you killed."

He thought for a moment that he had misheard or that she was joking but he saw that she was deadly serious.

"You and your brother betrayed me," she explained. "I cannot forget that. And I cannot allow you to kill Venutius. Do not return to Brigantia, Calgacus."

"I hope you get what you deserve from your marriage," he told her angrily.

Her expression was hard, unforgiving. "Then we understand each other," she said.

Calgacus shook his head. "I don't think I will ever understand you," he said.

Sword in hand, he swung away, stepping out through the doors, turning his back on her and walking away into the night.

Chapter XVII

"Where do we go now?" Runt asked when they returned to the copse where they had left their horses.

Calgacus, who had not spoken since leaving Cartimandua's hall, said, "We go west."

"We could go north," Runt suggested hopefully.

Calgacus stopped, regarding his friend curiously. "North?"

Runt seemed faintly embarrassed at having made the suggestion but he explained, "There are tribes beyond the Brigantes. We would be far away from the Romans and there are bound to be some chieftains who would welcome a couple of warriors." He shrugged. "It's an option, Cal. Most people think we are dead, so why go back to the Silures?"

"Because I must," Calgacus said. "I am the King of the Catuvellauni now. Caratacus' coin has passed to me. I must continue the fight."

"You may be the king, but you have no tribe and no land."

"I have you."

Runt gave a soft, wry laugh. "Do you really think the two of us can beat the Romans?"

Calgacus reply was instant and decisive. "Yes. I know how to do it, Liscus. I can beat them. I know I can. Once we raise an army, I will prove it."

Runt regarded him thoughtfully for a moment. "All right," he said. "We'll go west. But we'd better move quickly. Venutius will be after us. He was trying to get close while you were talking to Cartimandua."

Calgacus frowned. "I didn't see him."

"You never see anything when she's in front of you," Runt said. "He was creeping round the side of the hall. I don't know how much he heard. He stopped when he noticed that I'd seen him."

"Then you are right. We had better get away from here," Calgacus said with a grimace. He heaved himself up into the saddle, settling between the comforting security of the high pommels. He wiped his brow, feeling the damp clamminess of sweat.

"Come on," he said. "There is nothing here for us."

They rode south and west, avoiding Roman patrols, stealthily skirting even the smallest settlement. After three days, they reached the River Deva which marked the limit of the Roman province. Stripping naked to swim alongside the horses, they crossed into the land of the Deceangli.

"Where to now?" Runt asked.

"Let's find Vosegus," Calgacus replied, naming the King of the Deceangli.

"Do you think he's still alive? He was pretty badly injured when we saw him at Caer Caradoc."

"I hope he is. I only met him a couple of times, but I liked him. He's a tough character. He won't surrender to Rome without a fight."

Now that they were out of Roman territory, they made faster time, reaching Vosegus' home within two days. It was a small place, a collection of roundhouses set in a wide, heavily wooded plain near the coast, home to the King of the Deceangli and a handful of his warriors. Vosegus, who had fled from the disastrous battle at Caer Caradoc with blood streaming from a wound in his side, was still bed-ridden when they found him. His family fussed around him but Vosegus barked at them to leave him in peace so that he could speak to his visitors in private.

"This wound is taking a long time to heal," he informed them. "But I'll be up soon enough." He gave Calgacus a sharp look. "What happened to Caratacus?" he asked. "I heard he got away from Caer Caradoc but that's all I know."

Calgacus briefly related how Cartimandua had refused to help and had handed Caratacus to the Romans. Vosegus swore bitterly when he heard the story.

"Bloody woman!" he said. "You never could trust the Brigantes but I didn't think she'd go that far. Caratacus was our best hope."

"Yes, but now that he is gone, I will do what must be done."

Vosegus studied him thoughtfully. "It will be hard to follow in the footsteps of a man like your brother," he said cautiously.

"Especially for one so young."

"I can do it," Calgacus asserted.

Vosegus remained unconvinced. "How? I know you can fight, but can you be a War Leader?"

Calgacus responded with a question of his own. "Will you continue to fight?"

Lying propped up on his bed, Vosegus eyed Calgacus carefully, clearly trying to evaluate how much he could trust him. "I have no wish to submit to Rome," he said. "But the Deceangli cannot stand alone."

"You won't be alone," Calgacus assured him. "I will raise the Silures. They will draw the Romans away from you. All I need is for you to keep enough pressure on the enemy so that they leave some troops in the north. If you tie them down by making small raids, they won't be able to concentrate their whole army against us in the south."

"That makes sense," Vosegus said thoughtfully. "What about the Ordovices? They are the most numerous tribe."

"I will speak to Cadwallon, but I don't expect much from him. He has no stomach for war, I think the best we can hope for is that he does not surrender to Rome."

"He's a frightened old woman," Vosegus said bitterly. "But some of his warriors may join us."

"Perhaps. But Cadwallon can still help us. He can supply food and weapons, and allow us to send messengers through his territory."

"I suppose he might agree to that," Vosegus said doubtfully. "But I wouldn't count on it."

"I can make sure he helps us," Calgacus said.

Both Vosegus and Runt looked at him in surprise. "How can you do that?" the Deceangli King asked.

"The druids will persuade him. Once I convince them to back me."

"You are going to Ynis Mon?"

"That's right. If I get the support of the Druid Council, all the free tribes will follow me."

Under his breath, Runt muttered, "By Toutatis, Cal!"

Vosegus said, "You've got balls, lad, I'll say that for you. There are not many who come back from Ynis Mon."

"I will come back," Calgacus vowed.

177

Ynis Mon, the sacred island, home of the druids, lay off the north-west coast of the western lands, separated from the mainland by a narrow strait. The island was large, almost a small kingdom in its own right. It had fertile fields and meadows, producing vast quantities of grain, herds of fat cattle, and huge flocks of sheep. It was also dotted with marshes, sacred pools and lakes where offerings were cast to beseech favours from the Gods. All across the island were groves of trees where the druids practised their rites and taught the lore to those chosen for a druid's life. For, above all, Ynis Mon produced druids. Here they lived and learned. Ynis Mon was the seat of their power, a place where only druids were welcome.

Calgacus and Runt were rowed across the choppy water, stepping out onto a sandy beach before trudging up to the grassy foreshore where a druid stood watching them with unfriendly eyes. Calgacus forced himself to appear outwardly calm as he walked up to the man. This was the first time he had been to Ynis Mon. According to Runt, it was likely to be his last.

"You don't need to come," Calgacus had told his friend.

"You know I won't let you go on your own," Runt said. "But this is a dangerous place, Cal. You've always said you never wanted to set foot here."

"I know. But things change. Myrddin was right. We need their help. And they need us."

He had tried to appear confident but as he clambered up from the beach towards the lone druid, he felt his heart beating faster. Ynis Mon was a place of dark mysteries, a place where few outsiders were ever welcomed.

A grim smile came to his face as he recalled how, if the Romans had not come to the lands of the Pritani, he would have spent his adult life on this island, learning how to become a druid. His escape from that fate was the only good that had come from the Romans' invasion.

The waiting druid frowned at the two warriors as they climbed up from the beach. The man, wearing an ankle-length druid's robe, was in his forties with a long, flowing beard and brown hair that fluttered in the sea breeze. He stood erect, his shoulders back, a long staff, taller than he was himself, held in his left hand. The dark wood of the staff was carved with circles and swirling lines.

178

Its curved top was fashioned in the shape of a dragon's head.

Calgacus noticed the staff but ignored it. His time with Myrddin had taught him to look at things critically, to see things for what they were. He had also heard Cethinos talk of the power of symbols. He recognised the staff for what it was; a device to frighten the uninitiated. The druid wielded it like a weapon of great power but Calgacus told himself it was merely a piece of shaped wood.

Drawing himself up to his full height, he confronted the druid. He told himself that he was a king. It was time to act like one.

"I need to speak to the Druid Council," he said gruffly.

"That is not possible," the man replied, giving Calgacus a haughty look.

"Then make it possible. I am Calgacus, son of Cunobelinos, brother of Caratacus."

The druid's expression of superiority was replaced by one of bemused uncertainty. "I do not know whether the Council will see you," he said.

Calgacus gave him a humourless smile. "Then find someone who does know. Or I will go back across the water and leave this place to the mercy of the Romans. Then you can explain to the Council why I left."

The druid flinched in the face of Calgacus' cold anger. This was not how visitors to Ynis Mon usually behaved. They normally came full of fearful respect, seeking favours. Most of them were permitted to go no further than the beach. Yet this tall, dark-haired warrior came with arrogant demands, expecting to be obeyed. The druid considered trying to face the man down and sending him away. He had done such things before to those who did not show proper respect. But the news of the disaster at Caer Caradoc and the subsequent capture of Caratacus was on everyone's lips and he knew that, as much as he would like to, he could not simply refuse Calgacus. After a moment's thought, he nodded. "Come with me."

It was a long, silent walk across the island, following narrow paths that wound through lush meadows. Small farmsteads dotted the landscape, slaves worked in the fields, gathering the harvest, while great herds of cattle grazed the meadows.

In other places the land was uncultivated, wild and rocky, or heavily wooded. From time to time they saw druids, sometimes accompanied by one or two young men or women, presumably students.

The two warriors received a few curious looks, but nobody spoke to them. Calgacus was glad of that. It had taken all his determination to bluster the druid into submission. Despite his determination to act like a king and War Leader, Ynis Mon still exerted an influence, still filled him with a sense of awe and wonder. For as long as he could remember, he had been taught that this place was special, that it was a holy place where ordinary men could not go. Whatever thoughts Myrddin had released in him, those teachings ran deep. In his mind, the very ground beneath his feet seemed alive with magic, pulsating with a power that was more than human. On Ynis Mon, it was possible to believe that the Gods truly walked the earth.

Fortunately, the long walk gave Calgacus time to grow accustomed to his surroundings and to steel himself for the tests that undoubtedly lay ahead. That initial encounter at the beach had given him confidence and reminded him that a. king should speak as if he expected to be obeyed. He had grown up among kings and War Leaders and had seen how they acted. He knew he must adopt that same behaviour, must act as if he were entitled to be here. Above all, he must not allow his inherent sense of reverence for this sacred place to prevent him doing what he must do or saying what he must say. He could not afford to let the druids, or Ynis Mon itself, intimidate him.

After more than three hours of walking, they reached a woodland, where they followed a winding trail that eventually led to a small village set in a wide clearing. Their guide called over a young woman.

To Calgacus he said, "This slave will show you to a house where you may wait. I will inform the Druid Council of your arrival." It was the first time he had spoken to them since they had left the beach.

The slave led them to a small roundhouse. It was clean and well-maintained but sparse in furniture. There was a pile of furs and knitted blankets over several mattresses stuffed with straw or bracken, and there were four small, three-legged stools arranged around the hearth stones. Kindling and blocks of peat lay within the hearth but there was no fire. There were no tools, no storage chests, no clay oven for baking, no loom for weaving wool, no quern stones or cooking pots. It struck Calgacus as an empty and soulless shell.

Soon, though, the slave returned, bearing hot embers in a clay pot. Carefully, she placed the glowing embers in the hearth. The kindling began to smoke, then a small hint of flame appeared. The slave knelt to blow on the embryonic fire until the kindling was well alight. Soon, the earthy aroma of burning peat began to permeate the emptiness of the house. Again, though, the woman said nothing, leaving without so much as meeting their gaze. When she returned a second time, she brought some welcome food and water.

"Thank you," Runt said. "What is your name?"

The woman shook her head and hurried out.

"Not very talkative," Runt said. "Quite pretty, though."

"Don't even think about it," Calgacus warned.

"It would take my mind off thinking about what they might do to us," Runt told him.

"Relax. We are here now." Calgacus gestured towards the food. "We may as well eat."

They scarcely had time to begin eating before the door was pushed open. Calgacus looked up to see the gaunt figure of Cethinos standing in the doorway.

The druid's thin lips twitched. "I was told you were dead," he said icily, as if Calgacus' survival was an irritating inconvenience.

Calgacus remained seated on his stool. He should not have been surprised to see Cethinos here but the druid's sudden appearance had startled him. He hid his dismay by biting off a chunk of dark bread and chewing slowly. Then he looked up at Cethinos.

"I was dead," he said through a mouthful of bread. "I went to the Underworld but I was allowed to return. It is my task to complete the work begun by my brothers. I have come here to claim the position of War Leader of the free tribes."

He swallowed the bread, hoping that chewing it had helped conceal any trace of the lie. Tell a lie convincingly, Myrddin had told him, as if you believe it yourself. He had done his best but Cethinos was a druid, trained to read people. Calgacus took another bite of bread, feigning indifference to whatever Cethinos might say.

The druid surprised him. Instead of challenging Calgacus' story, he turned his attention to Runt, asking sharply, "Is this true?"

Runt squirmed under the druid's harsh, interrogatory stare but he managed to nod his head and say, "I saw it. He was gone from the world of light, into the Underworld. Then he returned."

"Swear it!" Cethinos snapped.

Calgacus thought that Runt's resolve would collapse under the old druid's intimidating glare. His friend had always been afraid of the old man. But Runt had learned from Myrddin, too. He swallowed, placed his hand on his heart and said, "I swear before Toutatis that what I have said is true. I saw it."

Cethinos frowned. He studied them closely, his eyes flicking from one to the other as if he were trying to find some proof that they were lying. Calgacus felt the old, familiar tingle of fear sweeping through him. Cethinos had haunted his days ever since he had been a young boy. He had escaped the druid's clutches on that fateful day when Caratacus had brought word of Togodumnus' death and when Beatha had been abandoned to her fate. He had escaped, but he had not forgotten. He knew his man, and recognised that the menace in Cethinos' eyes was very real.

The awful silence dragged on. Calgacus was tempted to say something, to fill the unsettling void, but he knew that was what Cethinos wanted. The old man was waiting for him to betray himself by saying too much. Cethinos had done that often enough when Calgacus was a boy. This time, he refused to accept the bait. He bit another chunk of bread and said nothing.

Eventually, Cethinos said brusquely, "I will tell the Druid Council. You will be sent for."

He turned, ducking out through the entranceway and pulling the door shut behind him. Calgacus immediately put a finger to his lips, signalling to Runt to say nothing in case Cethinos had waited outside the door in the hope of overhearing something. Runt closed his eyes, muttering soft prayers.

Calgacus took his gold coin from under his shirt, closing his fist around it, hoping that it would act as a talisman to protect them from whatever Cethinos and the Druid Council had in store.

"Thank you, Liscus," he said softly.

Runt could only nod his head as he sagged with relief. He buried his face in his hands as if he expected Toutatis to strike him down for swearing a false oath. It took him a long time to recover his usual composure.

The afternoon passed with frustrating slowness. Eventually, another druid arrived. He was younger than the others they had seen, perhaps little more than thirty years old, with a beard that was a dirty brown rather than grey. With a curt demand for them to leave their weapons behind, he ordered them to follow him.

He led them out of the small woodland village, following a wide, well-trodden pathway between the trees. The woods were thick here, the trees crowded together, ancient trunks festooned by tangled growths of ivy and smeared by patches of moss. The branches above their heads were so dense that the afternoon sunlight barely penetrated them. It was as if the druid was leading them down a long, dark tunnel.

After about fifty paces, the path widened into a small, shadow-filled clearing. The druid walked unhesitatingly to the far side, towards a gateway the like of which Calgacus had never seen before.

A wooden archway, wide enough for two men to walk abreast, towered over their heads, its thick posts decorated with carved images of skulls. Calgacus hesitated as they approached. He heard Runt, half a pace behind him, swearing softly.

"You must go in here," the druid intoned, one hand motioning towards the dark entrance that seemed to lead into nothing but gloom.

Calgacus' eyes were drawn to the skulls. They are only symbols, he told himself. They are there to frighten you. He knew this, but still he could not ignore the brooding menace of the gateway. The trees that loomed dark and damp on either side only served to add to his sense of apprehension.

"The Druid Council awaits you," their guide said, his voice impatient.

Calgacus took a deep breath. Instinctively, he felt for the gold coin under his jerkin and shirt. Through the leather and wool he could feel its round solidity. Recalling the fateful step he had taken when he had entered the Cave of the Wind, he stepped through the arch.

The path turned almost immediately, opening out into a small, secluded clearing. The grass was dark and thick, the small oval of the grove entirely shadowed by a roof formed by the interlocking branches of the massive trees that stood all around them. In the centre of the small bowl of the glade was a large, flat stone, its roughly oval shape matching the grove around it. Nearly smooth on its upper surface, it had ragged, irregular, uncarved edges. It was supported on two massive rocks. As Calgacus approached, he saw that the surface of the stone was stained dark by streaks of long-dried blood. He heard Runt whisper a supplication to Toutatis, but he ignored the altar stone. It was, he told himself, like the druid's dragon staff, like the skulls on the dark portal, a symbol designed to frighten them. Whatever happened in this place, he could not permit himself to be frightened.

Nine druids waited at the far end of the tiny glade. Three were sitting on high-backed chairs. Three more stood on either side of the seated men. Three, the number of power, the mystic, indivisible number. Tellingly, the Druid Council comprised three times three. Another symbol, Calgacus thought. Ynis Mon reeked of symbols.

Calgacus scanned the waiting men and saw that Cethinos was standing at the end of the group to his right, his thin face set in a permanent scowl. After a first glance, Calgacus made a point of not looking at him. His former teacher may have achieved his ambition of joining the Druid Council but Calgacus refused to acknowledge him.

The druid who sat in the centre was a very old man, his skin wrinkled and blotched, his limbs thin. But his hair and beard were full and his eyes were alert, shining with intelligence.

"I am Maddoc," he said in a surprisingly strong voice. "Head of the Druid Council. Welcome to Ynis Mon, Calgacus, son of Cunobelinos."

Calgacus bowed his head briefly, acknowledging them but refusing to be deferential. He needed to be strong; to act like a King.

"I thank the Council for meeting with me," he said. He thought his voice sounded weak, as if the air in the grove had sucked all the confidence out of his words.

Maddoc replied, "We are told that you claim to have been returned to the land of the living. That you were in Dis's realm but were sent back. Is this true?"

"Yes." He almost believed it himself now. And it was not wholly a lie. When he had stepped into the Cave of the Wind, he had genuinely believed it was an entrance to Dis's realm. Still, he forced himself to keep his hands at his sides, to make no attempt to touch his face in case the nine old men detected his falsehood.

He expected Maddoc to question him about the Underworld but the old druid asked, "To what purpose? Why should Dis permit you to return?"

"Because I know that I can defeat the Romans. That is the task the Gods have given me."

"There are those who have claimed that before now," Maddoc said, although not in an unfriendly way. "Your brother was one."

"My brother made a mistake, by his own admission. I will not make the same mistake. We cannot fight the Romans the old way. We must fight on our terms. I know that I can do this. I intend to return to the Silures but I need the support of other tribes. For this, I ask your help. I have already spoken to Vosegus of the Deceangli. He assures me that he will fight on. I will go to Cadwallon next."

"You presume much," Maddoc said. "By what right do you claim to lead the war?"

"Because I am the last of the sons of Cunobelinos," Calgacus said. He paused, making sure he had their attention, then made his last roll of the dice. "I am the only one who can keep the Romans from marching all the way here and destroying everything on this island. If you wish to stop them, you must trust me. There is nobody else who can do this."

"You can prevent the Romans from coming here?" Maddoc asked. "How?"

"By stirring up the Silures. If we create enough trouble in the south, the Romans will not attack in the north. They will be too busy fighting us. Then we will lure them into the hills and destroy them."

There was no reaction from the druids. They sat or stood, stone-faced and immobile, watching him with unreadable eyes.

In a voice that sounded completely reasonable, Maddoc said, "There are those among us who believe that the best way to ensure the Romans are defeated is to make a sacrifice of royal blood."

Calgacus could not prevent himself looking at Cethinos. The old druid stared back implacably. Turning back to Maddoc, Calgacus asked, "You mean me?"

Maddoc nodded, his expression calm. "The greater the sacrifice, the more chance there is of the Gods answering our prayers. We often ask people to give up their most prized

185

possessions for purposes that are far less important than the safety of all the free tribes. A sacrifice of royal blood, offering one of our finest warriors, a son of the great Cunobelinos, would surely be effective."

Calgacus ignored the sharp exhalation from Runt as he fought down his own panic. An image of himself lying on the grove's altar stone filled his mind, driving all other thoughts away. He closed his eyes, telling himself to remain calm. He must not allow himself to be terrified into dumb inaction. He knew he must answer this threat.

Speaking as calmly as he could, he said, "The Gods must be honoured. Everybody knows that. But we have made many sacrifices and none have worked."

"We have not yet sacrificed anyone of royal blood," Maddoc said firmly.

"But if you shed my life, I will not be able to lead the war against Rome. I am more use to you alive than dead. To sacrifice me would go against the wishes of Father Dis himself. That is why I was sent back."

A shadow of a smile crossed Maddoc's face, as if he approved of Calgacus' answer. He said, "We will deliberate on what you have said. Return to the house that has been set aside for you. You will be sent for."

Calgacus wanted to say more but he knew he would only be repeating his arguments. He had done all he could. Maddoc's faint smile gave him hope that it had been enough. Signalling to Runt to follow, he left the glade with trembling knees, returning to the roundhouse as quickly as he could.

"By Toutatis, Cal," Runt gasped. "I nearly wet myself when we went in there."

"Me too."

"You could have fooled me. You were as cool as ice. But Cethinos wants your blood. A royal sacrifice!" He shook his head. "We should not have come here."

"Cethinos won't get my life. Maddoc knows he needs me."

"I hope you are right. But what if you are wrong?"

"I'm not wrong."

"I know, but what if you are?"

"I suppose we will find out soon enough."

It was dark by the time they were called back to the glade. Nothing had changed except that burning torches had been lit, set in brackets atop short stakes around the perimeter of the glade. Other than that, everything was the same. Even the nine men sat or stood in identical positions, as if they had never moved.

Calgacus had thought he could not possibly feel any more anxious than when he had first set foot in this dark place but he was wrong. Cold sweat prickled on his back and his mouth felt as if he had chewed cold ashes from a dead hearth. The threat of being sacrificed felt very real indeed. He dared not look at the blood-stained altar stone.

With his heart racing, he stood in front of the Druid Council, trying to read their decision in their faces.

Maddoc gazed up at him. Without preamble, he said, "It is agreed that you may return to the Silures to lead the war. We will send word to the other tribal leaders, especially Cadwallon of the Ordovices, that we expect them to support you."

Calgacus could not help exhaling loudly with undisguised relief but Maddoc held up a warning hand.

"There is a price," the druid said.

"What price?" Calgacus asked, feeling his heart sink once more.

"First, to show your commitment is true, you must offer up the most precious possession you have."

Calgacus was caught off guard. "I have nothing of any value," he said.

Maddoc said, "You have a gold coin of Cunobelinos, do you not? A precious heirloom."

Of its own volition, Calgacus' hand moved to his throat. "Yes," he said, his eyes flicking to Cethinos, who bared his teeth in a grim smile, telling Calgacus that he had informed Maddoc of the coin's meaning.

"You will give it to me," Maddoc commanded. "It will be cast into one of the sacred pools as an offering."

The old druid held out his hand, palm upwards, refusing all negotiation.

Reluctantly, Calgacus tugged out the coin from under his shirt. He looped the cord over his head, then placed his talisman in Maddoc's waiting hand. Maddoc closed his fingers around the shining gold, barely glancing at the coin.

"Very good," the old man said. "Now, the second condition of our support for you." He paused, his brown eyes staring into Calgacus' face. "You have until midwinter after next to achieve a great victory. Do you understand? You have what is left of this year and all of next year. If you have not delivered the great victory we require by then, if you have not shown yourself worthy of being a War Leader, you will be brought back here so that your life may be offered to the Gods."

Among the druids, only Cethinos showed any emotion. When Calgacus looked at him, the druid's mouth split in a feral grin of triumph.

Chapter XVIII

With Vellocatus in tow, Venutius walked to the roundhouse that had recently housed Caratacus and his warriors. It was now home to some new arrivals. He rapped a hand on the door and pushed his way inside.

There were six men in the house, all big, brawny warriors, their arms decorated by tattoos of eagles, bears or horses. They looked round angrily when Venutius strode into the house but relaxed when they saw who it was. Most of them returned to the hot food they were spooning into their mouths, but one man, a stocky, thick-waisted character of medium height but broad in the shoulder and with arms as thick as small trees, put his platter down and stood, extending a meaty hand. He gave a smile that revealed a mouth of crooked, yellowing teeth. His nose was squashed and misshapen, remnant of a long-forgotten fight and his eyes were small and furtive.

"Hello, Cousin," he said, his voice coarse and grating.

"Welcome, Segomou. I am glad you got here at last," Venutius said, clasping the man's hairy forearm. "I have a job for you."

Segomou frowned. "We only just got here," he growled.

"It is important, Cousin," Venutius said. "You will be well rewarded. When you return, I will see that you are given land and many head of cattle."

"Gold and women would be preferable," Segomou said.

Venutius shrugged. "As you wish." He signalled to Vellocatus who handed Segomou a small bag that clinked with the unmistakeable sound of coins. Venutius said, "Roman silver. Take it as part of the payment."

Segomou weighed the bag appreciatively. "So, who do you want killed?" he asked. Behind him, his men chuckled.

Venutius replied, "His name is Calgacus. He is a Catuvellauni."

Segomou's brow wrinkled as he scratched at his stubbled chin. "I know that name," he said.

"He is the brother of Caratacus."

"I thought it sounded familiar," Segomou said, adding without hesitation, "Where do I find him?"

"You will need to track him. That is why you must go as soon as possible. He left here three days ago, heading west. I believe he intends to join the Silures."

"That's a long way," Segomou observed. "It's not easy to track a man after so long. And we'll need to cross Roman lands. That will make it harder."

"You will catch him eventually. He is not a man who hides. He will proclaim his presence everywhere he goes."

Segomou shrugged. "All right. We find him, we kill him. Anything else?"

"Bring me his head." Venutius cast a sidelong look at Vellocatus. "I thought he was dead once before but he has an annoying habit of surviving."

"No problem. What else can you tell me about him?"

"He is a big man; very big, with black hair. He wears a southern-style moustache. He is also a formidable warrior. You will need to take care."

"I always do," Segomou said with a sly grin. "No matter how good he is, he won't be able to stop a knife in the back."

"His shield-bearer is a small man," Venutius said. "He is dangerous too. If you can, kill him as well. He is the sort who would come seeking revenge if you leave him alive. Killing him will save any complications later."

"Do you want his head brought back too?" Segomou enquired.

"No. And I don't want Cartimandua to see Calgacus' head, either. His death must remain a matter between you and I."

Segomou gave a throaty chuckle. "How is your new bride anyway?" he asked. "I only got a brief look at her but she's a pretty one."

"She is," Venutius agreed.

"So when do you want her—"

Venutius held up a warning hand. "Not for a while yet," he said.

"Suit yourself," Segomou shrugged.

"So can you leave in the morning?" Venutius asked.

Segomou rubbed at his chin. "I suppose so. Can you send some women over? We could do with some company tonight if we are to leave so soon."

"I'll see what I can do. But you must not harm them."

"We wouldn't do that, would we lads?" Segomou laughed.

"Then I wish you good hunting," said Venutius. "Make sure Calgacus dies."

"Have no fears, Cousin," Segomou said. "He's as good as dead already. Just make sure you send those women over here tonight."

Venutius nodded and left as quickly as he could.

As they walked back towards Cartimandua's hall, Vellocatus said, "I know he is your cousin, Lord, but I do not trust him."

"Neither do I," Venutius admitted. "One day I will have to have him killed, but for the moment he is useful. We can trust him in this, though."

"I hope you are right, Lord."

Venutius laughed. "You know that looks can be deceptive, Vellocatus?"

"Yes, Lord."

"Well, with Segomou they are not. He looks like a brute and he is one. Did you notice that he did not even ask why I want Calgacus dead?"

Vellocatus nodded, although the truth was that he had missed that. "Yes, Lord."

Venutius said, "That is because he does not care. Segomou enjoys killing people. For him, hunting men is no different to hunting boar or deer. He does it because he enjoys the chase and he likes killing. That is why I can trust him to dispose of Calgacus."

"I hope he succeeds," Vellocatus said fervently. "I do not like the thought of a man like Calgacus remaining alive, however far away he may be. One day, he will come for us."

"You need not worry. Segomou never fails." Venutius paused before adding softly, "Now hold your tongue. There is Cartimandua."

The Queen had left the hall, intending to retire to her private dwelling, the house she now shared with Venutius, but she stopped when she saw the two men crossing the open space towards the great doors.

"Have you spoken to your cousin?" she asked in a disapproving tone.

Venutius treated her to a smile of innocence. "I have. I told

191

him he must leave tomorrow."

"Good, I do not like the look of him."

Venutius feigned indifference. "He is not all bad," he said lightly. "But he is greedy. I expect he will return from time to time, seeking favours."

"Just keep him away from me," Cartimandua said firmly. "If he does come back, he had better not cause any trouble or I will see his ugly head removed from his shoulders."

"Don't worry, my love," Venutius said soothingly. "He will leave in the morning."

Segomou and his five followers rode out of Isuria early the following day. They rode with swords at their sides, shields on their backs and long spears in their hands. Most of them wore thick, leather jerkins but Segomou wore a battered coat of chainmail over his clothing. Their horses were laden with sacks of food, and water skins hung from the rear pommels of their saddles. They were prepared for a long journey.

The first part was slow and dangerous. To reach the Deva, they needed to cross Roman-held territory. Cavalry patrols roamed the land and foot soldiers were still hunting rebels among the recently-conquered Cornovii. Work parties were building roads or constructing wooden forts and watchtowers. Avoiding them was not easy but Segomou and his men were well versed in travelling unseen. Once or twice Segomou was tempted to raid a small column of supply wagons but these were usually well guarded so he resisted the lure of plunder and kept moving west.

Once across the Deva, the hunt began in earnest. Segomou soon learned that Venutius was correct. Everywhere he stopped, people had heard of Calgacus, Some had seen him pass only a few days earlier. The trail led him to the home of Vosegus, King of the Deceangli.

"What do you want with Calgacus?" Vosegus asked when they found him. He was sitting at the door of his roundhouse, wrapped in a thick cloak despite the summer warmth. When he moved, his face contorted with pain from a serious wound in his side.

Segomou replied, "We heard he was looking for warriors to join him."

"You are Brigantes?"

"Aye, but not all Brigantes agree with what the Queen did to

192

Caratacus. We decided we would like to see some real fighting."

Vosegus nodded, his eyes taking in the array of weapons, the rough, easy brutality of the six horsemen. He said, "He passed this way. He said he was going to join the Silures."

"How long ago was that?" Segomou asked.

"Three days."

Segomou nodded. "Then we had best move on," he said. "My thanks to you."

The six Brigantes turned south, away from the coastal plains, into the high, rugged hills.

"We should have stayed the night there," one of the men, a balding thug named Narcollus, said to Segomou.

"No. He didn't trust us. And there were too many warriors around for us to have any sport. We'll find easier pickings in the mountain villages."

Segomou's prediction was correct. That evening they found a small settlement, no more than half a dozen homes perched on a hillside. The village had a ditch and stockade but there were not enough men to offer resistance to Segomou's heavily armed war band. Unable to send the riders away, the villagers invited them in, fearfully offering food and shelter. Once inside, Segomou demanded women and these, too were offered, or offered themselves, to ward off the unspoken but very evident threat of violence.

The small war band repeated their tactic for three more nights, always selecting isolated places where there were few people, using threats to take whatever they wanted. They replenished their supplies and helped themselves to any valuables that took their fancy. When anyone objected, swords were drawn.

"We could take some of the women with us," Narcollus suggested.

"No," Segomou told him. "Maybe once the job is done, but not until then. They'd only slow us down."

Narcollus' heavy brow furrowed. "If the job gets done," he said. "We've lost his trail. Nobody's seen him at any of the places we've stopped. Maybe that fellow Vosegus lied to us."

Segomou shook his head. "Venutius said the same thing. Calgacus is going south, to the Silures. There are a thousand routes he could have followed. We'll find him sooner or later."

They continued southwards, stopping briefly at a high,

193

mountain fort which was surrounded by multiple ditches, enclosing many roundhouses. This, they learned, was the home of Cadwallon, King of the Ordovices. There were too many armed men for Segomou to feel comfortable about staying long, but he asked whether anyone had seen a man named Calgacus recently.

"No," Cadwallon replied. "He has not been here."

Segomou thought the man looked nervous at the mention of Calgacus' name, but his response was not what the Brigante assassin had expected. A man like Calgacus would surely have visited an important chieftain, even a portly, timid king like Cadwallon. The fact that he had not come this way was disturbing.

Making hasty excuses, Segomou left Cadwallon's mountain fortress. For the remainder of the day he was in a thoughtful mood. A few more days' easy travel would take them to the hill country of the Silures but there was still no trace of Calgacus. It was as if the man had vanished from the face of the earth.

That night, Segomou's spirits were raised when they found an isolated farmstead in a long, mountain valley. The farmer was a young man, barely twenty years old, with a pretty wife and two baby girls.

"We need shelter for the night," Segomou told the farmer.

The young man had fetched a spear from his home and stood protectively in front of the door while his wife stood behind him, her face pale and tense. She held one of her daughters in her arms while the other clung to her skirts.

"We have no room for so many," the farmer said nervously.

Segomou laughed, He dismounted, walking towards the farmer. "I was not asking," he said, "I was telling."

"We have nothing here," the farmer said, his voice rising with fear. "We can barely feed ourselves. You should move on."

"We'll stay," Segomou said as he advanced on the young man, drawing his sword.

The farmer waved his spear, trying to ward him off but Segomou swung his sword, using it to knock the spear aside. The farmer's wife screamed as Segomou backhanded the blade, taking the young man in the face. The farmer staggered back, blood spraying from his shattered skull. Segomou hacked again, cutting into his chest. He yanked the blade free, leaving the man lying on the ground, moaning softly, blood frothing from his hideous wounds.

194

The woman ran inside the house but there was no safety there. Segomou's men leaped down from their horses to follow him inside as he pursued the young woman. She screamed hysterically as he dragged her children from her. The two girls, the eldest only two years old, were carried outside while their mother was pinioned in Narcollus' powerful grip.

Segomou grabbed at her dress, ripping it from her, revealing her body.

"I'd advise you not to struggle," he told her. "It will only make things worse for you."

The woman screamed again. Tears ran down her face as she called for her children. She kicked and pushed, frantic to escape but Narcollus held her firmly.

Segomou punched the side of the woman's head, stunning her. When she opened her dazed eyes, she saw the men who had taken her daughters come back into the house, their daggers dark with blood.

She did not scream. She had no more screams left. She sagged helplessly, knowing that what remained of her life would be short and brutal. She did not care. There was nothing left for her to live for.

Segomou unbuckled his belt, letting his sword drop to the ground. Then he began tugging his long coat of chainmail over his head.

"Me first, lads," he said. "But don't worry. We have all night. You'll all get a turn."

Narcollus pushed the woman to the ground while Segomou loosened his trousers. He laughed. The search for Calgacus could wait until morning. They would find him eventually. Until then, Segomou wanted to make this trip worth his while.

195

Chapter XIX

It was too late in the evening for Calgacus and Runt to return to the mainland, so they were compelled to spend the night in the small house on Ynis Mon. The same slave woman they had seen before brought them more food and a pitcher of beer but she silently waved off Runt's invitation to spend the night with him.

"Don't you ever think about anything else?" Calgacus asked.

"I think I need some fun after today," Runt said.

"Well, you must be losing your touch. She turned you down flat."

"That's the least of our worries. Were you listening to the condition they put on you? By Toutatis, Cal, they're determined to put you on that altar stone. I bet it was Cethinos who persuaded them about that part of the deal."

"I'm sure you are right. But they'll be disappointed. I'll give them their victory."

"You'd better. But I suppose we can always flee to the north if things go wrong."

"I'm sure they have druids in the far north, too," Calgacus said. "If we don't beat the Romans, we won't be safe anywhere."

"That's a cheery thought," Runt grumbled.

Calgacus tried to appear positive. The sentence that Maddoc had pronounced had brought home to him the true price of failure. He tried to dismiss it from his mind, knowing he could not afford to dwell on it. He had witnessed sacrifices more times than he cared to recall. He could not help thinking about them now.

In some ways, being sacrificed on an altar stone was relatively quick. The druids would slit the victim's throat, then cut open his chest and belly to examine the entrails. Cethinos had always maintained that they could read the will of the Gods in what they saw inside a freshly slaughtered victim.

"The intestines, the heart, liver and kidneys reveal much to the trained eye," the druid had once told the young Calgacus. "The innards of a man are much the same as those of a goat or a bull.

They can tell us a great deal."

Calgacus had been sceptical when he was young and remained so now, especially after what old Myrddin had told him. The thought of Cethinos ripping his body open to probe around at his guts made him shiver with revulsion. Yet he suspected that, if they were to sacrifice him, he would suffer the triple death that was reserved for special offerings. He had only witnessed that once and hoped never to see it again.

A victim of the triple death would stand, naked, in a holy place. After he had been ritually cleansed and purified by smoke and water, and drunk some powerful concoction that induced a euphoric, trance-like state, a druid would tighten a garrotte around his neck, squeezing the life from him, choking him. But before he died, a second druid would smash a small club onto his skull, then a third would slash a ceremonial dagger across his throat. His body would then be cast into a sacred lake, a dark cave or a deep marsh while his spirit travelled to the Gods, bearing the hopes and prayers of the people.

Calgacus had seen it done and the knowledge that it might happen to him now hung over him like a dark cloud. At least Maddoc had given him a way to avoid that fate. If he won, if he proved that the Romans could be beaten, if he could drive them back, he would live.

He decided that, if the worst happened, if he failed, he would not resist the druids. The Pritani were taught that there was nothing to fear in death. If he died, he would go to the Underworld where he would meet Togodumnus again. He would see his father, who had been an old, crippled man when Calgacus had been a boy. In Dis's realm, Cunobelinos would be young and strong, as he had been when he had forged the Two Tribes of the Catuvellauni and the Trinovantes into the strongest people on the island. In the Underworld, Calgacus would even meet his mother, who had died when he was too young to remember her. There would be others there to greet him, too. Verran and Beatha, who must have died when the Romans stormed Camulodunon. And Caratacus who, if not already dead, would soon be ritually strangled in a dark, dank dungeon in Rome.

No, he thought, apart from a transitory and fleeting pain, there was nothing to fear in death. Yet, as Myrddin had said, the desire to live outweighed the desire to reap the ephemeral rewards of the afterlife. If death came, he would face it without fear but he would not meekly surrender to Cethinos' desires. He would prove himself. He would show them what he could do. He would fight and he would win.

Runt asked, "Are you all right?"

"I'm fine. We should get some sleep. We'll leave as soon as it's light."

The night passed uneventfully, although Calgacus' mind was too full of images of sacrifice and war to allow him much sleep. But nothing disturbed the dark stillness beyond the walls of the small house. He had half expected to hear the sound of drums and mystic chanting but Ynis Mon was as peaceful as anywhere he had ever been.

In the morning, another young druid accompanied them back to the beach where a small curragh was waiting. The hide-covered, wooden-framed boat was paddled across the strait by two men who lived in the small village that sat on the shore of the mainland opposite the sacred island.

Once safely ashore, they recovered their horses and equipment from the local chieftain. Calgacus paid the man in bronze rings, then prepared to leave. Before fastening his breastplate, he took Caratacus' gold coin from his pouch and hung it around his neck.

"It's just as well Cethinos didn't know about that one," Runt said. "He'll be mightily pissed if he ever finds out you tricked him."

"I didn't trick him. Anyway, this is appropriate. Now I have the coin my father gave to Caratacus. The mantle of leadership falls to me."

"As long as it doesn't fall any further," Runt said glumly.

"Cheer up," Calgacus told him. "We are going to start a war that the Romans will never forget."

They mounted their ponies and set off, leading the string of pack horses behind them as they headed south-east, angling towards the hills. It seemed a long time since they had left Brigantia but they still had a long journey ahead of them before they arrived among the Silures.

The following day, as they were plodding up a narrow hillside track, Runt spotted a lone horseman pursuing them.

"Whoever he is, he's in a hurry," he said.

"Let's wait for him and see what he wants," Calgacus said. As a precaution, he drew his sword, laying it across the front of his saddle.

The rider turned out to be a messenger from Vosegus of the Deceangli. His horse was lathered with sweat, the man himself tired by his long chase.

"I thought I'd catch you sooner," he said. "Vosegus wanted you warned."

"About what?"

"A man named Segomou is looking for you," the messenger recited. "He is of the Brigantes. He has five warriors with him. He said they wanted to join you but Vosegus did not trust him. He sent me to warn you."

Calgacus exchanged a look with Runt, who shrugged.

"I have never heard of this man," he said to the messenger. "But I will watch for him."

"Vosegus told the man you were heading south," the messenger added.

"That explains why he hasn't found us yet. Give Vosegus my thanks for the warning."

The messenger nodded wearily before turning his horse and riding away at a sedate trot.

"I don't like the sound of that," Runt said.

"Me neither. I trust Vosegus' judgement."

"Brigantes," mused Runt. "Venutius, do you think?"

"I wouldn't be surprised. I suppose this Segomou may be genuine, but he may have been sent to kill us. Let's keep our eyes open, but don't forget why we are here. Come on, I want to find Cadwallon."

A light rain was falling as they wended their way through the mountain valleys, seeking Cadwallon. The clouds hung low over the hilltops, sending a steady, persistent drizzle to soak them. When they found Cadwallon's hilltop home, deep in the midst of the mountains, Calgacus was genuinely pleased to see the king, if only to get a chance to dry out.

The King of the Ordovices welcomed them to his home, offering them the warmth of his hearth fire, giving them hot broth and warm, dark bread. They accepted the food gratefully, sitting cross-legged by the fire, surrounded by a gathering of Cadwallon's warriors and advisers.

Despite the apparent warmth of the hospitality, an uncomfortable air of tension hung over the house. They all knew that it was the Ordovices who had been the first to run from the disastrous battle at Caer Caradoc and Calgacus felt that the men were waiting for him to cast their cowardice in their faces. He knew that a wrong word would only inflame the Ordovices' pride, creating more problems. While the memory of Cadwallon's flight still rankled, Calgacus decided it was time to forget the past for the sake of the future.

"I am glad to see you, Cadwallon," he said. "We need to make plans for continuing the fight."

Cadwallon nodded thoughtfully. Realising that Calgacus was not about to make any accusations, he relaxed a little, although the thought of continuing the fight obviously troubled him.

"Where is Caratacus?" the king asked nervously.

"The Romans have him," Calgacus said with undisguised bitterness. "Cartimandua of the Brigantes betrayed him."

That brought angry mutterings and more than a hint of dismay, but Calgacus silenced the men by saying, "That does not mean we are beaten. Caratacus wants us to continue the fight."

"You want us to fight the Romans again?" the King asked. His eyes were wide with surprise and reluctance.

Calgacus shook his head. "I am going to the Silures. The Druid Council has charged me with continuing the war. What I need from you is weapons, horses, food. I need the supplies that will allow me to concentrate on fighting. And I need to know that you are watching the hills in case the Romans try to cut through the mountains."

"You think they might do that?" Cadwallon asked anxiously.

"No. I intend to make sure that they have all their attention turned on the south. But I need to know that someone is guarding my back. Just in case."

Cadwallon managed a weak smile. "So you want swords? Horses? Food?"

"That's right. Can you provide these things?"

"Of course." The King's tone betrayed his relief. Now that he knew he was not being asked to fight, he seemed almost eager to help. As a result, the bargain was quickly struck and nobody's pride was offended. Cadwallon gave them a bed for the night, and a slave girl each to keep them warm.

"The man's a weasel," said Runt in disgust.

"He's scared," Calgacus told him. "He's spent his whole life with the druids close by, telling him what to do. Now he's got the Romans on the other side of him and he's afraid of them. He's caught between the two and he doesn't know which way to turn."

"He'll not fight if the Romans come for him," observed Runt.

"I know. But why should they come through these mountains? That's the hard way. Once we stir things up, they'll come after us."

"That's something to look forward to, then," said Runt.

In the morning, Cadwallon presented them each with a new cloak and some blankets. He also gave Calgacus a fine new sword to replace the old, battered one he had carried at Caer Caradoc.

"It is a very fine gift," Calgacus said as he examined the blade. "Thank you."

"Use it well," Cadwallon told him.

The King wished them well, promising he would send the supplies they needed. Then, almost as an afterthought, he said, "By the way, there was a man here yesterday. He was looking for you."

Calgacus' eyebrows rose. "Does this man have a name?" he asked.

"He said his name was Segomou. He had five warriors with him. He said they wanted to join you."

"So where is he now?"

"He went south," Cadwallon said. "He had heard you were going to the Silures, so he is looking for you there."

Calgacus tried to sound unconcerned. "Well, maybe we will catch up with him soon."

Leaving Cadwallon's village, they followed the trail south, with Calgacus deep in thought as he rode. It was clear that the journey they had made to Ynis Mon meant that Segomou, instead of following them, was ahead of them. He studied the trail carefully, watching for any signs that the mysterious Segomou might be lying in wait.

Later that day, as they passed through a long, narrow valley, they saw a solitary roundhouse nestled at the foot of a steep hill. A small field of stunted barley stalks lay below the house, the crop having been harvested and the stalks left for livestock to graze on.

"Maybe we'll get a bed for the night there," said Calgacus.

"What's that outside the door?" Runt asked.

Calgacus shaded his eyes. "Birds?" he suggested.

201

The unusual sight made them cautious. The nearer they approached, the more Calgacus sensed that something was very wrong. The small farm was too still, too quiet.

As they rode up to the house, a flock of carrion crows scattered noisily, cawing in alarm, wings flapping furiously as they left the bodies they had been feeding on.

"Oh, by Toutatis," Runt groaned. "What has happened?"

"Leave the horses here," Calgacus said, "The blood might spook them."

They dismounted, drawing their swords. Runt fetched Calgacus' shield from a pack horse and handed it to him. Slowly, they walked up to the house.

A man lay on his back outside the door, his chest and face smashed by the unmistakeable cuts of a heavy sword. Flies buzzed around the wounds and crawled over his face. His eyes had been pecked out by the crows, leaving bloody, gaping sockets. Beyond him were two smaller figures, both of them with their throats cut, both bodies gnawed and mutilated by birds and animals.

Calgacus made for the door.

"Be careful, Cal," Runt called softly.

Calgacus' face was grim as he said, "The birds would not have stayed if there was anyone left alive."

He went into the house, knowing what he would find. The young woman, not much more than a girl, lay on her back in a pool of blood. She was naked, her face, arms and legs bruised and cut but she had died because someone had stabbed a dagger into her chest, leaving a ragged open wound between her breasts.

Feeling sick, Calgacus went back outside.

Runt was squatting down, running his fingers across some faint marks on the ground.

"Five, maybe six horses," he said. "Perhaps more."

"Six," Calgacus said.

"Segomou?"

"Who else? It is too much of a coincidence."

"So what do we do?"

"We put the bodies in the house and we burn it. The least we can do is give them some sort of a funeral."

"And then we go after Segomou?"

Calgacus face was hard, his eyes burning with cold fury. "And then we go after Segomou," he agreed.

202

Chapter XX

Annwyl was scared of the six big men who arrived at the farm late in the evening. Max, the old sheepdog, barked at them until Annwyl's father snapped at him to be quiet. Annwyl could tell that his father was frightened of the men too, though he tried not to show it. The visitors all wore thick leather jerkins. They carried spears and long, heavy swords. Their leader had a coat of chain mail, made from thousands of tiny ringlets, each one carefully stitched to the leather undercoat to provide a protective cover, proof against most weapons. He also had a sour expression, an ugly, squashed nose and small, greedy eyes.

"My name is Segomou," he said to Annwyl's father. "My men and I need shelter for the night." The way he spoke made it plain that it was not a request.

"You are welcome," said Annwyl's father. "My name is Bebb."

"The boy is your son?"

"Yes. This is Annwyl."

The man named Segomou quickly lost interest in Annwyl. "We need food," he said to Bebb.

They crowded into the roundhouse. Bebb sent Annwyl outside, telling him to make sure all the pens were securely shut. Annwyl protested. He knew that the animals were safely stored for the night and it was wet and cold outside. Ignoring his protests, his father pushed him out of the door, clearly anxious to keep him away from the warriors.

Pulling the hood of his cloak over his head against the rain, Annwyl went to the three small, stone-built pens. The goats were safe, the two pigs were safe. Their small flock of sheep was penned in, the gate firmly shut. He checked the tiny coop to make sure that their few chickens were secure. Everything was as it should be, but he had known that already.

The six horses the men had brought were tethered together off to one side. There was no shelter for them but they were not his concern, he thought, although he frowned when he saw that the warriors had not even bothered to remove the saddles. Annwyl knew very little about horses because his father was too poor to own one, but he knew enough to be sure that the animals would develop sores if the saddles were left on their backs for too long. The six visitors obviously did not care about that.

Out of habit, Annwyl scanned the hillside in case a wolf or a fox might be prowling around but there was nothing to be seen except the huge rocks which, much to Annwyl's disgust, were the main crop the narrow valley produced.

Bebb's farm was a poor place. The soil in the valley was so thin they could grow hardly anything. A few stunted beans and kail were their only crop. So they tended animals instead, trading their wool, hides, eggs and goats' milk for flour and vegetables. It was hard, unrelenting work that had sent Annwyl's mother to an early grave and threatened to do the same for his father. Bebb was already thirty one years old and looked worn out by the constant drudgery of trying to provide enough food for the two of them.

Annwyl looked north, along the valley. The clouds loomed low, hiding the tops of the hills that pressed in on either side. The tiny stream trickled its way along the marshy floor, passing the farm on its way down into the next valley where it provided water for the village. Annwyl went to the village with his father once every sennight to barter the little produce their farm provided. They never went any further than the village. Sometimes, in the summer when the weather was fine, Annwyl would climb the hills. From the top, he could see forever, yet all that was visible in any direction was an endless vista of more hills, more valleys. In all his eleven years, he had never ventured any further.

Standing in the rain and the gathering gloom, he thought he saw a movement at the far end of the valley. It was only a brief, fleeting glimpse and what he saw might have been nothing more than a shadow. But it had moved. Annwyl wiped the rain from his face, peering into the distance but whatever he had seen was no longer there. It might have been a man on a horse. It might have been nothing. He went back inside, glad to get out of the rain.

His father had given the men a meagre meal. They usually had barely enough for the two of them, but the men demanded more, so Bebb went out and took one of the chickens, the oldest one. He wrung its neck, then set about cleaning and gutting it. There was not much meat on the bird, but it kept the men happier for a while.

Annwyl looked enviously at their swords. He wanted to hold one, to see what it felt like to be a warrior, but the men looked rough and fierce and he was too frightened to ask permission, so he sat quietly, watching and listening.

"Where's your wife?" the leader of the men demanded of Bebb.

"Dead," the farmer replied dourly.

The man grunted, disappointment in his eyes. Then he asked, "We are looking for a man called Calgacus. Has he passed this way recently?"

"Nobody passes this way," Bebb told him with a shake of his head.

The man muttered darkly to himself. One of his companions said, "We've lost his trail."

"We'll find him soon enough," the leader said.

"I hope so," the other man grumbled. "I've had enough of riding around in the pissing rain looking for him. I just want to find him and kill him as quickly as we can."

Annwyl listened, enthralled. "Who is this man you are looking for?" he piped up.

Bebb hissed at him to be quiet, apologising to the men for the boy's impertinence, but the stocky man with the mail coat gave Annwyl a look that chilled him to the bone.

"He's my enemy," Segomou said coldly.

The men eventually settled down for the night. Bebb made Annwyl sleep beside him, keeping the boy against the wall of the roundhouse, away from the strangers. Unused to the presence of so many other people in the house, it took Annwyl a long time to fall asleep.

He woke before dawn, as he always did. Pulling on his trousers and shirt in the darkness, he crept outside, gathering up the old wooden bucket that stood by the door. Max, his tail wagging, followed him as he pushed aside the weighted cowhide screen that hung inside the doorway and pulled the door open as quietly as he could. He was relieved to see that the rain had stopped at last, though it had left the ground soaked and soggy so that his feet sank into the mud of the yard. The sullen clouds that covered the sky told him that more rain would follow soon.

With Max darting happily around him, Annwyl crossed the

yard then walked down to the tiny river where he knelt to fill the bucket. Struggling back up the slope, water sloshing around in the bucket, he heard Max growl and bark at something. Annwyl snapped at the dog to be quiet, but Max continued his throaty growl, holding his body low to the ground.

Annwyl looked around but could see nothing. It was probably a fox somewhere nearby, he thought. He scolded the dog, bringing him obediently to heel as he lugged the heavy bucket back up to the house.

As he approached the door, the hide cover twitched aside and the leader of the warriors, the man who called himself Segomou, stepped out. He had left his mail coat inside, but he had strapped his sword belt around his waist. Max growled again.

The man looked at Annwyl with an unfriendly glare. "Where's your privy?" he demanded.

"Over there." Placing the water bucket on the ground, Annwyl pointed to a small wooden fence across the yard, beyond the pen that housed the pigs.

The man grunted, shivering in the damp morning air as he walked across the yard, past the pig pen. Max continued to growl. Annwyl looked around again, trying to see what was bothering the dog. He could hear movement inside the house as the rest of the men got up. Perhaps it was that. Then his breath caught in his throat as he saw the other warrior.

Like a silent shadow, a tall man crept from behind the stone wall of the pig pen. He was one of the biggest men Annwyl had ever seen, with long, dark hair that fell over his shoulders, and a dark moustache framing his mouth. He carried a shield on his left arm and a huge longsword in his right hand. The dull glint of a bronze breastplate was visible beneath his cloak. With barely a sound, he moved to stand between the privy and the roundhouse.

Annwyl stood, transfixed by the sight. The big warrior was barely twenty paces from him. The man shot the boy a look that froze him to silence. Max barked again, but Annwyl clapped him quiet.

Segomou finished relieving himself, turned and stepped out through the rickety fence. He stopped in his tracks when he saw the tall warrior facing him.

Annwyl heard the big man say, "Are you Segomou?"

The shorter man nodded. "Who are you?"

"I am Calgacus. I hear you are looking for me."

Annwyl jumped when he heard movement behind him. He sensed the other warriors as they began filing out of the doorway. The first one hissed a whisper of alarm back to the others. Slowly, they crept out as quietly as they could, drawing their long swords.

Annwyl wanted to shout a warning to the man called Calgacus. He was facing one man, but there were five more creeping up behind him. He was a big man, but some of the others were almost as large and he could surely not defeat six warriors.

Annwyl's heart was pounding, but he was too frightened to say or do anything. One of the warriors placed a meaty hand on his shoulder and whispered, "Stay quiet."

Calgacus still faced Segomou, apparently oblivious to the men behind him.

"So why are you looking for me?" he asked.

Segomou gave him a wicked grin. "King Venutius wants you dead."

"Cartimandua said I was free to leave," Calgacus said.

"What she doesn't know won't hurt her," replied Segomou with a shrug of his shoulders.

"So you've been sent to do Venutius' work for him?"

"That's right." Segomou's dark eyes narrowed.

Calgacus said, "Well, what if I—"

He moved, faster than Annwyl had ever seen anyone move. Segomou was caught completely off guard, expecting Calgacus to keep talking, but Calgacus' sword flashed through the air to take the shorter man in the neck, almost decapitating him. Blood sprayed as Segomou toppled. Before his corpse had hit the ground, Calgacus whirled, following the momentum of his mighty blow. He spun, then stopped, facing the five warriors who were suddenly frozen, shocked by the ease with which their leader had been killed.

"Who wants to be next?" Calgacus asked them, his teeth bared in a wolfish grin.

Annwyl heard his father come out of the door. The farmer put his big arms round Annwyl's shoulders. Both of them stood watching. Max barked excitedly, but Bebb shouted at him to be quiet and lie down. The dog, ever obedient, did as he was told and lay at Annwyl's feet, tail swishing angrily. Annwyl was too astonished by the speed and power of Calgacus' movements to do anything other than gape open-mouthed.

The five men hesitated. Calgacus faced them without fear, his eyes watching them carefully. Then one of them let out a yell as he charged wildly at Calgacus.

He was a young man and his inexperience killed him. Calgacus stepped forwards, raised his shield then swung his sword to hack the Brigante down in one smooth, almost graceful, movement that was brutally fast and utterly deadly.

The other four men were nervous now. One of them said, "Spread out. He can't take us all." He gestured with his free arm, waving at his comrades to move to either side.

Annwyl held his breath. Then Max barked again as he jumped up excitedly. Annwyl caught the dog, holding him tightly as another man, a small warrior carrying a sword in one hand and a wickedly sharp hunting knife in the other, burst from hiding behind the roundhouse and sprinted across the yard.

The four Brigantes heard him too late. Two of them were down in an instant. The third parried the small man's sword, but the long knife moved, fast as a striking snake, taking him in the chest. The last of the warriors might have had time to strike a blow but he fell under Calgacus' blade before he could move.

Following the ringing clash of weapons and the awful cries of the fallen, there was sudden silence. Even Max ceased his barking.

Annwyl heard Calgacus say to his companion, "You timed it perfectly. Thank you."

The little warrior replied, "Well I was waiting for your signal. I reckoned when you cut his head off, that was probably it."

Calgacus laughed. "Yes, there's a nice edge on this blade."

Stepping past the corpses, he walked purposefully towards the roundhouse. Annwyl felt his father's grip tighten around his shoulders. Max barked furiously but the man called Calgacus ignored him.

"Are you harmed?" he asked.

Bebb shook his head, unable to speak.

Annwyl could hardly believe what he had witnessed. It had all been over so quickly that it seemed almost like a dream. Only the crumpled bodies of Segomou and his men told him that it had been all too real. He looked up at the tall warrior.

"Who are you?" he asked in wonder.

"I am Calgacus. War Leader of the Silures."

They buried Segomou and his men in a shallow grave half way along the valley, covering them with a pile of the rugged landscape's plentiful rocks. Bebb and Annwyl helped cover the grave. Then Calgacus sent Annwyl to the far end of the valley to fetch his horses which were tethered in a small copse.

Back at the farm, Runt sifted through the plunder they had taken. There were rings and brooches, and a small bag of silver Roman coins.

"Blood money," he said, holding up one of the coins for Calgacus to see. "Venutius must really hate you."

"The feeling is mutual," Calgacus grunted.

"Well, for the moment, he's helped us. All this stuff will come in useful."

Calgacus was pleased with the haul they had taken. Together with the horses and weapons they had brought from Brigantia, he now had plenty of gifts he could distribute. A War Leader was expected to give rewards to those who followed him into battle. By sending Segomou to kill him, Venutius had unwittingly helped to assure Calgacus' status as a gift-giver.

He offered Bebb one of the swords but the big farmer shook his head. "What would I do with a sword?" he asked. So they left him two of the horses and some jewellery, more wealth than the man had ever seen in his life before. The rest of their booty was piled onto the other horses. Segomou's coat of mail was much too small to fit Calgacus and too large for Runt, but it was valuable, so they took it with them.

Annwyl approached him nervously as they made ready to leave. "Can I come with you?" he asked.

Calgacus looked at his earnest face. The boy was small and wiry. His eyes were filled with a look of anxious pleading. "Please?" he begged.

Calgacus glanced to the boy's father. He saw the look of despair on Bebb's face. Looking back at Annwyl, he asked, "How old are you?"

"Eleven."

A memory flared in Calgacus' mind. A memory of himself at Annwyl's age, approaching Caratacus who was sitting on a stool, oiling and cleaning his sword in preparation for setting off to fight Verica of the Atrebates. Calgacus had asked his brother the same question that Annwyl had now posed to him. He smiled when he recalled Caratacus' response.

Slowly, Calgacus drew his sword. He turned it, presenting the leather-bound hilt to the boy, recalling what his older brother had once said to him.

"If you can hold this out straight in one hand for a count of fifty heartbeats, you can come with me."

Annwyl's eyes gleamed, just as Calgacus' had done when Caratacus had handed over his huge sword. The boy gripped the heavy weapon in one hand, stretched out his arm and began counting. The sword wobbled erratically as his young muscles strained under its weight. He managed to count to fifteen before the tip of the heavy blade fell to the earth.

Gently, Calgacus took the sword back. The boy had done well, considering his slight build. Calgacus himself had managed to reach a count of twenty-six before dropping Caratacus' sword.

"When you can hold it for a count of fifty, you can come and join me," he told Annwyl. "Until then, stay here and grow strong."

Annwyl's eyes filled with tears. He nodded miserably, then watched the two warriors ride away, leading their train of captured horses. He heard his father calling to him, telling him that there was work to be done, but Annwyl stood watching until Calgacus had disappeared from sight. For the first time in his life, Annwyl had seen a glimpse of a world far beyond the confines of their narrow, rock-encrusted valley, a brief vision of a life that promised more than relentless drudgery. He had been afraid of the six Brigantes but his fear was as nothing to the wonder of seeing Calgacus fight. For Annwyl, it was as if a door had been opened, showing him what might be possible. Dreams filled his young head, visions of glory and fame that called to him.

One day, he thought, I will be a warrior, just like Calgacus.

Chapter XXI

Rhydderch's home was situated near the border territory between the Silures to the south and the Ordovices to the north. When Calgacus and Runt arrived at the gates, the rugged chieftain's usually surly face broke into a broad grin.

"Nodens be praised!" he exclaimed. "I thought you were dead!"

"Not yet, although we came close once or twice. How are you, Rhydderch?"

Rhydderch's face crumpled into a mass of worry lines. "Well enough. But I'm hurting." He tapped at his chest. "In here."

"We are all hurting," Calgacus agreed. "But it is time to do something about it."

"That sounds good," Rhydderch said. "I am glad the Gods have preserved you. Welcome to Caer Gobannus."

The settlement was not large, consisting of a score of roundhouses protected by a ditch and rampart beside a small stream on the gently-sloping south side of a long, ridge-shaped hill. It was named Caer Gobannus because Rhydderch's father had been famed for his skill at forging swords and had claimed that the God of Smiths had blessed him with his talent. The old sword-maker had passed away many years before, but the name of the settlement had stuck. Other men continued the work, producing metal tools and weapons. Although small, and with many other hilltop settlements and valley farms dotted around the district, Caer Gobannus was an important place and Rhydderch remained an influential chieftain among the Silures.

More importantly for Calgacus, Caer Gobannus, although well situated, was not easy to get to. The rugged hills of the high country lay a short way to the south. To the north, a river wound its way through marshy reed beds and to the east were thick forests. Even the Roman army would have difficulty reaching them here.

Rhydderch listened to the news of Calgacus' adventures with

mounting anger and dismay that turned to a savage joy when he heard that the Druid Council wanted the fight to continue.

"We nearly beat the bastards at Caer Caradoc," he growled. "We would have done if the Ordovices hadn't run like deer fleeing from hounds."

"What is done, is done," Calgacus said. "But now we are going to fight them properly. This time, we are going to beat them."

"Good. What do you need from me?"

"A place to stay. I'd like to base myself here if I may."

"Of course. My home is yours."

"Thank you. But I will also be travelling. I want to visit as many chieftains as I can. I need to gather warriors so that we can launch our attack when Spring returns."

"Why wait so long?" Rhydderch asked.

"Because I want to be sure of winning. We will raise an army over the winter. Cadwallon will send supplies of weapons and food. But don't worry, we won't let the Romans off lightly. The Governor is in the north just now. I think we can do enough to let him know that the Silures are not beaten."

"What did you have in mind?" asked Rhydderch.

Calgacus grinned. "Do you have any Roman wine?" he asked.

Rhydderch shook his head. "No."

"Then I think we should go and get some."

"You want to trade with them?" Rhydderch frowned.

"No, my friend. I do not intend to trade. Can you find twenty men who would accompany me on a raid? If we can start with a success, it will encourage more men to join us."

Rhydderch laughed. "Give me a day and I will have them here," he promised.

With Runt and twenty young men of the Silures, Calgacus rode eastwards, passing into the Roman province. The frontier was watched by patrols and a series of watchtowers that the Romans were constructing, but there were many places a small force could pass undetected. They swam across the Hafren at night, hid until daybreak, then moved on.

By mid-day, Calgacus had located the perfect spot for an ambush. In a wooded valley, a long, rutted track wound its way towards a distant Roman encampment that lay out of sight beyond a low, wooded ridge.

"This will do," he said. Quickly, he issued his orders. Two men were detailed to lead the horses back into the trees, over the crest of the hill that bordered the track. The rest were split into two groups. Runt took half of the warriors to the far side of the track while Calgacus kept the rest with him. They squatted or lay down among the trees, concealing themselves in the long grass and ferns, or hiding behind hummocks in the uneven ground. Calgacus drew his sword. Now all they could do was wait.

A Roman cavalry patrol rode past a short while later. There were five men, each holding a long lance and bearing a small shield on his left arm. Calgacus saw them coming and signalled to his men to let them pass, to remain hidden. The Romans trotted through the woods without stopping. The horses sniffed and tossed their heads nervously, probably having scented the hidden warriors, but the riders pressed on, heading towards the fort. They soon vanished beyond a turn in the path.

The Silures waited.

The supply wagons rumbled into view as the sun was beginning its slow descent towards evening, its rays slanting through the trees into the eyes of the Romans. There were three wagons, each with a driver seated on the bench and with two soldiers marching alongside. The wagons were pulled by oxen who trudged along with docile steadfastness, their tails swishing at flies, their heads lolling from side to side.

The soldiers looked bored, their heavy spears held over their shoulders, their faces red and sweating. They paid little attention to their surroundings.

Calgacus smiled grimly to himself. The Romans, like most people, used river transport whenever possible, especially for heavy goods. But sooner or later, most of their army's frontier posts had to be supplied by wagons. That was especially true along the Hafren, where the river Goddess regularly sent a great wave rushing up the river from the sea, a wall of water that forged its way against the usual flow. The Silures, whose ancestors had lived with the river for more years than anyone could count, knew that these waves, or bores, coincided with the tides. The Romans, unused to tidal waters, were terrified of them, fearing that the Gods were sending the waves to prevent them crossing the river. For the moment, the new fortress the legions had built at a place they called Glevum, and all the minor forts and watchtowers that they

213

were constructing further upriver, were supplied by regular convoys of wagons.

It was a dull, routine task. The soldiers trudging along the track must have thought they were safe, that the task of escorting the heavily-laden wagons was a nice, easy job that entailed an afternoon of boredom and perhaps sore feet at the end of it. Calgacus intended to show the Romans that none of them were safe.

He waited until all three wagons were in the trees. He could sense the expectant eyes of his warriors on him, waiting for his signal.

A Roman soldier was passing below him, barely five paces away, the steady tramp of his footsteps masked by the rumble and squeak of the heavy carts. Without a word, Calgacus sprang to his feet and launched himself out of the woods. He smashed into the soldier, sending the man reeling against the side of the wagon. As the Roman shouted in alarm, Calgacus' heavy sword turned his face to pulp.

The wagon stopped. There were shouts and screams as the Silures swarmed out of the trees, swamping the defenders. Spears flashed, men leaped with knives eager for blood, and the Romans died. It was all over in a few, brutal moments.

In the almost unnatural stillness which followed the fight, Calgacus looked around carefully, his blue eyes quickly taking in the scene, checking on his men. He clucked his tongue in disappointment when he saw the crumpled body of one of them sprawled on the ground, clearly dead. The rest of them were largely unhurt, having suffered only a few cuts or bruises, and they were already busy ransacking the three wagons.

He nodded in satisfaction when he saw that some of the men were slitting the throats of the oxen to prevent them dragging the heavy carts away.

Calgacus crouched to wipe the worst of the blood from his sword on the grass, then wiped it again with a small rag he had tucked into his belt. Ever cautious, he looked around once more, checking for any signs that the attack had been witnessed or that the Roman cavalry might be returning. The sun, which had hampered the Romans as they trudged along the forest path, now dazzled his view to the west. He shaded his eyes, studying the distant ridge. It was clear.

214

Satisfied that there was no immediate danger, he sheathed his sword, glancing casually at the body of the man he had killed, now lying face down on the rutted track. The sight meant little to him except a quiet satisfaction that he had killed the man quickly and efficiently.

Looping his shield onto his back, he walked round to the rear of the nearest wagon. Runt was already there, grinning happily.

"There's so much stuff we'll never carry it all," he said.

"Take what we can," Calgacus ordered. "Spill or scatter the rest."

He cast a cursory glance over the contents of the wagon. Runt was right; there was far too much for them to carry away with them. The wagons were laden with wooden crates, leather sacks, and the large jugs that the Romans called amphorae. Inside the various containers were wine, grain, hard baked bread, salt, olives, olive oil, salted meat, vegetables, picks, axes, saws, shovels, hammers, nails, strips of leather, bolts of cloth, sandals and even a few army helmets.

The tribesmen, knowing what to do, were cutting the cloth and the leather sheets that had covered the wagons. They scooped or poured food out of the heavy and unwieldy crates and amphorae onto the newly torn strips, hastily tying them up to create small bundles which could be carried more easily. They would not leave the surplus for the Romans. What they could not carry, they spoiled. Some men scattered the extra food across the grass for the animals and birds to feast on, others simply trampled or urinated on it, laughing as they did so.

They found the guards' packs, hauled out the waterskins, emptied them, then refilled them with wine. Some men took a drink of the dark liquid but Calgacus shouted at them to stop.

"You can have it later!" he told them. He did not want any of the men becoming drunk before they were safely away. He was still nervous. He had chosen this site because it was remote but he knew they were vulnerable while they were plundering the wagons. He prowled the length of the small convoy, eyes and ears alert for any signs of danger.

Near the leading wagon he found two of the tribesmen crouching over the bodies of fallen Romans, sharp knives gleaming in their hands. He called to them, "Leave the heads! We need to carry food and supplies, not trophies."

The men scowled. "How will anyone know we have killed our enemies if we do not take back their heads?" one of them asked in a surly voice.

"You tell them to ask me and I will tell the tale of your bravery. Right now, taking back food, clothes and tools is more important than showing off how brave you are. Leave them."

The men pushed their knives away. Under Calgacus' stern gaze, they reluctantly went to join their comrades who were looting the wagons. Calgacus gave an irritated sigh. Taking the heads of dead enemies was an ancient tradition. Warriors were proud of the number of skulls they could adorn their homes with. Calgacus himself had done the same when he had killed his first Roman. The head he had taken was a symbol that he had become a warrior. He knew that symbols were important but he had learned that actions were more important. This time, the fallen Romans would keep their heads.

He moved quickly back down the line of wagons, telling the men to hurry. He found Runt, rifling through the corpse of one of the soldiers who had been escorting the convoy. Hefting the short Roman sword he had taken from the lifeless hand of its former owner, Runt gave a few tentative mid-air swings and thrusts, testing the feel of the blade.

"I think I'll keep this," he said with a satisfied smile when he saw Calgacus approaching.

"It's a bit short," Calgacus pointed out in a derisory tone.

"So am I," Runt laughed. He wandered over to another corpse, stooping to pick up a second fallen sword. "Maybe two would be better," he said to nobody in particular. He held a sword in each hand, weighing them thoughtfully. Grabbing the belts and scabbards from the corpses, he looped the two swords over his shoulders so that they hung at his hips, one on either side.

"You look ridiculous," Calgacus told him, trying not to laugh.

"You're just jealous that you don't have the style to carry it off yourself," Runt replied with a smile. "That meat cleaver you call a sword suits you, though."

"Maybe you *should* keep them," Calgacus conceded. "The Romans will probably die laughing when they see you coming."

The exchange brought a round of laughter from the tribesmen. The success of the ambush had raised everyone's spirits. Calgacus was pleased, but he knew this was no game. He clapped his hands,

216

demanding their attention.

"We need to get going," he called. "Now!"

Runt swore suddenly, stepping away from the body he had just relieved of its sword. "By Toutatis! This one's still alive."

"Leave him," Calgacus said. "Maybe his friends will find him before he bleeds to death."

"It would be kinder to kill him," Runt said as he gazed down at the injured man.

"Killing defenceless men is druids' work," Calgacus replied tersely. "Come on. It's time to go."

Runt did not argue. He had no qualms about killing wounded men. Most people would have thought nothing of it. But Runt knew that the sentence of doom that hung over Calgacus had only served to harden his conviction that a warrior should not harm those who could not fight back. Without so much as a backward glance, Runt left the soldier lying on the ground with his life ebbing slowly out of him.

Calgacus barked orders, telling the tribesmen to gather up their bundles of stolen supplies. Every man, including Calgacus, took as much as he could carry.

He briefly considered setting fire to the wagons, but dismissed the idea. A plume of smoke would only attract attention and the iron tools they had been forced to leave behind would not be greatly damaged by a small fire anyway. There was precious little else left for the Romans.

He smiled to himself as he lugged his heavy sack of plunder into the trees. One small raid would not defeat the Romans but it was a start. It would show that the invaders could be hurt, that they were not invincible.

Soon, he would deliver a greater blow but for now he had done enough. It was time to disappear.

Chapter XXII

As winter drew near, Venutius was forced to admit to himself that Segomou must have failed. The moon had waxed and waned three times since his cousin had ridden away but he had still not returned, nor sent any word. Worse, news was slowly filtering back that the Silures were once again causing trouble for Rome and that Calgacus was very much alive. Venutius supposed there was a slim chance that Segomou had simply been unable to get close enough to Calgacus to kill him while leaving himself an opportunity to make his escape, but he knew that Segomou, although a resourceful and cunning man, was not overly patient. It was unlikely that he was simply biding his time. No, Venutius decided, something must have happened to Segomou.

The Brigante king considered his next move carefully. Calgacus was far away, and it was likely that, sooner or later, the Romans would crush him, just as they had crushed everyone else. But the wretched man was developing a nasty habit of turning up alive when he was supposed to be dead. Venutius had no wish to spend his life looking over his shoulder, waiting for a knife in the back. Then again, a fool like Calgacus would probably come for him openly with a challenge to meet him in single combat. That prospect did not appeal to Venutius either. He had seen Calgacus fight and had no illusions about the outcome of any contest between himself and the big Catuvellauni. Besides, any man who could best Segomou was to be feared.

Almost as bad as the worry about Calgacus seeking revenge on him, was the knowledge that Cartimandua, whatever she might say, still had feelings for the man. Venutius knew she did, though she had denied it when he had challenged her. But she had let Calgacus go when she could have ordered him slain, which proved something. And the news that he still lived and was raiding the Roman province had made her smile, a fact that had further irritated Venutius.

Venutius' plans for his own advancement meant that he would

218

need to dispose of Cartimandua at some stage, although for the moment he was still consolidating his power, not to mention enjoying his nights with her. But pleasures of the flesh could be found elsewhere. Beautiful as she was, Cartimandua was only one woman. If he could find a way to remove her without sparking a civil war among the Brigantes, he would soon find someone else to share his bed.

That still left the problem of how and when to get rid of the Queen. Segomou would no longer be able to carry out the deed, thanks to Calgacus.

Calgacus. Everything always came back to him. The man was a living problem but a thought struck Venutius that there might be a way to turn things to his advantage.

Cartimandua still had feelings for Calgacus. That was obvious. Venutius wondered what she would do if she were to hear of Calgacus' death.

She would be upset. Perhaps she might even become so distraught that she would be suicidal. Of course, she would need some assistance to actually commit suicide, but Venutius was sure he could arrange something suitable. That, he thought, would neatly dispose of two problems at once. He mentally patted himself on the back. He liked that idea.

It also fitted well with the wishes of several minor chieftains of the Brigantes. Already, men had come to him privately, whispering of their discontent at Cartimandua's pro-Roman stance. Venutius had soothed them, assured them that he shared their concerns, and asked them to be patient. The number of dissenters was growing but, as yet, he did not have enough backing to make an overt move against the Queen. How much simpler it would be if she were to kill herself in grief over the death of her former lover. Venutius would become the undisputed leader of the Brigantes at a single stroke. Then he could placate the dissidents by pointing out that even the mighty Calgacus could not defeat Rome. If any of them refused to be placated, they could be disposed of. After all, Venutius knew who they were.

So Calgacus must die. The problem was how to achieve that. Venutius could not afford to wait for the Romans to get round to it. He needed something more certain.

He had tried the direct approach but that had clearly failed. Something more subtle was called for. He needed an ally. He smiled to himself when he realised where he could find one.

Once the idea came to him, he wasted no time. He made some excuses to Cartimandua about needing to travel back to his home in the north. He should have been annoyed when she did not argue with him, when she made no effort to dissuade him, or even to offer to accompany him. But he was only mildly irritated, because he needed to be away from her for a while.

He also left Vellocatus behind, ostensibly to look after his interests in Isuria but mainly because the tall shield-bearer was becoming a liability. Venutius decided that he could not afford loose tongues and he had discovered that Vellocatus was poor at keeping secrets. Cartimandua had already made some veiled references to Segomou, trying to prise a confession from Venutius about what his cousin had been ordered to do.

He suspected that Vellocatus had told the wretched woman everything. The man's vanity left him vulnerable to someone like Cartimandua. A few softly whispered words, perhaps a gentle kiss or a lingering look and Vellocatus was foolish enough to tell her anything she wanted to know. This time, Venutius decided, his shield-bearer would know nothing of what he planned.

Taking a handful of chosen, trusted warriors, he set off, well wrapped in furs against the winter chill. At first he headed north but he soon cut west, making for the coast, seeking out a small fishing village. The fishermen rarely ventured far offshore during winter, but the simple expedient of threatening to kill their families and burn their homes quickly brought them round to seeing things Venutius' way. Ignoring the risk of storms, he set sail, following the coast south, then past the vast salt flats at the mouth of the Deva and westwards until they reached Ynis Mon.

It was a cold, wet, miserable journey, but they reached the sacred isle without mishap, drawing ashore in a small cove where a dozen small boats and curraghs were beached. The druids may have discouraged visitors but they were practical men. They permitted some fishermen to make their homes on the island's coast and they allowed traders to stop here, secretly bringing goods from further north or from the land of Erin that lay across the western sea.

Venutius stepped onto the rainswept shore and sought out the druid who oversaw this small community.

Announcing himself, he said, "I wish to speak to Cethinos. It is a matter of some urgency."

The druid scowled at him. "You do not summon druids to speak to you, lord or not."

Venutius took some small beads of black jet-stone from his pouch and handed them to the druid. "Then please accept these tokens as evidence of my loyalty. But I must speak to Cethinos."

The druid considered the offering. It did not take him long to make up his mind. "I will send a message to him," he said as he scooped up the precious stones.

Venutius kicked his heels for a night and a day, finding shelter in a small roundhouse which he and his men were forced to share with some sailors who manned a small trading ship. On the second day, accompanied by squally showers of icy rain, Cethinos arrived. Ordering everyone else outside, Venutius welcomed the druid into the house where they sat facing each other across the smoking hearth fire.

"I had not thought to see you here," Cethinos said gruffly. "I hope it is as important as your message implied."

"It is. I have a proposal to make which I think will be of mutual interest. Should you agree, I have many valuable items which can be cast into the sacred lakes as offerings, to ensure the success of the venture."

Cethinos was immediately attracted to the idea of valuable offerings. Proper respect for the Gods was essential. But he knew men well enough to know that Venutius must want something important in return for such lavish gifts.

"What does the proposal concern?" he asked.

"Not what. Who. Calgacus."

Cethinos' expression turned frosty. "What about him?"

Venutius took a deep breath. "He has threatened to kill me."

Cethinos said nothing, but merely continued to stare at him.

Feeling slightly discomfited under the druid's stony glare, Venutius went on, "I gained the impression when we spoke last that you, too, have no reason to love him."

"He is an arrogant fool who defies the will of the Gods," Cethinos agreed.

Which meant, Venutius knew, that Calgacus defied the will of the Gods as interpreted by Cethinos. He smiled again. "I have heard that he leads the Silures. Do you know whether this is true?"

"It is true. He has the blessing of the Druid Council."

221

Venutius hesitated. He had not expected that. For a few moments he was unsure how to respond to this startling revelation. The implications were clear. Calgacus had come to Ynis Mon, seeking the support of the druids. Venutius had not thought the Catuvellauni capable of such a daring move. It threatened to undermine his entire plan. He had hoped that Cethinos would have a free hand to deal with Calgacus but if the Druid Council had given the big warrior its blessing, everything had changed.

Frowning, he said, "That makes things difficult. I would not like to go against the wishes of the Druid Council."

"The decision was far from unanimous," Cethinos said. "There was considerable support for a proposal that he be offered as a sacrifice to the Gods, but others wished to allow him time to prove himself. Maddoc granted him a year's grace during which he is to win a great victory. If he fails, he will be sacrificed."

Venutius rubbed his chin while he tried to take in this information. A year was a long time to wait and if Calgacus failed to win his victory, there was no guarantee that he would not flee from the druids' vengeance. With little to lose, he might come after Venutius. That was not a risk that the Brigante chieftain was willing to take. His frown faded as he saw a solution to his problem.

He said, "So is it fair to say that I would like to see Calgacus dead and that you would like to see him offered as a sacrifice?"

Cethinos pondered the question for only a short time before nodding his head. "That would not displease me," he said.

"Then I think it can be done," Venutius told him. "In fact, it should be done. His constant raids on the Romans can only have one outcome. You know that. The Governor might have been content to rest where he is but if Calgacus provokes him, he will bring his army west and this time he will not stop until he has crushed all resistance. The Silures will fall, then the Ordovices. Once they are defeated, Ynis Mon will be threatened."

Cethinos sat rigidly, giving only a slight nod of his head. "Go on," he said.

Venutius was growing in confidence now. He continued, "It would suit both of us, as well as the others among the druids who agree with you, if Calgacus could be sacrificed earlier. Say, at midsummer? His death then would ensure that the Romans do not march against the western tribes."

Cethinos' eyes sparked with interest but he showed that he was no fool. He had offered many sacrifices that had failed to halt the Roman advance. Cautiously, he said, "Nothing can be certain. If he dies, the Romans may still cross the Hafren."

"Not if someone were to deliver his head to them. If some chieftain among the Silures submits to the Governor, pledges peace and delivers Calgacus' head, the Romans will not attack. We should learn from what Cartimandua achieved when she handed over Caratacus."

"That might work," Cethinos conceded thoughtfully.

"It *will* work," Venutius said confidently. "It cannot fail."

Privately, he did not care whether his suggestion worked or not. As long as Calgacus died, his own aims would be achieved. But he could tell that, for all Cethinos' apparent disinterest, the druid was intrigued.

"You overlook one problem," Cethinos said. "Calgacus will not willingly submit to being sacrificed. Not when he has been granted a year by the Council."

"I never overlook things," Venutius said. "We can trap him."

"How?"

"There was a girl who was sent here a few years ago. She was to be trained in the lore. Her name is Senuala."

Cethinos tugged at his long beard. "I think I know her. What of it?"

"She is Cartimandua's sister."

Druids rarely admitted that they did not know something and Cethinos was no exception. He asked, "What does that signify?"

"She can help us. It should not be difficult to persuade her that Calgacus tried to betray her sister and her entire tribe. That is the simple truth. If you could also persuade her that Calgacus is a heretic, a man who defies the Gods, that should be sufficient."

"You wish me to send her to Calgacus?" Cethinos asked as he sought to grasp Venutius' plan.

"Yes. If she can get close to him she can achieve two things for us. First, she can get him to admit his heresy. Secondly, when the time comes, she can drug him so that he is unable to resist when you come for him. You will be able to offer him at midsummer. You will save the free tribes from destruction."

Cethinos' thin lips twitched in the beginnings of a smile. "If Senuala tells the Druid Council of his heresy, they will not dare punish us. It is our duty to rid the people of those who show disrespect to the Gods."

"Exactly!" Venutius said eagerly.

"But how can we be sure that Senuala will be able to get close to him?" Cethinos asked.

"That should be easy enough," Venutius told him. "Calgacus may be a warrior, but he is soft. If we present him with a woman who is being abused, he will not be able to resist helping her. Then, if she is even remotely like her sister, she will be able to find a way to get into his bed. After that, he will be helpless."

Cethinos nodded gravely. "He has always been soft," he agreed.

"We will need a way of getting her to him without him suspecting her."

"That should be easy enough to arrange," Cethinos said. "I know a man who can help us with that."

Venutius said, "Excellent. In that case, the only problem arises if Calgacus fights the Romans before mid-summer. It is unlikely, but he is an unpredictable man. We should not discount the possibility that he might actually be able to win a victory."

Cethinos considered the problem. "We could sacrifice him sooner. The Spring equinox would be a good time, I suppose. Or perhaps Beltane. But midsummer would be better. A sacrifice of royal blood made on the longest day would be very powerful."

"And the more time Senuala has, the easier it will be for her to lull him into our trap."

"In that case," Cethinos said decisively, "I will ensure that no matter what he achieves before midsummer, the Druid Council will deem it insufficient."

Venutius grinned. "Then we have him."

Cethinos waved a cautionary hand. "Do not gloat before we have achieved our goal," he warned. "Nothing is certain. Still, it is a good plan and one that a dullard like Calgacus will never see through. He views the world in black and white, without subtlety."

"The girl will need to play her part well," Venutius said.

"She is training to be a druid. She will be able to convince him easily enough."

Venutius bowed his head, acknowledging the truth of the old man's statement.

Cethinos narrowed his eyes. "Who else knows of this?" he

demanded.

"Just the two of us."

The druid relaxed slightly, tugging at his beard thoughtfully. After a short moment of reflection, he said, "Then I will speak to the girl."

"So we have a bargain?"

Cethinos' smile was genuine as he said, "We have a bargain."

Venutius' broad smile mirrored that of the old man. It had been a bold gamble coming to Ynis Mon but it had paid off. He emptied his belt pouch, presenting Cethinos with trinkets of gold, silver and dark jet which could be thrown into the sacred lakes as offerings to the Gods. Then he made his farewell and set off for Brigantia, feeling immensely pleased with himself. Things were falling into place. All he needed to do now was return to Isuria and await the news of Calgacus' death.

Chapter XXIII

Winter brought rain and gales, buffeting in from the west. Some old roundhouses collapsed and a few low lying villages were flooded, but such things were normal and the people simply rallied together to build new homes for those whose houses had been destroyed. After midwinter, the rains subsided and the wind died. Now there were frosts, severe enough to turn the ground as hard as iron and coat everything white. The pale winter sun, lying low in the sky, often failed to clear the frosts for days at a time.

A few flurries of snow hinted at worse weather to come, but when it did snow, only the mountain tops were covered white, to the dismay of the children and the delight of the adults. Caer Gobannus escaped with little more than a thin sprinkling of white that soon disappeared. Still, winter was a time for staying warm, for conserving food until the Spring arrived. This winter, Calgacus also made it a time for preparing his war.

He and Runt had settled in Rhydderch's hillside village for the winter. Rhydderch had had a small roundhouse built for them, but Runt had soon moved in with a young widow named Sula. Her husband had gone to Caer Caradoc but had not returned, leaving her with a two-year-old son, her mother and her elderly grandmother to care for. Runt spent most of his time in Sula's home, which left Calgacus with a house to himself.

On the morning that the slave trader arrived, he was sitting outside the door, wrapped in heavy furs, sipping a hot and rather tasteless tisane he had brewed, running over his plan in his mind. Runt, always uncomfortable when he came across slaves, wandered over to tell him of the man's arrival.

"Is he buying or selling?" Calgacus asked unenthusiastically.

"Probably both."

The slaver rode on a small horse, trotting slowly into the open space at the centre of the village. Behind him rode an armed guard, followed by a coffle of half a dozen slaves on foot, with another armed guard riding at the end of the line. Rhydderch, as head man, went to greet his visitor.

Calgacus watched from a distance. He had no interest in slaves. Idly, his eyes took in the slaver, a short man, dressed in many layers of clothing against the chill, his hair balding, a smile fixed on his lips as he greeted Rhydderch effusively, treating him like an old friend. Calgacus had seen his type before, and had little time for men like that. He looked disinterestedly along the line of slaves. And his heart missed a beat. There, in the middle of the coffle, iron manacles around her wrists and ankles, stood Cartimandua.

He was on his feet before he realised that it was not her. The way she stood had seemed familiar, and her long, dark hair had fooled him, but as soon as he took a second look, he saw that it was not her. This girl was taller, her face more rounded, her cheekbones less prominent than the sculptured beauty of the Brigante Queen. Only her dark hair and blue eyes bore any resemblance to Cartimandua.

But Calgacus had jumped to his feet and the slave trader had not missed his interest. With a quick word to Rhydderch, the man scurried over, all smiles and beckoning arms.

"Greetings, Lord," he said, smoothly. "I am Phennarcos, a dealer in slaves. And in other trifles." His voice sounded as oily and insincere as the man himself looked. "I see something has caught your eye. May I be of service to you?"

Calgacus wanted to shake his head but the girl had turned to face him with a look of desperate longing on her face, a look that was as stark as a cry for help. She caught his gaze and held it, silently beseeching him.

He pointed at her. "Who's the girl?" he asked brusquely.

"Ah, you are a man of taste, I see," Phennarcos said. "She is quite outstanding, is she not? Such a rare beauty. Come and see."

He tugged at Calgacus' arm, urging him towards the slave coffle. Calgacus soon found himself standing in front of the girl. She had lowered her head now, looking down at her feet. Her long hair, lank and dirty, hung around her face, concealing her features.

"Who is she?" Calgacus asked again.

"She can be whoever you want, Lord," said Phennarcos with a sly smile. "A princess of the Caledones, perhaps. Or a Gaul. Or a priestess from far away Greece."

Calgacus scowled at the man. "Just tell me," he said sharply.

227

"Of course, Lord. Of course." Phennarcos fawned. "But I regret that I do not know very much about her. Her last master called her Senuala and claimed she was of the Votadini."

Calgacus turned to the girl. "Is that true?" he asked her.

When he spoke to her, the girl lifted her gaze enough to glance at Phennarcos, seeking permission to reply. The slaver nodded his assent.

Lowering her head once again, she said softly, "Yes, Master."

"Would you like to see her naked?" Phennarcos asked, scenting a sale and eager to please.

"No," Calgacus replied sharply. "How much do you want for her?"

"Well, she is quite special, Lord. I was hoping to sell her to a very wealthy man for a considerable sum."

Runt protested. "Calgacus! What are you doing? You don't need a slave."

Calgacus ignored him. "How much?" he asked the slaver.

Phennarcos' eyes widened. "You are Calgacus?"

"Yes."

"Then I am sure we can work something out," smiled Phennarcos. "I was considering taking her to the Romans, to see if I could find a wealthy man there who might want to buy her, but, to be frank, the bottom has fallen out of the Roman market in the last year. They took so many slaves when they conquered the Cornovii. But for a famous lord such as yourself . . ." He gave Calgacus another greasy smile. "Perhaps we can go somewhere more private where we can work out a deal?" he suggested.

Runt touched Calgacus' arm. "Cal, this is foolish. Leave her."

Phennarcos, oblivious to Runt's protests, produced a large iron key which he used to unchain the girl from the coffle. Taking her by the arm, he followed Calgacus back to his roundhouse. Runt tagged along, his sullen glare making it clear that he was unhappy.

Once inside the house, Phennarcos shoved the girl to one side where she stood silently, head bowed, rubbing her wrists where the manacles had chafed her skin. Phennarcos sat with Calgacus beside the small hearth fire and the bargaining began. Calgacus eventually parted with almost all of the silver coins, rings and brooches that he had gathered over several years of plundering Roman soldiers. They clasped forearms to seal the deal and Phennarcos left, hurrying back to his horse and leading the

228

remaining slaves away as quickly as he could, apparently not interested in doing any more business.

Runt watched him go then turned back into the house. "No wonder he's in such a hurry to get away. He probably thinks you'll chase after him when you realise how much you've paid him."

"It doesn't matter," Calgacus replied. "I can get more from the Romans."

"And what are you going to do with her?" Runt asked, indicating the silent girl with a jerk of his head.

"I don't know," Calgacus admitted. "But maybe you could ask Sula to give her a wash and some fresh clothes. I'll pay."

"With what?" Runt asked sourly. "You've got precious little left." He threw up his hands. "Oh, come on, girl. Let's get you cleaned up for your new master."

He took Senuala's arm. She followed meekly as he led her outside, leaving Calgacus alone by his fire.

Sighing, Calgacus ran his fingers back through his hair. He was not sure why he had bought the girl. It was not the initial, mistaken belief that she was Cartimandua, although that was what had first caught his attention. It had been the lost, haunted look on her face, the silent plea for help. It reminded him of the young woman of the Ordovices who had been raped and murdered by Segomou; it reminded him of little Beatha, abandoned to the Romans after he had persuaded Caratacus to spare her life; it reminded him of Aemilia, the Roman girl he had held prisoner for his own, selfish purposes and whom he had failed to keep hidden. Three young girls and he had not been able to help any of them.

He rested his chin on his hands. He knew why he had bought the Votadini girl, but he had absolutely no idea what he was going to do with her.

Senuala returned as the sun was setting. Runt showed her to the door, but did not come in with her. With a curt farewell, he returned to Sula's home.

Senuala stood, unmoving, just inside the doorway. Calgacus looked at her. Her hair had been washed and combed, her face cleaned of grime and she was wearing a long, grey, woollen dress with a thick shawl wrapped around her shoulders. Her feet were encased in new shoes that were lined with lambswool.

He waved her in. "Come and sit down," he told her.

229

She did as he ordered, taking a stool opposite him, on the other side of the small fire. She said nothing, keeping her eyes downcast, pulling the shawl around her and warming her hands by the fire.

Unsure of what to say, he asked her, "Are you hungry?"

"No. Sula gave me some food."

"That's good."

"She said you are a rotten cook," Senuala added by way of explanation, showing the first spark of character he had seen from her. She quickly lowered her eyes, showing that she had learned that pride or insolence would be beaten out of a slave, although she had clearly not lost all of her self-esteem. And she was right about his cooking. He could not argue with Sula's assessment of his culinary skills.

"So tell me about yourself," he said.

Senuala kept her eyes fixed on the fire. She asked, "What do you want to know?"

"Everything. Where are you from? How old are you? How did Phennarcos get hold of you?"

Senuala looked up. Her expression was calm, betraying nothing. Speaking with barely a trace of emotion in her voice, she said, "My people are the Votadini. I was captured by Brigante raiders four years ago when I was thirteen. I have been a slave ever since. What more is there to know?"

"You have been a slave for four years?"

"Yes."

"But you still don't know enough to address me as Master?"

She flinched. "I am sorry, Master."

Somehow, Calgacus felt more embarrassed than she did at the reprimand. He had not meant it to sound quite as harsh as it had come out, but although she scarcely moved and she spoke quietly, he gained the impression that she was testing him, trying to see how far she could go.

"What about Phennarcos?" he asked. "How did he get hold of you?"

"My last master got a new wife. She did not like me, so he sold me."

"I can understand that," said Calgacus, studying the smooth perfection of her skin and her full figure which even the heavy shawl could not disguise. Senuala was enough to tempt any man and no woman would want a slave like her in the house.

"The Votadini," he said. "They live to the north, is that right? Beyond the Brigantes?"

She nodded. "Yes."

The Votadini, thought Calgacus, were one of the lucky tribes. They had no direct contact with Rome. Yet that had not stopped Senuala being taken captive. As in so many things, old Myrddin had been right about that; the tribes were just as capable of enslaving their neighbours as the Romans were. The difference was only one of scale.

"May I ask a question, Master?" she said, keeping her gaze lowered.

"Of course. What is it?"

She lifted her face, looking into his eyes with an unexpected show of boldness. "Why is your friend Liscus angry with me?"

"He is not angry with you. He is angry with me."

"Because you bought me?"

"Yes."

"I don't understand." She stared a challenge at him.

"Neither do I," he sighed. "And you forgot to call me 'Master' again."

She dropped her gaze immediately. "I am sorry, Master. Please do not beat me."

"I won't beat you," he said, annoyed with himself for reminding her of her status again. "But by all the Gods, I don't know what I am going to do with you."

"I am sure you will do whatever you want," she said, adding after a short pause, "Master". She folded her hands in her lap, looking down again.

"You were of noble birth," Calgacus said.

Senuala stiffened. She looked up. "What makes you say that?"

"Your hands. They are not rough and worn. You have never worked in the fields."

A faint smile played around her lips. "Most of my masters have not kept me just to be a mere field slave."

"That, I can believe," he said. "So what am I going to do with you?"

"You could free me," she suggested, her eyes once again shining a bright challenge.

Calgacus studied her face but this time she did not look away. He told himself she was only a slave. He could do whatever he wanted and she would have no alternative but to obey. Obedience or death were a slave's only choices. Yet he knew that if he forced her to his bed, he would be little better than Segomou and his thugs who raped and killed solely because they could.

"What would you do if I freed you?" he asked her. "Would you go back to your people?"

"How would I get there?" she retorted. "I would be enslaved again before I had travelled a day or two."

That, he knew, was true. A woman, especially one as good-looking as Senuala, could never travel far on her own.

"So what would you do?" he asked again.

"I have not thought about it," she said. "It is best not to think too much about freedom when you are a slave."

"Every slave thinks about it," Calgacus scoffed.

"Well, I would not sleep with you, for one thing," she stated boldly.

He laughed. "I think you have just given me an excellent reason to keep you as a slave."

"As I said, Master. You will do whatever you please."

Calgacus thought for a few moments. "What I really want is for Runt not to be angry with me. He was a slave once himself. That is why he is angry. He disapproves of anyone being kept as a slave."

Calgacus stood up, stretching his back and legs. Senuala gazed up at him, watching his every move expectantly.

He said, "I need Runt's friendship more than I need a slave. You are free."

Senuala blinked in astonishment. "What?" The word came out as little more than a hoarse whisper.

"You are free." He waved a hand at her. "That is what you wanted, isn't it? You are no longer a slave."

Her dark eyes filled with tears. She brushed them away with her delicate fingers. "Do you mean it?" she asked in a voice that was suddenly thick with emotion.

"I wouldn't say it otherwise. I may be many things, but I am a man of my word. You are free."

Senuala whispered, "Thank you." She looked at a loss. "But what will I do?"

"You can do whatever you want," he told her. "That is what being free is all about. You can go and find someone who will take

232

you in. Sula is a good woman, though her house is getting rather crowded now. And there are plenty of young men who would fall over themselves for a wife like you."

"Men like you?" she asked him.

Calgacus shook his head. "I need a wife even less than I need a slave. I am under sentence of death from the druids if I don't beat the Romans in battle. I have no time for a wife right now. If I did have one, she is likely to be a widow by next midwinter."

"So you don't want me to stay here?" she asked, her dark eyes watching him closely.

"No. Yes. I don't know."

"You make yourself very clear," she said with a hint of a smile.

"You are free to do as you please," Calgacus told her. "I need to talk to Liscus."

Hurriedly, he opened the door and stepped outside into the cold darkness. He took a deep breath and exhaled loudly, his breath steaming away in swirls in the frosty night air. Despite the chill, his face was burning.

By the light of the moon, he made his way through the village to Sula's home. He heard voices from inside. Rapping his knuckles on the door, he called Runt's name. After a moment, the door opened and Runt peered out.

"Calgacus?"

"I've told her she is free," Calgacus said.

Runt beamed at him. "That is good."

"She needs somewhere to stay. Will you and Sula take her in? Just until she finds somewhere permanent."

"Of course. If that is what you want." Runt sounded sceptical.

Sula came to the door, pushing out to join them. A short, big-breasted woman who bustled vivaciously around most people, she rarely spoke directly to Calgacus unless he asked her a question. Runt had once told him that Sula was afraid of him because he was always grim and brooding. Now, she smiled.

"I always said men are fools," she grinned. "She will stay with you. She did nothing but ask questions about you all the time we were washing her."

"She was a slave then," Calgacus replied. "Now, she is free."

Sula smiled. "You should go home," she advised him. "Talk to her."

233

So Calgacus wandered slowly back to his house, his emotions confused and conflicted. He ducked through the low entrance, hastily pulling the door shut after him to keep out the cold night air.

Fresh wood had been piled on the fire which was burning brightly, filling the circular house with warmth. By the flickering firelight, he saw Senuala, lying under the furs and blankets of his bed.

She leaned up on her elbow, exposing a bare shoulder. He saw her new dress lying neatly folded on one of the stools. Seeing him, she moved the blankets aside invitingly.

"I decided to stay," she said with a smile.

Chapter XXIV

"She's good for you," observed Runt, happy for his friend's good fortune, as well as for his recent good mood. In the weeks since Senuala's arrival, Calgacus had been more content than he could remember. He had bustled and organised as much as ever, driving the warriors on in their preparations, but he had done it with more humour than before. Even Sula had commented that he seemed less grim.

"I wish she was as happy," Calgacus said. "There is something bothering her, but she won't say what it is."

Runt laughed. "She's a woman. For one thing, there is bound to be something bothering her, and for another, she will expect you to know what it is without her having to tell you."

Runt had considerably more experience with women than Calgacus did, so he expected that the little man might be right, but he still harboured a nagging doubt about Senuala's happiness. In only a few short weeks, she had transformed his roundhouse, persuading some of the carpenters to provide her with a new table, two stools and a chest to keep clothes in. She had hung a blanket behind the door to keep out draughts and insects and draped other blankets over taut strings so that the house could be partitioned for privacy and comfort. When the first signs of an early Spring began to show, she hung garlands of flowers above the door and from the oak beams of the roof.

She had quickly shown that she was a much better cook than Calgacus and she was also skilled at making herbal drinks.

"Where did you learn to do that?" he asked her.

"When I was young, I knew a druid. He showed me how to mix drinks to help fight minor ailments, to help people sleep, or just to calm and relax the mind." She shrugged. "It is nothing special."

That was one of the few things she had ever revealed about her past. For the most part, she refused to talk about her life, saying the memories were too painful.

She may not have wanted to talk about her past life but she was full of questions. Whenever she was alone with Calgacus, she wanted to know all about him.

He told of growing up in Camulodunon; of helping Runt escape from the Roman trader, of Verran and Beatha, and of his older brothers.

"You had a lot of brothers," she said.

"Four," he confirmed. "They were half-brothers really, although they never treated me any different. Apart from Adminius. He was the oldest."

"You didn't like him?" she asked, snuggling closer to him under the blankets.

Calgacus shook his head. "He would have been king but he was greedy. When my father fell ill, he wanted to seize power without waiting for the old man to die, but my other brothers opposed him. So he fetched an army from among the Cantiaci, telling them that my father was dead."

"Was there a battle?" she asked. "Did your other brothers fight him?"

He laughed. "No. My father crawled from his sick bed. Togodumnus held him while he climbed onto his chariot. When the Cantiaci saw him, they knew Adminius had lied, so they refused to fight for him. He ran away to Rome, so Togodumnus became king when my father died."

"Adminius does not sound like the rest of your family," Senuala observed, encouraging him to tell her more.

"No, but he got his wish. When he came back, it was with the legions behind him. He helped kill Togodumnus. The last I heard, he was ruling the Catuvellauni like a Roman Governor." Calgacus gave a bitter smile. "One day I will kill him."

Senuala was silent for a long time. Then she said, "So you are the last of the sons of the famous Cunobelinos."

"Yes. Togodumnus was killed by Adminius and the other traitors; Caratacus and Talacarnos are prisoners of Rome. They are probably dead, too."

She leaned over him, kissing him. "Do not worry," she said. "You will be the greatest of them all."

He reached for her, pulling her close. "I love you," he said softly.

In reply, she slid on top of him, pressing herself against him.

"Prove it," she whispered.

Much as Calgacus wanted to be with Senuala, he had a war to fight. By the time the early festival of Imbolc had passed, he had over six thousand warriors who had pledged themselves to the fight. But a third of those warriors were young men, scarcely more than boys. Many of them had just turned fourteen and did not have the strength to wield a spear properly. Calgacus knew that they would have no chance in a straightforward fight against heavily armed Romans but he had no intentions of fighting a straightforward battle. Instead, he had devised a plan that would make best use of the men he had.

He had spent the winter months riding through the rugged hills and valleys of the Silures' heartland. Men had flocked to join him, encouraged by the success of his raids, attracted by his victories, lured by the fact that he was brother to the Great King, Caratacus. He gained men and he gathered supplies to feed and arm them.

Cadwallon had been as good as his word, sending swords and spears, along with salted beef and sacks of grain. Calgacus had the weapons distributed among the warriors and the food stored in secret locations scattered throughout the Silures' territory.

Then he summoned some of the chieftains to Caer Gobannus, men he could trust to follow his orders and to lead the warriors. Like Rhydderch, these men felt the shame of the defeat at Caer Caradoc and were desperate to avenge Caratacus.

The Silures had no king. They were ruled by many chieftains, each of whom refused to acknowledge any of his neighbours as stronger than himself, but when the tribe was threatened they came together under a War Leader. Now they came to follow Calgacus.

They met in the valley below Caer Gobannus where many of the warriors who had come to join the war had built themselves temporary shelters. Sitting alongside Rhydderch was Hillinos, who had brought nearly seven hundred men to join the fight. Then there was Tannattos, who grumbled at everything but fought like a demon. These three, with Runt, formed Calgacus' council of war.

"So how do we win a great victory?" Tannattos asked. "Some Romans have already crossed the Hafren. They are building forts and staying in them, blocking the valleys. We can't beat them if they don't come out to fight."

"We could try luring them out," Hillinos suggested.

237

"How?" Rhydderch asked.

Hillinos shrugged. Nobody had any suggestions.

"We don't have to lure them out," Calgacus said after he had let them consider the problem for a while. "We will attack them. We will destroy one of their forts."

"You're crazy!" Tannattos declared. "That can't be done."

Runt nodded his agreement. "Even Caratacus couldn't do that," he said.

Calgacus smiled. "It hasn't been done before, but I think I know how we can do it." Using a short stick to scratch outlines on the earth, he told them his plan, explaining how they could achieve the impossible.

Tannattos shook his head. "Well, I still say it is crazy, but it's worth a try."

Calgacus scanned the faces of the other men. None of them raised any objections.

"All right," he said. "I want to be ready to strike before Beltane. That gives us around two moons to prepare." He pointed at Hillinos. "Can you get thirty men practising with bows?"

Hillinos frowned. "Bows are for hunting animals. You can't kill a man at much over thirty paces with a bow, and it takes a lot of practice to use them well. Anyway, they'll be useless against the Romans. They wear too much armour."

"We don't need to kill them," Calgacus said. "We just need to keep their heads down. I want a group of men who can fire arrows quickly, and can keep firing."

Hillinos agreed that he would see to it, although he did not look convinced as to the sanity of the idea.

Calgacus turned to Tannattos. "We have a lot of young men, new warriors. I'd like you to take charge of them, no matter what village they come from. You will lead the diversion."

"You mean I don't get to fight?" Tannattos asked, unhappy at the prospect.

"I mean you will be an essential part of the plan. For this to work, everyone must play a part. We have to find a new way of fighting them. Forget the ideas about glory and proving how brave you are. This is no time for that. We must fight together, the way the Romans do. This plan needs some men who are very fit to carry out the diversion. The young men are best suited to that, but an older head must lead them. Will you do this?"

Tannattos thought about it for a moment, then reluctantly nodded his head. "I'll do it."

"Good. Rhydderch, we'll need ladders and we'll need a way to cross the ditches. Can you get men working on that?"

"No problem," agreed Rhydderch. "There are plenty of men who are skilled at working with wood."

Finally, Calgacus looked at Runt. "And you, Liscus, get the most difficult job of them all."

As the days slowly lengthened, Calgacus drove the warriors harder. Only the chieftains knew the details of the plan. The others were simply told that they were preparing to fight a battle unlike any other. To win, they must run faster than they had ever run before.

Tannattos reluctantly supervised the training of the younger warriors. He did it well but he constantly grumbled about their lack of skill and experience. When Calgacus ignored him, he complained about the lack of swords.

"They don't need swords for what they have to do," Calgacus told him. "But the more experienced warriors do need them."

Seeing that Calgacus would not be swayed, Tannattos turned to moaning about the weather, which had turned wet again.

Ladders and ropes were made, walkways of planks were nailed together and warriors were taught how to fight against men wearing armour. The hill and river plain around Caer Gobannus became an armed camp as the war host gathered. Similar camps were scattered through the neighbouring valleys because Calgacus knew that having too many men congregated in one place would lead to disease breaking out.

While the men trained, Calgacus prowled everywhere, issuing commands, offering advice and giving encouragement. He spent the daylight hours constantly on the move yet there never seemed to be enough time. Beltane, the early summer festival, was fast approaching.

Beltane was a time of celebration, a sign that the season had turned, that the hardship of winter was over and that vibrant, green life had returned to the land. By the time Beltane came around, the sun rode high in the sky and the long winter nights were forgotten. It was a time for sowing seeds, for tending the new-born lambs, foals and calves. On the feast day, huge bonfires would be lit high

239

on a hill and the cattle would be driven between them, symbolising movement through a gateway into the new year. Everyone was busy at Beltane, far too busy to fight a war. The campaigning season did not start until after Beltane. Everybody knew that, even the Romans.

"Must you go?" Senuala asked as she wriggled close to him under the covers.

"Yes."

"But it is so early in the year. The druids gave you until midwinter to win your victory. Why do you have to go so soon?"

"Because I must."

She cuddled into him, wrapping her arms and long legs around him. "I don't want you to go," she said, her tone pleading. "Stay here with me."

He kissed her forehead. "You know I cannot stay. But I will come back. You can be sure of that."

"I will pray to Nodens to watch over you," she said. "But I have a bad feeling about this, Calgacus. Please do not go."

"I must."

She cried then, pulling away and refusing to let him touch her, shaking off his hands when he reached for her. Angry, he rolled away, turning his back to her, letting her cry herself to sleep.

"I don't understand her," he confided to Runt the following morning.

"Don't bother trying," Runt advised airily. "You'll never understand women."

"That helps a lot. I wish I knew what is bothering her. I know she doesn't want me to go but I get the feeling there is something more."

"Wrong time of the moon," Runt said. "One sennight in every four, women get really irritable. You should know that."

"It's not that."

"Maybe she's pregnant," Runt suggested.

"She says not."

"Then maybe it is because she is not pregnant."

"It's not for the want of trying," Calgacus said gloomily.

"In that case, you'd better concentrate on what we need to do," Runt said. "Forget her for a few days until we get the job done. This is not going to be easy, you know."

"We can do it. We're almost ready. It's time for you and your men to prepare."

Runt had chosen thirty men for the crucial part of the attack. He had drilled them all winter, driving them as hard as he could, explaining over and over again what they needed to do. Now, with several hundred of their comrades gathered on the grassy slope outside the gates of Caer Gobannus to watch, they were to have their hair cut short and their faces shaved. They were not happy about it. Runt was none too pleased either, especially at the thought of losing his moustache.

"You get to keep yours," he accused Calgacus.

So Calgacus went to the stool first, telling the barber to shave off his moustache. The warriors laughed as the barber first trimmed the long hairs, then applied oil before scraping his razor deftly across Calgacus' face, giving him a shave which, for the first time since he had been old enough to grow one, included removing his moustache. He twitched his lips, felt the smooth skin with his fingers, then stood up. The men cheered and laughed.

"What about your hair?" Runt asked. "You should cut that too."

"Not this time," replied Calgacus.

Runt was next to sit on the barber's stool. He too was shaved, then his hair was cut short, the barber trying inexpertly to give him a Roman hair style. Shaving was one thing, but few of the tribesmen ever cut their hair short, so the end result of the barber's attempt was rather uneven. Still, the watching men applauded when Runt stood up.

The rest of his chosen men followed him without argument. When they had all been shorn of their long hair, Calgacus addressed them, making sure that the other warriors could hear.

"You men have the most dangerous job," he told them. "The whole plan depends on you. If you fail, we all fail. You have been chosen because I believe you are men who will not fail. You will make this work. We are all relying on you, and I know you will not let us down."

He thought it was a poor speech, but there were more cheers and now the shaven men wore their short hair as a mark of pride. It denoted them as men apart, men who would dare to do what no other men had ever done.

241

Senuala folded her arms across her chest when she saw Calgacus' clean-shaven face. He could see that she was still angry with him but her stance softened slightly when he asked her what she thought of his new appearance.

"It makes you look younger," she said grudgingly.

"That was the point of wearing a moustache," he told her. "I am the War Leader. I am supposed to look older. I am supposed to look fierce, to scare my enemies."

She reached up to run her fingers along his upper lip and down the sides of his mouth where the hair had grown. Her gentle touch suggested that she might have accepted that she could not change his mind about going to war.

"It suits you," she declared. "Or it will once the pale skin has turned a bit darker." Before he could protest at her mockery, she reached for him, pulling his face down so that she could kiss him. "You don't need a moustache to make you a fierce warrior," she assured him.

He kissed her back, relieved that she had apparently forgiven him.

"We will soon find out," he said.

Because the time was suddenly upon them.

Runt and his chosen men left first because they had the greatest distance to travel. They rode horses, with other riders accompanying them to bring the mounts back when Runt led the men deeper into Roman territory on foot. Calgacus wished his friend luck.

"We'll see you in six days," he said, clasping Runt's hand.

"Depend on it," Runt said. "Just make sure you are there. We're going to look awfully silly if we try this without you."

"We'll be there."

Calgacus watched his friend ride off, taking the first steps in the plan that Calgacus had devised and which would lead either to glory or disaster.

The following day, Calgacus and Rhydderch led a long, ragged column of men southwards, into the hills. Messengers went to the neighbouring valleys, calling the warriors together from their far flung camps. Gathering up their weapons, the Silures marched to war.

Chapter XXV

The Romans were always building. Calgacus and his men had been watching them all winter and had been amazed at how much they constructed. Even in poor weather, they built things. Over the winter, much of their effort had been put into building the massive fortress beyond the river Hafren at the place they called Glevum, constructing a permanent home for thousands of legionaries who guarded a river crossing.

Now, despite their initial fear of the tidal bore that regularly swept up the Hafren, the Romans had pushed across the river, into the broad, green flatlands that bordered the estuary where it joined the sea. They were building smaller forts and watchtowers along their frontier to guard their province from the Silures, forcing the tribesmen back into the hills. In many of these forts the soldiers built wooden homes for themselves, setting up long, rectangular barracks. In other, less permanent camps, they shivered in tents through the bitter winter.

But it was not only forts; they were building roads to connect these forts, roads that ran straight, through woodland, over hills, across rivers; roads that grew in length at astonishing speed, often several hundred paces each day. It seemed that nothing could stop the Romans when they started building.

It was the soldiers who did the construction work. The legionaries were trained not just to fight, but to build everything. They built their own fortified camps and they built the roads, digging the ditches, piling up the layers of gravel and rock, then laying shaped cobbles until they had a paved route along which they could march with a speed that few armies could hope to match.

The men making these roads would quickly construct a small fort for themselves, a base to protect them at night while they built a stretch of roadway during the day. After a few days they would abandon the camp, march along the road they had just completed and build another fort. It was never-ending, hard, back-breaking

243

work. It was what the legionaries did better than any men alive.

As they pushed inexorably inland, their supplies were brought to them by ox-drawn wagons that rumbled along the new roads. The further the roads pushed along the frontier, the longer that supply line grew. That, Calgacus fervently hoped, would give him the opportunity he needed.

Calgacus was nervous. There was a watchtower on the far hill, away to the northwest, and another perilously close by, to the southeast. He had selected his target carefully, knowing he had to take advantage of the cover provided by the thick woodlands, but to reach that target he had to move five thousand men through the woods, over the hill and down to the fort without alerting the Roman sentries in the watchtower. If he had been leading a small raiding party of twenty men, it would not have been a problem but he had so many warriors that he felt certain they would be detected. He wished there was some other way to get close to the fort, but his scouts had covered every blade of grass in the area and he knew that there was no other choice.

He let Rhydderch lead the way, with Hillinos bringing up the rear while he patrolled the column, constantly whispering to the men, reminding them, especially the inexperienced men, to remain silent.

They reached the top of the hill by late afternoon. Slowly, going down in small groups, they made the descent, through the thick woodland, trying desperately to make no noise. By the time the sun was sinking low, away to their left, Calgacus was at the foot of the slope, with his men strung out along the foot of the hill, concealed far back among the trees.

Taking Rhydderch with him, Calgacus crawled forwards to the edge of the forest until he found a spot where they could peer out from behind a bush. Two hundred paces distant was the dark bulk of the Roman encampment.

Like all Roman forts, this one was well protected. It had a double ditch and a high rampart of earth, topped by a wooden palisade of stakes. Sentries patrolled the rampart, their long javelins carried over their shoulders. There were four gates, one on each side, but the north and south gates were not centred; they were closer to the eastern side of the fort. Peering along the wide valley, Calgacus could see the trackway coming from his right, leading to the fort's eastern gate. He could see the track but, from where he lay hidden, the gate was concealed from his view.

He looked left and right. The valley stretched out in both directions, wide and open. The Romans had a clear view of anyone trying to approach from either east or west. To the north was open country too, but to the northwest a steep hill jutted skywards. Near the summit of that hill, overlooking the western approaches to the fort, was a watchtower. Calgacus knew that there were always eight men in that tower, with at least two of them permanently on watch, looking to the west for any sign of attack by rebellious tribesmen. He allowed himself a satisfied smile. The Romans were watching the west but he already had five thousand warriors behind them.

He studied the fort again. He could not see over the wall, but he had had men watching these Romans for many days. Every fort was built the same way. He knew that there were lines of tents inside, all neatly ordered, enough to shelter nearly five hundred legionaries who spent their days building the road along which their supplies would come. Each night they went inside their camp, closed the gates and slept securely in the knowledge that nobody had ever managed to breach a properly fortified Roman camp.

Calgacus stared at the fort as if he was willing the walls of earth and wood to collapse before his eyes. The enormity of what they were about to attempt came home to him as he watched the patrolling sentries, saw how high the ramparts were.

He was twenty two years old. If he wanted to live beyond his twenty third birthday at midwinter, he needed to achieve the impossible.

He nudged Rhydderch, signalling that they should return to the dark woods to wait out the night. There would be no camp fires, no singing, not even any speaking above a whisper. In the fading light, picking his way through the dark shadows of the trees, Calgacus moved among his men, reminding them over and over again that they must remain silent. Discovery now would mean defeat.

When it was too dark to move around safely, he sat down, drank some water, chewed on some stale bread and cheese, then tried to sleep. He had done all he could. The warriors were in position. Now, everything depended on Runt.

While Calgacus was leading his army through the hidden pathways of the forests, Runt and his thirty shaven men were setting a trap. The Roman road was a line of grey against the green of the wide earth, pointing like an arrow to the western frontier. There were precious few places for an ambush because the Romans were learning that trees close to the road could hide tribesmen, so wherever the road ran through woodland, they had cleared the trees back for at least fifty paces on either side. Runt had been forced to set a different kind of trap.

He knew that the supply convoy would come this way, just as he knew there would be at least a dozen soldiers escorting it. Surprising them would not be easy. Killing them all would be even more difficult. He and Calgacus had wrestled with the problem for a long time, suggesting and discarding ideas. The plan they had come up with was, Runt knew, extremely risky. But it had to work. Without it, Calgacus and the main force would have no way of getting into the fort.

Carefully, Runt looked around, checking that everything was in place. There was a small bridge, crossing a narrow stream. A man could splash across the stream in three strides with the water barely reaching above his ankles, but over the countless years that the water had run its course, it had gouged a deep, steep-sided gully for itself, with few easy places for a wagon to cross. The Romans, determined as ever to keep their road as straight as possible, had built a bridge. It, too, was a small thing. Piers of stone had been sunk into the earth at either side of the ditch and long planks of wood had been laid across them, then secured in place by heavy brackets and thick, iron nails that were as long as a man's hand. The result was crude by Roman standards, but it served well enough. In time they would build a proper bridge of stone, but, for now, the legionaries had moved on to build the next section of roadway.

Runt had four swordsmen hiding under the small bridge. They were cramped, uncomfortable and wet, but they could not be seen by anyone coming along the road. On the north side of the road was a wide stretch of soggy marsh land. Hidden in the long grass, lying on the wet ground, tufts of grass tucked into their clothing to aid their concealment, were another ten men.

The rest of the chosen men were busy. They had chopped down three trees, lopped off the larger boughs, dragged the fallen trunks to the side of the road, near the bridge, and were using small axes to trim them. Runt stood on the paved roadway, acting the part of an overseer. He was unarmed. His two newly-acquired Roman swords lay hidden among the swords of his warriors, beneath bundles of cloaks at the roadside.

Old Myrddin had told Calgacus to let the enemy see what he wanted them to see. Runt hoped that the approaching Romans would simply see a gang of men chopping wood.

The convoy, though, was late. The road remained empty for as far as he could see. Few tribesmen would use it, he knew; the Romans did not allow their subjects to move around the country freely. The roads were for the army and for imperial messengers. This far out near the frontier, there was very little traffic. Runt told his men to rest. There was no point in tiring themselves when there was nobody to see them. He stood on the road, looking eastwards.

It was late afternoon before he saw a dark spot in the distance, a small cloud of dust rising above it. With a shout, he set his men working again, playing their parts. He called to the men hiding in the marsh grass to stay down and to keep still. Then there was nothing else to do except wait for the wagons to reach him.

There were four large carts, each one laboriously pulled by two oxen. Great leather sheets covered the contents of the wagons, protecting the precious supplies from the elements. Runt tried to count the soldiers, although it was difficult with them coming straight down the road towards him. At least a dozen, he reckoned.

"Keep working!" he called to his men as he turned to face the oncoming convoy.

He stood his ground, a few paces short of the bridge. He wanted them to come to him, to bring their wagons close to where his men lay hidden.

The convoy rumbled towards him. When it reached to within twenty paces, the leading soldier signalled the wagons to halt, while he approached Runt. He was carrying a long spear and a large, oval shield, wearing a short sword at his right hip, a helmet on his head and a coat of chain mail over tunic and trousers. His eyes glanced around suspiciously as he came to see what was going on.

Runt stepped towards him, arms held away from his body to show the man that he was unarmed.

"Are you the lumber wagons?" Runt asked in a loud voice.

247

"You're early. We haven't got it all ready yet." He gestured towards the men chopping at the great logs. "It will be a while yet."

The soldier blinked in consternation. "What lumber?" he asked. "Our wagons are full."

"Oh. They said that wagons would come for the timber. But we have a lot still to do."

"Well, get out of the way so that we can pass." The soldier looked and sounded irritated, flicking the tip of his spear towards where Runt's men had dragged one of the long tree trunks on to the road, partially blocking the way.

"Of course." Runt hesitated. "I don't suppose you have any wine you could sell us?"

"No." The soldier was annoyed, but no longer suspicious.

Runt, looking over the man's shoulder, saw the rest of the soldiers relaxing, chatting to one another in a desultory way while their commander tried to get the road cleared. He waved his left hand, signalling to the men hidden in the long marsh grass, telling them to wait. The movement distracted the soldier. He glanced to the side to see who Runt was waving to.

Runt seized the opportunity. His right fist crashed into the soldier's cheek, sending the man staggering back. Runt, moving with the speed that made him so deadly, instantly had his left hand on the man's sword, pulling it free of its scabbard. It found the soldier's throat before the man could regain his balance.

The warriors, expecting Runt's move, dropped their pretence and charged to the road. Some carried their axes, others grabbed for the swords hidden under the cloaks. The men under the bridge, already armed, scrambled up the muddy bank to join the charge, yelling wildly as they ran.

Runt switched the sword to his right hand, sprinted towards the first wagon, dodged past the oxen and jumped up to cut down the panic-stricken driver. A spear came for him, but he kicked it aside, then jumped down to kill the soldier with a vicious slash across his throat. It was a clumsy stroke, but the man's chain mail meant that he was too well protected to risk a thrust to the body.

The soldiers were running now, trying to form ranks, but they were in two groups, separated on either side of the wagons. Runt's men swarmed at them, heading for the men on the side furthest from the marshland. The soldiers all turned to face them, the group on the far side of the convoy desperately trying to crowd through between the wagons. The oxen snorted, alarmed by the smell of blood, the movement and the shouting. For a moment the battle turned frantic and bloody, the Romans using the superior reach of their spears to fend off their attackers. Then the warriors who had been hidden in the long grass of the wetland, charged in behind them, overran the wagons and caught the Romans in a deadly trap.

It was over quickly. The men who drove the wagons were slaughtered and the soldiers were finished off without mercy, leaving an eerie silence hanging over the scene. For a moment nobody moved, then Runt began shouting commands, reminding his men of what they needed to do.

"Get their armour off! Hurry!"

The Roman corpses were quickly stripped, their armour and weapons distributed as warriors tried to find coats of mail that would fit. There were fifteen Romans, so there were not enough uniforms to go round, but they had expected that. As the bodies were stripped, the corpses were carried the long walk to the trees where they were dumped out of sight. Then the wagons were unloaded, the supplies hauled away to the woods, creating space for the men without uniforms to hide under the leather sheets.

Two of the warriors had been wounded. Runt offered them the chance to make their own way home, but both elected to stay, joining the men in the wagons.

Under Runt's constant prompting, the warriors worked with nervous speed, exchanging small, unfunny jokes as they prepared to take the place of the Roman convoy. Runt caused some hilarity when, even though he had grabbed the smallest coat of mail, he still found it hanging low, almost to his ankles. He joined in the laughter, clucking his tongue in disappointment, but there was nothing for it. He was the only one who spoke Latin, so he had no option but to wear the oversized armour.

Facing his war band, he announced, "All right, lads. You are the shaven men, the chosen ones. But for the moment you are Romans. Try to act like them. Remember what I taught you. Now let's get moving."

Hefting the heavy Roman spear over his shoulder, he led them along the road on the long trek to the fort.

They stopped at nightfall, making camp beside the road. Sitting by the fire, Runt went over the plan with them once more, making sure they knew what to do, rehearsing the few Latin commands he might need to give them.

"What happens if the rest of the men haven't got there?" one warrior asked.

"They'll be there," Runt assured him. But that was his worry, too. If Calgacus had not managed to get several thousand warriors through the woods undetected, Runt and his men would be marching to their deaths. He had to believe that his friend would be there. Yet even if he was not, Runt was not afraid. Calgacus had saved him from a life of slavery and no matter how often he fought alongside his friend, he knew that he would never be able to repay that debt.

Calgacus needed a victory to escape Cethinos' machinations, so Runt would do whatever was needed to help him. Calgacus had asked him to do this, and Runt had agreed, knowing the risks. He might die, but he was determined that, whatever happened, he would never be a slave again.

He had stood there, covered in filth from the pig sty, facing Togodumnus, king of the Two Tribes. People clustered around, gawping at him, laughing at him, at the joke the king had made about his diminutive size, and the new name he had been given. At the time he had not known who these people were, just that they were laughing at him.

The two girls, the tall, red-haired Bonduca and the blonde Beatha, giggled and pointed. In an extravagant gesture, Bonduca held her nose with one hand while she waved the other under it as if to dispel the unpleasant smell.

"He stinks!" she declared.

Togodumnus stared down at him, rubbing his chin thoughtfully. "What is your name?" the king asked.

"Liscus."

"You were a slave of Rubius, the trader?"

Runt nodded. "Yes, Lord."

"Why did you run away?"

Runt thought that was a silly question. "I wanted to be free," he said.

Togodumnus nodded. "And Calgacus helped you?"

"Yes."

The king's gaze took on a sharp look. "Did you run, or did he engineer your escape?"

"I ran. He found me and helped me hide."

Togodumnus nodded. "Well, what am I to do with you?"

Cethinos spoke in a tone that suggested he was bored by Togodumnus' needless concerns. "He should be held as a captive for when we require a sacrifice," the druid said, as if the solution should be apparent to everyone.

Runt felt his legs go weak when he heard the old man's words. He gave the druid a terrified look, unable to speak, but Calgacus shouted to the king, "No! Cethinos always says that! Liscus is not a prisoner. He will be my friend."

Togodumnus held up one hand, stifling any more protests. "I think it is up to Liscus to decide whether he will be your friend. But I agree; to kill him, or even to imprison him again, would be a poor reward for such a brave act. The Romans are not renowned for letting slaves escape." He rubbed his chin again. "Well, you are here now. I suppose I must welcome you to the Two Tribes of the Catuvellauni and the Trinovantes."

Cethinos had rolled his eyes in disgust, but Calgacus had put an arm round Runt's mud-stained shoulders and said, "Ignore him. He just likes sacrificing things, but he can't do anything to us. Togodumnus will not let him."

How things have changed, thought Runt as he stared into the fire.

Somewhere in the darkness an owl hooted, snapping him out of his reminiscence. Some of the men looked up, alarmed. Owls were birds of ill omen, their calls harbingers of doom.

"A warning from the Gods!" a man hissed nervously. "Someone is going to die."

Feigning a confidence he did not feel, Runt said, "Yes. The Romans."

He hoped he was right.

251

Chapter XXVI

Runt's men marched before dawn, following the road by the pale light of a waning moon. The wagons moved painfully slowly, the wheels rumbling along the cobbled surface, creaking and groaning. No wonder the Romans were often caught unawares, Runt thought. The noise of the wagons, the thudding of the oxen's hooves, the tramp of the men's hob-nailed sandals, all served to drown out any other sound.

On and on they rumbled, passing the small milestones that measured out one thousand paces, one Roman mile. As they walked, Runt prayed to Camulos that Calgacus and his men were ready and waiting.

He turned his head frequently, watching the eastern horizon behind him for the first signs of dawn. He knew they must get the timing of their approach right. Too early and it would be too dark to see anything, too late and the Roman troops would be up and about their daily business. He had been over the distances and times again and again when they were planning this. He must judge this correctly or the plan would fail. He knew the distance from the bridge to the fort, he knew how fast, or rather, how slowly, the wagons would move. But still he worried. So much depended on them getting this right.

The sky behind the tiny convoy grew gradually lighter, the hills and trees standing out from the night sky as darker silhouettes. Runt urged the drivers to make the oxen move faster, but the beasts seemed to have only one, frustratingly slow, pace. As the first rosy fingers of dawn slowly appeared in the sky, the birds began their singing and chirping to greet a new day. Runt felt the cold sweat of anxiety on the back of his neck. Then, as they crested a low rise, the paved road petered out, becoming a simple, wheel-rutted trackway, with the valley, still dark with night's shadow, stretching out ahead of them.

And there, in the middle distance, was the black outline of the fort, its position marked by the flickering of the torches on the

252

ramparts.

Runt breathed a sigh of relief, knowing that he had got the timing right. They were committed now. This new day would bring glory. Or death.

Calgacus felt as if he had lain awake on the hard earth all night, but he must have slept because Rhydderch had to nudge him awake with his foot.

"Nearly dawn, lad," the veteran warrior whispered.

Calgacus wearily pushed himself to his feet and stretched his muscles. All around him men were waking, preparing for the battle. He knew that many of them would not have slept at all that night. The knowledge that you are going into battle in the morning is not conducive to sleep. He moved quietly among them, whispering messages of good luck, telling them that he knew they would do well, reminding them again and again of the need for silence. There was quiet laughter when one man retched, vomiting up the contents of his stomach.

Calgacus found Hillinos and his archers among the trees.

"We're ready," Hillinos assured him.

"The ladders and boards?"

Rhydderch whispered. "Just behind you."

"Then let's go and watch for Runt," said Calgacus.

He and Rhydderch crawled to the edge of the woods again, peering out at the fort. They could see the flickering flames of torches on the ramparts. The distance seemed so much greater now, he thought. There was a lot of open ground to cover between their hiding place and the fort.

The sky grew lighter, a trumpet blared out a call from inside the fortress and he knew that the Romans would be stirring in answer to the summons. The men would be crawling from sleep, preparing their morning meal. Soon they would don their armour and come out to begin building another stretch of road, but for a short while they would be vulnerable, wearing only their tunics, unprepared for battle. They had no need to be prepared, of course; they were safe, protected by the ramparts. Nobody had ever breached a fortified Roman camp. They knew it could not be done.

Rhydderch nudged Calgacus' arm, pointing eastwards. There, coming over the low rise, was a small convoy of wagons. The leading soldier, a short man, lifted his spear high in the air, then lowered it. Silhouetted against the skyline, he raised the spear again, then a third time.

Calgacus grinned. "That's Runt! He did it."

Relief flooded through him. He had not realised just how nervous he had been, how much tension had gripped him.

Rhydderch bared his gap-toothed grin. "By Andraste's holy tits, this crazy plan might just work."

Calgacus returned the grin. "Of course it will. Did you ever doubt it?"

"Just so long as you believe it, we'll do the same," chuckled Rhydderch.

"Go back and tell everyone to move closer to the edge of the trees, but remind them to stay out of sight."

Still grinning, Rhydderch slipped silently back into the woods.

The wagons approached the fort. All around him, Calgacus could hear the rustle of movement as his warriors edged closer. He moved back, seeking the cover of a large tangle of brambles. Crouching behind the bush, he rose to his knees, then took his shield from his back, looping it over his left arm. Then he drew his sword.

Soon, he told himself. Soon.

The gates swung open as Runt approached at the head of the supply convoy. A Centurion stood at the gateway, idly swishing his vine staff that served both as a mark of his rank and as a useful implement for beating obedience into the soldiers.

"Where the bloody hell have you been?" he demanded brusquely as Runt marched up to the gates. "You should have been here last night."

"We were attacked, sir," said Runt. "We had to fight off some barbarians. We lost two men."

The Centurion scowled. He knew that the barbarians had been increasing their raids over the past few months, though most of the attacks up to then had been some distance to the south. He could hardly complain if the men had fought off an attack and still managed to get the supplies through, but he was not about to congratulate them either. The men guarding the convoy were mere auxiliary troops, not yet Roman citizens, certainly lower in status than the citizen legionaries he commanded. He scowled at the little man who led them, rolling his eyes in disgust at the man's sloppy appearance and his over-sized coat of chain mail.

Grudgingly, he ordered, "Get the wagons in and get them unloaded."

"Yes, sir!" Runt waved the wagons forwards.

The Centurion stood aside as the convoy rumbled and creaked its way into the open space behind the gates. Runt also stood to the side, watching the wagons pass, taking up position near the Centurion and two of the sentries.

His heart was beating fast. Tannattos should have shown himself by now. Even as the thought went through his mind, he heard the cry from the far end of the camp. Heads turned. Men pointed and the Centurion snarled a curse.

"What is it?" Runt asked, feigning confusion and managing to step in the Centurion's way.

"The bloody savages are attacking the watchtower!" the Centurion barked, pointing his staff up at the hill to the northwest.

Runt turned to look. Up on the hill, so small as to be nothing more than a swarm of dark dots on the high slopes, hundreds of men were rushing up to the watchtower. A flag was waving from the top of the tower, signalling to the fort far below. In the fort, a trumpet blared an urgent tune, calling men to arms.

Turning back, Runt saw that the fourth wagon was at last in the gateway. He nodded to the driver who immediately hauled on the reins and jammed the brake lever into place, stopping the wagon in the centre of the open gates, preventing the soldiers from swinging them shut.

The Centurion whirled round. "What are you doing?" he demanded angrily.

In answer, Runt rammed his spear into the man's throat, driving it up into his skull. The Centurion let out a brief, strangled gasp then toppled backwards, his hands going to the wound, grasping the shaft of the spear, his eyes gaping as his life ebbed away. Runt ignored him, knowing that the wound was fatal. Releasing his grip on the spear, he drew his sword. He had leaped past the falling Centurion and killed one of the sentries before the stunned man had time to react.

The shaven men joined the slaughter, cutting down the rest of the surprised guards. At Runt's shouted command, the men in the wagons threw the leather covers aside and leaped out, swords at the ready. They cut the traces of the oxen, jabbing at the beasts to

255

alarm them and send them stampeding into the fort.

Runt quickly organised his armoured men into a wall, guarding the gate while the other warriors grabbed flaming torches from the gateway, hurling them at the lines of tents.

Legionaries, many of them still eating their breakfast, others half dressed in their armour, whirled in confusion. The trumpet blast had called their attention to the western gate, towards the watchtower that was under attack, yet now there were enemies inside the camp, maddened oxen charging through the ordered ranks of tents, warriors wielding flame and swords, rushing at them. Most of the Romans had not had time to fasten their complicated armour, and were completely unprepared for what was happening around them. The camp, usually so orderly, was in chaos.

Then the men on the south wall began shouting and pointing.

"Go!" Calgacus shouted. He knew that only the nearest men could hear him, but the rest would follow as soon as they saw him break cover. He charged out of the trees, pounding across the uneven ground towards the fort. Behind him, he heard the footsteps and breathing of hundreds of men as they streamed after him.

There was no shouting, no war cries, no chanting. The Romans were distracted by the feint attack on their watchtower, caught unawares by the convoy guards suddenly turning on them, and nobody in the fort was looking south. Calgacus and his men had two hundred paces to cover to reach the fort, and another fifty to get to the open gate before the Romans overwhelmed Runt and his shaven men and closed the gates again.

The tribesmen dashed across the valley. Calgacus was wearing his heavy breastplate. He was big enough to run even with its weight, but some men were already passing him. He did not mind. They had to reach the gate quickly and the fort seemed such a long way from the trees.

The sentries had seen them now, were shouting in alarm. He could only imagine the confusion inside the camp. He was relying on the commanders not knowing where the greatest danger lay, not being certain which threat to deal with first. His men were streaming towards the gate now, thousands of blue-painted, half naked warriors brandishing spears and swords. Some had plastered their hair with lime, spiking it up in fierce, white manes. Others had stripped to the waist, revealing painted designs of ferocious, snarling beasts that matched their own feral expressions.

Calgacus reached the wide ditches at last, grateful that he could stop his headlong run. Breathing hard, he urged his men to run on, waving his sword, sending them along the eastern edge of the fort to the open gate. He fought down the urge to join them; he was the War Leader and his task was to direct the next stage.

He turned, looking for Hillinos and his group of archers. They were close by, running hard to join him. He pointed his sword at the high rampart of the south wall.

"Keep their heads down!" he yelled.

The archers hurriedly formed a rough line, facing the fort. At Hillinos' command, they began loosing arrows in ragged volleys. The sentries on the wall ducked behind their shields. Arrows arced over the ramparts, falling inside the fort. That would add to the confusion, Calgacus thought.

He whirled, looking for the men with the ladders and boards. They arrived, breathless, flinging the long boards across the first ditch. Calgacus cursed when he saw that the boards were not quite long enough and had fallen some way down into the ditch, but his warriors charged on regardless. Men jumped on the boards, running across to leap up the other side and fling more boards over the second ditch. Other warriors simply charged down the slope of the ditch, splashed through the muddy water in the bottom and clambered up the other side. Normally, this would be suicidal, but Hillinos and his men were still firing, keeping the Romans' heads down and few javelins were being thrown at the attackers.

In moments, ladders were slammed against the wooden palisade. Some warriors scrambled up while others clawed their way up the earth bank to haul out the wooden stakes of the palisade. A handful of Romans tried to charge, to throw them back, but there were too many tribesmen and the wall was swept clear.

Hillinos threw down his bow and drew his sword.

"Open the gates!" Calgacus yelled to him.

Hillinos waved a hand in acknowledgement, then charged across the ditches, yelling at the men on the wall to open the gates. His cries were answered as the south gate to the fortress was hauled open to reveal a cluster of dead Romans who had been swamped by the rampaging tribesmen.

Calgacus screamed at his warriors to charge into the camp.

Yelling wildly, they ran in, baying for blood, swords waving.

Letting them go, Calgacus turned to run for the eastern gateway, where Runt had first made the breach for them. Warriors were still crowding in through the open gates, desperate to join the fight. Calgacus shoved and pushed, roaring at them to get out of his way. When he reached the entrance, he could scarcely believe he was there. They had breached the fort.

He felt a savage joy at what they had achieved. But now they had to finish the task. He knew that victory depended on his warriors killing as many Romans as they could as quickly as possible. He had seen the Romans snatch victory before. They must not be allowed to do it again. But as War Leader, he could do no more. It was time for him to join the fight.

The wagon had been dragged clear of the gateway, allowing room for the warriors to surge into the camp. Runt stood just inside the fort, looking ridiculous in a mail coat that was far too big for him. He held a bloody sword in each hand. All around the entrance corpses were piled, most of them Romans, although several of Runt's shaven men had been killed or wounded trying to hold the gate. But they had done their job and they had held it.

Runt shouted excitedly when he saw Calgacus. "Cal! We are winning!"

The camp was being devastated. Tents were wrecked, some burning. Bodies lay sprawled on the ground, weapons and armour were scattered everywhere. Terrified oxen stampeded through the fort, adding to the chaos. Someone had freed the officers' horses and these too were galloping around, desperately seeking a way out of the camp, bowling men over in their panic.

In the midst of the wreckage, men were still fighting, in small groups or singly. This was war the way the tribes knew it. There were no ordered ranks here, simply warriors facing each other in a fight to the death. The Romans were hopelessly outnumbered, unable to form their solid ranks, deprived of their armour. In ones and twos, they died as hordes of screaming Silures swarmed mercilessly over them.

Calgacus looked at Runt and his surviving shaven men. "Well done!" he told them.

"Let me get out of this stuff," Runt said, dropping his swords to haul the mail coat off over his head. He threw it to the ground, picked up his swords and said, "Let's finish them." His eyes were sparkling.

They ran through the camp, seeking out pockets of resistance, finding none. As soon as they saw any Roman still alive, dozens of tribesmen would rush at him and hack him down. Five thousand warriors had attacked five hundred unprepared legionaries, and they were slaughtering them.

Yet the sounds of fighting continued, out to the north side of the camp, beyond the ramparts. Calgacus and Runt charged out of the fort again, following the unmistakeable noise of battle. They stopped when they saw a knot of Romans gathered on the north plain, shields interlocked, standing their ground, surrounded by a snarling mob of warriors. An officer, wearing a red-plumed helmet, was rallying his men. There were barely fifty of them left alive, but they were formed up and they were armed. Many had no armour, but they held their huge shields and they gripped their swords with the grim determination of men who knew they must fight or die.

The Romans must have known the fight was hopeless. The Silures had charged them once and been thrown back, but more and more tribesmen were gathering and no men could stand for long against such overwhelming numbers. Yet their officer was shouting at them, shoving men into place, and, against all reason, preparing to march away, attempting to punch an escape route through the mass of tribesmen.

Calgacus lifted his sword. "Kill them!" he shouted.

He ran at the wall of shields and his men ran with him. He had done this before, at the battle of Caer Caradoc where he had leaped over the wall to smash into the Roman column. He had charged the Roman shields and he had broken through. He did it again.

He crashed his shield into the line with reckless fury, using his weight and speed to push back the man facing him. A sword stabbed at him from the man on the right, but his own sword was longer, his movement faster and he hacked the man down. He had created a gap. Screaming death, the Silures poured into it.

Calgacus battered another legionary down, then faced the Roman officer. The man showed no fear. He was older than Calgacus, almost middle-aged, a veteran soldier. He held his sword ready, feinted, then thrust. Calgacus blocked with his shield then swung his heavy blade. The Roman dodged back but Calgacus

259

used his immense strength to turn the swing into a thrust, slamming the point of the blade into the man's chest, ringing on his armour, making him stagger.

Warriors streamed past, ignoring this fight, allowing Calgacus the honour of killing the enemy's leader. He stepped forwards, rammed with his shield, felt the Roman's sword crash against the leather cover, gouging into the wicker frame beneath. Calgacus twisted his left arm, forcing the Roman's sword arm aside while he jabbed his own sword with as much force as he could muster. The longsword was not an easy weapon for close combat, it needed room to swing, but Calgacus was big enough and strong enough to use it to thrust, and his muscled arm drove the blade straight for the Roman. It took the man in the thigh, cutting through the protective leather strips of the man's skirt.

The Roman screamed, stumbled and Calgacus smashed his heavy blade down on his helmet, battering him to the ground. Shouting in savage victory, he sent a final, savage thrust into the back of the man's neck.

He spun, looking round for more enemies, but the battle was over. Tannattos and his young warriors were pelting down the hill, breathless from a headlong run, furious that they were too late to join the slaughter.

On the blood-soaked field, the warriors looked at one another, as if they could not believe that there were no more Romans left to kill.

Rhydderch appeared, practically jumping with excitement. "We did it, lad! We did it!" he shouted.

Then the chanting began.

The warriors had been forbidden to chant before the battle. Silence and surprise had been essential. Now they began to stamp their feet, bash swords and spears against shields, beating out the ritual that normally preceded a battle.

"Bouda! Bouda! Bouda!"

The chant echoed around the valley.

Bouda.

Victory.

Then the chant changed.

"Calgacus! Calgacus! Calgacus!"

Grinning hugely, Runt pointed a triumphant sword at Calgacus as he joined in the chanting. Calgacus lifted his own sword and shield in the air, raising his arms high in the early morning sunlight. He threw back his head, yelling defiant victory, an incoherent cry of savage joy. He had done the impossible. He had breached a Roman fort.

He had given the druids the great victory they demanded.

Chapter XXVII

Sitting in the dim light of his large office, listening to the drumming of rain against the wooden shutters, Governor Ostorius Scapula frowned as he read the despatch.

Outside, the colony of Camulodunum was being drenched by yet another of the incessant showers of rain that plagued the pestilential island of Britannia. Yet the Governor's frustration with the weather was nothing compared to the growing horror he experienced as he read the tattered scroll by the flickering light of a small oil lamp.

When he had finished, he lowered his hands, holding the parchment scroll loosely on his lap. He sat quite still for a long time, staring at the despatch as if willing it to change what it had told him. When he eventually looked up, his face was pale.

Standing stiffly on the other side of the desk, Anderius Facilis waited for an outburst of fury. But for once, Scapula appeared remarkably calm. Then Facilis noticed that the Governor had gone beyond mere anger. His face was grim with an icy rage that stiffened every muscle, making his skin look taut and deathly pale. When he spoke, Scapula's voice was full of barely controlled outrage.

"An entire cohort? In a fortified camp?"

"Yes, sir."

"They cannot all be dead."

"It is always possible that a few were taken captive, sir," Facilis offered. "But the body count was, I am told, precise. Unfortunately it was not possible to identify many of the bodies. The barbarians took their heads, you see."

Scapula tossed the parchment onto the desk. "They are savages," he said in disgust. The habit of head-hunting was just one of the many things he hated about the Britons.

"Yes, sir," Facilis agreed.

"What about the neighbouring forts? Did they not send men to help?"

"They did, sir, but it was too late. The barbarians were gone by the time they got there."

"Someone blundered," Scapula growled. "There is no other way the barbarians could have stormed a fort. Someone blundered and the savages got lucky. It is as well that the Camp Prefect was among the dead or I would have him executed for incompetence."

Facilis said nothing. He had read the despatch and quizzed the messenger who had brought it. There was no doubt that the barbarian assault had been a savage, merciless one. Yet the men from the nearest watchtower had reported that the attack had been co-ordinated and obviously well planned. The Silures had struck at dawn, wiped out the garrison, then run off westwards before reinforcements could arrive.

Facilis suspected that those reinforcements had not hurried too much and he could hardly blame them. The Centurion commanding them had claimed that they had driven off the barbarians but the report from the watchtower said that there had been several thousand Britons. He doubted whether they would have run from a couple of hundred legionaries. It sounded to Facilis like a well-planned and brilliantly executed attack. While he was appalled at the fate of the legionaries, he felt a grudging respect for the Britons. To destroy a Roman fort was unprecedented and it seemed to him that luck had played very little part in it. He held his tongue, however, knowing that the Governor would not want to hear such disloyal thoughts.

Resting his elbows on the desk, Scapula placed his head in his hands.

"I informed the Emperor that Britannia had been pacified," he said in a low, hoarse whisper. "When I sent Caratacus and his family to Rome, I was awarded triumphal honours."

"Yes, sir," Facilis agreed. He understood the Governor's concern. Only the Emperor or a member of the imperial family could celebrate a formal triumphal march through the streets of Rome, but a successful general like Scapula was sometimes permitted to wear a laurel crown and a purple toga as a mark of his success in battle. These privileges only lasted one month but he was also entitled to erect a statue of himself in the Forum at Rome as a permanent reminder to every citizen of his success.

Such honours were not given lightly, and only when a great victory had been achieved. Facilis knew that Scapula was worried that his acclamation as a triumphant general had been premature.

Scapula sat back, sighing deeply. "I said it before, Facilis. This place is a nest of vipers. If you turn your back for an instant, trouble will flare up. You need look no further than that nonsense with the Brigantes last year."

"Things in the North seem to have settled down now, though, sir," Facilis ventured cautiously.

Scapula exhaled loudly. "Perhaps, but I wouldn't count on it. One day we are going to have to deal with the Brigantes. I don't trust that Queen of theirs. She is too clever by half."

"She did give us Caratacus, sir."

"That's the only reason I'm prepared to leave her in place," Scapula said. "That and this latest problem." He waved an exasperated hand at the discarded despatch. "By Jupiter, we seem to spend our time racing from one part of this damned island to another, constantly putting out fires."

"It is not all bad news, sir," Facilis said. "Camulodunum has settled down. Since you had the protesters enslaved, there has been no more trouble over the taxes."

"A minor victory," Scapula responded. His voice was still gruff but his face grew a little less tense at the reminder of his success.

Under its Latinised name of Camulodunum, the town that had once been the home of the kings of the Catuvellauni and Trinovantes was now, nominally at least, the provincial capital. It was a growing settlement, with a population of retired legionaries who were busy establishing a proper Roman town. Streets were being laid out in a no-nonsense grid pattern and there were plans for a theatre and bath house. The old, scattered roundhouses of the barbarians were being swept away to make space for the new town. Camulodunum would soon become entirely Roman.

The colony was also home to the great temple. Construction was well under way; the massive foundations laid and the walls already rising to an impressive height. In time, the townspeople would be able to come here to worship the Emperor Claudius as a God. It would be the largest, most impressive temple north of the Alps and it had been Scapula's idea.

"Yes, this place is coming along nicely," the Governor conceded. "But I am thinking of moving my headquarters to Londinium. It is more central and has better communications with

Gaul and the rest of the Empire."

"Would you like me to find some suitable accommodation there, sir?" Facilis asked. That, he knew, would be no easy task. Londinium was a new settlement, a burgeoning river port on the north bank of the Tamesis. The Governor was correct about its location but it was still a small place compared to Camulodunum.

"Not until we get this latest problem sorted," Scapula said.

The Governor had recovered his composure now. Facilis could see that he was still angry but he had mastered his initial fury and was now thinking about how to deal with the Silures.

Facilis was pleased that Scapula had calmed himself. The Governor's temper was notorious but there was little doubt that they were facing the greatest disaster the island province had ever seen, and they could not afford to lash out angrily. This situation required a cool head. Facilis saw it as his duty to keep the Governor calm enough to make rational decisions instead of angry ones.

"How would you like to proceed, sir?" Facilis asked.

"This is serious, Facilis. I will deal with it personally."

Facilis nodded. Scapula lived by the creed, *delegatus non potest delegare;* someone to whom a task has been delegated may not delegate that task to anyone else. The Emperor had appointed Scapula as Governor, had delegated the task of defeating the rebels, and Scapula knew that he must finish that task personally. He was ultimately responsible for what happened in the province.

Clasping his hands together on the desk in front of him as if to prevent them shaking with anger, Scapula asked, "What is Valens doing?"

"Awaiting your orders, sir," Facilis replied.

Scapula grunted. Manlius Valens was Legate of the Second Legion *Augusta*, whose men had been massacred in the fort. Valens was a solid, dependable sort, but not a man inclined to act on his own initiative. Still, on this occasion, that suited the Governor. Revenge would be dealt out by Scapula himself.

"Send him a despatch. Tell him to do nothing until I arrive. But he is to prepare his men for a campaign. I want to exterminate that wretched tribe. Every last man, woman and child of the Silures will be put to death. Tell him that."

"Yes, sir. Shall I tell him when to expect your arrival, sir?"

Scapula frowned. "I need to check on the Iceni. I don't want

265

them causing any more trouble while I am away in the west. Seeing as I am near their territory anyway, a personal visit to Prasutagus should ensure he remembers who is in charge. We'll go west after that. Tell Valens to be ready to march by midsummer. That should give us plenty of time to wipe out the Silures before winter."

Facilis nodded. "Midsummer. Yes, sir. And the other legions?"

There was a pause while Scapula considered this. He had four legions, more than virtually any other Governor in the Empire. He could hardly approach the Emperor with a request for more troops, especially when he had been awarded triumphal regalia for winning the war. But the truth was that he needed all those men, and more, just to hold the wretched place down.

Britannia, Scapula mused, was like the many-headed Hydra; as soon as he cut off one head, another sprang up to strike at him. Or like a constantly bubbling pot that needed something to hold the lid down to prevent the water boiling over. No matter what he did, the pot kept boiling.

His legions were spread out, covering the frontier between the province and the barbarians. If he moved any one of them, trouble would almost inevitably flare up immediately. He sighed with frustration.

"The Ninth must stay at Lindum," he said, thinking aloud. "I still need them to keep an eye on the Brigantes. The Ninth is also handily placed should the Iceni cause any problems."

"Yes, sir," Facilis agreed. "And the others?"

"Tell the Fourteenth and the Twentieth to launch punitive raids, starting at midsummer. Every village, every farm, every settlement of any sort within three days' march to the west of their bases, is to be destroyed. Kill or enslave everyone. A touch of atrocitas will keep the Ordovices and Deceangli in line. But I don't want them launching any major offensive. They are simply to control the territory opposite them."

"Yes, sir. Does that mean that you propose to defeat the Silures with only the one legion?" Facilis asked. "The Second is under strength now, in light of what has happened."

"They will be enough!" snapped Scapula. "They will be burning with desire for revenge."

"Of course, sir," Facilis agreed smoothly. "I will send the orders without delay."

266

Facilis left the Governor's office with a feeling of relief. All things considered, Scapula had taken the news of the disaster remarkably well, but his retribution, when it came, would be terrible. Scapula was a straightforward man, raised in the Roman tradition. If he wanted to crack a nut, he would use a hammer. If that failed to work, he would simply fetch a bigger hammer. Subtlety was not a trait that was often found amongst the Romans.

Facilis almost felt sorry for the Silures. Rome's neighbours were treated to either *clementia* or *atrocitas*, clemency or atrocity. The Silures were about to discover just how bad *atrocitas* could be.

Chapter XXVIII

Calgacus had wanted to travel to Ynis Mon, to stand before the Druid Council so that he could see the old men's faces when he proclaimed his victory. Runt had thought that was a bad idea.

"You'll be putting yourself right into their hands," he said. "If Cethinos has his way, they'll find some excuse to keep you there this time."

Senuala agreed. "What if they say this victory was not enough?" she asked. She clung to him, her eyes pleading. "Don't go," she said insistently. "Stay here with me."

Calgacus was sure that he had done enough to prove that he could beat the Romans, but in the face of his friends' emphatic arguments, he asked Rhydderch to take the news to Ynis Mon for him.

Rhydderch frowned uncertainly. "Ynis Mon is a dangerous place," he said.

"Less dangerous than facing the Romans," Calgacus pointed out. "And you are taking good news."

Rhydderch nodded. "All right, I'll go," he agreed unenthusiastically. "I'll leave right after Beltane."

The tribe held a great celebration, combining the Beltane festival with a victory feast. Everyone got drunk, even old Gwalchmai, the oldest of the chieftains of the Silures. He had praised Calgacus to the skies, offering him a farm stocked with many head of cattle. Calgacus had laughed, telling the old man that he was a warrior, not a farmer, but that he would keep the offer in mind.

Senuala had sat beside him, smiling and laughing, her arm linked with his. He had given her some gold rings that he had looted from the Roman camp. She had been embarrassed at his show of generosity, but she wore them proudly.

The warriors had taken a huge amount of booty from the wreckage of the fort, everything from iron tools to horses, from tents to huge amphorae of wine and olive oil. They had also taken a vast number of weapons and armour. Few of the Silures valued the short Roman swords or the heavy armour, so Calgacus sent most of those with Rhydderch, telling him to deliver them to Cadwallon to be melted down and reforged into proper weapons.

Some of the heads of the dead Romans were presented to the local druids who took them away to their secret caves and woodland groves where they would be added to the druids' collection of grisly trophies as offerings to the Gods. Other heads were kept by the warriors as their own, personal proof of their bravery.

After the feast, Calgacus stumbled back to his house, half supported by Senuala. She helped him undress then climbed into bed with him. When he drunkenly grabbed at her, nuzzling her breasts, she at first tried to fend him off but eventually submitted to him. He did not care that she was reluctant. He was drunk and he was full of excited pride at what he had achieved. He wanted her and he took her, oblivious to her unwilling, passive acceptance.

He woke the next morning with his head thumping from the effects of the beer he had consumed. Senuala lay beside him, staring up at the smoke-darkened rafters.

"How are you feeling?" she asked, not turning to face him.

He groaned. "Good food, good drink and a good woman. It was a perfect night. But I am suffering a bit now. I could do with a drink of water. My mouth feels horrible."

"It serves you right," she said, quite matter-of-fact. "You were very drunk."

"It didn't affect my performance, though. Did it?" he said with a salacious leer.

"No. You were very . . . potent."

"That's me," he agreed.

She moved to face him, her expression clouded by a deep frown.

"Why did you not present a Roman head to the druids?" she asked.

"What?" His befuddled mind struggled to grasp the unexpected question.

"I know you killed some Romans. Runt told me you fought their leader in single combat. If you killed him, why did you not bring back his head?"

Calgacus shrugged. "I am not interested in trophies," he said.

269

"I am only interested in winning. What does it matter?"

"You should have presented his head to the druids," she said, her tone disapproving. "Or do you not honour the Gods?"

"Of course I honour the Gods," he said, wondering why she was making a fuss over such a trivial matter. "It's the druids I have little time for."

He sensed her whole body stiffen, as if in outrage. He could hear the hardness in her tone when she asked, "Is that because of what they have threatened to do to you?"

"Partly. But mostly it is because I have witnessed what druids do to innocent people in the name of the Gods."

"You cannot say such things!" she gasped, horrified by his admission. "The druids ensure that the Gods watch over us, that we are kept safe."

"Then they haven't done a very good job," he snapped, feeling his temper rising in the face of her condemnation. "They are always offering sacrifices but the Romans keep advancing, taking more and more of our land and enslaving our people. I'd respect the druids a lot more if they offered themselves up as sacrificial victims instead of telling everyone else what a privilege it is to be sent to the Gods."

He stopped, seeing the appalled look on her face. He expected her to launch an angry response but her expression changed, becoming suddenly sad. She lay back, blinking her eyelids, saying nothing.

After a long, thoughtful pause, she eventually said, "If the druids ever learn of what you have said, they will kill you. It would be best if you kept such thoughts to yourself."

"It was you who asked," he said, more sharply than he should have. He reached out to place a hand on her bare shoulder. "I didn't want to lie to you," he told her in a more gentle voice.

She said nothing and he thought she might have begun crying again. Bewildered, he struggled out of the bed and went in search of a drink of water.

Once they had observed the rituals of Beltane, the Silures returned to war, rampaging across the frontier, raiding and plundering as they pleased. More warriors flocked to join them, attracted by the news of the great victory. Some men of the Ordovices arrived at Caer Gobannus, declaring that they wished to fight alongside the

Silures, to fight with the mighty Calgacus. And while the tribesmen plundered the province, the Romans withdrew to their mighty fortress at Glevum, not daring to come out.

Calgacus took part in a few raids, but he was basking in the glory of his achievement, waiting for word from Ynis Mon that the sentence that hung over him had been lifted.

He managed to patch up his quarrel with Senuala. She was attentive to him, passionate when they made love, dutiful in keeping the house, but he knew that his admission regarding his attitude towards the druids was troubling her. Neither of them mentioned the matter again but he felt that something in their relationship had changed and that she blamed him for it.

"Maybe you should marry her," Runt suggested. "Most women want to go through a hand-fasting."

"Not until I know what the Druid Council has decided," Calgacus replied. "Anyway, she's never mentioned that. And she keeps picking faults with me."

"She's a woman," Runt said airily, as if that explained everything. "As long as she keeps your food hot and your bed warm, don't worry about anything else."

"That works for you, does it?"

Runt pulled a face. "Most of the time. But you know me. I never usually stay with the same woman for very long. Sula is starting to mention that young Gillarcos needs a proper father."

"Gillarcos is a good boy," Calgacus said. He had little experience of dealing with three year old boys, but Sula's son, Gillarcos, always seemed good-natured enough, although he did have a tendency to tease the village dogs.

"I know he is," Runt said. "But I don't think I want to be a permanent father."

"And I'm asking you for advice," Calgacus mocked. "It sounds like you have more problems than I do."

"At least I can just walk away from mine if it comes to it," Runt said. "She won't be happy, but I can handle that." He gave Calgacus a pointed look. "Could you walk away from Senuala?"

"Of course I could," Calgacus replied, just a shade too quickly.

Runt laughed. "No you couldn't."

The influx of new volunteers allowed many of the warriors to return to their homes. There were crops to be sown and livestock to be tended. Barley, oats and rye did not grow by themselves, kail and beans needed care to prevent weeds from strangling them. The small, dark-fleeced sheep needed to be plucked for wool, and lambs and bullocks must be selected for slaughter.

This was also a time for repairing homes, replacing thatch, mending fences and dry-stone walls. While the elite warrior-class could afford to remain under arms, there was always work to be done by the poorer men.

Knowing that the war was far from over, Calgacus instituted a system that allowed some men to spend time at home while others remained with the war host. These warriors spent their time watching the borders, carrying messages and practising their warcraft.

Calgacus rode through the valleys and climbed the hills to watch for any signs of a Roman attack. He visited their abandoned watchtowers and patrolled the banks of the Hafren. He kept himself busy but all the time, he waited for Rhydderch to bring an answer from Ynis Mon.

It was more than a full turning of the moon before Rhydderch eventually returned. He rode through the gates of Caer Gobannus with a grim expression on his face and with a druid accompanying him.

When they heard Runt's call, Calgacus and Senuala hurriedly got dressed before going out to meet the returning head man.

Rhydderch dismounted in the centre of the village where he was mobbed by his wife and daughters. He looked up, saw Calgacus but could not meet his gaze.

With the entire village gathering to watch, the druid also dismounted. His long, curly hair and full beard were brown, flecked with grey. He was short and plump, his stern face flushed with either exertion or worry. Rhydderch, still embracing his wife, answered the druid's unspoken question by gesturing towards Calgacus. Proudly oblivious to the stares of the villagers, the druid walked over to where the tall warrior waited for him.

The druid's eyes went appraisingly to the slim figure of Senuala, standing beside Calgacus. Then he looked back at the tall, dark-haired warrior.

"I am Cadwgan," he announced. "You are Calgacus?"

Calgacus could tell from the way the man spoke and acted that he was not bringing good news. He felt an emptiness in the pit of his stomach as he answered the druid's haughty question.

"I am," he confirmed.

"I bring word from the Druid Council." Cadwgan said rather pompously. He hesitated as if unsure of himself. After a moment, he cleared his throat and went on, "Your victory over the Romans is acknowledged as a good start to your campaign. But it is not the great victory we require."

Runt made as if to grab the druid's robe, but Calgacus was faster, flinging out an arm to pull his friend back. He faced Cadwgan, towering over the plump druid.

"So my doom still stands?" he asked, his voice harsh.

Cadwgan's initial haughtiness had deserted him. With his eyes nervously flickering towards a potential threat from Runt, he nodded. "That is correct," he said.

"So what do I have to do to win a great victory?" Calgacus demanded angrily. "Kill every last Roman single-handed? March to Rome and kill the Emperor? Tell me what it is you want from me!"

Cadwgan visibly flinched under Calgacus' anger. "It is not for me to say," he managed to reply.

Calgacus stared at him until Cadwgan blinked and lowered his gaze.

"I think you should get out of my sight," Calgacus told him, "before I reach down your throat and pull your rotten heart out."

Cadwgan looked horrified. "I am a druid!" he protested. "You may not threaten me with violence."

Calgacus laughed scornfully. "What have I got to lose? It seems to me that your masters want me dead anyway. Will they kill me twice?"

Cadwgan tried to regain some composure but the tall warrior scared him. He had been taught that nobody dared harm a druid, yet this man was openly threatening him. Worse, the look on the big warrior's face left Cadwgan in no doubt that he was more than ready to carry out his threats. Cadwgan was also uncomfortably aware that other warriors had left the camp that lay outside Caer Gobannus and had followed him in through the gates, anxious to hear his message. Even without looking at them he could tell that their mood was one of simmering violence. He resorted to one of the standard responses he had been taught to use.

"It is not your place to question the will of the druids," he said as firmly as he could.

Calgacus looked around at the villagers who were watching intently. "Do you hear the message from the druids?" he called out so that they could all hear. "We have not done enough. We have done what no other tribe has ever been able to accomplish and yet the druids, sitting safely on their sacred island, far from the dangers we face, have decreed that it is not enough." He paused, allowing a muttering of discontent to ripple around the crowd. "The druids are convinced that the only way to win is to lay me on an altar stone and shed my life."

There were shouts of anger at this. He glared at Cadwgan who was anxiously licking his lips. Calgacus stared him in the eyes as he said, "I can beat the Romans. I have proved it. If I have to prove it again, I will. I will give you your victory so that you may sleep safely at nights. The Silures will shed their blood for you while you stay out of harm's way and bravely slit the throats of people who cannot fight back." He jabbed a thrusting finger at Cadwgan's chest as he added, "You go and tell the Council of Druids that."

Runt began stamping his feet and clapping his hands in rhythm. He started the chant that the other warriors quickly took up.

"Bouda! Bouda! Bouda!"

Cadwgan, startled by the hostility, looked around, dismayed when he saw that even the women were joining in the chant. They were chanting for victory, but he could not tell whether they were calling for victory over the Romans, or over the druids. If it was the latter, it was an unprecedented display of disobedience.

Then the words changed.

"Bouda! Calgacus! Bouda! Calgacus!"

Calgacus stood, triumphant, daring the portly druid to oppose the will of the people.

Cadwgan mustered his courage. "I have delivered my message," he said over the noise of the crowd and with as much dignity as he could muster. "I will leave you to think on it." He walked over to Rhydderch. "You have somewhere for me to stay?"

Rhydderch, looking distinctly uncomfortable, nodded. "My home is yours. My wife will show you."

Rhydderch's wife and daughters dutifully led the druid to the head man's roundhouse. The echoes of the villagers' victory chant followed him.

Rhydderch frowned as he watched Cadwgan's retreating back, then he shook his head sadly and walked over to Calgacus.

"I am sorry," he said. "I tried to tell them, but they were determined that what we did was not enough."

"Maybe they are right," Calgacus said grimly. "The Romans are bound to want revenge. We killed a few hundred, but they have thousands more. Maybe we do need to do more."

"I don't think we have any choice," said Runt with a bitter half-smile.

Senuala had stood silently at Calgacus' side, but now she let out a stifled sob before hurrying back inside the house. Calgacus made as if to go after her, then stopped, turning to look back to Runt and Rhydderch.

"Send men to fetch Tannattos, Hillinos and the other chieftains. Get scouts out to find out what the Romans are doing. We have plans to make."

Without waiting for them to acknowledge his orders, he turned back to follow Senuala.

She was sitting on a stool beside the fire, her hands covering her face. He could see her shoulders trembling.

"What is it?" he asked, squatting down beside her. Outside, the sound of the chant had died away, leaving a quiet, ominous stillness.

Senuala lowered her hands to look at him with red-rimmed eyes. "What do you think it is? You are going to die."

He put his arm around her shoulders. "I am not dead yet."

"One way or another, you will be," she said hoarsely. "You cannot escape your destiny."

"Are you a soothsayer?" he asked, surprised at the conviction in her voice.

"The druids want you dead," she said. "The Romans want you dead. How can you escape?"

He pulled her close. "That is easy. All I need to do is kill all the Romans. That will force the druids to release me from their sentence."

"Nobody has ever defeated the legions," she said through her tears.

"Nobody has done it yet," he agreed.

She put her head on his shoulder and cried.

275

That night she made love to him as if it was the last night they would ever have together. Yet in the morning her tears returned and she could barely speak to him. Her reaction to Cadwgan's message surprised him. She had cautioned him that the Druid Council might reject his claim to have won the great victory they demanded, yet now that they were faced with the reality of the decision it seemed to have hit her particularly hard.

Unable to calm her, Calgacus gave up trying. With a frustrated sigh, he went in search of his chieftains. He had a war to plan.

Cadwgan watched Calgacus leave, heading out of the gates to the lower ground where many of his warriors were camped. The other men of the village, including Rhydderch and the little man they called Runt, followed after their young War Leader.

Cadwgan sighed with relief. This was not turning out at all the way he had expected. He could not believe how furious the people had been, how unrepentantly violent Calgacus' mood had been.

At forty years of age, Cadwgan was an old man by Pritani standards, yet young for a druid, and only just starting out on his life. He had passed the final rites only a short time ago, just before Beltane, a feat that had left him feeling immensely pleased with himself. He had stood before the Druid Council, reciting from memory great tracts of lore, including tales from the past and the exploits of the Gods. Then he had been quizzed on herbal lore, on the illnesses of the body and spirit and what cures were prescribed for each ailment. Finally, he had sacrificed a lamb and had examined its entrails, explaining to the nine old men what he had found and what each organ signified.

Looking back, Cadwgan wondered how he had got through all that without making a single mistake. He had waited for the Council's decision with trepidation but at the end of the long ordeal, Maddoc had welcomed him as a fully-qualified druid. His forehead had been smeared with blood from the lamb he had sacrificed, then each of the Council members had presented him with some token of his success, a set of divining rods, a bronze dagger, a staff, herbs and potions. It had been the happiest day of Cadwgan's life.

Later, when Cethinos, a member of the Druid Council, had come to him, asking him to deliver the Council's message to Calgacus, he had been ecstatic. It would be the first time he had left Ynis Mon since he had been fourteen years old. Not only that, he was carrying a message from the Council of Druids to a War Leader. It was an important mission, and he was honoured to be granted such a privilege.

He never questioned why he had been chosen for such an important task. Then Cethinos had taken him aside to explain his other mission.

Cethinos had been one of Cadwgan's teachers, helping him through the final stages of his preparations for the vital rites of passage. The old druid was well respected, fierce in his devotion to the Gods. Without his mentoring, Cadwgan knew he would have struggled to become a fully fledged druid. He owed Cethinos a lot. Now Cethinos had demanded payment of that debt.

Cadwgan had been left in no doubt what was required. He was rather afraid of Cethinos, but he had dared to question his commands, saying, "But I thought Maddoc had given Calgacus until midwinter?"

"Things change," Cethinos had replied dismissively. "When the Romans are defeated by the will of the Gods, Maddoc will realise the wisdom of what we have done."

Cadwgan had no more arguments to offer in the face of Cethinos' rigid certainty. Reluctantly, he had agreed to carry the second, secret message and now the time had arrived to deliver it.

Satisfied that the warriors would not return for some time, he made his way towards Calgacus' small roundhouse. He rapped on the door. From inside, he heard a woman's voice.

"Wait a moment!"

He did not wait. Pushing the door open, he ducked inside. He caught a glimpse of Senuala's naked back as she pulled her dress over her head. She whirled in alarm as she heard him come in.

"I asked you to wait!" she snapped, hastily pulling her dress around her.

"I do not have much time," he said. "Cethinos demands that you be ready."

She bit her lip nervously. "When?"

"Midsummer. As planned. Cethinos will be here himself."

Senuala bunched her fists. "I think Cethinos might be wrong about him," she said.

"Cethinos has known him a lot longer than you have. Calgacus is a crude man, a man who disobeys the will of the druids. You

277

saw that yesterday when he incited the people against me. He has no respect. He threatened me. He condemned himself by what he said to me."

"I know," she said. "But the people respect him. Perhaps they even love him. All the warriors are devoted to him."

"Their faith in him is misguided," Cadwgan insisted. "Remember how he betrayed your sister's trust."

Senuala lowered her head, nodding sadly.

"What is wrong?" he asked.

Senuala gave a slight shrug and shook her head. "I just got a fright when I saw you yesterday. Somehow, it brought home what I had been asked to do." She gave him a forlorn look. "Calgacus is a good man. He is brave and he is honourable."

Sternly, Cadwgan said, "You are mistaken. You saw what he is like when he threatened me. Tell me, has he said anything else to you? Has he spoken out against the true faith?"

She nodded mutely.

"Then what we are doing is justified," Cadwgan said. "The man is not to be trusted in anything he does. He defies the Gods. That can only bring disaster to us all."

"Can we not give him until midwinter?" Senuala persisted, her tone desperate and pleading.

Cadwgan walked towards her. He grabbed her, squeezing his chubby fingers into the flesh of her upper arms.

"A bargain has been struck. There must be a sacrifice of royal blood. Only that way will the Romans be defeated. You gave your word to Cethinos. You swore an oath that you would see this through."

"That was before I knew him!" Senuala said, her voice almost a sob.

Cadwgan gave her a sharp look. "Does he suspect you?" he demanded.

Senuala shook her head. "I convinced him I am upset that he might die," she said softly, as if she hated herself for the deception.

"Good. You should not mistake sleeping with him for loving him," Cadwgan warned. "You have been with many men on Ynis Mon."

Senuala's face took on a look of revulsion. "They were druids. Old men. It was not as if I had a choice. The Gods demand such things of their servants."

"And you have no choice now. You are doing the Gods' will. If you defy Cethinos in this, your soul will be damned forever in the afterlife. You gave your oath willingly. You must remember who you are. Steel yourself against this renegade warrior. He must die, for the sake of all the free people. If he does not, the Gods will never aid us in this war and we will all perish. What is one man's life against the lives of all the free people? You must do this."

Senuala dropped her head meekly. "He will resist," she said softly. "He will not go quietly. He knows the taste of my medicines. He will know if I give him something to make him sleepy."

Releasing his grip on her arms, Cadwgan fished inside a pouch that hung on his belt. He pulled out some small, red berries.

"Use these," he told her.

Senuala stared at the berries. "They could kill him," she said in a horrified whisper.

"Only if you give him too many. They will just make him too ill to resist." Taking her hand, he placed the berries in her palm. He paused, then asked, "What shall I tell Cethinos? Will you be ready for midsummer? Will you complete your sworn task?"

Senuala stared at the deadly fruit in her hand for a long time before she spoke.

"I will be ready," she whispered.

Chapter XXIX

Out in the wide, tree-bordered valley, in the centre of the camp where the warriors were gathering once again, a young man sat confidently among the chieftains as though he was entitled to be considered one of them. His name was Gutyn and he was sixteen years old. He had the dark, curly hair and swarthy looks so typical of the Silures, and he also exuded an air of complete confidence in his own ability. He was, Calgacus recognised, a born leader, a young man who could think for himself. Despite his youth, men were already clamouring to join him, to follow him.

"So what are the bastards up to?" Tannattos asked.

Gutyn smiled. "They are preparing to attack us. The Governor has said that he will kill every man, woman and child of the Silures."

Hillinos gave a mocking laugh. "They could try!"

"They have done that sort of thing before," Runt cautioned. "I have heard of such things. My own people were all but destroyed in my great-grandfather's day. If that is the Romans' intention, they will not stop until they have accomplished it, no matter how long it takes."

"So what can we do to stop them?" asked old Gwalchmai, his voice betraying his concern.

"We can kill them," said Calgacus evenly. He looked at Gutyn's youthful face. "I need to know when and which way they are coming. Can you watch them and send word?"

"I can do better than that," Gutyn assured him with an easy smile. "I will find out what their plans are before they march." He paused, studying the faces of the older men as his words sank in. He laughed at their puzzled expressions.

"They keep slaves," he explained. "Slaves hear things. All I have to do is talk to those slaves."

"You will go into the Romans' camp?" Calgacus asked.

"Perhaps not inside the fort itself," Gutyn admitted. "But you can get into a lot of places with the right words and a friendly smile."

"Then do what you can," said Calgacus. "I also need to know how many of them will come."

"One legion," Gutyn said instantly. "The Second Augusta. They are under strength, so they only have around four thousand legionaries, plus one hundred cavalry and six catapults. There will also be around five hundred auxiliary troops, mostly cavalry."

The chieftains looked at Gutyn in amazement.

"How do you know all that?" asked Calgacus.

Gutyn smiled his radiant smile. "I asked."

In the legionary fortress at Glevum, the Legate, Gaius Manlius Valens, was doing his best to hide his concerns from the Governor.

"We are ready to march when you give the word, sir," he said.

"Good," Scapula replied wearily. "I have had a long and tiring journey. I will visit the bath house and rest this evening. Tomorrow we will make our plans and we will march the following day."

"Very good, sir. Will you dine with the officers this evening?"

"Of course. I shall look forward to it."

The Governor left, heading for the legion's bath house, a gaggle of clerks and slaves following in his wake. Valens wondered whether he should prime one of his tribunes to ask the Governor why only one legion was being used for this assault. He dared not admit it to the Governor, but he knew that the men's morale was low. The loss of one of their cohorts, wiped out to the last man, had seriously shaken them. None of them wanted to be on this miserable island with its savage barbarians.

Though he could not show his feelings openly, Valens could not blame the soldiers. It was true that the legionaries wanted revenge, but the thought of marching deep into the territory of the Silures was enough to worry the best of them. Valens would have felt a lot happier if the Governor had brought another legion with him. The Silures were only barbarians but they would not be easy to defeat. At least one of their leaders seemed to know how and when to fight.

With a sigh, Valens decided it would be better to keep his thoughts to himself. The Governor was in a determined mood and Valens knew better than to show the man any sign of weakness. Aemilius Pudens, Legate of the Ninth, had already been sent home, if not in disgrace then certainly under a cloud of disapproval.

Valens had no wish to join him.

He knew there was no point in arguing with the Governor. It was plain that Ostorius Scapula was convinced there could only be one outcome to this campaign. They were Romans. They would march and they would smash the barbarians as they had done so many times before. What could possibly prevent them?

There was a narrow valley, a deep combe with a steep, rocky wall on the south side and a forested slope on the north. Calgacus walked the slope, moving along the trees, checking that there would be enough cover for his warriors.

"It's just what we are looking for," he said to Runt. "There's plenty of cover and lots of dips and hollows for the men to hide in."

"Only if we can get the Romans to march through the defile without sending scouts into the trees," Runt pointed out.

Calgacus nodded. "We need some bait."

He looked westwards, away to his right. The defile ran straight, then opened out into a narrow, grassy plain that was surrounded by high hills. He pointed to the far side of the open ground.

"If they saw we were camped on that slope over there, what would they do?"

Runt studied the distant hill. "They'd head through here as quickly as they could to get to us. They'd want to reach the open ground quickly so that they can deploy for an attack before we block the end of the pass."

"If we have a group of horsemen harassing them and then fleeing through here that would also draw them on. They wouldn't waste time checking these woods."

"You're probably right, but there is one problem."

"What's that?"

"If we are camped on that hill, we can't be hiding in these trees at the same time. Or had you forgotten that?"

Calgacus grinned. "I hadn't forgotten. Come on, we need to get back. I want men building a camp over there as soon as we can."

Runt shook his head. "Is this another one of your crazy plans?"

"It's not any crazier than the last one," Calgacus assured him.

"Oh, good," said Runt.

It took them a day of hard riding to get back to Caer Gobannus. Calgacus sent messengers to gather the war council, then went home to see Senuala. When he ducked through the door of his house, he was surprised to discover the stout druid, Cadwgan, in his home. He and Senuala both looked embarrassed to be seen together.

"What are you doing here?" Calgacus demanded angrily.

Cadwgan's hand moved up to nervously brush his fingers against his nose. "I merely came to wish you good luck in the coming battle," he said, seeming flustered.

"I thought you wanted me to lose, so that you can have your sacrifice at midwinter," Calgacus retorted.

"Not at all," Cadwgan protested. "We both want to see the Romans defeated. All that is at issue is the manner by which that victory is achieved. We know that sacrifice is the proper way to ensure success."

"I never fail to be amazed at how easily you druids speak of killing people," Calgacus said with heavy sarcasm.

Cadwgan bristled angrily. "Shedding a life as an offering to the Gods is no mere killing," he protested.

"The victims end up dead just the same," Calgacus replied, surprising himself at how much his argument sounded like something old Myrddin would have said.

"That is blasphemy!" Cadwgan said, shocked at what he had heard.

"I think it is self-evident," Calgacus told him. "I also think you should leave now, before I throw you out."

Cadwgan stared back at him for a moment, then made for the door.

When he had gone, Calgacus said to Senuala, "What did he really want?"

"As he said, he wanted to wish you well."

"I find that hard to believe," he said. "He's lying about something."

Senuala waved her arms in a gesture of helplessness. "It hardly matters now, does it?" she retorted. "You have proved to him that you are a heretic. Whatever you do now, it will never be enough in the eyes of the druids."

Calgacus knew that she was right. He had allowed his anger at Cadwgan to loosen his tongue too much. But what was said could not be brought back, however much he might regret his words. Then he realised that he did not regret them. He might live to regret the consequences of having said them, but he had meant what he said.

Shrugging off the problem, he said, "The man's a pompous fool, incapable of thinking for himself."

"No," Senuala said heatedly. "He is doing what he thinks is right."

"He is doing what he has been told to do," Calgacus countered.

"Now you are being silly," she snapped irritably. "You know that Cadwgan has no choice but to follow the Council's orders."

"Everybody has a choice," Calgacus said bitterly.

His words seem to sting her. "Like you when you chose to betray Cartimandua?" she asked testily, catching him unawares with her question.

He froze. He saw the challenge in her expression and the tense way she stood as she waited for his answer.

"That was different," he replied.

"How was it different?" Senuala asked angrily. "You said you loved her, yet you betrayed her. You deliberately tried to bring the Brigantes into a war with Rome even though you knew that was not what she wanted."

"Who told you all this?" he demanded. "Was it that druid?"

She shook her head angrily. "I was a slave of the Brigantes. Everyone there knows the story."

Calgacus hesitated. He knew her well and he thought he detected a lie, although she was doing her best to conceal it.

He said, "You never mentioned it before."

"Why should I?" she retorted. "I have no wish to hear about the other women you have slept with." Her eyes narrowed as she continued her accusation. "Or was that part of the ploy? Did you sleep with Cartimandua just to get her on your side? Did you tell her that you loved her? The same way you told me? Will you betray me the way you betrayed her?"

"It wasn't like that!" he shouted. "I did what I did because I had to! I was trying to save all the free tribes."

"So you didn't love her at all? You were just using her?"

"Forget her!" he snapped. "She means nothing to me now."

"So you did love her?" Senuala persisted.

"Perhaps," he admitted angrily. "At least, I thought I did. But she certainly does not love me. She has threatened to kill me if I ever go back there."

"You lied to her!" Senuala raged, her arms waving in front of his face. "What other lies have you told?"

Calgacus' fist was raised before he could stop himself. Senuala did not flinch. She simply stared up at him.

"Is that your answer to everything? Are you going to beat me now for daring to argue with you? Are you?"

Slowly, Calgacus lowered his fist. "I have no time for this," he muttered. "I don't know why you care so much about what happened between me and a woman I will never see again, but I have a war to plan. The Romans are coming and I need to stop them or we will all be dead."

Furiously, he spun on his heel and stormed out of the house.

Senuala watched him go, her own anger matching his. The difference was that she did not know who she was angry at. She felt trapped. She wished that Calgacus had hit her. That would have given her a reason to hate him instead of hating herself.

Calgacus arrived at the war council with a face like thunder.

"Trouble?" Runt asked.

"Just woman trouble," Calgacus told him sourly as he took a seat in the circle of chieftains.

"Is there any other kind?" Runt asked.

"There's Roman trouble," Calgacus snapped. "That's what we are here to sort out."

The other men glanced at one another, intimidated by Calgacus' dark mood. By unspoken agreement, they turned their attention to the Romans, not daring to pry into his private affairs.

Calgacus noticed their apprehension. Dismissing his thoughts of Senuala and her constant fault-finding, he told them what he wanted done. He soon became engrossed in the detailed planning. Tasks were allocated, questions asked, problems raised. Calgacus' head was soon spinning. It was not simply a case of telling six thousand warriors to go to a certain place and prepare for battle. Men needed food and water, horses needed fodder. The war host was spread across several valleys and would need to come together at exactly the right time and place without alerting the enemy to their presence. The Silures were experienced in such things now but over-confidence could be as much of a problem as

285

inexperience, so Calgacus insisted on going over everything several times to make sure that everyone understood what was required.

Gutyn arrived, flamboyantly leaping from his lathered horse, bringing confirmation that the Romans were marching, just as he had warned them.

"They have crossed the Hafren," he reported. "They are heading for the hills but they are burning and destroying everything in their path."

"How fast are they marching?" Calgacus wanted to know.

"Not quickly. They are making sure that they leave nothing alive in their wake except any slaves they may take." Gutyn frowned as he added, "Most of the folk who live in the lowlands are abandoning their villages and heading for the hills."

"So we are going to see a stream of refugees who will need shelter and food," Calgacus said. "That will place more strain on our resources and we are stretched enough as it is."

Rhydderch said, "I hate to admit it, but at least Cadwallon is still sending us food. If not for that, there would already be a desperate shortage."

Calgacus turned to old Gwalchmai. "Can you take charge of looking after the people who are fleeing ahead of the Romans? Make sure they are provided with shelter and as much food as we can spare?"

"I can do that," Gwalchmai agreed instantly. He was too old to fight, but he was desperate to do something to help.

"Then the rest of us need to prepare for battle. Delaying the fight will only make the food situation worse."

Picking up a small, pointed stick, Calgacus sketched a map on the earth, outlining the combe he had found.

"You know this place?" he asked Gutyn, tapping the crude diagram.

The young man nodded. "You want me to lead them there?"

Calgacus wished all of the warriors were as quick to grasp things as Gutyn was.

"That's right. We are going to let them see a camp on the far hill, over here." He scratched the stick, indicating the hill opposite the end of the combe. "I need them to come straight through the pass without stopping."

"When?" asked Gutyn.

286

"Midsummer is in two days. The men want to see the ceremony before marching. If we leave as soon as the ritual is completed, we can be there by the afternoon of the second day after that."

"That's no problem," said Gutyn. "They will take at least six days at the rate they are going. Maybe longer."

"Good. Harass them as much as you can without getting yourself caught. Slow them down if you can, but lead them on. Make sure they follow you."

"Consider it done," Gutyn said confidently.

Calgacus turned to Tannattos. "You, my friend, need to leave now. We need a convincingly large camp built on that hillside. Lots of fires, lots of shelters. Your men need to convince the Romans that there are thousands of them instead of hundreds."

Tannattos, as usual, complained about the task. "We will miss the sunrise ceremony," he pointed out.

Calgacus waved his protests aside. "Then you will have to miss it," he said testily. "Find a druid and have him perform your own ceremony if you must. But get there quickly and get building."

Tannattos reluctantly agreed. "But when the battle starts, we will be too far away again."

"As soon as it starts, you get there as quickly as you can to block the end of the pass," Calgacus told him. "I want the Romans to have only one way out, and that is back the way they came."

The discussions went on late into the long summer evening as Calgacus did his best to answer every question, no matter how trivial. When the sun began to sink towards the west, he decided to spend the night at the camp fire. Runt did the same.

"Sula's not very happy at the prospect of the Romans coming this way," he explained. "We had a bit of an argument."

Calgacus could sympathise. He had no wish to return home just to get into another fight with Senuala. He told Runt what had happened.

"Ever since that druid, Cadwgan, arrived she's been on edge. Arguing all the time."

Runt said, "I wonder why he was talking to her. It doesn't make sense."

"I don't know," Calgacus growled. "But he's up to something. If I see him tomorrow, I'll gut him."

287

But the next day Cadwgan, and all the druids, were noticeably absent.

"They are probably over at the circle, preparing for tomorrow's ceremony," Runt suggested.

Calgacus nodded. There was a small circle of stones that sat on a spur of the hill that housed Caer Gobannus. He had seen it from a distance but had never visited it. He knew that, like all such circles, it was used by the inhabitants of several of the local farms and settlements as a meeting place. It would have served that purpose for as long as people had lived here; a place where people came together to negotiate and resolve disputes under the watchful eyes of their ancestors. The circle was a gateway between this world and the next, a place where the spirits of the ancestors could guide the decisions of those in the mortal world. It was also the place where the midsummer sacrifice would be offered to Alaunos, the sun god.

Calgacus said, "I don't care where they are, as long as they stay out of my way."

He and Runt spent the entire day on horseback, moving from one valley to another, visiting the villages and the camps, telling the men to be ready. At each camp he told the men to gather for the sunrise ceremony with everything they needed because they would be marching as soon as the ritual had been completed. He made sure that everyone knew of the Governor's boast that he was going to wipe out the Silures. That was as good a boost to morale as he could ever have come up with himself. The Silures' pride would never allow them to back down from a challenge like that.

Everywhere they went, men asked questions. What should their families do? What about their livestock? How many Romans were coming? Patiently, Calgacus tried to answer them all, to assure them that they would defeat the invaders and that their families would be safe. Many of the men were older than he was, but they all looked to him for advice and encouragement. It made him realise the weight of the responsibility he had taken on. It was, though, a responsibility that he accepted.

He fingered the gold coin that hung around his neck. It told him that he was a son of Cunobelinos, the last of the brothers who still opposed Rome. He had been born for this.

Still, it was a long day and he was tired when he and Runt returned to Caer Gobannus late in the evening. It was not quite dark, but bats were already fluttering overhead, chasing insects through the darkening sky. Camp fires dotted the valley, and the sound of distant singing drifted on the breeze. Everyone would be up and about early, long before dawn, to make the trek to the sacred circle. Many people would not sleep at all this night, knowing that they were going to war in the morning.

"I'd better go and make my peace with Sula," Runt said as they tethered the horses. "I'll see you before sunrise."

Giving his friend a wave of farewell, Calgacus walked to his own house, apprehensive about the reception that awaited him. He told himself not to be concerned. He was a War Leader. He had spent all day giving orders to his warriors; he could surely deal with one young woman. Determinedly, he pushed through the doorway, ready to show his authority if Senuala wanted to argue with him again.

He saw that the fire had been stacked high for the night. Smoke hung amid the rafters and a warm wave of heat hit him as he went in. There was a platter of food set out on the table. Beyond, against the far wall, Senuala lay in the bed, a look of profound relief on her face when she saw him.

"I was worried you might not come back," she said. "It is getting late."

"I've been busy," he replied, pleased that she seemed happy to see him.

"There is food if you want it," she said. Then she pulled the blankets aside, revealing that she was naked. She smiled as she patted the furs. "Or you can come to bed."

Once again she had surprised him. He smiled. It was the easiest decision he had had to make for two days.

Chapter XXX

It was still dark when Senuala woke him. She was already up and dressed, a shawl wrapped around her shoulders against the chill of the night. She had placed some wood on the fire to boil some water and was busy mixing a drink.

"We need to leave soon," she said, her voice flat and unemotional.

Calgacus lay in the bed, unwilling to move out from the warmth and comfort of the covers. He watched her admiringly as she stirred the drink.

"You are very beautiful," he told her.

She did not look at him, did not respond to the compliment in any way. Even in the dim, flickering glow of the fire, he could tell from the stiff way she was standing that, once again, she was distracted and unhappy. There was a tension about her, an almost visible aura of apprehension radiating from her. It was much more than unhappiness, he thought. There was nervousness in her every move. She was trying hard to appear normal but he knew her too well to be fooled.

"You don't need to worry," he told her. "I'll be back in a few days and then we will celebrate another victory. If it will make you happy, I'll even bring back some Roman heads and present them to Cadwgan to take back to Ynis Mon."

Senuala gave a weak smile. "That would be good," she said with little conviction.

He sighed. It seemed there was no way he could reach her when she was in this sort of mood. Frustrated at his inability to understand her, he clambered out from under the blankets and hurriedly dressed. He pulled on his trousers and boots, then tugged his shirt over his head before slipping on his leather jerkin, tying the fastenings tightly. He reached for his breastplate, shield and sword, but Senuala walked softly to him, holding a steaming mug.

"Drink this first," she said. "It will help you get through today."

He took the mug, sipping at the liquid. It was hot. He swallowed only a tiny amount, but the taste of it struck a chord in his memory. It was tantalisingly familiar.

"What's in it?" he asked.

"Just some herbs," Senuala replied. She sounded calm, but her face still wore its expression of barely suppressed anxiety.

He knew that something was wrong, but he also knew from the past months of unanswered questions that she would not tell him what it was, so he took another sip. As the steaming liquid touched his tongue, the memory returned.

In a burst of insight, he remembered where he had tasted this before. It had been in Myrddin's cave, when he had chewed the mistletoe berries to make the paste the old hermit had used to catch small birds. The realisation almost made him drop the mug.

He stared at Senuala, saw that she was watching him intently through fearful eyes. Moving to the table, he carefully put the mug down.

"It's too hot," he explained. He remained outwardly calm, yet inside, he was churning with the dreadful certainty that she was trying to poison him. He did not know what to do, did not know how to confront her with the accusation. To give himself time to think, he went to pick up his breastplate, to dress for the war.

"You don't need that!" Senuala said quickly. "You are going to a sunrise ceremony, not a battle."

"I am marching to a battle straight afterwards," he replied, picking up the heavy, bronze breastplate and holding it in place. "Can you help me with the straps?"

She came stiffly, reluctantly, fastening the straps unwillingly. When she was at last done, he looped his sword belt over his shoulder. Finally, he hung his shield into place over his back.

He looked at her. Her face was pale, her eyes wide.

"Let's go," he said.

Instead of making for the door, Senuala hurried to the table and picked up the mug.

"Drink this before we go," she said.

He did not take the mug from her. He placed his hands on his hips, looked into her dark eyes and said, "No, I don't think I will."

He studied her carefully, saw the fear in her eyes.

"Please! You must drink it!" she begged.

"Why? Why must I drink it Senuala? You know I will die if I

291

drink that."

Silence.

It was the awful silence of realisation. Senuala stared at him, biting her lower lip so hard that he thought she might draw blood. Her eyes were damp with threatened tears.

"I would not do that to you," she whispered, so softly that he could scarcely hear her.

"No? Then tell me why I must drink it."

She did not reply. He reached out, taking the mug from her unresisting hands. With deliberate slowness, he poured the steaming contents on to the floor, soaking the straw and rushes at his feet.

Senuala lowered her head, standing helpless before him.

"You are supposed to drink it," she said. "It will be worse for you now."

He dropped the mug to the sodden floor, then reached for her, holding her by the arms. Angrily, he demanded, "What will be worse? Tell me!"

He shook her as if he could shake the answer from her.

"They are coming for you," she cried at last. "You were supposed to drink it so that you would be too ill to resist them."

"Who is coming?" he insisted.

"The druids." She paused. Quietly, she added, "Cethinos."

He was so surprised that he released his hold on her. His mind reeled, unable to understand.

"Cethinos? Why?"

She put her head down, lifted her hands to spread her fingers across her forehead, as if she was trying to drive the thoughts from her mind.

"Because you are to be sacrificed when the sun rises."

He felt as though she had stabbed him in the guts. Her words cut him as deeply as any blade could have done. He placed a hand on the table for support, the new table she had had made for them. She had made a home for them and now she had tried to kill him.

She had tried to help Cethinos sacrifice him. He needed to know why.

"Maddoc said I had until midwinter," he managed to say, desperately trying to understand what was happening.

Senuala shook her head. Tears were running down her cheeks now.

"Maddoc does not know. Cethinos made a deal with Venutius. Venutius hates you and Cethinos wants a royal sacrifice. They planned it together."

"And you helped them? Why would you do that? Tell me!"

She reached for him, stepped towards him but he angrily pushed her arms away, refusing to offer any comfort for her distress.

Sobbing, she said, "They told me you were a cruel man, a renegade, a traitor who tried to kill Venutius and who betrayed Cartimandua."

"And you believed them?"

"Why should I not? They are powerful men. When Cethinos told me, I wanted to help them."

Calgacus was fumbling for questions, desperate to learn the whole story. "I don't understand," he said plaintively. "Why did you want to help them? How did Cethinos find you?"

The words poured out from her now that she had begun her story. "Cethinos has known me for a while. I was on Ynis Mon, training to be a druid. I have been there since I was fourteen years old." She swallowed as she made the confession. "Cal, I am not Senuala of the Votadini. I am Senuala of the Brigantes, daughter of King Volisios. Cartimandua is my older sister."

Her admission stunned him. "Her sister?"

"Phennarcos, the slave dealer, knew. He would have given me to you for nothing if he had to. It was all just a performance for your benefit."

"You have lied to me for all this time?" His anger was rising now, driving away his confusion. "Why not just kill me while I slept? You had plenty of opportunities."

"No, I would not do that. You don't understand. Cethinos needs you as a sacrifice. Only that way will the Romans be defeated. He told me to stay close to you and to give you something so that you would not resist. I am sorry, Cal. I truly am. I thought you would keep me as a slave and that I would hate you for it. That would have made this easier. I did not know you would free me as soon as we met. But you have spoken against the druids. You admitted your lack of faith to me, and to Cadwgan. I had to do this. I had no choice."

"There is always a choice," he told her coldly. "And you have made yours. I thought . . ."

293

His voice trailed off, lost in a maelstrom of false dreams and dead hopes. He had thought that she loved him. Now he knew it had all been an act, part of an elaborate trap set for him by Venutius. A trap into which he had walked willingly, just as Venutius must have known he would, because he had been beguiled by her beauty, by her helplessness and her willingness to share his bed.

He was still wondering what to do when he heard a commotion outside, the sound of raised voices. Runt was shouting, demanding to know what was happening.

With mounting anger, Calgacus grabbed Senuala's arm and roughly dragged her to the door. She squealed in protest as he gripped her tightly, shoving her out in front of him.

When he followed her outside, he saw the druids waiting for him.

Torches lit the crowd that had assembled in the centre of the village. There were a dozen druids, Cethinos standing at their head, Cadwgan beside him. Runt confronted them, demanding to know why they had come. Rhydderch stood with the men and women of his village, watching with concerned expressions on their faces. Warriors coming up from the valley joined them, puzzled as to why the druids were in the village instead of waiting at the stone circle.

Calgacus saw the surprise on Cethinos' face when he stepped out of the house, recognised the flash of fear in the old man's eyes. He did not allow the druid time to regain his composure. Grabbing Senuala's arm, he flung her at him. She staggered, falling to the muddy earth at Cethinos' feet.

"Here is your faithless spy, Cethinos!" he shouted. "She has, as you can see, failed in her task. You should take her away before I change my mind and kill the treacherous bitch."

Runt gaped at Calgacus. He did not understand what was happening, but he did not ask questions. Stepping aside, he took up his usual position at the tall warrior's side.

Cethinos stared fixedly, while Cadwgan bent down to help the sobbing Senuala to her feet, putting a protective arm around her shoulders.

Nobody spoke. The only sounds were the crackling of the flaming brands and Senuala's quiet crying.

Cethinos soon recovered his composure. He pointed a long, bony finger at Calgacus.

"You are required for the sacrifice," he intoned. "Royal blood must be shed, or we are all doomed. This is the will of the Gods. Will you continue to defy them?" He spoke in a loud voice, addressing the crowd of villagers as much as Calgacus. "Disaster awaits us all if you do not go to the Gods on behalf of the people. I say again, you are required for the sacrifice. This is a great honour for you. You must come now."

In the expectant hush that followed, Calgacus swore, telling Cethinos exactly what he could do with his great honour.

The crowd gasped. Nobody had ever heard anyone defy a druid the way Calgacus had just done. Even his earlier confrontation with Cadwgan had not been so filled with scorn and hatred.

Senuala looked stricken with grief as she gazed at Calgacus imploringly. She could not speak through her tears. Even Runt shifted uncertainly.

Calgacus' mind turned to Myrddin. The hermit had already saved his life three times; once from his wounds, then by giving him the story of how he had escaped Dis's realm, and again this morning when he had recognised the taste of the deadly mistletoe berries. Now he gambled that the old man's advice would save him again.

There was a part of Calgacus that knew instinctively that his sins were being counted in the spirit world and would haunt him in the afterlife. That part of him feared that Cethinos was right, that he should surrender himself to the druid's will to ensure victory. But the greater part of him was consumed by anger. Maddoc had given him until midwinter. Yet Venutius and Cethinos had devised a plan to kill him before that time had elapsed, before he had had the chance to defeat the Romans. Above all, Senuala had tricked him, offering feigned love so that she could earn his trust before betraying him.

He recalled what Myrddin had told him. The Gods, the old man had said, do not listen to men or druids. Sacrifices do nothing except spill wasted blood and keep the druids in power. The old hermit's ideas were shocking, but Calgacus had come to believe them. Besides, he told himself, if Myrddin was right, then what difference did it make that he had lied? What difference would it

295

make if he lied again?

Myrddin had also told him to let his enemies see what he wanted them to see, to use their own beliefs against them. Cethinos, he knew, was his enemy. Cethinos believed absolutely in the Gods, in their desire for wealth and blood to be offered in sacrifice. He believed implicitly that the Gods guided and helped the people through the intercession of the druids.

Calgacus decided that he could use those unflinching beliefs against his old nemesis. He would not go meekly to his death to satisfy Cethinos' blood lust. Slowly, he raised his own arm, pointed back at Cethinos, using the druids' own methods against him.

"Do you know why your spy failed, Cethinos? Shall I tell you?"

He had everybody's attention now, but he concentrated on Cethinos to the exclusion of everyone else. He continued, not allowing Cethinos the chance to speak.

"I had a dream last night. In that dream, Camulos and Nodens, the war gods, came to me. They said that I would lead the Silures to a great victory. But they told me that I would only do this if I refused the first drink I was offered when I woke. They told me that if I took that first drink, I would die, leaving nobody to lead the tribe in the coming battle. You say it is the will of the Gods that I am sacrificed. I say that is only the will of Cethinos, who has been paid by Venutius of the Brigantes, a man who is so cowardly that he dare not fight the Romans himself.

"Venutius is happy to let the Silures die for him, while he sits in comfort, drinking Roman wine. He bribes druids to dispose of his enemies for him because he dare not stand against them himself. And you accepted his bribes because you are blinded by greed which you disguise as devotion to the Gods.

"My death under your knife is not the will of the Gods. The will of the Gods is that I fight and that I win. I can prove this. They came to me in my dreams. How else would I know not to drink your bitch's poison?"

Cethinos blinked, speechless. Around him, the other druids looked uncertainly at one another.

Then Runt clapped his hands together, breaking the awful silence.

"Calgacus! Bouda! Calgacus! Bouda!"

For a short moment his was the only voice, then Rhydderch joined him and other men quickly took up the refrain. The warriors thumped the butts of their spears against the ground, stamped their feet. The women clapped their hands, all of them chanting in support of Calgacus. Those at the edges of the growing crowd, too far away to have heard what had been said, still joined in the chanting, filling the air with the sound of their support for Calgacus.

Calgacus shouted at Cethinos, "Go! Sacrifice a ram or a bull as you usually do. Leave the fighting to me, just as you usually do. And take your traitorous slut with you. The two of you are well suited."

Senuala cried, "No!" She reached an arm towards Calgacus, but Cadwgan held her tightly and pulled her back.

The crowd was closing in, slowly jostling the druids. Cethinos, alarmed at the hostility in the villagers' faces, turned away, hurriedly pushing his way back through his brother druids who quickly followed him towards the gates. Cadwgan pulled Senuala away as he went after them.

Calgacus saw her turn back, saw her hold out her arm again, beseeching him. Her lips moved, framing his name, but he could not hear her over the noise of the crowd. He stared back at her, his face impassive. Then Cadwgan pulled her and she disappeared among the druids as the crowd closed in behind them, still chanting.

Runt heaved a sigh of relief. "By Toutatis, Cal. What was that all about?"

"She is Cartimandua's sister. She was sent here to drug me so that Cethinos could shed my blood this morning."

Runt whistled in astonishment. "That explains a lot. Do you want me to go after her?" he offered. "To bring her back?"

Calgacus shook his head emphatically. "After she tried to kill me? No. She made her choice. Let her live with it. I'm sure she'll get on well with Cethinos. I hope I never see her again."

"I thought—" Runt began.

"You thought wrong," Calgacus interrupted. "I'm just thankful she is not as ruthless as her sister."

The crowd was moving away, heading out of the village towards the circle of stones where the sunrise ceremony would be performed. The sound of chanting could still be heard on the night

297

breeze but the song had changed. Now, the people were singing in praise of Alaunos, the sun god.

Rhydderch walked over, a nervous look on his face. "I've never seen anything like that before," he said solemnly. "Did the Gods really visit your dreams?"

"I've already proved that, haven't I?" Calgacus responded. "You'd best go to the ceremony. I think I'll stay here."

Rhydderch nodded. "That's probably a good idea."

With a small wave of his hand, he followed the crowd out through the gates, heading round the hill to the circle. Soon, only Calgacus and Runt were left in the village. Only the sounds of the animals and the faint crackling of fires gave any indication that Caer Gobannus was a place where people lived.

"I suppose that means we have to win now," said Runt. "What with the Gods having visited you and everything."

"Win or die," Calgacus agreed, ignoring his friend's sarcasm. "But it was always going to be that way, Gods or no Gods."

They went back into Calgacus' house where they brewed a tisane, and sat beside the fire, saying little. When they heard the birds begin the dawn chorus, they went outside to greet the sunrise.

They stood in silence, looking to the east. The sky slowly changed from black, to grey, to blue as the sun crested the horizon and began its trek up into the heavens on the longest day of the year.

The two of them shared a reflective moment as the sun climbed slowly over the distant hills. When the first rays struck the altar stone, the victim's throat would be cut and the crowd would let out a great cheer. If there had been a roar of acclamation from the distant circle, they had not heard it.

Calgacus did not care. He breathed deeply as the moment passed. The sun was up and he was still alive. It promised to be a fine day, a good day to go to war.

They waited for what seemed an age for the people to return from the ceremony. When they arrived, they did so in a sombre mood. Midsummer was usually a time for celebration, but the crowd of men, women and children slowly returning up the hill to the village was virtually silent. Calgacus watched them, surprised to see that Rhydderch, who led the long queue of people, was accompanied by the druid, Cadwgan. Both men wore grim expressions as they walked through the open gates towards him.

298

"What's wrong now?" Calgacus asked Rhydderch. He nodded rudely towards Cadwgan. "And what is this piece of horse dung doing here?"

Rhydderch looked at him sadly. "It is Senuala," he said.

"What about her?"

"She is dead."

Chapter XXXI

Ostorius Scapula never slept for more than five hours each night. The Governor's mind was always racing, busy with thoughts of what needed to be done. He believed that it was better to be up and about doing them than lying awake thinking about them. Even on the longest day of the year he was awake and dressed before dawn.

By the light of an oil lamp, he sat in his campaign tent, eating a breakfast of figs, idly contemplating the wonders of the Roman Empire which allowed figs to be brought all the way here, to the middle of nowhere, beyond the end of the civilised world, so that he could eat them for his breakfast. Rome, he thought to himself, was an empire like no other.

"Things are going well," he observed to Valens.

The Legate of the Second Augusta, his eyes still heavy from lack of sleep, was sitting opposite Scapula, alongside the Governor's aide, Facilis. Scapula thought the Legate was less than enthusiastic about this campaign, an attitude he intended to alter by driving the man on to great accomplishments. Not quite as great as Scapula's own deeds, of course, but Valens had family connections in Rome and one never knew when such connections might prove valuable. Once the Silures had been crushed, Scapula would see out his term as Governor before returning to Rome as a hero, with a military reputation second to no man living. Once he was back in Rome, who knew where fate would lead him? Having men who owed him favours, men like Valens who had wealthy and influential relatives, would do Scapula no harm at all.

Stifling a yawn, Valens said, "There has certainly been little opposition so far, sir."

Valens found it difficult to conceal his lack of enthusiasm. He understood the need for atrocitas, but he saw little to be pleased about in the burning of a handful of mud huts and the confiscation of cattle. It was a job that had to be done, but it was not something he took pleasure in.

The Silures had no large towns, no major settlements, so it

seemed to Valens that the summer was likely to be a never-ending succession of destroying small, undefended villages or storming fortified hilltop settlements. All he really wanted was for the campaign to be finished quickly and with as few casualties as possible.

"The barbarians are scared of us," Scapula said affably. "They do this every time, you know. They run as we approach, they make small raids, letting us know which way they are going. Then they wait for us at some site they have chosen, give battle and we defeat them."

"It sounds very straightforward," Valens said. "But these are men who destroyed one of our camps. We should not treat them lightly."

Scapula shuffled irritably. "I do not treat them lightly, Valens. But they are barbarians; nothing more. They got lucky once. That will not happen again. The Britons are entirely predictable, I tell you. They may be cunning, but they have no concept of strategy, no idea how to win a war." He gave a mocking laugh. "They think that holding high ground makes them invincible. What they do not realise is that the object of war is to destroy the enemy. High ground or low ground, it does not matter. What counts is striking hard and fast, wherever you find the enemy. We showed the truth of that at Caer Caradoc last year. Is that not so, Facilis?"

"Indeed it is, sir," Facilis agreed dutifully.

"We shall do the same again this year," Scapula said confidently. "Once we find their army, we will attack. It may take us a while to track them down but once we find them, it will all be over quickly. These savages never learn."

"The men are looking forward to getting to grips with them," Valens said, feeling that he needed to say something positive. "At the moment, we have seen nothing except their cavalry."

Scapula turned to Facilis. "Their horsemen are still shadowing us, making small raids when they can?"

Facilis nodded. "Yes, sir. So far, they have been nothing more than an annoyance. Our own horsemen outnumber them so they are keeping well clear, always just ahead of us."

"You see?" Scapula said to Valens as he waved a fig at him. "Entirely predictable. Mark my words, Valens. When we see their camp, we shall go straight for it. I will send in the legionaries, hard and fast. The British vermin will break and run. They always do.

They are brave right up to the point where our swords are at their throats, then they run like children. This time, let us hope that the terrain allows our cavalry to pursue them and cut them down. After that, we will burn their crops, take their cattle and their women, and destroy their homes. We shall put an end to the Silures."

Valens nodded deferentially. "I look forward to that day, sir," he said.

Facilis smiled. The Governor, too, was predictable, he thought. As always, he was using a hammer to crack a nut. Yet this could indeed be a hard nut to crack. Privately, Facilis shared Valens' concerns about what they might be facing this time. He hoped that Scapula's assessment was correct. So far, the campaign mirrored the one they had fought the previous year, with small groups of barbarians watching them, launching pin-prick attacks and leading them into the hills where, if the Governor was correct, their main force would be waiting.

The Silures were apparently playing into Scapula's hands, doing exactly what he wanted them to do. Yet Facilis knew it was a mistake to assume that any enemy would do what was expected. He could not help wondering what surprises the barbarians might have in store for them. He had an uneasy feeling that men who could plan and execute the destruction of a Roman cohort that was entrenched within a fortified camp would not be foolish enough to resort to tactics that had failed them before.

Facilis shivered. Surely, he thought, the Britons were not that stupid. But the Governor believed that they were and, so far, there was no evidence to show that Scapula might be wrong. Facilis had no reason to doubt the Governor except a vague, unsettling sense of foreboding. He instinctively knew that Valens shared his concerns but the Legate had tried to caution the Governor and had been quickly over-ruled. There was no profit in continuing to argue with a man like Scapula.

Facilis supposed that his own worry may have been nothing more than a reaction to the dreadful fate of the slaughtered cohort. He had tried to visualise the sight of nearly five hundred corpses, each one with its head hacked off. He had tried, and he had failed. It was too awful to contemplate. He raised his hand to his throat, as if to reassure himself that his own head was still attached to his body, lowering it self-consciously when he saw Valens glance at him.

In his mind's eye, Facilis had a brief, awful picture of his own head stuck on a pole, just like the fence of skulls that he had seen lining the bank of the Sabrina at the battle of Caer Caradoc. He shivered again, telling himself not to dwell on such images. He was letting his imagination rule his rational mind. No matter what the Silures did, they could not defeat an entire legion. Nine years of warfare in Britannia had proved time and time again that the Britons simply were not capable of facing the legions in battle.

There was, Facilis told himself, nothing to worry about.

The interior of the tent began to lighten as the sun rose. Outside, the horns sounded, calling the soldiers from their sleep. The barking of centurions echoed dimly around the camp as they roused the sleeping men for another day of war.

Scapula popped the last fig into his mouth chewing slowly. He dipped his fingers in a small bowl of tepid water, then dried them on the towel that one of his slaves handed to him.

"Well, gentlemen," he said. "Another day dawns. Let us hope that this one brings us closer to the enemy. We must press on."

Another slave handed the Governor his sword which he buckled around his waist. Then he was given his helmet with its ornate, red crest of died horsehair. He placed it on his head, fastened the chin strap and gave the other officers a fierce smile.

"Come," he said. "It is time to show the barbarians what it means to incur the wrath of Rome."

Chapter XXXII

Despite himself, despite the knowledge that Senuala had tried to kill him, Calgacus felt the shock of Rhydderch's news like a body blow.

"Dead? How?"

Rhydderch looked away, unable to speak.

Disconsolately, Cadwgan said, "She offered herself as the sacrifice in your place. She is of royal blood, so Cethinos was happy to agree. He shed her life at sunrise."

A cold fury came over Calgacus. "Where is Cethinos now?" he demanded, his eyes narrowing.

"He has returned to Ynis Mon," said Cadwgan. "I think he fears your vengeance."

"Too bloody right," Calgacus breathed angrily.

"He has a good head start on you," Rhydderch said. "Besides, you may not harm a druid."

"And we have more important things to do than chase him," Runt gently reminded them.

Calgacus was aware that the villagers and the gathering warriors were watching him anxiously, waiting to see how he would react. They must have all witnessed Senuala's sacrifice.

"Why did she do it?" he asked.

Cadwgan said, "She kept repeating that she had betrayed you and that you had rejected her. I think she believed that if the Gods had warned you against her, then she must have acted wrongly."

Cadwgan did not need to voice the thought that the same thing had occurred to him. He looked up at Calgacus' stern face and saw the anger burning in the big warrior's eyes. Once again, Cadwgan had the terrible feeling that Calgacus might be capable of ignoring the absolute taboo on harming druids. The big warrior looked ready to strike him down on the spot.

Hurriedly, the druid continued, "But there is more. At the last, just as the sun touched her and the knife was about to open her throat, she called out your name so that everyone could hear." He

304

paused, swallowed nervously, then added, "That is why I am here. I only know you from what Cethinos has told me of you. I need to know why she would call your name before she died. I would like to accompany you in this war. I need to understand."

Calgacus looked down at the short, plump druid. It was obvious that Cadwgan was afraid of him, but the druid stood his ground despite his fear. Calgacus did not speak for a long moment while he battled with his own emotions. He wanted to lash out at somebody, or something. Cadwgan was the obvious target for his fury, yet he knew that it took courage to do what the druid had done in returning to him with his news. Cadwgan had perhaps been as much a victim of Cethinos' plotting as he and Senuala had been. His former conviction in the rightness of what he had done, in what Cethinos had tried to do, had certainly been shaken.

Eventually, Calgacus said, "You can come, but if you start any of your nonsense, I will surely let the Romans take you. You know they kill druids on sight."

Cadwgan nodded, his relief almost palpable. "As you wish."

Runt said menacingly, "And if I so much as think that you have come to finish Cethinos' work, I will kill you myself."

Cadwgan looked at him with sad eyes. "Cethinos is well respected on Ynis Mon, but it seems to me that he has not acted as a druid should. I swear by Matrona, by Nodens and by Epona that I will no longer do his bidding."

Something in the way Cadwgan spoke calmed Calgacus' rage a little. He drew himself up to his full height, took a deep breath then said in a loud voice. "We have a war to win! Let's get moving!"

Without waiting to see whether anyone would follow, he strode away, turning his back on the village. He did not look back.

Runt gave Rhydderch and Cadwgan a sharp look, warning them to let him speak to Calgacus alone. He hurried to catch up with him, almost jogging to keep up with the angry pace Calgacus was setting.

"It's not your fault, you know," he said.

"I know that. But there was no need for her to sacrifice herself."

"Perhaps she thought there was nothing left for her after you threw her out. Despair is a terrible thing." Runt glanced up at his friend, then added quietly, "I think she loved you."

305

Calgacus grunted. "If you are trying to make me feel better, it's not working. If she ever loved me, she had a strange way of showing it. She tried to kill me."

"There is that," Runt conceded. "But just make sure you don't do anything stupid because you are angry."

"I am not angry!" Calgacus shot back.

"If you say so."

"All right, I am angry," Calgacus admitted. "I'm angry because she is dead. I'm angry because she tricked me. Because Cethinos tried to kill me. Because Venutius put him up to it. I think I have a right to be angry, don't you?"

"Well, as Myrddin once said, you do seem to attract a lot of enemies," Runt said with a weak smile.

"Yes, and we have more of them to tackle very soon. That's the worst of this whole thing."

"Aye, it will be tough to beat the Romans this time."

"Not that," Calgacus told him irritably. "We can beat them all right. It's just that, when we do, Cethinos will be able to claim it is because he sacrificed someone of royal blood. The bastard's got me whatever happens."

Runt considered that for a moment. "In that case, maybe you should let the Romans win," he suggested.

"Not a chance."

Runt grinned. Calgacus was in a foul mood and when that happened, somebody usually suffered. The Romans had picked a bad time to get in his way.

"You really think this plan will work?" he asked.

"Of course it will work," Calgacus snapped.

"Good. Then let's go and kill the bastards."

Calgacus' temper had barely eased by the time they reached his chosen battle ground two days later. Men hurried to obey when he barked his commands at them, fearing to question him in case he turned his temper on them. Even the fact that things were well in hand did little to soften Calgacus' mood.

They discovered that Tannattos and his men had made a good start on the camp. There were hundreds of camp fires, and scores of small shelters. Some enterprising men had even used pieces of wood and old clothes to fashion crude, man-sized models, imitation warriors. A group of men could stand close together,

306

each holding two of the fake warriors, making it appear that there were three times the real number of defenders. It would only work from a distance, but that was all that was required.

Yet for all that had been achieved, Calgacus still picked fault, demanding more fires, more shelters. "And we need a ditch and rampart," he ordered.

Tannattos grumbled but set his men to work. The newly arrived warriors were drafted in to help.

Calgacus needed to know where the Romans were so he and Runt, with an escort of thirty warriors, left the bulk of the army constructing the fake camp while they set off eastwards to find Gutyn. They walked the length of the deep combe, across the wide plain at its eastern end, then skirted the hills to head into the next valley.

A solitary horseman, riding in the opposite direction, met them. It was a messenger from Gutyn, a tall, thin-faced young man named Baddan. He told them that Gutyn was not far away, setting a trap for the Roman foraging parties.

"The Romans are camped further east," he informed them. "We saw where they set up their flags. They are at least a half day's march from here."

Calgacus nodded. The Romans always sent a party out ahead of their marching troops to find a site where the legion could camp for the night. These men would plant small flags in the ground, marking where the boundary of the new camp would be and where the principal tents should be pitched. When the legionaries arrived at the chosen site, they would dig a ditch, throw up an earth wall, and set wooden stakes on the top of the rampart. The practice never varied. Every tent was pitched in the same location in every camp. Imagination, Calgacus thought, was not a Roman trait. But efficiency was, and they were only half a day away. That was not far.

He detailed one of his warriors to go back to inform Rhydderch, then said to Baddan, "I want to speak to Gutyn."

Baddan replied, "If we go to him, we will warn the Romans and ruin his trap. But there is a place I know where we can hide and watch."

Dismounting, he led them up onto the hillside, following a winding route among straggling gorse bushes. It took them until late afternoon to cross a shoulder of the hill from where they could look down on the valley. Baddan led them along the hillside then pointed down to a small hollow.

"We can wait in there," he said.

They scrambled down into the long depression. The hollow was a large dip in the hillside, big enough for all of them to stand upright while remaining out of sight of anyone further down the slope. Calgacus and Runt lay on the steep bank, peering out over the rim of the depression, looking down into the valley.

Baddan joined them. He pointed along the valley, saying, "Gutyn is in the village."

The valley was broad, well watered by small streams. It was green and fertile, good farmland, but devoid of any real cover beyond a few clumps of trees dotted here and there. Near the western end, not far below their hiding place, sitting on a low rise, was a small, stockaded village. It was deserted. No fires burned, nothing moved. There were no people, no animals. The fields and meadows around the village were empty, the crops abandoned to the crows. It was, Calgacus thought, a ghost village.

He looked at Baddan sceptically. "Are you sure he is there?"

"He is there. He sent the horses over the hill, well out of sight. He wants to catch their scouts."

Calgacus looked up to the sky. The sun was sinking low as late afternoon turned to early evening. Half a day's march to the east, the Romans would be at their camp site, digging their defensive ditches, preparing to settle in for the night. But while the legionaries worked, their scouts and foraging parties would be out, checking the way ahead, not only seeking the Silures but also looking for fodder for their horses and any supplies they might be able to gather for the soldiers.

They waited.

Runt, eagle-eyed as ever, saw them first. A group of fifteen horsemen were riding along the valley. They came at a canter, fast enough to travel quickly without tiring the horses, yet slow enough to prevent them running headlong into danger. They rode straight for the tiny village. As they drew nearer, Calgacus could make out the bulges of the nets they carried behind their saddles, used for carrying fodder and whatever plunder they could find. He signalled to his men to stay down, warning them to keep quiet. The village was several hundred paces away, below and to their right, but he knew how far sound could carry.

The Romans reined in their mounts outside the stockade. Their leader was being cautious. He signalled to two men to dismount and go inside first.

Calgacus whispered under his breath, "That's ruined it."

"No," said Baddan. "Gutyn has left the first few houses empty. And he's left a jug of wine for them to find."

"Where on earth did he get that from?"

"He stole it from their baggage train a couple of days ago," grinned Baddan.

The two Roman scouts moved slowly, carefully peering in through the open door of the first house. One of them went inside, emerging a few moments later carrying a large amphora which he held up triumphantly. His comrades immediately urged their horses into the village, satisfied that the inhabitants had fled, and eager to loot whatever had been left behind. Most of the riders dismounted, spreading out to search the houses for plunder. Some clustered round the man with the wine, producing small mugs that they wanted filled.

Without warning, the village erupted as warriors streamed out of the houses. They flung themselves at the Romans, each soldier being attacked by at least two warriors. Spears and swords flashed as the dark swarm of Silures hunted their enemies.

On the hillside above the village, Baddan thumped a fist to the ground in delight. "That's how to do it!" he exclaimed.

The fight was over quickly. Three tribesmen were cut down, but the Romans were slaughtered. Only two of them, still on horseback near the entrance to the stockade, managed to escape. They wheeled their mounts and raced away, abandoning their comrades to their fate.

In the village, Gutyn was organising his men. They searched the bodies of the Romans, quickly gathering up anything of value, then grabbed as many of the horses as they could. Some of the animals bolted, following the two fleeing riders, but Gutyn's men caught several of them and piled looted weapons and armour on to their backs. Before the two escaping horsemen were out of sight, Gutyn and his men were already leaving the village. It was as impressive an ambush as Calgacus had ever seen.

"Let's go and meet him," he said, pushing himself up.

"Wait!" Runt said urgently. He pointed to the far end of the valley. "There are more cavalry coming!" he warned. "Lots of them."

Calgacus instantly dropped to the ground. Peering down the slope, he quickly checked the distances with an experience born of many years of war.

"They'll catch them!" he hissed. He grabbed Baddan's arm. "Go down there and tell Gutyn to head up this way. Tell him to go along the hillside just below here. He is not to join us, just go along below us so that the Romans follow him. We can take them by surprise as they pass beneath us. Understand?"

Baddan nodded. He sprang to his feet, leaped over the edge of the ridge and ran down the slope.

Runt shot Calgacus a worried look. "There are about fifty horsemen coming. We have thirty men on foot."

"Gutyn has forty men," Calgacus said, slowly drawing his sword. "And we will take them by surprise."

"Oh, that's all right, then, "said Runt. "For a moment I thought you were going to do something crazy again."

Ostorius Scapula had been growing increasingly impatient. He had told Valens that the barbarians were predictable, and that was true. He knew that campaigns such as this, designed to exterminate a whole tribe, took time to accomplish. But he desperately wanted to find the barbarians' main force so that he could destroy it.

Burning deserted villages was satisfying, but it did not bring the savages to battle; they simply melted away into their misty, rain-soaked forests and rugged, windswept hills before his men could close with them. Surely they would stand and fight soon? He knew that he would eventually defeat them if he destroyed all their homes and burned all their crops. If that happened, the barbarians would starve over the winter and he would have wiped them out just as he had promised. But such a slow, laborious victory brought no glory.

Scapula wanted to return to Rome as a true hero, a mighty conqueror. His earlier success had been tarnished by the rebellious Silures' refusal to know when they were defeated. He needed to show the world how a Roman general repaid such rebellion. With every day that passed, Scapula grew more impatient to bring the enemy to battle.

The legion was digging in for the night, building the marching camp where they would stay safely until they resumed the march at daybreak. Scapula, bored and frustrated at the lack of an enemy to crush, had decided to ride out to see whether he could find any sign of the barbarians. With the fifty horsemen of his personal guard, he headed west, riding through the seemingly endless succession of valleys. Then, just as he was considering turning back, he met two panicked riders from a foraging party.

The men's horses were lathered, the terrified riders breathing hard. In halting words, gasping for breath, they told the Governor about the ambush that had killed thirteen of their comrades.

Scapula looked along the wide valley to the tiny village, some two miles away. From this distance, it was hard to tell whether there were any men there but if the rebels had been in the village only a short time ago, perhaps he could catch them. Was that movement he could just make out, he wondered? Drawing his sword, he yelled a word of command, clapping his heels to his horse.

Calgacus dropped down the side of the gully, telling his men to stay down but to be ready when he gave the word. Then he scrambled back up to lie on the rim again.

Runt had pulled out his sling and was scrabbling around, picking up pebbles, weighing them in his hand.

"This is madness," he said quietly so that only Calgacus could hear.

Calgacus nodded grimly. He knew the odds.

"I know. But I won't hide here just to watch Gutyn and his men be slaughtered."

Runt sighed. That was why men followed Calgacus, he knew. But this promised to be a fight that could turn into a disaster. Surprise or not, men on foot could not beat men on horseback unless the foot soldiers stayed close together in a solid formation of spears. Even then they could do no more than drive the horsemen off. Here, Gutyn's men were scattered along the hillside while their own warriors would lose all cohesion as soon as they broke from their hiding place.

Runt was philosophical about their prospects of success. This was what being a warrior meant. If they stayed hidden, or ran, while their fellow tribesmen were in danger, they would no longer be warriors, they would be cowards. It was better to die fighting.

He risked a look over the edge of the gully. Baddan, arms

311

waving, was bounding down the slope in great leaps. He had not reached Gutyn, but the young chieftain had seen him, had looked back and spotted the Roman horsemen who were closing on him rapidly. Baddan was pointing furiously as he ran, yelling instructions.

Gutyn, quick as ever to understand, frantically signalled to his men. They began climbing the slope.

Some of Gutyn's men led horses. A few of them heaved the plunder off the high Roman saddles and jumped up onto the animals' backs. Other warriors grabbed hold of the saddles and clung to them, running alongside as the riders galloped off westwards. The men who were precariously clinging on risked falling but were able to use the superior speed of the horses to carry them away to safety. Still, Gutyn had around two dozen men on foot. He yelled at them to abandon any plunder they were carrying and to run.

Baddan skidded to a desperate halt, then turned to lead them up the hill, angling to their right so that they would pass below the gully where Calgacus lay hidden. Gutyn cast an anxious look back over his shoulder. It was going to be desperately close.

Scapula urged his horse on. He held his long cavalry sword out straight ahead of him, pointing the way. He could see the enemy now, fleeing from his vengeance, trying to climb the hill. They would not escape him. There was no cover on the slope, no rocks, no forests. The surface was steep and uneven, but he would still catch them. They had nowhere to hide.

He had, he knew, started the gallop too soon, so the horses were already tiring, but they were still faster than a man going uphill on foot. He shouted with delight. This was war; this was glory. The thunderous noise of the horses filled his ears, the wind whipped on his face as he surged towards a fleeing enemy. This would be a story he could tell to his admirers for years.

When he reached the foot of the hill, his horse almost stumbled as it adjusted to the slope. He urged it up, digging his heels into its sides, yelling at it to go on. His arm ached with the effort of holding the weight of the long cavalry sword, the spatha which gave a man on horseback greater reach than the short gladius used by the legionaries, but the pain in his muscles evaporated as he caught up with a barbarian straggler.

The man tried to dodge aside as Scapula's horse reached him, but the Governor hacked down, catching the savage on the shoulder, the sword cutting deep into him, smashing through his collar bone. The man shrieked as he fell away in a bloody mess. Scapula wrenched his blade free as his horse surged past the barbarian. Yelling with delight, the Governor charged on up the slope in search of a second victim.

Calgacus watched as the leading Roman cut down the fleeing warrior. The Roman wore a long, red cloak, a helmet with a red plume and a bronze breastplate that shone like gold in the bright evening sunshine. Calgacus gripped his sword, waiting for the right moment. The Roman officer was passing below him but he had outstripped the rest of the riders and to attack now would mean Calgacus would spring the trap too soon.

He watched as the gleeful Roman swung at another warrior, sending the man tumbling down the hill. Calgacus swore softly. Looking to his right, he watched the approaching horsemen as they galloped along the hillside. At last, he judged it was time.

"Now!" he yelled.

He jumped to his feet, launching himself over the rim of the gully, heading for the officer. He heard his men scream their war cries as they hurled spears at the Roman horsemen before leaping down to follow him.

There was a whirr as Runt swung his sling. He was as accurate as ever, sending the stone slamming into the Roman officer's helmet with a metallic ring that Calgacus could hear over the furious noise of the fight. The Roman fell sideways. His horse reared as it felt him involuntarily pull back on the reins. The sudden shift of weight made it slip on the steep slope, sending man and horse down with a crash in a jumble of flailing legs.

Somehow, the man avoided being crushed by the horse as he fell from the saddle and was thrown clear. He scrambled up to his hands and knees. Another stone from Runt's sling hammered into his arm, and he fell again.

Calgacus hurtled down the slope, leaping in great bounds. A warning shout from Runt sent him skidding to one side as a horse charged at him. He swung his sword, aiming for its face, forcing the beast to rear in an attempt to avoid the blow. The rider swung his sword but missed, then Calgacus was past him and running

313

again, going for the officer. As he ran, he heard Runt call, "It's Scapula!"

The words galvanised him. Scapula. The Governor who had sworn to exterminate the Silures. Calgacus jumped over a tussock, staggered as he landed, but kept going in a wild, headlong charge which he would not be able to stop. Horses were coming from his right, trying to reach the fallen Governor, but Calgacus was closer and moving faster than he had ever run before. They would not catch him.

He reached the Governor's fallen horse. It was struggling, shrieking in pain, unable to rise because it had broken a leg. Calgacus jumped, somehow missed the animal's flailing legs, planted his left foot on the horse's writhing body and leaped again. Scapula, further down the slope, was slowly rising to his feet, blood dripping down his left arm, his helmet battered and dented. He was dazed, injured and unarmed.

Calgacus had no time for qualms. The man might be unarmed but he was hardly helpless. Shouts and thuds of hoofs told Calgacus that the Governor's men were rapidly closing in. Calgacus jumped again, swinging his sword as he sailed through the air towards the Roman. He had time for only one blow.

Scapula saw him coming, tried to jump aside as Calgacus hurtled past him, but the sword smashed into his side, wedging deep into the metal of the Governor's bronze breastplate. Calgacus went whirling past, yanking at the sword, trying to pull it free. It came loose, but he was past the Governor now, his arm was flailing behind him and he lost his grip on the weapon. He slipped as he landed and lost his balance, falling to hit the ground hard. Unable to stop, he tumbled down the slope.

The fall saved his life. Horsemen were wheeling round the Governor, forming a protective barrier. One of them had aimed a blow at Calgacus' head but had missed as the warrior careered further down the slope. Calgacus was dimly aware of the riders as he rolled and slid down the hill. The large shield on his back caught, snagged on something unseen, twisting him awkwardly, turning him over. His face ground into the grass and earth while his fingers scrabbled uselessly for a hold. Mercifully, he slid to a stop, face down, his head lower on the slope than his legs.

He pushed himself up, stabs of pain coming from every part of his body. Spitting grass and earth from his mouth and wiping dirt

314

from his cheeks, he turned to look back up the hill. He was amazed at how far he had fallen. Up above, he saw that the Romans were fleeing. They had grabbed the Governor, thrown him onto a riderless horse and were charging away down the hill as fast as they could go. There were still enough of them to have won the fight, but the Governor's fall meant they had had enough. Calgacus laughed aloud with relief as he watched them go.

Runt arrived, coming down the hill quickly, although far more carefully than Calgacus had done on his mad charge. The little man held Calgacus' sword.

"Are you all right?" he asked in a concerned voice.

Calgacus grinned. "Twisted my ankle a bit. Nothing broken, but I think I'll have a few bruises."

"I thought I told you not to do anything crazy," Runt said as he handed back the sword. "How can I protect you if you go and do stupid things like that?"

"I got him, though," Calgacus said with satisfaction as he wiped the sword clean. He tutted as he saw a nick in the blade where it had caught in the officer's armour. But for the first time since he had heard of Senuala's death, he was smiling. "I got him good. Are you sure it was Scapula?"

Runt nodded. "I heard the riders shouting that they had to protect the Governor. It must have been him."

"Well, he's a dead Governor now."

"He's still alive," Runt said. "At least, he was when they picked him up."

"Damn! Are you sure?"

"I'm afraid so."

Calgacus swore. "Well, he'll be out of action for a while, at least."

He looked back up the slope. There were several Romans lying dead, but a scattering of Silures as well, with other warriors nursing wounds. It would have been far worse if the Romans had not been intent on rescuing the Governor. He knew they had been fortunate.

Gutyn came bounding down to greet them, grinning hugely. "Magnificent!" he said. "That was a sight to behold. One man charging a hundred Roman cavalry on his own. I've never heard of such a thing. You are the greatest warrior I have ever seen."

"No," said Runt. "He's just the luckiest. And the craziest."

315

Chapter XXXIII

Calgacus presented Gutyn with a new sword, one just arrived from Cadwallon's forges. The young warrior was immensely proud and lost no opportunity to show it off. He was also keen to regale anyone who would listen with the tales of his ambush and Calgacus' attack on the Governor. By the time morning came, Calgacus heard that Gutyn and his men had killed forty Romans in the village while he himself had slain ten cavalrymen single-handedly, scaring off the other two hundred.

Cadwgan was puzzled. "Why does he say these things? Everyone knows he is exaggerating."

"Of course they do," Calgacus said. "But we didn't bring back any Roman heads to be counted, so even if he told the truth, they would still think he was exaggerating and would discount his deeds to nothing." He shrugged. "It is the way of young men."

Cadwgan laughed. "You speak as if you are an old man, Calgacus. Yet you are younger than many of the men who follow you."

"War makes old men of us all," Calgacus commented.

"Yet you still fight."

"What else would you have me do? We either fight or we become Roman slaves."

Cadwgan peered closely at him. "I think I am beginning to see why Cethinos fears you," he said. "You make men believe they can do things through the force of their own will."

Calgacus frowned. "Why should Cethinos fear that? I think he fears me because he knows that he has lost his power over me. He knows I would not be afraid to tear his rotten heart out."

Cadwgan flapped his pudgy hands anxiously. "Don't say things like that! You should not be so disrespectful to druids, you know. What I meant was that Cethinos knows that our actions are controlled by the Gods. If men start believing they can do things for themselves, then they might start thinking that they do not need the Gods. These are dangerous thoughts."

Calgacus wondered how Cadwgan would cope with speaking

to Myrddin for a day or two. The druid was earnest in his beliefs, yet anxious to understand the world outside Ynis Mon. He was obviously starting to see that the two were not always easily reconciled.

Calgacus found himself growing to like Cadwgan, so he resisted the temptation to throw some of Myrddin's more heretical views at him. Instead, he said, "When the battle starts, it will be won by men with strong arms and strong hearts. If you watch, you will see more blood spilled in one day than in a lifetime of making sacrifices to the Gods. And you will see only men fighting. There will be no Gods there."

Cadwgan wagged a finger at him. "You do not know that. You said yourself that the Gods came to you in a dream. Just because you cannot see them, does not mean that they are not there, guiding you, protecting you."

"He has me to protect him," said Runt. "And his own crazy luck."

"You call it luck," replied Cadwgan. "I prefer to call it the protection of the Gods. Perhaps Camulos still watches over you."

"Well, perhaps you can ask the Gods what the Romans are up to," said Calgacus. "Gutyn's scouts say they are just sitting in their camp, doing nothing."

He stood up, stretched, and peered eastwards. All around him, hidden in the trees and bushes, his men lay or sat, idly waiting for the Romans to march into their trap. Everything was ready, but the Romans were not coming.

Calgacus turned to Runt. "Send someone to find Gutyn, will you? I have a job for him."

In the heart of the Legion's camp, an anxious crowd of medical orderlies huddled around the Governor's bed. One of them withdrew, moving away to talk to Valens and Facilis who were watching from the doorway of the large tent, concern etched on their faces. The orderly looked grave as he faced them.

"His arm is broken, but we have set the bones," he said in a low voice. "It should heal, although the break is a bad one and the stone that hit him has caused a lot of damage to his muscles. His head is also badly bruised, and he may have concussion. But the wound in his side is extremely serious. There has been a lot of bleeding. Several ribs are broken and I fear his lungs have been

317

pierced. I am not sure he will survive this."

"We cannot sit here for long," said Valens. "Will he survive a journey back to Glevum?"

The orderly gave a slight shrug of his shoulders. "I cannot say. He is very weak. But he is asking to talk to you."

The orderlies dutifully moved away as the two officers approached the cot. Scapula was lying swathed in bloody bandages. His face was grey, the skin taut. His hair lay plastered around his face, lank and dull. When he opened his eyes, they could see that he had been heavily drugged. Yet he tried to focus on Valens.

"Have you found their camp yet?" he asked in a whisper so faint that they could barely hear.

"No, sir. We are waiting for you to recover before we move on."

Scapula croaked, "Don't wait for me. Go after them. Pursue them as far as it takes. When you find them, go straight for them. Kill every last one of the savages."

He coughed with the effort of speaking and his face contorted as a spasm of pain shot through him. He closed his eyes. After a moment he opened them again.

"Have you found their camp yet?" he asked.

Facilis leaned over the bed. "Not yet, sir. But we are pursuing them, as you ordered."

Scapula gave a weak smile. "Good. Kill them all," he said softly.

Facilis gently pulled Valens away from the bed, allowing the orderlies to return to tending the Governor.

"We need to send him back," he told the Legate. "I don't think the journey could be any worse than leaving him here."

Valens nodded. "I will have a wagon prepared. You can take his personal guard and half the cavalry. They are of little use in these wretched hills anyway."

Facilis nodded. "You had better find their army and destroy it. Once he recovers, he will not be happy if the Silures have not been wiped out."

Valens wondered what he was supposed to do if the barbarians did not stand and fight, but he realised that he had no option except to follow the Governor's orders.

"We will march in the morning," he said to Facilis.

It was, he felt, the best thing he could do. Rumours about the skirmish that had nearly killed the Governor were already spreading throughout the camp. The Silures were madmen, the stories said. On foot, they attacked cavalry on open ground, and they won. Men were saying that the barbarians were led by a giant who could carve his way through men and horses like an invulnerable god of war. Valens did not believe that, but something had unnerved the men of the Governor's bodyguard, and somehow one of the barbarians had evaded them to strike down Scapula. Such things started the whispering.

Now, some men were saying that they had seen strange portents, a dove chasing an eagle, a goat with two heads, a raven perching on the Governor's tent.

Valens had ordered his Centurions to clamp down on such stories, to punish any man heard repeating them. He doubted whether it would do any good. Once men got it into their heads that the omens were against them, it was difficult to change their minds.

Valens called the aquilifer to him. The Legion's standard-bearer was an experienced soldier, a trusted man, perhaps the most important man in the Legion. He bore the Second Augusta's eagle into battle.

"Sir?" the aquilifer asked, giving a punctilious salute.

Valens spoke to him as one soldier to another. "I want you to make sure that the Eagle is well guarded," he said. "I want no mishaps, no slips, trips or other unfortunate accidents."

The aquilifer gave him an offended look. "Of course not, sir."

"Good. We are only facing barbarians, after all."

"Yes, sir."

The aquilifer left, clearly annoyed by the Legate's words, but Valens did not regret speaking to him like that. It was not unknown for an aquilifer to drop the eagle standard, or to trip and fall while holding it. If that happened, the soldiers would refuse to march because it was the worst of all omens if their standard fell, a clear warning from the Gods not to fight. Valens now knew that if any such accident did occur, it would signal a genuine omen, not a contrived one.

That evening, while he prayed to his family's Gods, Valens also poured a libation to Mars, god of war, beseeching his aid in the coming battle. It always helped to have a powerful deity on your side, especially when others had seen portents of doom.

Dawn broke reluctantly through a blanket of grey clouds that masked the sky as far as the eye could see, shrouding the summits of the surrounding hills in a dull fog. A light but persistent drizzle fell on the camp, the sort of rain that Valens had grown to hate during his time in Britannia. On days like this he would step out into the rain thinking that it was not too bad, only to find shortly afterwards that he had been soaked by its unrelenting persistence.

He watched as the Governor was carried to a covered wagon where he was laid on a bed of furs. The wagon set off, surrounded by over a hundred cavalrymen. Facilis nodded a curt farewell as he led the Governor on the long road back to safety. Valens was now in command of the war effort.

The legion was up and preparing to march, packing away the tents, loading the mules of the baggage train, dismantling the wooden palisade of stakes. Then Valens heard the warning shouts. Cursing, he hurried to the earth rampart, peering westwards.

He saw around fifty barbarians on horseback, riding the small, ugly mountain horses they favoured. They galloped and wheeled, circling towards the camp to hurl javelins and insults, riding away laughing and whooping with delight. The missiles were clumsily thrown and did no damage, but the riders ventured ever closer with each circuit. When they had thrown all their javelins, they merely mocked the Romans as they rode past.

Valens fumed. He wished he had some archers. There were, he knew, some Syrian auxiliaries in Britannia, men who were skilled with the bow, but they were far away to the north. The Roman army generally disdained the use of bows, viewing them as cowardly weapons, although Valens thought they were no more cowardly than the catapults and ballistas the army used quite happily. Archers had their uses, he thought, but Scapula was a traditionalist and had brought no bowmen on this campaign.

Wishing would not solve the problem, Valens knew. He turned to his signaller.

"Summon the auxiliary cavalry. Get them to drive this lot away."

Each legion had a cavalry *ala*, usually around a hundred and twenty men. The Second *Augusta* now had barely thirty horsemen left, after the losses they had suffered and the need to provide an escort for the wounded Governor. But there was an auxiliary unit accompanying the legion, two hundred Tungrians sworn to the service of the Empire. Valens considered them a poor lot, but there were more than enough of them to scare away these annoying barbarians.

The Tungrians took forever to get ready, but at last they swept past the fort, charging at the rabble of barbarian riders. The Silures immediately turned tail, galloping away as soon as they saw them coming. The Tungrians, mounted on bigger horses, gained on the fleeing tribesmen, but the Silures had a head start and the auxiliaries could not catch them.

Valens watched as the two groups of riders disappeared round the spur of a hill, vanishing into the murk. "The Legion will march!" he ordered.

The Second *Augusta* was a good legion, experienced in war. Their morale had suffered recently, but when Valens gave the order to march, they fell into the routine that had been instilled in them over years of training and warfare. Valens felt proud as he watched them. His horse was brought to him and he mounted, taking his place near the head of the column, beside the legion's eagle standard.

The *aquilifer* gave him a curt, challenging nod of greeting, as if to prove that Valens' warning had been a waste of time. He held the eagle high, letting the legionaries see it. Below the winged eagle, the long staff bore a plaque with the legend, "SPQR", which stood for *Senatus Populusque Romanus*, "The Senate and the People of Rome".

The men took pride in that. They represented Rome in their mission to bring the Empire's civilising influence wherever they went, though the truth was that it had been many years since the legions had enforced the will of either the Senate or the people. They fought for the Emperor, the man who paid them and who demanded their loyalty. The Emperor had decreed that Britannia should be conquered, so now the men of the Second Augusta were marching to complete that conquest, to crush the last of the tribes who stubbornly resisted the civilisation that Rome was intent on imposing upon them.

This, Valens mused, was a historic moment. This was the moment when he, Gaius Manlius Valens, would fulfil the Emperor's wishes.

Chapter XXXIV

"Gutyn's coming!"

The word flashed along the lines of men who lay hidden on the wooded hillside. Calgacus immediately sent his chieftains scurrying along the slope, dodging among the trees and the thick undergrowth, telling the warriors to lie down, to remain hidden. The last thing Calgacus wanted was for them to betray their presence too soon.

"If anyone so much as breaks wind before I give the signal, I will personally cut his balls off!" he told them. "Stay silent. Stay down. Don't even look at the Romans until I say so. If they see us, we are all dead, so keep out of sight."

In the face of Calgacus' savage determination, the warriors crouched or lay on the hillside, not daring to move.

Calgacus took a position behind a tree, screened from below by thick foliage and the fine mist and drizzle that filled the morning air. From this vantage point he watched as Gutyn and his men rode along the combe, splashing through the puddles, throwing up muddy spray as they galloped past in a clatter of hooves. Behind them came a horde of Roman cavalry.

Calgacus turned to Runt, "Pass the word. Leave the cavalry alone. Let them pass."

Gutyn and his men raced out of the combe into the grassy plain at the western end. The Romans galloped after them, but their commander slowed before they were half way along the narrow defile. Calgacus, barely sixty paces from the leading rider, smiled to himself as he imagined the cavalry officer's thoughts. There, up ahead of the Roman horsemen, was the Silures' camp.

On the far hillside, beyond Gutyn's tiny force, dark shapes were moving as thousands of men gathered at a long defensive ditch that had been dug around the lower slopes of the steep hill. The poor visibility helped mask how many men there were in the camp but, as Calgacus had hoped, it looked as if there were several thousand.

The Roman commander obviously thought so, too. Gutyn's horsemen had wheeled again, circling to face the Romans, daring them to continue the chase, but the leading cavalryman waved his hand high, gesturing in a circling motion. The riders tugged on the reins, wheeled their horses around and galloped back out along the narrow, rain-soaked valley.

Calgacus gave a satisfied smile. He turned to Cadwgan who was crouching beside him.

"We've got them," he announced confidently.

The cavalry thundered through the hills, hurrying back to meet the marching legion. The commander hastily saluted Valens, then turned his horse to ride alongside the Legate.

"We have found their camp, sir." The man said in his atrociously coarse, guttural accent.

"Where?"

The man pointed into the rain. "Straight through this valley. Then there is a narrow pass. The camp is at the far end, on a hillside. They have dug themselves in."

"How many of them? Is it their main force?"

The Tungrian nodded. "It's a big camp, sir. I'd say at least five thousand of them."

Valens gave a satisfied smile. The barbarians had done exactly what the Governor had predicted. But the Legate remained cautious. He quizzed the cavalryman mercilessly, trying to understand the lie of the land. Once he had an idea of what to expect, he asked, "Do we have time to get through this pass before they block it?"

The cavalryman looked doubtful. "Not if they leave their camp."

"Then go and make sure they stay behind their ditch," Valens ordered him. "We will get through as quickly as we can."

While the Tungrians rode off again, Valens summoned the Legion's Centurions and Tribunes to him. Quickly, he outlined what the cavalry had seen. He turned to the senior Centurion, the primus pilus, the First Spear, the man who led the first century, a double century comprising one hundred and sixty of the most experienced legionaries.

"Set a fast pace," Valens told him. "We need to get through that pass quickly. Once on the other side, we will form up and attack without delay."

That was what the Governor had told him to do. The barbarians will hold the high ground, Scapula had said. Go straight for them. They will run because they are barbarians; they always run when confronted by the power of the legions.

The Centurion clapped his hand to his chest in salute. In moments, the legion was marching again.

It took them half an hour of splashing through the continual rain before they reached the narrow pass. It was rocky, uneven and rutted, with puddles everywhere. The steep hillside on the left loomed high and forbidding, its upper reaches hidden by the low clouds. To the right was a dark, thickly wooded hill. The combe looked a dangerous place, but beyond the far end, over a mile away, Valens could just make out the small lights of hundreds of fires, marking the site of the barbarians' camp.

One mile. One thousand paces separated him from the enemy.

He wanted to get there quickly. The narrow defile troubled him but he could see the Tungrian horsemen gathered at the far end, guarding the approach to the barbarian's position, keeping the way clear. Scapula's command rang in his head. *Strike hard and fast.*

Valens waved to the senior Centurion. "Go on! The cavalry have been through this place twice. There is no danger."

With mounting expectation, Calgacus watched as the legion marched into the narrow defile. Away to his right, the Roman cavalry were sitting, watching the fake camp, while Gutyn's horsemen rode up and down in front of the hill, giving the Tungrians something to look at.

The Roman horsemen did not move. They sat on their horses, wiping the rain from their faces while they waited for the legionaries to arrive. On the hill, Tannattos and his men were chanting and singing, beating on drums and waving spears up and down. The ghostly call of a carnyx sounded, its eerie cry muffled by distance and rain.

Calgacus turned his attention back to the column of marching soldiers. Each legionary carried his shield and two javelins. They also had heavy wooden cross-poles on which they hung all the paraphernalia a soldier needed: spare clothing, eating utensils, plates and mugs, water skin, spades, picks, wooden stakes and wicker baskets. Over a century earlier, a Roman general named Marius had reformed the way the legions fought, insisting that the men carried much of the gear they needed. Ever since, the legionaries had called themselves "Marius's Mules".

Yet even with the men carrying these burdens, they still needed a baggage train. Behind the legion came their mules, laden with tents, food and other assorted essentials. Then came their siege equipment, and wagons carrying yet more supplies.

A small rearguard detachment of soldiers brought up the rear of the official column but behind them came the camp followers, the traders, artisans, slaves, whores and thieves who followed every army wherever it marched.

Calgacus had no interest in the followers. He concentrated on the leading men. The legionaries marched through the narrow pass four abreast, each century under its own standard. Behind the first group came some men on horseback and the legion's standards, the eagle and another bearing an image of the Emperor. Then came more soldiers, more standards, all tramping along the rough floor of the valley, heading towards what they believed was their enemy's encampment.

They marched in silence, keeping in step even over the rutted, uneven ground of the pass. There was no singing, no marching songs. The only sounds were the tramp of marching feet and the drumming of rain on armour, shields and packs.

Runt leaned close to whisper into Calgacus' ear. "They won't all get in. The valley is too short."

Calgacus nodded. He had noticed it too. He could either let some Romans leave the far end of the pass or he could trap the leading men and leave some stranded at the back. He quickly considered the options. The leading men were the best troops, the most experienced soldiers. He decided he could not afford to allow them to leave the defile. If they were able to form up, they could turn the tide of the battle.

He had his shield ready. Slowly, he drew his long sword as he peered down through the rain at the marching column. From their hiding places among the trees warriors watched him, waiting for the signal.

He raised his sword high, paused, then slashed it down.

"Now!"

The hillside erupted in a torrent of frenzied violence. The bushes and shrubs were torn aside as thousands of warriors leaped out to charge down the slope at the exposed column of marching men.

A hail of missiles preceded them. Spears, slingshots, arrows, even rocks were hurled down at the marching Romans. The legionaries carried their shields on their left side, offering no protection against the sudden and unexpected onslaught from their right. Dozens of them fell injured or dying while the rest whirled in confusion. Before the startled legionaries could rally, the Silures were among them, their spears and swords dealing death.

Calgacus had concentrated his forces in the centre of the valley where they could outnumber and overwhelm the Romans. He charged in, hacking and bludgeoning men down under his great sword. Beside him, Runt was more economical, yet just as ferocious and deadly. The Romans were weighed down by their heavy packs, unable to form their usual ranks, and terrified by the sight of this huge barbarian storming among them. Bewildered by the attack, they fought not as legionaries, but as individuals. They fought and they died.

Valens, near the western end of the valley, was flung from his horse when a javelin caught the beast in the neck. He landed on the hard ground with a thump that forced the air from his lungs and left him dazed when his helmet struck a rock. Screaming tribesmen ran at him, brandishing wickedly sharp spears. He tried to stand, then fell back as Roman sandals and shields filled his vision. His men were gathering round him, protecting him. He heard the *aquilifer* yelling frantically for the legion to rally.

Valens was hauled roughly to his feet to gaze into the grizzled features of the senior Centurion.

"Which way do we go sir?" the man asked in a wondrously calm way, apparently oblivious to the carnage all around them.

Valens was too stunned to understand the question. "Which way?"

"Forward or back?" the Centurion wanted to know. He ducked as a stone whistled past his head, glaring at the impertinence of the barbarians.

Valens was buffeted and jostled as the legionaries around them braced to withstand a charge. He staggered, held upright only by the press of men around him and the Centurion's vice-like grip on his shoulders. His head was ringing, filled with the sounds of screams and yells. In his confusion, he focussed on the last word he had heard.

"Back?" he mumbled, trying to grasp what the Centurion was asking him.

That must be wrong, Valens thought. Surely the Governor had said they should attack?

"Back it is, sir," the Centurion said smartly. He barked orders to the men of the First Century who instantly locked shields and began the nightmare journey back through the blood-soaked valley.

All along the narrow pass, hemmed between the steep cliff behind them and the marauding tribesmen in front, the Romans were in disarray. The Silures had smashed into them so viciously and so unexpectedly that all cohesion had gone and the battle had degenerated into a series of savage, merciless brawls.

Only the men of the First Century retained any semblance of order. They locked their shields over their heads in the testudo formation, marching, slowly, ponderously, but remorselessly, back along the valley.

The testudo, or turtle, was normally reserved for assaults on towns or cities where missiles would be dropped from above. The men in the centre of the column raised their shields above their heads, forming a protective roof. The men on each side formed walls of shields and only the men at the rear were unprotected. Yet this was not good enough to protect them from the madness that threatened to engulf them now. The Centurion yelled at the men of the rear rank who turned about, forming a wall of shields at the back of the formation. These men were now forced to walk backwards. Their comrades in the next rank reached back, grabbed their belts and pulled them, determined not to allow a gap to appear in the formation. It was desperate, slow, difficult work, but the formation held together while missiles rained down on the covering of shields and tribesmen hurled themselves uselessly at the solid phalanx. In obedience to the grim shouts of the Centurion, the Romans ground their way back down the pass, tramping over the bodies of the fallen, sweeping tribesmen aside and making space for other legionaries to join the safety of the shielded column.

Calgacus took a moment to regain his breath. He surveyed the devastation all around him. There were no Romans left standing near him. Away to his left, the fighting continued, but the sweat, rain and mist made it virtually impossible to see what was happening. He was about to summon his men to charge that way when he heard Runt yell a warning. He whirled as Runt grabbed his arm, tugging him back up the slope.

Calgacus looked, appalled, to where Runt was pointing. From their right, a mass of Roman shields was forcing its way along the valley floor, resisting every attempt to break it.

Calgacus swore under his breath. If that formation reached the fighting further along the valley to their left, the Romans might be able to rally. There would still be several hundred soldiers who had not entered the pass, which meant that the tribesmen now risked being caught between the two groups of Romans.

He watched, helpless, as the Roman cocoon of shields made its ponderous way eastwards. He called out, telling his men to withdraw, to re-form. What he needed to break that formation was a solid punch of his own, yet his men were scattered and tired. It would take precious time to gather them. Time in which the Romans moved ever further eastwards along the combe.

The testudo passed beneath him, scant yards away. The Romans made no attempt to attack anyone. Their sole aim was to stay together until they escaped from the deadly confines of the pass.

Runt whirled his sling, sending a stone smashing harmlessly against the wall of shields. The Romans would not break and Calgacus saw victory slowly evaporating before his eyes. To his left, tribesmen were scattering as the testudo approached them. As they scrambled back onto the hillside, they eased the pressure on the Romans at the end of the pass, allowing the embattled legionaries to escape into open ground where their rearguard was forming, preparing to launch a counter-attack.

Calgacus knew that he needed to do something to retrieve the situation, but he could think of nothing that would break the solid phalanx of legionaries.

Then he heard the shouts.

Through the mist and rain, jogging at a steady pace, jumping over the dead and wounded, came Tannattos and his men, the young warriors who had manned the fake camp. Calgacus could not think how they had managed to evade the Roman horsemen, but they were here, and Tannattos' sword was dark with blood. The chieftain bared is teeth in a savage grin as he saw Calgacus. His men had been desperate to fight, to show that, despite their youth, they were true warriors. Now they had their chance.

Calgacus caught Tannattos' eye. He pointed his sword at the rear of the Roman testudo. Yelling a savage war cry, Tannattos led his men straight for the retreating Romans.

When Calgacus was still scarcely more than a boy, Caratacus had taught him that a charge should not be met standing still. A running man has momentum and power. A defender, standing still, risks being knocked down and killed. If a counter-charge was not possible, then at the last moment, a charge should be met by a forward movement. The Romans facing Tannattos' charge were not just standing still, they were already moving backwards. If they stepped forwards to meet the onslaught, they would leave a gap between them and the rest of their column, a gap the Silures would stream into. The legionaries in the rear rank had no choice but to continue their slow, backwards march.

With a crash that reverberated around the defile, the tribesmen smashed into the rear of the column. Swords flashed, men fell and a gap appeared as a legionary stumbled and was cut down. In an instant, the Silures poured in to the rear of the column, stabbing wildly, swarming over the Romans. The soldiers who had thought themselves safe in the centre of the shelter of shields, suddenly found their enemy was amongst them.

Panic, the foe of every army, set in. Calgacus felt a fierce surge of joy as he saw legionaries do what no Roman soldiers had done since they had first arrived in Britannia. They broke and they ran.

"Kill them all!" Calgacus shouted.

His voice was lost in the cacophony of battle but it did not matter. The Silures scented victory. They had no need of orders. They stabbed and they ran, hunting down their enemy.

Legionaries threw away their shields and weapons, hoping they would be able to escape more easily if they were not encumbered. For most, it was a vain hope. They ran a gauntlet of tribesmen who rushed at them, bowled them over and stabbed relentlessly.

A few soldiers held their ground, standing back to back in

small clumps, knowing they could not escape. They fought desperately but they were hopelessly outnumbered. Calgacus smashed into one small group of soldiers, scattering the legionaries who were quickly butchered.

He searched for the eagle standard, saw it further along the pass, surrounded by a small knot of legionaries who were running desperately, their numbers dwindling as men were picked off. Calgacus ran towards them but the pass was almost blocked by hundreds of warriors, choked by heaps of dead and dying men, by abandoned packs and discarded weapons. By the time he forced a way through to the end of the combe, the eagle had reached the sanctuary of the Roman rearguard.

Calgacus stopped, breathing hard while he quickly took in the scene. More than a quarter of the Legion had not yet entered the defile when the attack had been launched. Some of these men had formed a defensive phalanx which provided a refuge for the survivors of the leading centuries who ran to join them, shoving through the ranks as they frantically sought to escape from the fury of the Silures.

Their arrival created more panic among the rearguard. Most of the legionaries in that formation had escaped the carnage of the defile. They were fresh, uninjured and drawn up, ready to fight, but the terror of their fleeing comrades was infectious. As hordes of barbarians streamed towards them, many men were seized by dread. Fearing that the rearguard would also be overwhelmed, they broke ranks and fled.

Calgacus knew that the battle was beyond his control now, but there was nothing he needed to do. Only a few hundred legionaries retained their discipline and they were in no mood to continue the fight. Clustering round their eagle standard, they were retreating, all thoughts of counter-attacking forgotten.

They were pursued by thousands of tribesmen who poured out of the valley to attack them. The Silures, elated by their victory, swarmed around the Roman formation, forcing the soldiers back, bombarding them with missiles, jabbing at them with spears, driving them on. In their wake the soldiers abandoned the baggage train and left the siege engines marooned in a sea of victorious tribesmen.

Runt, gasping for breath, wheezed. "We did it. By Toutatis, Cal, we did it."

Calgacus felt his throat constrict. His arms and legs were suddenly weary, his sword almost too heavy to lift. But Runt was right. They had done it. They had defeated a Roman legion.

It was more than a victory. The Romans had left more than half of their soldiers dead or dying in the slaughterhouse of the defile. The survivors were escaping as the Silures grew tired or were distracted by the prospect of plunder but that did not matter. All that mattered was that they had won.

Calgacus stood in the pouring rain, watching the red and yellow shields retreat into the mist.

Chapter XXXV

In the aftermath of the victory, Calgacus felt curiously deflated. While the tribesmen hunted their fleeing enemy remorselessly across the plain and through the hills, he sat on the wet hillside, sheltering under the spreading leaves of a huge oak, looking down on the human debris that littered the pass.

The dead lay everywhere, often piled on top of each other. Women and children moved among them, knives ready to finish off any Roman who still lived, hands ready to loot whatever they could find of value.

Picking his way along the combe, Cadwgan found Calgacus sitting with his shield on the ground beside him and his sword across his knees as he wiped it with an old piece of cloth.

The druid felt slightly in awe of the young warrior. Cadwgan knew implicitly that the victory had only been possible because the Gods had willed it, but it had been Calgacus who, by the sheer force of his will, had held the warriors hidden, silent and uncomplaining in the dank wetness of the woods. His conviction and confidence had made the warriors believe that they could achieve the impossible. It was no wonder, Cadwgan thought, that Cethinos hated the young prince. The Gods may have made the victory possible but it was Calgacus who had been the driving force. Cadwgan was no stranger to violence, for the world of men was a violent place, but he had never witnessed anything to match the ferocity and savage power of the assault Calgacus had unleashed on the Romans.

"You have done a great thing," he volunteered as he ventured to stand under the long boughs of the tree.

Calgacus looked up at him with heavy eyes. "Tell that to Maddoc," he said.

"I will."

Calgacus shook his head slowly. "This time I will tell him myself."

Runt looked up anxiously. "You should not go to Ynis Mon,

Cal," he said. "Cethinos will be there."

"I am tired of having this hanging over me. I cannot do any more than I have done."

Cadwgan said, "It is a great victory. I will tell Maddoc this. As for Cethinos, he has had the sacrifice he demanded. I am sure you will be released from the doom pronounced on you."

"But Cethinos will take the credit," said Runt bitterly. "He will say that we gained the victory because of his royal sacrifice."

"Yet, it was Calgacus' name Senuala called out before she went to the Gods," Cadwgan pointed out. "She showed Cethinos, as she showed the warriors, where their hope lay. I think he will find it difficult to take too much credit."

"I don't really care," Calgacus said wearily. "What's important is that we have won. And at what cost."

That cost had been horribly high. More than two thousand Romans had been killed in that small pass, yet the tribesmen had lost nearly a thousand of their own. Among the dead was young Gutyn, killed when the Tungrian horsemen, seeing the awful fight in the pass behind them, had charged away, desperately seeking an alternative way out through the hills. They had cut through Gutyn's small force and galloped out the other side, riding off as quickly as they could. Gutyn had tried to stop them and had died in the attempt.

Tannattos was dead too, killed in that last, furious attack on the column, a Roman gladius taking his life at the very moment of his victory. His young warriors had avenged him, but Tannattos would not grumble again.

Rhydderch had survived, although with the loss of two fingers of his right hand. Despite their triumph, he was bemoaning the fact that he would not be able to hold a sword again.

Yet in spite of the losses, the Silures were exultant. They had pursued the fleeing Romans through the rain, cutting down stragglers, seizing the baggage train.

Half of the Legion survived, the Legate Valens among them, yet they were beaten and demoralised. The eagle standard had formed a rallying point that had held the remnants of the shattered legion together until they had marched all the way back to the camp they had occupied the previous night, where they dug themselves in, abandoning their wounded, leaving behind their siege weapons and an enormous quantity of supplies.

The Silures gleefully covered the catapults with oil and set them ablaze, sending dark pillars of smoke into the still raining sky while they danced around the weapons' funeral pyres. Wagons and packs were plundered but there was simply too much for them to carry it all away.

The tribesmen took few prisoners, and most of those they did capture were the women they had caught among the camp followers, women who were now dragged into slavery for the men's pleasure. Everyone else who was caught met a quick and violent death. The elated tribesmen soon began the grisly task of collecting the heads of the fallen while their bards began composing songs to commemorate the victory.

Calgacus' fame would be sung throughout the lands of the free tribes.

Several days later, what remained of the Second Augusta crossed the mighty Sabrina and returned to its fort at Glevum. The men were tired, battered and hungry as they marched sullenly back to where they had started the summer campaign. In the wake of the retreating legion, the Silures raided across the western edges of the province, looting and burning at will.

Valens was too numb to consider any course of action except reaching safety. His Tungrian horsemen had found their way home, reporting a desperate fight against hordes of barbarians which had prevented them from coming to assist the Legion. Valens accepted the report without argument, mainly because he had used a similar version of events in his own letter to the Governor.

He had worried that Scapula might be waiting for him at Glevum but the Governor had been taken to Londinium, sparing Valens the ordeal of reporting his defeat in person. It was a small consolation. However hard he tried, Valens could not disguise the enormity of what had happened. He sat at his desk, slowly scratching the quill across the parchment. He read it over, then tore it up, holding the scraps over a candle to burn it. It would not do, he realised, to tell the Governor that he had simply obeyed his instructions. That would imply that the fault was Scapula's. He reached for another piece of parchment and began writing again, choosing his words more carefully.

This time, he wrote that they had been ambushed by over ten

thousand barbarians in difficult terrain which did not allow them to deploy properly. Despite the difficulties, they had managed to withdraw in good order, killing a great number of the enemy, although not without serious loss of men and equipment. Valens was forced to concede that the legion could not claim victory, yet he assured the Governor that it was not a disaster. Once the legion was brought back up to strength, they would march again. Some standards had been lost, but the eagle had been saved, so the legion, although scarcely at half strength, had not been destroyed.

Valens sighed. What he had written was true, but he knew that the men were so shattered by their defeat that they would not be ready to fight for a long time to come.

He signed the letter, sealed it and sent it off to Londinium by fast messenger. Now all he could do was await the response. That was not a happy prospect. No matter how much he dressed it up, the battle had been a catastrophe and Scapula was not a forgiving man. Valens was the Legate; the responsibility was his. The best he could hope for now was a dishonourable return to Rome. And what was life in Rome without honour, he wondered?

He sat in his quarters, contemplating his future while the rain drummed against the shutters. The weather was as bleak as his mood.

The journey to Ynis Mon took over two weeks because Calgacus was in no hurry to confront the Druid Council. Despite Cadwgan's eager promptings for haste, they travelled slowly, making frequent, lengthy stops.

One of those stops was to visit Cadwallon and give him the news of the victory. The king of the Ordovices gave a lavish feast in Calgacus' honour, demanding that the tale of the battle be told to all his leading warriors. Cadwgan obliged, rehearsing the story he would tell to Maddoc and the Council of Druids, recounting Calgacus' cunning and bravery, describing how the Romans had fled from the fury of the tribesmen.

It was indeed a great victory and news of it must have spread throughout the Roman province because the other legions had hastily withdrawn to their forts, ceasing the devastation of the land which the Governor had ordered. The spirit of resistance was growing again because the free tribes had been shown that the Romans could be beaten.

Cadwallon went so far as to promise more warriors should Calgacus want them for the next year's campaign.

"The man is still a weasel," Runt opined sourly as they rode north from Cadwallon's homestead. "If the Romans ever decide to come this way, he will not stand against them."

"He will if I am standing behind him," Calgacus asserted.

When they reached the north-west coast, they made the short sea crossing to Ynis Mon where Cadwgan led them across the island to meet the Druid Council. Once again, they walked under the skull-carved gateway that led into the deep, dark grove with its blood-stained altar stone. Once again, the nine members of the Druid Council awaited them.

Cethinos glared at Calgacus with a face like thunder. His expression turned even darker when he looked at Cadwgan.

Maddoc, seemingly oblivious to Cethinos' mood, inclined his head in a slight bow as Calgacus stood before him.

"Welcome, Calgacus, son of Cunobelinos. What news do you bring?"

"I have delivered your great victory," Calgacus replied, forcing himself to be polite. "The Silures have destroyed a Roman legion and driven the enemy back beyond the Hafren. I ask to be released from the fate you decreed for me the last time I was here."

Maddoc glanced at Cadwgan. The younger druid said, "It is true. I witnessed the battle myself. An entire Roman legion was routed, leaving hundreds of dead behind them in their flight. They abandoned all their supplies and fled back across the Hafren. It was truly a great victory."

Calgacus had expected another delay while the council deliberated, but Maddoc surprised him with a smile. The old man's weathered face seemed to shed years as he beamed up at him.

"Then you have fulfilled your task and the doom of sacrifice is lifted."

It was as simple as that. In an instant, Calgacus had defeated not only the Romans, but also the doom of the druids. The weight of it lifted as a fierce thrill of exultation surged through him. He could not resist a triumphant look at Cethinos. His nemesis stared back, unrepentant.

"The victory was gained thanks to a sacrifice of royal blood," Cethinos said coldly. "It was as I have always said it would be. Though the victim was one who showed more honour than

Calgacus."

"Perhaps you could explain how that victim came to be where she was?" Calgacus retorted. "I am sure her sister would like to know the truth of the matter. Perhaps I should go and tell her."

Cethinos stared back with an expression as hard as stone. Maddoc stood, waving a hand at him, commanding him to remain silent.

The senior druid looked at Calgacus and said, "You have done well, Calgacus. You should return to the Silures to prepare for whatever the Romans do next. You have won a great victory, but they have not been driven from our lands."

"I will need more men if I am to do that. But I expect that will not be a problem now."

"Indeed not," Maddoc agreed. "Men are always eager to join a victorious War Leader." Reaching up to place a hand on Calgacus' shoulder, he went on, "Walk with me a moment."

He led Calgacus across the grove, circling round the altar stone, out of earshot of the others. In a low voice he said, "Many things have changed since Caer Caradoc. Some of them have been changed through you. More changes will come, for we will send word to Cartimandua of what has happened to her sister. Who knows what her reaction will be?"

A look that might have been sadness crossed Maddoc's expression. "Senuala was a girl of such promise," he said softly.

"She was tricked into doing what she did," Calgacus said. "Cethinos went behind your back."

"Leave Cethinos to me," Maddoc said.

Calgacus heard the disapproval in the old man's voice. Somehow, he resisted the temptation to look over at Cethinos. "What will you do to him?" he asked.

"That is my business," Maddoc replied. "Do not concern yourself with Cethinos. Nor with Cartimandua. I understand you are under sentence of death if you return to Brigantia. Is that not so?"

"That is what Cartimandua said when I saw her last," Calgacus confessed.

"You do seem to have a way of making powerful enemies, don't you?" Maddoc's eyes sparkled with amusement. "I think I will send Cadwgan with the message to Cartimandua. He seems to have developed a sense of himself since he left here. I have never

337

seen him so full of confidence. I suspect you may have had something to do with that. But while that may be a good thing, too much exposure to you would, I think, be not so good for him." He considered for a moment. "Yes, I think Cadwgan would be the ideal person to take that message, don't you?"

"I trust him to tell the truth," Calgacus offered.

"The truth?" Maddoc's eyebrows shot up. "What is the truth? Every man can tell the truth as he sees it, and yet tell a very different story to that of his neighbour. There are very few absolute truths in this world."

Calgacus gave a half smile. "You remind me of someone I met a while back."

"Oh? A druid?"

"No. He was not a druid. Just an old hermit. He had some very strange ideas, but he taught me a lot."

"You have some strange ideas, too," Maddoc said softly. "I would suggest that you keep them to yourself in future. For all our sakes."

Calgacus gave Maddoc an earnest look. "You leave the Romans to me, and I will leave the Gods to you," he said.

"You are an arrogant young man, Calgacus," Maddoc said with a smile. "But then, I suppose you have a lot to be arrogant about."

"I am proud," Calgacus corrected him. "Not arrogant."

"As I said, there are many truths. Now, you should go. But remember, you cannot change the world by yourself."

Calgacus smiled and nodded, but he recalled Myrddin once more, and as he watched Maddoc return to the other members of the Druid Council, he whispered to himself, "Just you watch me try, old man."

Chapter XXXVI

The feast of Lughnasa marked the height of summer. After a leisurely journey back from Ynis Mon, Calgacus and Runt returned to Caer Gobannus just in time to join the celebrations.

"It's a bit different to last year," Runt observed with a cheerful smile.

Calgacus did not reply. He wished he could forget the events of the previous Lughnasa. But Runt was right. This year was different.

Rhydderch welcomed them, announcing that several villages were meeting together at the nearby stone circle where they would eat and drink, sing and dance in the presence of their ancestors.

"You must come," he told Calgacus, rather uneasily.

"We will be glad to join you," said Calgacus, understanding Rhydderch's concern. The stone circle was where Senuala had died. She was buried there, beside the altar stone. Calgacus, though, was determined not to show grief at her death. She had, after all, tried to kill him. Nonetheless, when he arrived at the stone circle he walked slowly among the large, irregular-shaped boulders until he reached the altar stone where he spent a few thoughtful moments, contemplating what had happened and what might have been.

"Are you all right?" Runt asked after a while.

"I am fine," Calgacus replied. "We won, didn't we?"

"Aye, we did. You did. You beat the Romans and you beat Cethinos. He won't bother us again."

Calgacus gave a half smile. He recalled how Cadwgan had come to him, all breathless with excitement as they were about to leave Ynis Mon, to tell him that Cethinos had paid the price for going against Maddoc's will. The druid who had stalked Calgacus' life for as long as he could remember had been banished from the lands of the free tribes, driven out in disgrace.

"I wonder where he went?" he mused.

Runt said, "Good riddance to him wherever he went. But if he has any sense, he will have travelled north, to the Caledones or the other Picts. Personally, I hope he went to the Romans. They will have crucified him."

"That would be a sight to see," Calgacus said. He lightly ran a finger over a dark stain on the altar stone. For a moment he was lost in memories but he knew it was time to forget the past, or at least to move on from it. He straightened, smiled and said, "Come on. Today is supposed to be a celebration. Let's get something to eat."

Leaving the mystic circle, they walked over to a large meadow nearby where the people were gathering, bringing food and drink, spreading blankets on the ground and digging fire pits for communal cooking. Some of them cast anxious eyes to the clouds. There were shouts of delight when a brief shower of rain confirmed Lugh's blessing. After that, the weather held fair and the sun blessed them with its warmth.

Soon it would be time to gather in the harvest, though it promised to be a poor one this year. The fine spring had turned to an unusually wet summer, causing the farmers to bemoan the damage to their crops. Still, Lughnasa was a time of celebration and the Silures were determined to enjoy themselves.

Calgacus was a guest of honour. Many chieftains came to pay their respects to him as he sat at the foot of a small knoll enjoying the food and the plentiful drink. Some of the chieftains brought their daughters to meet him, suggesting that he might like to consider them for his next wife. Calgacus smiled and thanked them, but said that he was not considering marriage just at the moment.

Old Gwalchmai scoffed at him. "A man needs a wife," he said, ushering forwards his own granddaughter, a fourteen year old girl with dark, curly hair. She looked at Calgacus through large, brown eyes which told him that she was nervous at meeting him.

"Perhaps soon," Calgacus said as politely as he could.

Gwalchmai said, "Well, you should know that the people have decided to grant you land, a farm of your own, with twenty head of cattle, a flock of sheep and five slaves to work the land for you."

"That is very generous," Calgacus said. He meant it. He was touched by their generosity.

"You will need a wife to look after the home for you," Gwalchmai persisted.

"I will think on that," Calgacus said. "We still have a war to fight, you know."

But he quickly discovered that nobody was interested in the war. The Silures had seen off the threat to their homes and they celebrated the fact that the Romans had been driven back across the great river. Their warriors had raided the Roman province, returning with many heads as trophies, as well as vast quantities of plunder, but Calgacus soon realised that they had no interest in doing any more. None of the chieftains, not even Hillinos, had any thoughts of greater conquest or of joining with other tribes to chase the Romans any further.

Rhydderch, still nursing his mutilated hand, said, "The war is won, Calgacus. It is time to enjoy the peace. All we wanted was to defend ourselves. There is no need to do any more."

"The Romans will come back," Calgacus warned, trying not to darken the mood of the day, but not wanting to allow the Silures to deceive themselves.

Gwalchmai shook his silver-haired head. "No, they will not. Not with an army, anyway. An emissary is on his way to meet us. He will be here soon."

"An emissary? What does he want?" Calgacus was immediately suspicious.

Gwalchmai smiled. "We will find out when he gets here. But I believe the Romans desire peace with us."

Calgacus' heart sank, then he felt a pang of guilt that he should be so much in love with war that the thought of peace filled him with dread. He made some excuses to Rhydderch and Gwalchmai, then went off in search of Runt, finding him sitting with Sula and her mother near the edge of the meadow.

Little Gillarcos was running around close by, chasing some older boys, squealing with delight. Calgacus felt awkward at interrupting, but Runt seemed pleased to see him. Sula, though, did not look happy.

"Is something wrong?" Calgacus asked.

Sula frowned but did not reply. Runt stood up. "There's a Roman emissary coming. Did you know?"

"I just heard. I was coming to tell you."

"He is coming to talk peace." Runt spat the word as though peace was something to be despised.

"Not everyone loves war the way you do," said Sula angrily.

341

"When men go to war, many of them do not come back."

She folded her arms across her ample chest, glaring angrily up at the two men. Sula's mother studiously kept her gaze on little Gillarcos, pretending that she was not listening to the angry exchange.

"Let's go for a walk," Runt said stiffly, gripping Calgacus' elbow and guiding him away.

"Problems?" Calgacus asked.

"We had a bit of a disagreement," said Runt resignedly. "Again."

"You and I seem to be in a minority here," Calgacus told him. "Everyone is talking about peace. Gwalchmai has given me a farm."

"That's nice."

"Yes. He wants me to marry his granddaughter."

"And what do you want?" Runt asked pointedly.

"I don't know," Calgacus lied. "Let's see what this Roman emissary says before we decide."

The problem, he thought, was that the things he wanted, he could not have. He had wanted Cartimandua, though he knew now that what he felt for her had been lust, not love. He wanted Senuala to be alive, because he had loved her, but she was dead and he had convinced himself that she had not loved him. She had made her choice when she tried to poison him.

He wanted Caratacus back to lead the fight against Rome, but his brother had been taken to Rome to be strangled for the gratification of the Roman mob.

If it came to that, he wanted to be back in Camulodunon with Togodumnus. Yet he knew that wishing would not make any of these things come true. The Gods may not have been as uncaring as old Myrddin believed, but they never granted wishes like the deep desires that Calgacus nursed. All of the things he wanted were gone, lost forever. All of the things he had; his strength, his reputation, the respect of the tribe, all of these he was unconcerned with.

He silently acknowledged that there was a void in his life. He had lost so much, had experienced so many failures, that the only thing driving him on was his hatred for Rome and the desire to see the invaders gone. Myrddin had been right about him; he knew only how to fight, how to kill. Runt was the only person who

342

seemed to share his feelings.

"We'll wait to hear what the Roman says," Calgacus repeated, as much to himself as to his friend.

The Roman arrived the following morning, accompanied by a troop of thirty horsemen and an interpreter. The emissary wore a toga, a hugely impractical outfit for crossing the hills and valleys of the western lands, but Calgacus recognised it for what it was. Like the staffs and carved gateways of the druids, like the moustache he had shaved off, it was a symbol. This man came to the Silures dressed for peace, not for war.

The chieftains met him in the stone circle, under the guiding eyes of their ancestors. The Roman probably did not appreciate the significance of the ancient site, Calgacus thought. Compared to the temples of Roman towns, the circle was a crude place, yet any decision made here would be sanctioned by the ancestors of the tribe and would be binding on everyone.

The Roman stood in the centre of the circle of chieftains, apparently quite unconcerned at any thought that he might be in danger among his enemies. Speaking through the interpreter, he introduced himself simply as Arminius. He praised the Silures to the skies, congratulating them on their bravery and on their recent victories. He told them that Rome admired brave adversaries and that the Emperor, recognising them as worthy opponents, desired peace with them.

Arminius gestured to two soldiers who brought out a heavy wooden chest which they carried to the centre of the circle. There, Arminius opened it ostentatiously to reveal a pile of silver coins.

"A gift from the Emperor as a gesture of our goodwill," he said with a friendly smile. "There is a promise of a similar amount each year, provided that the peace between us is maintained."

A flurry of conversation arose as the chieftains nodded in appreciation. It was a generous gift the Romans offered.

Calgacus rose slowly to his feet. As he did so, the conversation died away. He asked the interpreter, "What about the oath sworn by the Governor to wipe out the Silures? Is that now forgotten?"

The interpreter, betraying some nervousness at Calgacus' belligerence, spoke hurriedly to the Roman nobleman who smiled pleasantly, answering smoothly, without hesitation. The interpreter relayed his words.

"Publius Ostorius Scapula, the Governor who made that promise, is dead. He died quite suddenly and unexpectedly. The noble Emperor Claudius Caesar has appointed Aulus Didius Gallus as the new Governor of Britannia. This gift and the promise for peace are offered by Governor Gallus on behalf of the Emperor."

Another buzz of voices ran round the circle of chieftains. Calgacus almost laughed. Scapula was dead. Unexpectedly. He supposed that the former Governor had probably not expected to be struck by slingshots, thrown from his horse and had his ribs crushed by Calgacus' sword. He also supposed that it would not do for the Romans to admit that the Governor had been killed by a barbarian, especially when the barbarians had allegedly been pacified. Scapula's successor had obviously decided on a different approach to the problem of subduing the Silures.

The chieftains appeared content, but Calgacus was not finished. He knew that the Silures were keen to agree a treaty with Rome but he did not want them to forget what Rome had done to them.

"This Emperor who offers us so much silver," he persisted. "Is he the same Emperor who executed the Great King Caratacus last year?"

A flurry of words was exchanged between the interpreter and the emissary. The Roman looked genuinely amused by the question. Calgacus could sense Runt straining to hear the words, but the two Romans spoke quietly and the Silures were making a great deal of noise, some of them repeating Calgacus' question angrily, demanding to know why they should trust the Romans. But when the interpreter spoke, his words stunned everyone.

"King Caratacus is not dead," he announced. "He was taken to Rome, along with all his family. There, he stood before the Emperor and made such a speech, full of pride and passion mixed with humility, that the Emperor's heart was touched. Caratacus persuaded Caesar that the Emperor's reputation would be enhanced more by showing mercy to a valiant foe than by having him killed. Claudius Caesar was so moved by his pleas that he granted the King his life. Caratacus and all his family are alive and well, living in Rome as guests of the Emperor."

Calgacus stood, mouth gaping in astonishment, while a wild cheer erupted all around him. Men leaped to their feet, shouting with delight. Runt punched the air in celebration.

344

Calgacus blinked rapidly as he felt his eyes begin to sting. Caratacus lived. The Great King, his brother, had reaped the rewards of mercy after all. He understood that being a guest of the Emperor meant that Caratacus was a prisoner. He would never see his brother again unless he too became a guest of the Emperor, but that was unimportant. What was important was that Caratacus was alive, along with Talacarnos and Rufinna. Against all hope, Caratacus was alive.

Calgacus recalled the memory of standing before his brother, shielding little Beatha, insisting that the king should grant mercy to those who could not defend themselves. Caratacus had reluctantly conceded that Calgacus had become a man that day, despite his youth. The king had sheathed his sword, sparing Beatha's life. Caratacus, the Great King, the fierce warlord, had learned the value of mercy from his younger brother. Then, when all else had failed, he had saved his own life and the lives of his family by pleading for mercy from Caesar.

Calgacus knew that it must have been hard for such a great warrior to stand before the Emperor as a supplicant, knowing that his life hung by a thread. Caratacus was a proud man. He would have faced death without fear, and would never grovel before anyone, but the Great King had somehow persuaded the Emperor to show clemency. And he lived.

Calgacus grinned like a fool until Gwalchmai waved at him to sit down.

After that, there were no more objections. Calgacus wanted to argue, wanted to deride the Silures for accepting a bribe, but the chieftains clamoured for peace and he knew it was futile to go against them. They had made up their minds from the start and all Calgacus' objections had been answered by the emissary's smooth words.

The Roman, still smiling his friendly smile, was sent on his way with promises of friendship from the Silures. The tribe had lost many men in the past year, had won great glory and had saved their land. They had achieved everything they had fought for. It was less than Calgacus had fought for, but he knew he would not be able to persuade them to continue the war. They were now, if not exactly friends of Rome, no longer enemies.

The long summer evening drew to a close with the sky glowing a wondrous red above the hills. Runt and Calgacus sat silently, side by side outside the door of Sula's roundhouse while she stayed inside, singing softly to Gillarcos to ease his way to sleep. Soon, Calgacus would have a far grander house, a farm of his own, with cattle and sheep and slaves. He would also have his pick of the young women for a wife.

In addition, Gwalchmai had promised him a share of the Roman silver. He already had plenty of coins plundered from the corpses of the legionaries, so the additional money would make him a wealthy man, a powerful chieftain. That should have contented him but he could not help thinking how much things had changed.

Until the Romans had come, coins had been of little practical use among the tribes. A man's wealth was still counted in cattle among the Pritani, but for small transactions, coins were becoming increasingly common. In the past, the tribes had bartered or used ringlets of iron or bronze, but coins were smaller and easy to carry. Above all, they were silver. Silver was valuable. The Romans offered coins knowing that men's heads would be turned by its lambent sheen and that the images of the Emperor that were stamped on the small discs would help to draw the tribes closer to the Empire.

Calgacus sighed. He may have shown the Silures how to defeat the Romans in war, but he was powerless against the beguiling lure of the wealth they had been offered.

Idly, he tugged the gold coin of his father, the coin that had once belonged to Caratacus, from beneath his shirt. He turned it over in his hand, slowly tracing his finger over the tiny horse carved on its surface. He had told Cartimandua that the coin reminded him of who he was. As he gazed at it now, the one thing he knew with certainty was that he was not ready to become a farmer.

As the shadows grew long over the village, Runt asked the question Calgacus knew was coming.

"What are we going to do?"

"I don't know."

"You have a farm to look after. You are a rich man now."

"I suppose so." Calgacus turned the gold coin over again, rubbing his thumb over the small design of a sheaf of wheat on its reverse side. The image reminded him of his brother,

Togodumnus, and his desire for a peaceful life, growing food and bringing wealth to the people. For Calgacus, that dream was long gone. Yet his father, a mighty warlord, had used the symbol of fertility on his coins. Was that a sign that he should put aside his sword and pick up a plough? He wondered what Caratacus would say about that. The fight was not over, whatever the Silures might think.

Runt went on, "The war here is finished. In a year, the Romans will be suggesting that some of the chieftains should visit their towns to see the buildings of stone. After that, they will point out that their Gods are really the same as ours, just with different names, then they will mention that it would prove our friendship if we built a Roman-style temple here in the valleys, and dedicate it to Mars Nodens. After that, there will be more Roman buildings. They will offer more silver, and gold too, and encourage us to speak Latin. In ten years it will be hard to tell who is a Roman and who is a tribesman. It is slower than conquest by force of arms, but it will work just the same. It is just another form of slavery."

"The two of us can't fight them on our own," Calgacus pointed out.

"I don't want to become a Roman again," Runt said, passion dripping from every word. "When I ran away that day, I hoped I would never have to look at another Roman. Now, I know I will have to fight to stay free of them."

"Everybody else seems happy to make peace with them," Calgacus said, trying to express his own doubts over what to do. "Maybe it is us two who are wrong."

Runt considered that for a moment. "Do you like fighting all the time?" he asked.

Calgacus turned to look at his friend, wondering where this was leading. "It's all I know how to do."

"But do you enjoy it? Would you go and pick a fight with someone just because you like fighting and because you are good at it?"

"You know I wouldn't."

Runt nodded as though he had just made a telling point. "So if you become a farmer and one of your neighbours decides he wants your land, what would you do? If he arrived at your door with a gang of warriors and told you that he was taking your farm and that you were his slave. What would you do then?"

347

Calgacus gave a wry smile. "You know damn well what I would do."

Runt smiled. "You are a warrior, Cal. The Romans are like that greedy neighbour. They want everything. If we roll over and let them take it, what does that make us?"

Calgacus nodded thoughtfully. "The truth is I don't think I am ready to become a farmer just yet. Besides, it would be difficult to settle down while Venutius still lives. I'm sure he won't give up trying to kill me."

"He's a mean one, all right," Runt agreed.

Calgacus did not have to think too hard to find more justifications for his desire to continue fighting. He had never bothered about the need to justify himself to others, but the doubts that the unexpected peace had raised in him meant that he felt a need to justify his instinctive reaction to himself.

"There are plenty of other people I still need to have reckonings with, too," he said. "Cogidubnus and Verica for a start."

"You've never even met them," Runt pointed out.

"No, but they helped the Romans and they killed Togodumnus."

Runt nodded knowingly. Blood ties called for vengeance for that death. He said, "All right. So, we need to deal with Cogidubnus of the Regni and Verica of the Atrebates."

"And my other half-brother Adminius," Calgacus added. "He's another traitor."

"All right. Including Venutius, that makes four people we need to deal with. But you can't get revenge on any of them if you are sitting on a farm here."

Calgacus rubbed his chin. "I know."

There was a fifth person they had not mentioned. He had not counted Cartimandua among his enemies. She had betrayed Caratacus, but Calgacus had also tried to betray her. Perhaps they were even. Perhaps not. She had promised to see him dead if he ever returned to her kingdom. But, as much as he wanted revenge on Cartimandua the queen, he doubted whether he would ever consider Cartimandua the woman as his enemy.

Runt sighed. "It sounds like we both have lots of reasons not to settle down," he said.

Calgacus asked, "What about Sula?"

Runt hesitated for a moment before saying, "She wants me to settle down. But I don't want to sit here waiting for the Romans to persuade us to become like them. I want to kill the bastards, not sit beside them like a friend."

"She could come with us," Calgacus suggested cautiously.

Runt shook his head. "I've already mentioned that. But she doesn't want to leave her home to live among other tribes."

They sat in silence for a moment. Calgacus felt relieved that he had made his decision. He knew that Runt had made up his mind, but he sensed that his friend's conscience was bothering him over leaving Sula. But they had to leave; the Silures had made peace which meant that this was no place for two warriors who wanted to continue the fight.

An idea struck him. He said, "I know someone who has just been given a farm that he doesn't want. Maybe he would give it to Sula. She'd be a rich woman."

"A rich woman without a husband and with a young son to bring up on her own."

"She's a good looking woman. She'll find plenty of suitors if she's rich. And there will be her mother and plenty of servants to help with the boy."

Runt nodded thoughtfully. "Are you sure this fellow you know doesn't want his farm?"

"Positive. He's decided to move on from here."

Slowly, Runt got to his feet. "I'll go and talk to her."

Calgacus sat alone as the sun finally sank into the west. The sky faded to dark blue and then to black. The stars were shining brightly by the time he heard the door opening behind him.

"I've just given away your farm," Runt said softly.

Sula followed him outside. Even in the dark Calgacus could tell that she was seething with conflicting emotions. Her anger at Runt had barely abated, but the gift Calgacus had offered was one of unimaginable wealth for a woman like her. She clasped Calgacus' hands, telling him that he was a good man, a kind man. Calgacus tried to brush it off as nothing. He promised that he would go to see Gwalchmai to make all the arrangements.

"But what are you going to do?" Sula asked them. "Where are you going?"

"We'll go north, to the Deceangli," said Calgacus. "Their king, Vosegus, has not made peace with Rome."

Runt gave a short laugh. "They haven't offered him peace because he hasn't defeated a legion."

"Not yet, he hasn't. But then he hasn't had us to help him."

Sula shook her head. "Do you two think of nothing but war?"

"It is what we do," Calgacus said. "There are a lot of people who don't want to be part of the Empire. We will help them stay free for as long as we can."

She looked at Runt with an expression of regret and sadness. Softly, she said, "Yes, I suppose it is what you do." She took a deep breath. "Well, you should come in and have some supper. You can't leave until morning."

"In a moment," said Runt.

She went back inside, leaving the two men standing in the darkness. Overhead, bats and moths flitted through the air and a fox barked somewhere out in the distance. They heard laughter and singing from one of the neighbouring houses. Everything was calm and peaceful. The war camps had gone from the valley, the warriors had returned to their homes, leaving only memories behind.

Calgacus wondered what his decision would have been if Senuala had been there to share the peace with him. Would he have stayed despite Runt's dire predictions of how the Romans would attempt to civilise them? They could still stay, he knew. There is always a choice.

He had made his.

"Are you sure about this?" he asked.

"Yes," said Runt emphatically. "I'm sure. Are you?"

"I'm sure. It is what I do."

With a laugh, Runt asked, "So which one of your enemies are we going after first?"

"I haven't decided yet. We can talk about it on the way north. There are so many to choose from."

END

AUTHOR'S NOTE and ACKNOWLEDGEMENTS

Although this is a work of fiction, the background to the story is broadly accurate. However, the passing of nearly two thousand years and the relatively sparse written records, all of which record events from the Roman perspective, mean that much of the history is open to interpretation.

The bald facts, as recorded by the Romans, are that the Emperor Claudius sent a massive invasion force to Britain in the year 43 AD. The short expeditions by Julius Caesar almost a century earlier and the aborted invasion threatened by Claudius' predecessor, Gaius Caligula, had had little real impact on the Celtic inhabitants of Britain but Claudius' invasion brought a dramatic and traumatic change to the lives of the island's people.

First Century Britain was not a unified nation as we would understand it today. Prior to the invasion, most of the native tribes were in a state of fairly constant conflict with their neighbours. Yet despite the Roman view of them as mere barbarians, there is evidence that their society was a sophisticated one which, although similar to the Gaulish tribes, had a uniquely British aspect.

The invasion itself was largely prompted by the need for a military victory to bolster the power of the new Emperor, Claudius. He had come to the throne through the will of the Praetorian Guard after the assassination of his nephew, the Emperor Gaius Caligula.

Many in Rome had wanted to see the restoration of the Republic, but the Praetorian Guard, whose purpose was to guard the Emperor, needed an Emperor to guard in order to justify their privileged position. While the politicians in the Senate spent a day and a night arguing over what to do, the soldiers chose Claudius as their Emperor, allegedly having found him hiding behind a curtain in the imperial palace, fearing for his life after Caligula's murder. When the rest of the army was bribed into swearing allegiance, few dared argue with the new head of state, and those who did were quickly disposed of.

Claudius himself spent only sixteen days in Britain, arriving to accept the surrender of several kings at the "capital" of

351

Camulodunon (Latin Camulodunum, modern day Colchester) before hastily leaving again to celebrate a triumph in Rome.

Reading between the lines of the ancient sources, it seems the Roman army did not have things all their own way during the early stages of the invasion. Had the British tribes acted together, they may well have been more successful in repelling the invaders. As it was, some tribes sided with Rome while others merely capitulated without a fight.

That the Romans were actively aided by some Britons seems almost certain. Cogidubnus of the Regni was certainly well rewarded by them and given a much enlarged kingdom to rule as a client king. Adminius, a son of Cunobelinos, may have been involved in some way, and Verica of the Atrebates also probably accompanied the invading Roman army. Verica's flight to Rome after being defeated by Caratacus was the catalyst for the Roman invasion, a convenient excuse for Claudius to bring Britain within the Empire by "restoring an ally to power", although Verica's fate is not recorded and he does not appear to have been installed as king of the Atrebates after the invasion.

As for those who resisted, Togodumnus, king of the Catuvellauni (and/or the Trinovantes depending on which interpretation is followed), was killed early in the campaign and his brother Caratacus, with whom Togodumnus seems to have shared some sort of kingship role, fled to what is now Wales.

With the collapse of the Catuvellauni / Trinovantes, the Romans swiftly conquered the south of Britain. Caratacus, doggedly refusing to give up, waged a successful guerrilla campaign for several years before eventually deciding to fight the fateful battle of Caer Caradoc. Frustratingly, although the ancient sources give a detailed and specific description of the battlefield, its exact location has never been positively identified.

After the battle, Caratacus fled to Cartimandua of the Brigantes, presumably with the intention of continuing the fight. Cartimandua, though, promptly handed him over to the Romans.

Very little is known about Cartimandua except that she was a powerful and charismatic queen. She, and her husband Venutius, had important roles to play in more of the great events of British history in the years that followed Caratacus' capture.

Caratacus is recorded as having other (un-named) brothers who were captured after the battle of Caer Caradoc, along with

Caratacus' wife and children. The King's speech to the emperor Claudius (or what is more likely a Romanised version of it) is recorded and is a powerful piece of rhetoric. Whatever words he actually used, they were effective because, unusually for a Roman war captive, he and his family were allowed to live out their lives in peace. It is said that when Caratacus saw Rome, he asked why, when the Romans had all these magnificent buildings, they coveted the Britons' humble huts.

In Britain, troubles continued. Unfortunately for Governor Ostorius Scapula, having claimed that the island was pacified once Caratacus was a prisoner, the Silures, who lived in what is now south Wales, had not read the script. The names of their leaders are not recorded which is a great pity, for they caused the Romans immense problems, showing a remarkable skill and bravery in their continuing struggle. After Caratacus' capture they grew almost recklessly aggressive. They carried out widespread raids, ambushed Roman foraging parties, overran at least one Roman camp and managed to inflict a defeat on a Roman legion, probably either the II Augusta or the XX Valeria Victrix. The extent of these Silurian victories may not have been quite as great as those I have allowed Calgacus but they were certainly serious reverses for the Romans.

In the midst of this continuing refusal on the part of the Silures to be conquered, Governor Scapula died suddenly and unexpectedly, reportedly worn out by the cares and worries of governing such an unruly province. His less warlike replacement, Aulus Didius Gallus, adopted a policy of peaceful appeasement.

Yet while Gallus brought a short period of relative calm, Britain was far from peaceful. It would be thirty years before another Roman Governor, Agricola, would again claim that Britain was conquered. His claim was perhaps stronger than Scapula's but still fell short of the whole truth. For a minor outlying province of the Empire, Britain was to continue to cause Rome problems that were out of all proportion to its size. The Romans were forced to maintain a force of at least three, and often four, legions in the province, more than ten per cent of their total army, an astonishing statistic, especially when one considers that the whole of North Africa, from the Egyptian border to the Straits of Gibraltar, was held by only one legion.

Some readers may appreciate a brief explanation of the principal Celtic festivals. Celebrations linked to the significant solar events such as the equinoxes and the midwinter and midsummer solstices go back to the very earliest days of human society. Many of the stone circles and other ancient monuments in Britain are aligned to one or more of these natural events. It seems almost certain that the Iron Age Celtic inhabitants of Britain marked them in some way, even if most of the ancient monuments pre-date the druids by thousands of years.

By the time of the Roman conquest, Celtic religion had moved on from merely marking the significant solar and lunar events. A pantheon of Gods had arisen, some of whom are very obscure. Other festivals had also joined the calendar. The four main celebrations of the Celtic world were Imbolc. Beltane, Lughnasa and Samhain, all of which have various forms of spelling. These can be roughly equated to the first days of February, May, August and November respectively.

So much for the history. As far as this story is concerned, students of early British history will no doubt have recognised the name of Calgacus and will have guessed that this fictional character faces many years of resistance to Rome. There are many battles for Calgacus to fight. Not all of those battles will be against Rome.

This story evolved over a period of three years. I am indebted to many people for their help and encouragement, particularly to Moira Anthony, Stuart Anthony, Moira Gee and Judith Murray, for their comments and advice on the various drafts. Thanks also to my wife, sons and daughter for putting up with my moments of distraction and the time spent ensconced in my study while trying to get all the ideas into some sort of cohesive narrative.

GA
February, 2012

Other Books by Gordon Anthony

All titles are available in e-book format. Titles marked with an asterisk are also available in paperback.

In the Shadow of the Wall*

An Eye For An Eye

Hunting Icarus*

The Calgacus Series:
    World's End*
    The Centurions*
    Queen of Victory*
    Druids' Gold*

The Constantine Investigates Series:
    The Man in the Ironic Mask
    The Lady of Shall Not
    Gawain and the Green Nightshirt

Charity booklet
    A Walk in the Dark

ABOUT THE AUTHOR

Born in Watford, Hertfordshire, in 1957, Gordon's family moved to Broughty Ferry in the early 1960s. Gordon attended Grove Academy, leaving in 1974 to work for Bank of Scotland. After a long but undistinguished career, he retired on medical grounds in 2008 without having received any huge bankers' bonuses.

Registered blind, Gordon had more time on his hands after retiring so, with the aid of special computer software, he returned to his hobby of writing and had his debut novel, "In the Shadow of the Wall" published in 2010. Gordon's books are now being read by a world-wide audience. As well as his historical adventure stories, he has ventured into crime fiction with some spoof murder mysteries in the "Constantine Investigates" series. He is also kept busy with speaking engagements, visiting libraries, schools and community groups to talk about his books.

In addition to his novels, Gordon devotes some of his time to raising funds for the RNIB. As well as visiting schools and social clubs to talk about his sight loss, he has self-published a charity booklet titled, "A Walk in the Dark", a humorous account of his experiences since losing his eyesight. The booklet is available free from Gordon's website www.gordonanthony.net All Gordon asks is that readers make a donation to RNIB. This booklet can also be purchased from the Amazon Kindle Store. Gordon will donate all author royalties to RNIB.

Now almost completely blind, Gordon continues to write stories and, in his spare time, attempts to play the guitar and keyboard with varying degrees of success.

Gordon is married to Alaine. They have three children. The family lives in Livingston, West Lothian.

You can contact Gordon via his website or by sending an email to ga.author@sky.com

Printed in Great Britain
by Amazon

32798670R00205